More Advance Raves for *The Street* from The Street:

"In *The Street*, Lee Gruenfeld has captured the insider's feel of the current business scene. In a compelling thriller that pits a dot-com entrepreneur against a government gumshoe, he takes the reader on a crooked road that leads behind today's *Wall Street Journal* headlines and into the heart of greed. This is a well-written page-turner that ranks with the best of the genre.

—Gerald Petievich, author of *To Live and Die in L.A.*

"Delusion, greed, and irrational exuberance combine to create one of the all time great works of fiction involving Wall Street."

—Kim Coggins, Senior Vice President–Investments, A.G. Edwards & Sons, Inc.

"A rollicking, pulse-quickening thriller that should be required reading in every business school and investment club in America."

—Charles G. Emley, Jr., former dean, The Peter F. Drucker Graduate Management Center

"As someone who led a successful, real Internet business success, I was amazed at Lee Gruenfeld's insights regarding what went on with the many dubious *dot-com*s. He has done a remarkable job of exposing the ugly underbelly of the feeding frenzy that continues to grip the U.S. Internet market, including the unholy alliance among entrepreneurs, venture capitalists, and Wall Street. His characterization of the financial news networks and securities analysts is especially apt and damning. Anyone who has an interest in technology companies, the Internet, and Wall Street and who likes a rollicking good story told with skill and daring, will not be able to put this book down."

—Henry R. Nothhaft, Chairman, President, & CEO, Concentric Network Corporation

"Lee Gruenfeld's *The Street* is a hilarious satire of Wall Street and an illuminating guide to the New Economy. It's also a brilliantly effective whodunit that will keep you excited through the closing lines. Gruenfeld has a novelist's eye and ear, he's a savvy observer of the economic scene, and he has the nowadays, unfashionable virtue of historical perspective. If you want to see clearly into the blinding world of Internet economics, *The Street* is a very good place to start; and once you've read this book, you'll never make an investment in quite the same way again.

—**Cathy Benko,** Global e-Business Practice Leader,
Deloitte & Touche

"Intelligent and insightful. A roller-coaster ride of financial shenanigans and a fiendishly clever tale of the mirage that is today's dot-com universe, with more than enough surprises to keep the pages turning into the wee hours of the night. Read this book, then rethink your investments before it's too late."

—**Richard Nehrbass,** Professor of Management,
California State University

"The situations in *The Street* are so true to life it's almost eerie. This is as close as most people will ever get to knowing what it was really like to start an Internet company in those heady days."

—**Kevin Nelson,** cofounder, DeltaNet

"Twists, turns, and intrigue in the new setting of dot.com mania and IPO insanity. This thriller carries a message: If you like high-risk investments, stick to lottery tickets."

—**Pierre-Rene Noth,** editor, *Rome News-Tribune*

THE STREET

Also by Lee Gruenfeld

THE EXPERT

IRREPARABLE HARM

ALL FALL DOWN

THE HALLS OF JUSTICE

As "Troon McAllister"

THE GREEN

THE FOURSOME

DOUBLEDAY NEW YORK TORONTO LONDON SYDNEY AUCKLAND

59.20   106.36   84.09

90.89   65.25   117.45

73.38 A NOVEL 9.68

85.15 73.45 49.68

THE STREET

LEWES GREENFELD

PUBLISHED BY DOUBLEDAY
a division of Random House, Inc.
1540 Broadway, New York, New York 10036

DOUBLEDAY and the portrayal of an anchor with a dol-
phin are trademarks of Doubleday, a division of Random
House, Inc.

Book design by Dana Leigh Treglia

Library of Congress Cataloging-in-Publication Data

Gruenfeld, Lee.
    The Street: a novel / Lee Gruenfeld.— 1st ed.
        p. cm.
    1. Wall Street—Fiction. 2. Stockbrokers—Fiction.
3. Government investigators—Fiction. 4. Securities fraud—
Fiction. 5. Internet fraud—Fiction. 6. Manhattan (New
York, N.Y.)—Fiction. I. Title.

PS3557.R8 S77 2001
813'.54—dc21   00-063922

ISBN 0-385-50150-1

IN MEMORY OF CHARLES A. PONZI

Back in the good old days, companies went public in order to raise enough money to expand. In exchange for giving up exclusive control, the private owners sold off minority ownership in the form of stock and used the proceeds to buy more steamships or build new factories or acquire other companies in the interest of empire building. In order to do that, investors traditionally insisted on seeing five years of audited financials and at least three years of consistent profitability.

But things had changed. Companies were going public primarily so their owners could cash in—or out, as was increasingly the case. And whereas the old-line industrialists steeled themselves to reluctantly cede ownership in companies they'd struggled to build up over decades, today's brand of entrepreneur gleefully jumped into the IPO fray so they could reap billions out of companies that sometimes hadn't even had a full year in business.

Nowhere was this practice more rampant than in the Internet arena. One company, an "incubator" called IdeaConnexion and run by CEO Burton Staller, was in business strictly to start up new Internet-based companies and then sell them off within twelve months.

James Vincent Hanley, who'd been involved in three of Staller's deals, spent his days gritting his teeth as he allocated blocks of shares in Internet start-ups, creating instant paper billionaires as he himself was forced to scrape by on subsistence wages of barely $300,000 a year.

On this April Fool's Day, Hanley was in a particularly foul mood. One of the phone reps in the department had run a gag ad in the *Wall Street Journal* announcing an IPO for a new company whose purported objective was to allow people to auction off their organs to patients awaiting donors. An hour ago they had all been having a good laugh, but since then Hanley's multiline phone had been jammed by calls from clients wanting to invest because the sham company was called *eBodyparts.com* and would be operating on-line. Hardly any of them even asked questions about the new venture. Some just wanted wire instructions for transferring funds. The phony ad hadn't even listed Schumann-Dallis as an underwriter, and people were practically breaking down the doors to dump money into it. One client called from a cell phone, and Hanley could hear him battling with two flight attendants who were trying to grab the phone away because they were still on departure from JFK.

Right now, every light on Hanley's phone console was blinking. His

APRIL 1

JAMES VINCENT HANLEY HATED HIS JOB
and therefore his life.

That combination was not terribly unusual, especially in the financial world, where what you did for a living could easily account for half your waking hours and the aftereffects could pretty much wreck the other half.

Hanley worked in the institutional sales division of Schumann-Dallis, a powerhouse nick-named "The Virgin" because the address of its monolithic black building was Three Maiden Lane in the Wall Street district of Manhattan. Hanley's specialty was moving great gobs of money around whenever a hi-tech company was involved in an IPO, an initial public offering, the process by which a corporation that was privately owned sold itself to the public at large.

PROLOGUE

THE STREET

I'd like to wrap my arms around the entire country, squeeze real hard and say, *"Will you for pity's sake just stop for a minute! This isn't Hula Hoops or Beanie Babies, this is real money we're talking about here! Too much more of this and we'll all be standing in bread lines again!"* But try telling that to people who think they've finally found the Can't Lose Casino.

—JUBAL THURGREN,
Enforcement Division,
Securities and Exchange Commission

I wouldn't even think of taking an Internet company public unless it was losing at least fifty million a year, minimum.

—ROBERT SCHUMANN,
Chairman, President and CEO,
Schumann-Dallis Investments

buddies were routing calls his way because Hanley was considered a chameleon with a gift for articulation that allowed him to instantly snap into whatever verbal mode the immediate situation required. He could spout utterly nonsensical but high-sounding business jargon in one breath, then turn around and banter in Brooklynese with a hot dog vendor in the next. The one thing he couldn't do very well was hide the intelligence and street smarts that made it all possible.

With no way to stop the ridiculous calls, he reached down below his desk and yanked the thick phone wire out of the wall, indelicately failing to release the little plastic retainer pin first and thereby taking some plaster with it, then sat and morosely contemplated the madness.

Geeks with half his brains were driving Ferraris to chic little food stores in Palo Alto to buy $1,500 bottles of balsamic vinegar. High school dropouts had their own fleets of Gulfstreams. One guy he knew, a run-of-the-mill programmer, had been having trouble getting phone connections to his parents in Vietnam, so the last time he'd gotten through, he'd just left the phone off the hook. The line had remained open, continuously racking up international long distance charges, for the last four months.

An industry segment that was barely identifiable at the start of the last decade was now driving the entire market. Companies that hadn't even existed a year ago, and which had laughably puny sales and frightening net losses, would go on the market at $10 a share and hit $100 by lunchtime, sometimes ending up capitalized at values several times those of venerable giants that had been founded a century before. Even a serious downturn in tech stocks, which should have served as a frightening warning to return some sanity to the market, backfired utterly: As the segment slowly and steadily recovered, speculators took it as a sure sign that this market was invincible and could rebound from anything, and they dove back in with renewed vigor. Investors never even read the required SEC filings; they just held out their checkbooks and asked the maximum amount they could buy. Announce a delay of one month in the shipping date of a new chip and the market's net valuation could drop by half a trillion dollars in a matter of hours.

Unthinkably large sums of money were being dumped into houses of cards whose foundations were not only perilously shaky but sometimes almost impossible even to define. It was vastly more out of control than the dizzying margin spiral prior to the horrific crash of 1929 that preceded a worldwide plunge into a decade of desolation, but what was really pissing off James Vincent Hanley was the fact that he was sitting in front of a (now defunct) phone in a windowless room on Maiden Lane in south Manhattan working his ass off eighty hours a week to funnel those truckloads of money into everybody's hands but his own.

Miserable and dejected, he half-listened as the broker in the next cubicle conducted an impatient, clipped conversation with a client.

"How the fuck should I know what they do, Harold. . . . What am I, a Caltech professor? It's an Internet start-up and I got eighteen more calls backed up here from people with their checkbooks out, so if all you're gonna do is ask me a lotta . . . okay . . . *okaaaay,* now you're talking! So how much . . . No, no, forget it. I said forget it! The max is a hundred thousand and . . . because those're the goddamned rules, that's why, you want me to lose my job? Now, you want in, or what? What? No, your wife can't also go in for a hundred thou. . . . Harold, your wife's been dead for two years! Harold . . . I'm hanging up, Harold! You hear me, I'm hanging up! Okay, that's better. I'm faxing you the wire instructions. The money's gotta be here in an hour or . . ."

Hanley stood up and looked into the cubicle on his left. Tony Favuzzo, headset stuck in his ears, punched a button on his phone, listened for less than two seconds, then rolled his eyes up at Hanley and dropped his head back wearily. "It was a joke, Mr. Thornton." He squeezed the mute button and said to Hanley wearily, "Another hour of this and I'm gonna auction my freakin' *soul* on-line." He let go of the button. "An April Fool's gag. Uh-huh. Yes, I'm sure it's actually a pretty good idea but . . . No, as far as I know, nobody's registered *eBodyparts.com* on the Internet yet. No, I have no idea how to . . . Certainly, Schumann-Dallis would be glad to handle the underwriting if you decide to . . ."

Hanley looked around. Cubicles stretched in all directions. The din of a hundred conversations floated upward, and all around the room drifted the unmistakable odor of money. Boatloads of it, moving from port to port and traveling so swiftly it left barely a trace in those places where it had set down momentarily before floating off again. Once there had been factories, railroads, oil wells, and real estate to denote where money, like a wolf urinating on a tree, had marked its territory. Great buildings, vast complexes, mighty steamships, even entire cities gave substance to the power of the dollars that had built them.

Now? *Whoopie!.com,* which consisted of barely more than a few dozen desktop computers and as many employees, was worth more on paper than Sears. Twice as much, if truth be told.

Hanley looked back at his own desk, his computer terminal, his phone, and the bits of plaster littering the space below his chair. The word "broker" came from the French *brocour,* one who "broaches" a barrel of wine and sells it off by the glass or bottle, and he wished he were in that business right now so he could guzzle his whole supply by himself.

"Mr. Hanley!"

He recognized the nasal voice even before he turned around. It was the president of one of the start-up companies Schumann-Dallis was handling. In existence for only eight months, it was about to go public.

"Arnold!" Hanley called back with unfelt amiability. He quickly reached for a book sitting on his shelf—a leather-bound copy of *A Financial History of New York,* one of several thousand Schumann-Dallis had given to all its employees the Christmas before—flipped it open and turned it upside down over the plaster mess on his carpet before turning and walking rapidly to make sure the new client didn't notice anything amiss.

"We're taking Mr. Plotkin on a little tour of the department, Jim," the senior account executive escorting the client said.

"That's nice." Hanley shook hands with the imminent billionaire. "Listen, let me take him around, okay?"

"You sure, Jim?"

"No problem. C'mon, Arnold."

As they left the account exec, Hanley said, "Arnold, you mind if I ask you something?"

"Sure, Mr. Hanley." The worldly unwise Plotkin still hadn't figured out that a corporate CEO and major client of the firm didn't need to address a salesman as 'Mister.' "What do you want to know?"

Hanley ran his hand through his hair. He was six feet tall, or at least he had been before he'd started this job. Now he felt like he'd shrunk an inch or two, whether from terminal ennui or a slightly stooped and beaten posture he couldn't tell. His thick, sandy hair, once a source of considerable pride, had become a nuisance of late, and he'd taken to letting it grow far too long before he cut it far too short, the better to stretch out the intervals between time-wasting haircuts. He'd even given up his participation in the compulsory young-Wall-Street-hotshots fashion competition, the stress of correctly anticipating the trends having overwhelmed the fleeting satisfaction of senseless victories. Only the overpriced haberdashers in lower Manhattan were winning that ongoing war, and he'd grown tired of subsidizing their prize money.

Now that he had the soon-to-be-legendary Arnold Plotkin all to himself for a few minutes, Hanley wasn't exactly sure what it was he wanted to know. "Look, I, uh, I'm not much of a technical whiz, see?"

"Yeah." Plotkin pushed his thick glasses higher on his face, grimacing and revealing badly neglected teeth in the process. He rubbed his nose and stepped nervously from one foot to the other. Here was a man—a kid, really—clearly more comfortable talking to his laptop than to people. "That's okay. Most people, they're not so smart in computers."

"Right. Okay, what you do, what your software does, it helps people find what they want on the Web, right?"

"Uh-huh."

"But there are all these search engines already. Dozens of them. I use them myself, and they're very good, so what is it your stuff does that's so different?"

"Jeez, Mr. Hanley," Plotkin said, scratching at the rear end of his worn corduroys. "You're gonna be part of the IPO team. Didn't you even look at our stuff?"

"What for?"

Plotkin blinked at Hanley a few times, realizing he'd been asked a good question. "Okay. Well, what happens is, sometimes a user enters some search parameters, and they don't say exactly what he thought they said."

"Like . . . ?"

"Like . . . okay, okay . . ." Plotkin bent forward and shook his hands, not unlike a first-grader called on to answer a question in class and struggling to find the right words. "Let's say you're writing a paper for school and you want to find out something about the planet Saturn, okay? Like maybe, I don't know, how big it is, okay?"

"Okay."

"Okay. So you go to a search engine and you enter in 'Saturn' and 'size,' and what it does, it comes back and it's got like five hundred sites and you click one and it says Saturn has a wheelbase of fourteen feet! Get it? You see what happened? It thought you meant the car, see? It thought you meant the *car* and it gave you the size of the wheelbase!" Plotkin giggled, sort of a cross between a snort and a death rattle, and pushed at his glasses again. Hanley nodded, and tried to force a smile of his own.

"What my software does," the Rockefeller-in-waiting explained, "it figures out what you really meant because it knows what other stuff you've been asking while writing this paper, and it knows what you really mean is the planet and not the car, and so what it does, it reformulates the query for you and submits it again."

He beamed triumphantly and folded his arms across his chest.

Hanley looked confused. "But all I had to do was go back and enter the word 'planet,' and maybe 'not car,' and hit it again. End of problem." Surely no piece of software could possibly do as good a job of searching for something as the user himself.

Plotkin's grin disappeared. "But you're a sophisticated user."

"Sophisticated?" Hanley exclaimed with unintended derision toward an important client. "My senile grandmother could figure that one out!"

"But she wouldn't have to," Plotkin argued. "My software would do that for her."

"That's all your stuff does?" Hanley sputtered in disbelief. "It figures out what it thinks somebody really meant and then does the search?"

"Actually, no," Plotkin said uncomfortably. "It doesn't do the search, just, uh, feeds it back to whatever search engine you were using in the first place." He sniffled a few times and added, "Only better."

Hanley could only stare at him incredulously. They were about to take this company public, probably to the tune of two billion dollars.

He didn't want to insult the client, but he had to understand. "Are you telling me that all your software does is something a user could learn to do himself, and better, in about fifteen minutes?"

Plotkin, who'd clearly had enough of this conversation, scratched his rear again. "Users are lazy and stupid, Mr. Hanley," he said as he began to turn away. "And there's no money in making them smarter."

And thus had this socially inept geek neatly encapsulated a key truth of an entire industry.

HANLEY WENT BACK TO HIS CUBICLE AND SAT DOWN. HE thought for a few minutes. He retrieved *A Financial History of New York* from beneath his desk and idly flipped through the pages as he swept away plaster dust, pausing at a particularly stirring introductory chapter entitled "The Great Tulip Catastrophe." He read it, then he went back and read it again, and then he thought some more.

That's when he got the first faint glimmer of "The Idea."

PART ONE

PART ONE PART ONE PART ONE PART ONE

When I was young, people called me a gambler. As the scale of my operations increased, I became known as a speculator. Now I am called a banker. But I have been doing the same thing all the time.

—SIR ERNEST CASSEL
Turn-of-the-century British financier

SEPTEMBER 15

"WHAT THE HELL DO YOU MEAN, 'HE declined!' "

Administrative aide Moira Framinghall squeezed her eyes shut and counted to three before forcing her voice to normal tones and answering Marshall Stratton's elephantine bellow. "He said, 'Thanks for the invitation but I must respectfully decline.' " She knew full well that the patiently delivered direct quote would tick him off, and also knew he'd have no grounds to criticize her response.

Stratton tore away the thick paper towel protecting his shirt and tie from the makeup being applied to his face and threw it forcefully to the floor. "Goddamnit, who the hell does he think he is!" Or at least tried to throw it, air pressure and static having intervened to pin the offending sheet comically to his hand, which only increased his theatrical ire and forced the makeup girl to turn away and smirk. "Another upstart entrepre-freaking-neur who thinks he can jack his own ass into the big time and ignore my show. Get him on the line!"

"He's not taking any—"

"I said get him on the phone!"

"Yes, sir." Framinghall dialed a number from memory and waited.

"Jerzy's. Shoot."

"This is Moira Framinghall from *Street Beat* on CBN."

"That's beautiful, Moira, and thanks for sharing. Four regulars and a dozen, right?"

"May I speak with James Hanley, please?"

"James—whaddaya hocking me, can you speak to James Hanley! You want four coffees and the doughnuts or what?"

"Uh-huh . . ."

"What '*uh-huh*'! Listen, I got customers lined—"

"Uh-huh . . ."

"Chrissakes, Moira are you gonna—"

"I see. Well, I'll let Mr. Stratton know, and thanks for your time."

"What the freakin'—"

"Gimme that!" Stratton growled, striding purposefully toward Moira's desk.

She hurriedly dropped the receiver onto its cradle. "Hung up. Sorry."

"Two minutes, Mr. Stratton!" a production assistant yelled.

"Sonofa—Where's Johnson?"

"Already on the set." The P.A. turned toward the makeup girl. "Is he—"

"All set," she answered, despite a pale patch on Stratton's cheek visible to every onlooker in the studio.

"Let's do it!" an overhead intercom rasped as the executive pro-ducer flapped her hands behind the glass wall of the control booth.

"Gonna shit-can that arrogant SOB's whole company before the show's half over," Stratton muttered as he walked onto the set.

"Good thinking there, Marsh," Ed Johnson said agreeably from be-hind the on-camera desk. "That way we can get rid of another half a mil-lion annoying viewers when they figure out we're idiots."

"Thirty seconds!"

"Bullshit." Stratton came around and took up the second seat. "One word from me and his stock'll drop thirty points." He scowled as the makeup assistant attacked him with a cotton puff, not seeing her knowing glance back at her supervisor when she spotted the off-color patch of skin she'd purposely left.

"There *is* no stock," Johnson reminded him. "Still a private company."

"Yeah, well I can still—"

"In five, four, three . . ." The production supervisor mouthed the last two words silently as he showed the count with his fingers held high in the air.

"Good morning, folks. Welcome to *Street Beat*. I'm Ed Johnson."

"And I'm Marshall Stratton. Dot-com dottiness is far from over, and just when you thought you'd heard every conceivable kind of self-aggrandizing pitch from zillionaires who still can't get a drink in forty-seven states, along comes something different."

"That's right, Marshall. The sounds of silence are fast becoming the loudest buzz on the Street, as everyone from Merrill Lynch to Barney Smith, my local paperboy, wonders what the story is on mystery company *Artemis-5.com*."

The blue screen behind them was blank in the studio, but to people watching television a succession of images appeared on it, each consisting of complex, fast-moving, computer-generated pictures culled from a spate of "image ads" produced by Internet companies. "While every dot-head with an advertising budget is spinning out expensive ads to convince us that they're the ones with the 'Next Great Thing,' *Artemis-5* founder James Hanley seems to have been exerting an equivalent amount of effort keeping everything about his company secret. He doesn't give interviews and doesn't even have a publicity department. It's my understanding his people are under strict orders to keep mum about whatever it is they're doing."

Stratton gritted his teeth but relaxed his jaw as soon as he saw himself on the studio monitor. "That's right, Ed. But here at *Street Beat* we've got the inside skinny and we're ready to share it with our viewers."

Johnson frowned and rechecked his script: *There are a few rumors in circulation, and while we can't confirm them* . . . Nothing about "inside skinny." He looked up at the control booth, but the executive producer shrugged helplessly.

"Seems Hanley has already received funding to the tune of at least thirty million dollars from some of the best-known venture capitalists in northern California," Stratton continued. "Obviously, some people know something and are willing to put their wallets where their knowledge is. It's breakthrough technology for sure and, amazing as it sounds, *Artemis-5.com* is already making its presence felt among the canyons of Wall Street. Ed?"

"That's right, Marsh." What choice did Johnson have at this point but to go along? "Yesterday morning a rumor floating around that Hanley had begun putting together a world-class board of directors caused a minor stall in some tech stocks, and—"

"*Whoopie!.com* plunged two and an eighth, didn't it, Ed?"

Plunged? "There was a slight drop, Marsh, although it's not clear that it was the *Artemis-5* rumor that precipitated it." As soon as the camera shifted back to Stratton, Johnson waved frantically at the control booth and repeatedly drew a finger across his throat. The executive producer nodded and began shouting orders.

"True enough, Ed, but the veil may be lifted next week, if the latest bit of gossip on the exchange floor has any merit to it. Seems there's a major announcement in the offing and we might at last learn what all the hoopla is really about. And if—" Stratton saw the large green clock over the control booth begin to flash. "Stay with us as we continue to discuss these developments, folks. Back in a minute."

"And . . . we're out!" the production supervisor yelled. "Back in ninety, people!"

Johnson yanked at his earpiece and slammed it onto the desk, causing several painful winces at the audio board in the control room. "What the fuck are you doing, Marshall!"

Stratton calmly began gathering several sheets of paper on the desktop in front of him. "What do you mean, Ed?"

"We don't have confirmation on the funding amounts, and nobody told *me* about any announcement next week!"

Tapping the sheaf of papers into alignment—they were all blank—Stratton shrugged off the objection. "I said it was a rumor, didn't I? What's the problem?"

"The problem is, you made it up! Why would rumors be floating around on the exchange floor when any IPO would start out on the NASDAQ and they don't even *have* a goddamned floor! What the hell do you think you're doing?"

"So we'll force the guy's hand a little. Where's the harm in that?" *And if there is no announcement—which of course there won't be—let Hanley explain why.*

ED JOHNSON WAS WRONG ABOUT ONE THING, AND THAT WAS that the New York Stock Exchange wouldn't be taking an interest in a budding hi-tech IPO. At the beginning of the next trading week, news reports flashing on the Big Board caused a higher than usual number of covert glances from floor brokers. As the week wore on, the glances were no longer covert, and by Thursday, the appearance of every new illuminated message nearly halted trading altogether until it could be ascertained that the news didn't involve *Artemis-5.com*. No market professional wanted to be caught short, to get a call from a client that began with those dreaded words, "I heard from someone else . . . ," meaning, "Why the hell didn't *you* know about it?" By the close of trading Friday, an acute state of collective exhaustion was apparent among exchange personnel, most of it caused by the torturous stress of anxiously anticipating something that never occurred.

Some of it morphed into anger and indignation, and resulted in protests to the Securities and Exchange Commission, which reported on Monday the reply it had received in response to its inquiries to *Artemis5.com*. "Ours is not a publicly held company," the terse statement began, "and has no obligation to respond to the SEC. Nevertheless, owing to the rash of irresponsible rumors surrounding *Artemis-5.com*, we state firmly that no announcement such as the one to which you referred in your inquiry was scheduled or even anticipated. Further, no officer of the company nor, to our knowledge any employee, has ever had a conversation with anyone associated with *Street Beat* aside from an administrative assistant who requested an interview, an invitation we declined. We were not asked by *Street Beat* to confirm or deny any of the rumors which were broadcast in the half hour following that phone call."

Marshall Stratton, of course, protested vehemently that he'd had no opportunity to check the rumors with *Artemis-5.com* because nobody from the company would speak with him. He told the *Wall Street Journal* that his failure to get anyone there to comment on the rumor of an announcement gave him reason to think it might be true. A young reporter at CBN, who asked him how he could make such an assumption when he'd just got finished saying he'd never directly put it to anyone at *Artemis-5.com* in the first place, was transferred to *Fashion Trends with Maven Rubinsky* and assigned to cover the new accessories line from the JCPenney factory in Haiti.

SEC Chairman George Peabody III thought this an appropriate occasion to point out that, yes, it was true that the Commission had limited authority so long as *Artemis-5.com* was in private hands and didn't issue fraudulent statements, but it might do for the company to remember that, the instant it filed its first notice of intent to go public, everything they said, signed, spent, transferred or solicited would be subject to scrutiny the likes of which Mr. James Vincent Hanley hadn't experienced since his last colonoscopy.

STRATTON HAD BEEN RIGHT ABOUT ONE THING, AND THAT was the fact that Hanley had managed to raise $30 million with very little effort. He'd chosen to skip the traditional round of "angel" financing from wealthy private individuals and instead headed straight for the venture capital firm of Caruthers & Osborne, whom he impressed not only with his financial acumen but his evident disdain for self-aggrandizing promotion. This was a serious businessman looking for serious money, and he had all the necessary computations and projections carefully calculated and fully supported. His knowledge of established (i.e., older than eighteen months) technology companies was encyclopedic, and he seemed to have gleaned out of that knowledge an uncannily perceptive synthesis of why they were so successful, lessons he'd brought to bear in creating *Artemis-5.com*.

Ashton Caruthers remembered well how Hanley had wrapped up his pitch, because he'd taken notes: "The company that will prevail is the one that successfully exploits today's paradigm of synergy between adding value via best practices and continually proving the customer proposition. We plan to empower the marketplace with just this kind of quality-driven strategy."

Following this leading-edge conclusion, Caruthers had sat back and said, "Why don't you write a book about all you've learned, James? Let everybody in on it?"

"I suppose I could do that, Ashton," Hanley had shot back without hesitation, "but don't you think it might be better *not* to let everyone in on it so we don't abandon the core paradigm at this mission-critical juncture and thereby erode the thirty million you're trusting us with?"

Which was roughly when Kenneth Osborne instructed his attorneys to begin drawing up the "term papers" for the first round of financing.

ALL TOO PREDICTABLY, YOUNG AND AMBITIOUS "STREET people" began appearing at Hanley's door. They were all impeccably dressed and coifed, the men wearing shirts custom made with monogrammed French cuffs in white even if the shirt was blue, loafers of top-grain butter calfskin, Rolex watches, Hermes ties and slicked-back, wet-look hair. Many of them were physically fit from hours of racquetball and squash played with murderously competitive intensity.

The women mostly wore the standard-issue MBA uniform: smart AK or DK jacket-skirt combos with silk blouses tied into flouncy bows at the throat, Ferragamo shoes that attempted to be both elegant and sensible but generally succeeded at neither, minimal but expensive jewelry and, for some reason Hanley had never been able to fathom, enough perfume to overpower people two subway cars away.

All of them, men and women alike, spouted financial jargon and traders' slang ("steents" instead of "sixteenths") and sported the knowing, crooked smiles of the nouveau insider, on the one hand reveling in their preeminent status when measured against the dockworkers and cabbies of New York and, on the other, miserable and bitter because of those who were rocketing up the ziggurat faster than they, never by virtue of superior intellect or skills but always because of happenstance or a shameless lack of ethics they themselves would never stoop to. It was this facet of Street reality that motivated many of them, especially those with expertise in the detailed minutiae of IPOs, to seek the Next

Great Thing and thereby rid themselves of the drudgery of actually having to work for a living.

Dozens tried to offer their services to Hanley's start-up without even knowing what business it was going to be in. Some were the jaded veterans of as many as half a dozen different jobs, jumping from one potential star to another, searching for the quick hit, none willing to stick it out over the long haul, because what was the point, when twenty-two-year-olds were retiring to Majorca with nine-figure stock portfolios?

Most of them had much the same line of approach in selling themselves to Hanley—"I returned twenty-six percent investing for my clients!"—and only the percentage changed from person to person. The twentieth time he heard yet another variation, Hanley couldn't take it anymore. "A goddamned brain-damaged parakeet could have made twenty-six percent!" he barked in irritation. "You couldn't have lost money in this market if you tried to do it on purpose!" He finally had a brass plaque engraved and placed in front of his desk facing outward. It read "Never confuse brains with a bull market," and put a quick stop to idiots telling him how brilliant they were for riding the same tide that had floated every other ship in the bay.

The Street people's faces merged in Hanley's mind, all of them stultifyingly conforming and mutually indistinguishable, with a single exception.

"WE'VE ALREADY MET, MR. HANLEY," LANCE MULDOWNEY SAID with an enigmatic smile.

"It's James. Jim when you know me better." Hanley held out his hand. "You do look familiar," he said as they shook, "but I can't quite—"

"The Virgin?"

"Schumann-Dallis, right! Investment banking, fourth floor."

"You got it. I'd only been there for a few months before you left."

"Nice to see a familiar face, Lance." Hanley waved him to a seat and they both sat. "The parade that's been trooping through my office, you'd think somebody was stamping them out on Second Avenue and shipping them all to me."

Muldowney laughed easily. "And they say we don't wear uniforms, right?"

"Right. So tell me why you're different."

The non sequitur intended to disrupt the easy informality didn't disrupt Muldowney one whit. "Can I skip the MBA and all the rest of the bullshit and come to the point?"

"Wish you would."

"Right now I'm still at the Virgin. I was put on the Burton Staller account just about the time you left."

That made Hanley take notice, although he tried not to show it. To be assigned to that significant an account after only a few months with the firm was unprecedented. "Rumor has it the SEC is looking at him pretty closely."

Muldowney caught the reaction but moved smoothly through it. "I heard they're looking at *you* pretty closely."

Hanley shrugged. "That's not exactly the freshest of news items."

"True." Muldowney rearranged himself slightly on his seat and dove right in. "James, you don't need any help running this place. Well, maybe you do, but that's not something I'd be much use for."

"Very forthcoming of you. But if you can't help me in running it, what can you help me with?"

"Selling it."

"Ah. And what makes you think I've designs in that direction?"

"Because running it isn't where the money is. You and I both know the vast majority of technology businesses are doomed almost as soon as they start. So you pull a couple three million a year out of it if you're lucky, and before you know it you're sitting on some antiquated technology because a couple of kids doing a high school science project somewhere suddenly make your whole company obsolete."

"That's how you see it?"

"That's how it is. Look at all the big money these guys are raking in. Hasn't got a damned thing to do with running a business. There's hardly a one of 'em making a profit. Hell, most of 'em don't even have any revenue!"

Muldowney leaned forward and put his elbows on the desk. "The money is in starting the company and selling it just as fast as you can."

"Maybe." *Definitely.* "How do you know I'm not in this for the long haul? Suppose I'm really interested in making a go of it. What are you going to do for me then?"

"Who says you can't be in it for the long haul?"

"I thought you were talking about selling it."

"Not necessarily lock, stock and barrel. Just selling shares on the market, taking it public. You can run it for the rest of your life, if you want. But you can grab a giant chunk of cash and reinvest it in the business right in the beginning by selling just a small piece and reduce your risk of ending up swigging Ripple on the Bowery later."

"And if I want to own it all and not sell any?"

"James, you got thirty big ones in venture funding. You don't even own all of it *now.*"

"I've got a loan option. I can pay them back with interest and a hundred percent of the shares stay with me."

"Never heard of something like that." Muldowney frowned as he considered it. "And I mean *never.* Why would they risk all that money for a capped return?"

"Promise of things to come, and there's a time limit on the option. Besides, that's the way I wanted it, so it was that or nothing." Hanley didn't mention the other part of that deal, which was that he had agreed not to offer participation to any other VC firm for the duration, and that the interest was a flat 20 percent. "So, what can you do for me if I pay it off and keep the whole company?"

"Not a damned thing," Muldowney answered, pushing away from the desk. "In which case I've wasted your time and I'll just leave." He made no move to do anything of the sort.

Hanley regarded him carefully for a few seconds, judging correctly that they'd now gotten the malarkey out of the way and could get down to business. "I've had fifty very smart, very ambitious people march through here in the last week alone. Let me ask this another way: What makes you so special?"

"Well, I'll tell you. I'm not interested in operations. I don't even want to know about the day-to-day business. What I know is IPOs. And I know them very well indeed."

Initial public offerings—the complex process by which a corporation sold a chunk of itself to the investing public in exchange for money it would need to fully realize its plans. Before the IPO, the proprietors of the company would very likely be tapped out and in debt, struggling to eke out the remains of whatever private financing they'd managed to obtain thus far and keep the place afloat. Within hours of a successful IPO, those same proprietors could be multibillionaires; by selling only a small piece of a very attractive company, they created a short supply in the face of huge demand, and the resulting imbalance meant that the shares they retained for themselves would swell in value as the public snapped up whatever was available on the open market.

"You and several dozen others I could name."

"That so?" Muldowney had lost none of his amiable arrogance. "How many of them worked on the *Whoopie!.com* IPO?"

As Muldowney grinned at him challengingly, Hanley looked up at the ceiling. "At last count," he said, looking back down, "four that I can remember offhand."

For the first time, some of the fullness seemed in danger of wafting out of Muldowney's sails. "Really."

Hanley nodded, guiltily pleased that he had managed to rattle Muldowney, however slightly.

But it took Muldowney just a few seconds to regain the upper hand. "And how many of those have a close friend in the Enforcement Division of the SEC?"

There was no longer any need for the pretense of this being a normal employment interview. Muldowney had Hanley now, and had him good.

It only remained for Hanley to discover the nature of the substance beneath Muldowney's considerable sizzle. "And I suppose you know just who over there has been assigned to bust my chops."

"Try me, Jim."

CHAPTER THREE

JUBAL THURGREN FELT LIKE AN IDIOT.

It wasn't so much that he was in a library, a venue stingingly ill-suited to his tastes and temperament even if it was on the main campus of the prestigious University of California at Los Angeles, nor that it happened to be the biomedical library, which made it even more inappropriate.

And it wasn't that he'd been uncomfortably ensconced in a study carrel for the past three-something hours trying to look absorbed as he leafed through the pages of a blazingly compelling page-turner entitled *Ribosome Sequencing Protocols for N-Stage Telomeres* while hoping that the outward signs of his urgent need to urinate might be mistaken for fierce concentration by the ascetic-looking graduate students who occasioned to glance at him with undisguised skepticism.

He'd been assured by younger colleagues that his dark suit would attract little attention, since it would simply be assumed that he ran with something called the Goth crowd at the eclectic school, but he was coming to understand that he'd probably been the butt of a practical joke by his bored compatriots. While the undergraduate population at UCLA may have freely sported every style from early Depression to neo-penal, one thing he'd learned over the past three hours was that post-doc molecular biologists ranked attention to fashion slightly below pinochle and creationism.

But that wasn't it either, because his was such a disarmingly nondescript appearance to begin with that clothes of any sort made him only slightly distinguishable from any wallpaper he happened to be standing in front of. He was about five-foot-ten when he stood up straight, of average build and average weight. He wore his salt-and-pepper hair in one of those banker styles that made it difficult to tell when he emerged from a barbershop whether anybody in there had actually done anything. His nose was not quite knobby and not quite aquiline, and his cheekbones were slightly elevated, not so you would notice that feature in particular but only that he seemed to have a perpetual look of mild curiosity. That air of inquisitiveness was enhanced by storm cloud–gray eyes ever on the alert, but it would have been tough to decide if they were questioning or simply recording. Overall, he was the picture of a Chandleresque gumshoe whose primary physical advantage was the ability to walk unnoticed among the more noticeable.

So it wasn't the somber clothes. The reason Jubal Thurgren felt like an idiot was because he was assistant director of enforcement of the Securities and Exchange Commission's Northeast division, ostensibly mandated to see to it that the overlords of U.S. industry, arguably the most powerful people on earth, toed the line as they trod the hallowed paths of capitalism, and here he was in the halls of obscurest academia staking out a bunch of kids who'd essentially played a prank.

He raised a questioning brow at Lewis Morosco, who was prowling the dusty stacks on the other side of the room. In contrast to Thurgren's appearance, Morosco's was striking. Although also under six feet tall, he was half Thurgren's age and in twice the shape physically. It showed in his face, his sharply etched features bolted onto pale skin that stood in bold relief against dark hair that fell over his forehead onto even darker eyebrows. His movements were decisive and economical, athletic and sure, giving off the air of someone for whom remaining calm really meant saving energy for action.

In response to Thurgren's raised eyebrow, Morosco pressed his hand over a flesh-colored earpiece attached to a coiled wire that ran down his neck and disappeared into his jacket, listened for a few seconds, then shrugged helplessly at Thurgren, who glowered back his dissatisfaction as though there was something Morosco ought to be doing to speed up the process before Thurgren wetted the floor.

He got the same response from the three other men positioned around the room, FBI agents all, and all with enough experience to have dressed in jeans and flannel shirts no more noticeable than the rows of books behind them. One of the special agents—the only one with anything to do as the interminable hours passed—took pictures with a silent, miniature electronic camera of each person who used the public computer terminal stationed just off the center of the room.

Two weeks ago the share price of an obscure, publicly traded company called EconoWeb shot from thirteen cents to over thirteen dollars in a single weekend. That kind of a jump in a moribund old stock had triggered a monitoring program at the SEC offices in Washington, D.C., which in turn triggered a call to the Enforcement Division. At first, Thurgren was inclined to shrug it off as just another symptom of Internet fever, the Ebola virus of the investment world, until he noticed that EconoWeb had nothing to do with computer technology: The "Web" in its name referred to a type of high-speed printing press used by newspapers and other large-volume printers.

A quick review didn't reveal any fundamental reason for that kind of escalation in the company's stock price, so Thurgren asked his wife, Genevieve, a forensic accountant with the FBI, to do a little lurking on the financial chat boards in her spare time. Genevieve quickly turned up hundreds of messages on four separate boards pertaining to a rumor that EconoWeb was about to be purchased by one of the heaviest-hitting players in the Internet industry. A phone call to EconoWeb's president showed that to be totally false, and it didn't take Genevieve long to discover that all the user names from which the chat room messages had originated were phonies.

Thurgren got a federal judge to issue a subpoena to *Whoopie!.com*, the Internet portal that hosted three of the chat rooms on which the messages had appeared, to disclose the locations of all the computers from which the messages were posted. To his astonishment, every one of the messages originated from only one computer, to which only five terminals were attached, all of them right here in the UCLA biomedical library.

One of them was within the field of view of a university security camera. Examination of the tapes, synchronized with the time stamps on the Internet messages, showed that only three people had been responsible for all the messages. Unfortunately, the faces captured by the low-resolution camera were not very clear and would likely enable a defense attorney to make a fairly good case for reasonable doubt as to the identities of the alleged perpetrators.

Earlier this morning an FBI technician armed with a federal warrant tapped into the cables feeding the public terminals and began monitoring the traffic emanating from each one.

None of the six people who'd used the machine since they'd begun watching had posted any messages to the financial chat boards, which wasn't too surprising, considering that the damage had already been done. But Morosco had suggested that, buoyed by their success, the trio might give it another shot, which was why Thurgren, trying to be the enlightened manager not averse to joining his troops in the field, was writing copious notes based on his study of *Ribosome Sequencing Protocols for N-Stage Telomeres* and trying not to either ruin his pants or choke Morosco to death.

Showing the flag was not the only reason Thurgren had decided to participate in this operation. He also wanted to get out in the field with Morosco, who'd joined the division only a year before but was already showing signs of being just the kind of man Thurgren thought should be actively encouraged in this kind of work. In contrast to the indentured civil servants whose life's ambition was to sink into the obscurity of the bureaucratic mire and lurk there until their pensions vested, Morosco was brash, ambitious and creative. This operation had been largely his idea and, as unlikely to succeed as Thurgren thought it was, he didn't want to discourage that kind of enthusiastic initiative.

On the other hand, he wanted to make sure Morosco's cowboy mentality didn't get out of hand. After all, their quarry typically dressed in pinstripes and didn't carry anything more lethal than a laptop computer, and anybody who thought that enforcing arcane securities regulations was going to be like dropping grenades on fleeing drugrunners needed to have his mind set right. Morosco could run the entire division someday, and Thurgren knew that grooming him for that position might be a veteran's only real legacy. Not that it would get Thurgren on the cover of *Newsweek*, but there were other sources of satisfaction for people who took their jobs, however uncelebrated, seriously.

If he didn't choke the kid to death first. Another student stepped up to the terminal and hit a few keys. Thurgren sighed as the FBI agent with the camera dutifully took a picture. Seconds later, a vibrating pager in Thurgren's pants pocket came alive. He looked to his right and saw Morosco, one hand pressed to his ear, nod and point to the terminal, a finger held up in the air: *Wait!*

Thurgren twisted in his seat and got a good look at the notorious criminal who finished typing and sat back, watching the screen. The desperado looked like a refugee from the high school audiovisual squad, one of those kids who scurried around helping the teachers set up VCRs and overhead projectors when they weren't entombed in airless rooms tinkering with homemade computers.

Even though Thurgren knew that a harmless-looking geek like this was capable of wreaking more havoc than a hundred Dillingers, he couldn't help tossing a sarcastic glance at Morosco—*I gave up my bowling night and traveled three thousand miles for this* nebbish?—who did his best to maintain a straight face as he listened intently to his earpiece, then nodded vigorously and raised a fist in the air.

Thurgren got up as casually as he could, stretched, and began walking toward the terminal. The student glanced at him briefly and then returned his gaze to the screen, rocking back and forth, his hands held prayerfully beneath his chin. When Thurgren didn't break off in another direction as expected, the rocking stopped and the kid looked up.

Thurgren halted about four feet away. "Yuri Levanovich?" he said sternly.

The student's face went ashen faster than Thurgren would have believed possible, then he jumped up so abruptly he knocked his chair over with a bang that reverberated loudly around the hushed room unused to such noise. Levanovich froze in a half crouch, his face radiating feral terror and despair. As his hands flew to his face, his eyes began darting around in desperation.

"Don't!" Thurgren commanded softly, flipping open his wallet and revealing his badge. From the corner of his eye he could see one of the FBI agents approaching, and hoped the man knew enough not to freak this cowering wretch who was reacting in a manner not untypical of white collar criminals who hadn't yet come to grips with the fact that what they were doing was illegal. If he behaved true to form, Levanovich would be sobbing and confessing and begging to be let go before they even made it out of the library.

"Mikhail!" Levanovich cried out suddenly, looking past Thurgren and waving his hands. "Mikhail, oh God oh Christ oh God! Please Mikhail, please, what are we going to—"

Thurgren turned to see "Mikhail" emerging from behind a stack. The newcomer, much taller than Levanovich, was already dropping the books he'd been carrying and was reaching into his jacket. Just as Thurgren recognized him from the grainy security photographs, Mikhail Yakovlev had a .45 Glock out and aimed right at his face, arms straight out and both hands wrapped tightly around the grip.

"Mikhail!" Levanovich cried out again piteously, shrinking even farther into himself as if trying to disappear right through the floor.

"Shut up!" Yakovlev hissed angrily as he strode forward, thrusting the gun at Thurgren and forcing him to step back. Yakovlev glanced momentarily at the screen, then at Thurgren, then back to the terminal as he began to hit some keys. But before he got too far, a whimper escaped from Levanovich and Yakovlev barked at him to stay quiet.

Thurgren felt his throat constrict and was sure his heart was going to explode through his chest any second. The gaping black barrel of the handgun threatened to swallow him whole, and he felt paralyzed as he visualized a bullet screaming out of that terrifying maw and tearing his face to pieces.

Yakovlev wasn't saying anything, just staring at him murderously as Levanovich covered his head with his hands and continued mewling helplessly. Somewhere deep within a brain that was otherwise preoccupied, Thurgren realized that Yakovlev was uncertain about what to do now, not having had time to think it through before he'd reflexively pulled his gun. Thurgren knew he ought to start managing the situation, but all he could think about was the gun still aimed at his face, and the only thing in the whole world he wanted or would ever want as long as he lived was to get Yakovlev to turn it away, and he didn't much care if both of these misbegotten felons escaped afterward and disappeared forever.

He saw Yakovlev's forefinger tremble as it played uncertainly about the trigger. Levanovich hazarded an upward glance and drank in the scene, then began sobbing even louder.

"Shut up!" Yakovlev repeated, anger and fear choking his voice as he tried to muster up courage and decisiveness by berating the pitiable wretch on the floor beside him.

But Levanovich wouldn't be silenced. "Mikhail!" he wailed, pumping his hand somewhere off to his right.

Sensing the movement, Yakovlev stepped quickly aside and looked behind him, spotting the FBI agent who'd been moving up slowly and was now only fifteen feet away.

Yakovlev took two steps back and swung the gun around.

"Whoa, easy!" the agent shouted as he stopped reaching inside his jacket and threw both hands in the air.

Yakovlev shifted the gun back to Thurgren, who'd just begun to feel guilty relief at the momentary reprieve, then back to the agent, then back to Thurgren. "Get over there!" he finally cried out as it dawned on him that he needed to move Thurgren and the agent together to cover them both.

"You don't want to do this, son," the agent said. "Right now you haven't hurt anybody and—"

"Shut up!" Yakovlev shrieked, pointing the gun at him. The tip of the barrel was shaking, and Yakovlev was working his finger nervously. Thurgren dimly recalled something he'd learned in a mandatory weapons training class about pull pressure and worn trigger springs on poorly maintained weapons, and hoped the setting on this gun was nice and tight lest one too many nervous twitches set it off inadvertently. Yakovlev had absolutely no idea how to end this, and hadn't reacted well to the agent's attempt to take charge.

"Listen to me, Yakovlev," the agent tried again.

At the sound of his own name, Yakovlev's eyes grew wide. *You know who I am!*

Thurgren could see that the agent's stock attempt to engender some familiarity had backfired; any thought on Yakovlev's part that he might get out of here without being identified, Levanovich having given away only his very common first name, evaporated, as did any lingering hopes Thurgren might have harbored about ending this quietly. He'd been prepared to tell Yakovlev to just turn around and walk away, but that was no longer an option. Realistically, it probably never was, given the presence of three FBI agents who'd rather die in a hail of bullets than explain to their superiors why they let a perp get away.

Thurgren didn't give a rat's ass about *his* superiors, and had no thought now beyond just wanting to survive this.

"Listen to me," the agent repeated.

Yakovlev, having failed to quiet the man down by threatening him, swung the gun back to Thurgren instead, looking back and daring the G-man to say something *now*.

"Okay." The agent held up his hands and pumped them at Yakovlev several times. "Okay."

Now what! Thurgren thought. He forced himself not to flick his eyes toward the other two agents and give them away. They were the only hope remaining, but it wasn't clear what they could do except gun Yakovlev down before he had time to react. It wouldn't have to be much of a reaction, either: With his finger poised at the trigger, any autonomic response and the gun still aimed at Thurgren's face would fire. Maybe the agents were waiting for Yakovlev to swing the gun back around toward the other agent, thinking they could nail him in the interim . . .

"*Nnn, nnthoothe me!*"

It came from somewhere off to the right, a barely comprehensible, heavily nasal and strained garble.

"*Thoothe me!*" again, this time accompanied by a heavy, awkward shuffling sound, as if a heavy bag were being dragged across the floor.

Lewis Morosco appeared from behind one of the tall bookshelves. Or at least Thurgren thought it was Morosco. His jacket was hanging off one shoulder, his tie was completely askew and one of his shirt buttons had come undone. His normally neat hair was sticking up in all directions and a trace of spittle ran down his mouth and on to a slack jaw that jutted sideways. Bent unnaturally to one side, Morosco was trailing one foot behind him, taking difficult steps with the other and dragging the back one along.

He had a heavy book in his left hand and waved it toward the computer terminal. *"Ek-thoothe me,"* he repeated yet again. His left eye half-closed and the other seeming to roll around in his head uncontrollably, Morosco painfully made his way across the space separating him from the computer.

"Stop!" Yakovlev cried out in alarm.

But Morosco didn't hesitate as he continued to move forward, and it wasn't even clear he'd heard the order to stop. "Hafta nyoos da kahpooter," he said, waving the book toward the terminal again as best he could. He was breathing heavily, huffing and snorting as though each breath was a great effort.

"I said *stop!*" Yakovlev looked from the agent to Thurgren, as though seeking guidance on what he was supposed to do about this pitiful apparition making his way inexorably toward him.

"Nuh-unnh," Morosco insisted, shaking his head so hard the saliva on his chin flew off in two directions. *"Nuh-unnh!"* He pointed at the terminal. "To'd you. I *to'd* you: Hafta nyooth da kahpooter!" Anger and defiance came over his twisted face and the labored breathing grew louder as he kept moving.

Yakovlev, mystified, could only stare at him. When Morosco reached the terminal he bent forward, supporting himself by leaning one hand on the counter holding the keyboard. Thurgren saw that the fingers of his hand were grotesquely gnarled, so that he was really leaning on his knuckles, and swaying uncertainly as he did so.

Morosco squinted at the screen. "Nnhh, hey! Hey, wha . . . ?" At that point he noticed Levanovich cowering on the floor. "Hey, ith thith your thtuff? I thaid *Hey! You!* Ith—"

Yakovlev, remembering that he hadn't finished erasing whatever Levanovich had left on the screen, stepped forward and shoved Morosco roughly aside. Morosco stumbled, choked out an undecipherable protest that went unheeded, and swung the heavy book he was carrying upward with blinding speed, slamming it into Yakovlev's hand so hard that the gun crashed into the man's face and knocked him backward off his feet.

Before anyone else had a chance to react, Morosco's free hand shot out and grabbed the gun, jerking it cleanly away just as Yakovlev crashed into the hard marble floor, blood from his freshly broken nose splattering around him. The FBI agent leaped forward to cuff him, and Morosco grabbed Levanovich by his shirt collar, hauling him to his feet as the other two agents appeared from behind the shelves.

"Who's the third guy!" Morosco demanded of the petrified nerd he was holding.

"Rudi Tscheschevsky!" Levanovich cried out without further inducement. "Rudi and Yakovlev, it was their idea! I swear to God!" He clasped his hands together pleadingly. "I didn't know Yakovlev had a gun, I swear to God!"

"I bet you didn't," Morosco said as he shoved Levanovich toward the two agents.

Thurgren had staggered away and dropped back onto the seat in the study carrel. The sweat that had poured from his armpits was now growing cold, and chills ran across his back and chest. He clutched his hands to his knees to stop them from trembling and tried to steady his breathing before he fainted.

"Hey, Jubal," Morosco said as he put a hand on his shoulder. "You okay?"

Thurgren nodded, taking several deep gulps of air before daring himself to speak. "Jesus H, Morosco . . . you could've got somebody killed!"

"Nah." With maddening calm, Morosco took a handkerchief from his pocket and wiped at his chin, then sat down across from Thurgren. "What was I gonna do, just stand there and let the sonofabitch start firing?"

"Who says he was going to?"

"Well, he had a gun, Jubal. That was my first clue. Hey, you don't look so good."

"Never had a gun pointed at me before. Pity's sake, Lewis: The guys we go after aren't supposed to carry guns!" Thurgren looked at Morosco's face, and was amazed to see him smiling and flushed with excitement.

Behind them, the FBI men were speaking into radios and hustling off the perps. Thurgren pretended to be absorbed in their activities, but was really trying to buy time to calm himself down.

"Some performance, huh?" Morosco was rebuttoning his shirt. "Coulda won me an Oscar for that one."

"Academy might have found it a little distasteful." Thurgren stretched a leg out to make sure it was still working. "What was that supposed to be, anyway?"

"Some harmless walking mess who couldn't possibly hurt Yakovlev. You see the look on the guy's face?"

"Walking mess?" Thurgren stretched the other leg out. "Candidate for a humanitarian award, you are."

The smile on Morosco's face faded slightly. "I save your life and you think I wasn't, what . . . *sensitive*?" When Thurgren only shrugged by way of response, the smile disappeared completely. "Tell me I'm not hearing this!"

"You just laid it on a bit thick, is all, Lewis. Like you were enjoying it or something."

"What was I supposed to do, Jubal! Phone up the human resources department and get guidelines on how to disarm a fucking punk without giving offense?"

"Forget it. Doesn't matter. Let's just get out of here. You've got a heckuva story to tell the boys in the office."

"See you downstairs," the FBI agent who was cuffing Levanovich called out.

Thurgren turned toward him, noting dark stains on Levanovich's pants and something running out over the kid's shoes just as the agent began pulling him away. "I need to go to the restroom," he said to Morosco, suddenly remembering the bladder that had been aching even before all of this started.

"Sure," Morosco said sardonically.

"Not to puke, you idiot. Just got to—"

"Sure, Jubal. No problem."

Thurgren rose shakily. "You did good, Lewis. What I said, forget it. Just being stupid, because you acted and all I could do was stand there."

The smile reappeared on Morosco's face. "Say, you think this'll be a first for the division?"

Thurgren knew what they would confirm when he subpoenaed the personal financial records of the trio and had Genevieve or another forensic accountant analyze them. They bought thousands of shares of the cheap EconoWeb stock weeks ago, using every penny they owned or could borrow. Then, after fraudulently driving the share price up to a hundred times its real value by posting phony takeover rumors on the chat boards, they dumped it all, using various cover accounts, and in a few hours made a small fortune before everyone else figured out that the rumors were false.

The division "first" Morosco had asked about referred to the fact that never before had fraud charges been brought against people who had no affiliation whatsoever with the company whose stock they were manipulating. "Yeah," Thurgren answered unenthusiastically. "We made history here today."

It didn't even seem to occur to Morosco that they'd almost gotten killed doing it.

SEPTEMBER 16

"The guy who's sniffing around your ass, his name's Jubal Thurgren," Lance Muldowney announced as soon as he was seated.

"I knew that already," Hanley responded, not having known that at all.

"Did you know they'd assigned it a case number?"

Hanley blinked several times. "No."

"Docket number zero one dash three eight four five nine. They've already had a face-to-face with your VC firm. Agent by the name of Swanson spoke with two guys there, one of whom was Ashton Caruthers his own self. You didn't hear about it because Swanson told him it was no big deal, no need to get you anxious over nothing, just routine, blabbity-blah."

A five-minute confirming phone call later, *Artemis-5.com* had a new employee, and James Hanley had his Sancho.

JUBAL THURGREN POURED A CUP OF COFFEE for himself, then held the pot out toward Lewis Morosco. "It's zero proof."

Morosco made a face and pulled his cup away. "Sense'a drinking coffee, it's got no caffeine in it?"

"If I hadn't told you, you couldn't have told the difference." He put the pot back and waited for Morosco to get a cup of the real thing, then they walked out of the break room and headed back to Thurgren's office to resume their weekly case review.

In the six months they'd been working together, Morosco had come to admire this boringly stolid, faux-hayseed assistant director of the Enforcement Division's Northeast operation. Despite the outward, Columbo-type appearance that gave the impression of impeded thought process and a hopelessly bland style of speaking designed not to inadvertently give offense to any of the thousands of diverse people he'd come into contact with in his previous professional incarnation, Thurgren had demonstrated time and again an uncanny knack for seeing several layers of implication beneath the surface of whatever situation they were up against. Some of this undoubtedly sprang from his experience as a "Big Five" partner who'd seen every kind of shenanigan it was possible for a corporation to play.

He'd left that lucrative and prestigious position after determining that any satisfaction he was feeling arose not from the hands-on demands of public accounting, of which he was doing progressively less, but from the career advancement process. Prescient enough to see that as an unrewarding and perpetually unfulfilling rut, he'd talked it over with Genevieve, knowing in advance what her response would be. She'd seen him grow more and more disillusioned with his vocational lot, and watched him biannually swap sets of company friends as his stature in the firm rose but enjoy them less and less. He was actually envious of the young associates working for him, newly minted accountants and MBAs who had their hands right on the pulse of the clients' businesses while he languished in partner meetings preoccupied with administrivia.

"There are few things in life more important, Jubal," Genevieve had said, "than being happy in your job. If you have that, you'll live forever. If you don't, you're a dead man walking."

"What can I do, Ginny? I can't return to the ranks and get my hands dirty again." Even if that were otherwise feasible, the arcane rules of public accounting made it near impossible for a partner to relinquish his ownership interest in the firm and return to being an employee.

"Quit," his wife responded.

"And do what?"

"You already know what. It's just a question of which agency."

He'd suspected that his talents were good for something other than keeping rich people's books when one of his clients was investigated for securities fraud. The SEC cowboys, even though still bean counters by trade, were the only ones really having any fun. The fact that Genevieve herself was a forensic accountant for the FBI just emphasized the point. She brought home exciting stories of bad guys brought to justice, and what was he going to do in return—regale her with rollicking tales of staff reviews?

Four years ago he'd joined the Enforcement Division—"going over to the Dark Side," his partners had called it—and if he'd thought before that a lot of people in corporate America were playing fast and loose with the rules, he was soon staggered by the scope of financial wrong-doing being perpetrated throughout the country. Most of it was harmless, at least from the very wide perspective of possible damage to the larger marketplace or the overall economy, but there were an awful lot of people making an awful lot of money by taking advantage of avenues and mechanisms not open to the ordinary citizen.

He couldn't have chosen a more fortuitous time to join up. The division had always moved along fairly briskly, settling 99 percent of its cases and occasionally making a splashy bust, but it wasn't until the explosion of Internet start-ups that enforcement moved to the forefront of the SEC. Securities regulators, whose main job was essentially to prevent the kind of crash that had occurred in 1929 and who naively thought that they'd seen it all, were terrified by the amount of money tied up in companies with little or no intrinsic worth. What Federal Reserve Chairman Phillip Goldwith had called "irrational exuberance" was in fact psychotic delusion, and the potential for devastating havoc to be wreaked on the economy if it were left unchecked was too awful to contemplate.

But it was difficult to contain. Like cocaine dealers who daily risked their lives for the astronomical profits involved, investors weren't interested in the long-term implications of reckless speculation when there were billions to be made right now, and again like cocaine dealers, they were ready and willing to fashion nooses for anyone who tried to stop them.

"What makes our lives tough," Thurgren was saying to Morosco as they walked the long corridor, "is that hardly any of it's illegal. How can you stop people from investing as much money as they want in anything they want, if the purveyors don't engage in any overt deception?"

Morosco slowed slightly to take a sip of the hot coffee before resuming the pace. "Kinda depends how you define deception, doesn't it?"

"And therein lies the problem," Thurgren responded, nodding his approval of Morosco's insight. "If somebody simply buys into a popular delusion, even perpetuates it, is he being deceitful?"

They stopped in front of an east-facing window. "See that building?" Thurgren said as he pointed toward the National Gallery. He leaned an elbow on the windowsill and took a sip of coffee. "There's a painting in there by a Russian guy named Malevich. It's called *Black Square*."

"What is it?"

"It's a black square."

"No, what I meant, what's—"

"I know what you meant. It's a black square. That's it. A one-armed monkey could've painted it in about ten minutes. And may have, for all I know."

"Modern art." Morosco shook his head contemptuously and raised his coffee cup.

"It's worth about two million bucks."

Morosco looked at him incredulously. "Bullshit."

Thurgren shook his head. "Now here's the thing: If someone who can afford it gets it in his head to pay a couple of million for a picture of a black square, who is anybody else to tell him he's crazy?"

"A lot of people!"

"True," Thurgren said, laughing. "But none of them are in a position to stop him, because there's nothing illegal about it."

"Gotta give you that."

"But now suppose that the person selling the painting tells a prospective buyer that it's *worth* two million bucks. Is he being deceptive?"

Morosco thought about it for a few seconds. "But art's a matter of taste. Somebody thinks a Picasso's worth fifty mill, who's to argue?"

"So you agree that it's worth whatever anybody's willing to pay, regardless of what you might think it's intrinsically worth, which is about ten bucks for the frame and paint."

"You mean it comes with the frame? Well, you didn't say that."

"Very funny." Thurgren pushed away from the window and resumed walking down the hall, Morosco in tow. "So what happens if a guy offers up some stock in a new company that's never had a nickel of revenue, doesn't even have a product yet, and he's asking half a billion for the shares?"

"Then he's fulla shit."

"Why?"

"Because the company isn't worth it, and before you say anything else, there's a difference between buying art and buying a business."

"And that is . . . ?"

"You can assess the value of a business objectively."

They reached Thurgren's office. "And that, my friend, is where you are dead damned wrong. Any calls, Nan?"

"About three dozen," his secretary answered.

"Fine. Hold them all."

"So, why'd you ask?"

"Habit. I'm educating my young friend here."

They went through the secretary's anteroom and into the office. "Why am I dead damned wrong?" Morosco asked.

"Something for you to remember," Thurgren said as he sat behind his desk. "There is only one determinant of the price of a stock, and that's what people are willing to pay for it."

"Obviously. That's your big lesson? But it doesn't mean the company is *worth* that."

"No? So what's it worth?"

"Couple ways to figure it." Morosco dropped into a chair and slouched, one leg thrown over the armrest. "All of its assets added up, some reasonable multiple of earnings, intangible assets as well . . ."

"Assets."

"Right. Everything that can be sold off."

"Suppose my company doesn't have a single asset other than the patent on a new drug that cures baldness and makes you lose weight. What's the company worth?"

"Well, that depends on whether it really works, if there are side effects, what it would take to scale up production . . ."

"In other words, somewhere between zero and a hundred billion dollars." Thurgren sighed. "Lewis, listen to me. When I was in B-school, I had an instructor who had us create a fictional company. He gave us data on what the company manufactured, what the raw materials cost, how much labor it required, what were the sales outlets . . . every bit of information you could imagine. Then he gave us two days to figure out what we should charge for the product."

"Sounds like a good teacher."

"He was. He let us work in teams, which we did for nearly forty-eight straight hours, came back bleary-eyed with our answers, and then he said not one of them was worth more than an F."

"Why?"

"Because the right answer was to charge whatever people were willing to pay. Nothing else was relevant, and the only real question was whether you'd be able to make money. It's the same thing with selling stock."

"But that means the share price has nothing to do with the underlying value of the company!"

Thurgren slammed a hand down on his desk. "Hallelujah!"

There wasn't very much the SEC could do about the explosion of paper fortunes that were based on corporate enterprises of dubious substance. It wasn't even clear that they *ought* to do something. After all, if people wanted to bet their money in the casinos of Wall Street rather than those of Monte Carlo, who was the government to stop them? As it happened, Thurgren and most of his colleagues were sympathetic to that hands-off philosophy.

But the SEC's mandate wasn't to protect the individual investor, it was to protect investors in general, as well as the integrity of the securities markets, occasionally by doing things that didn't seem fair, like suspending trading or forcing brokerage firms to "make markets" in certain stocks. The Federal Reserve had a lot of clout, too, and attempted to keep everything steady by methods such as adjusting interest rates.

The issue facing regulators now was the extent to which the new investing atmosphere threatened the market, even though it might seem that nothing overtly illegal was being perpetrated. Lots of start-ups had tested the bounds of prudence, usually by going public prior to realizing any profit, or by filing dubious but legal patents on "business practices" and then vigorously challenging their infringement. While many of those cases were still winding their way through the courts, it was only rarely that they seemed to affect stock prices very much. Even Microsoft, whose very existence was threatened when a federal judge ruled it a monopoly, lost only a dollar in share price the day that decision was announced, and didn't start really hitting the skids until the punishment phase began. It was Thurgren's belief that, when the investing community as a whole began ignoring traditional and reliable warning signs in its mad rush to eviscerate the golden goose, there was a case to be made that some levelheaded intervention was warranted.

But the new trading realities presented a new obstacle: The outer limits of the powers of federal regulators had never really been tested, and it wasn't very likely that the citizenry would sit still for any such exercises when the economy was the strongest it had ever been. What they needed was a test case, and *Artemis-5.com*, were it to go public, had all the makings of a possible candidate.

Right now, however, more mundane business was at hand. "Where do we stand with Talisman Media?"

"Open and shut," Morosco replied. It was an insider trading matter in which a corporate officer had sold a large block of his stock when he found out that an overseas subsidiary was about to fail.

"Nothing's open and shut."

"We got a smoking gun, Jubal." Morosco dug around in a manila file folder and produced a few sheets of paper. "A copy of an e-mail the guy received and the paperwork that shows he'd sold off within an hour of receiving it. Conclusive proof he'd traded based on information not available to the general public."

"What bothers me isn't our evidence, Lewis. It's the guy's defense. He's saying that insider trading is the only thing that really protects the small investor."

"A total crock," Morosco said.

"But it isn't. Supposing that some fixed-income retiree had decided to buy a bunch of Talisman shares with the grocery money. Then the subsidiary fails, the stock price goes down and he takes a big loss. But this insider, he knew that in advance, so he started selling off, which dropped the price of the stock. *Now* if the old guy buys, he buys in at a lower price, one that more accurately reflects the true worth of the company. Why? Because the guy who started selling off based on inside knowledge, he helped make sure that whatever was known about the company was already reflected in the price. Insiders regulate stock prices to make them more fair, because they always know what's going on."

"But this guy makes a fortune because of his access to information no one else has. Is that fair?"

"Think of it as his fee for making sure things stay on an even keel."

"Give it up, Jubal. You're not serious."

" 'Course not. But in a warped kind of way, he's got a point, because the net effect of insider trading is that it protects small investors."

Morosco shook his head but wasn't worried about Thurgren's commitment to pursue the case. He knew well his boss's philosophy, that an uncontrolled market would inevitably destroy itself, and that insider trading, left unchecked, would hasten that process. As SEC Chairman George Peabody III liked to say: "A free market doesn't mean a market without rules. It means that everybody plays by the same rules." "Trouble with you, Jubal, you always try to see both sides of every issue. Mighty bad *ju-ju* in a cop."

Thurgren grinned, then said, "What about our friend Burton?"

Upon hearing the IdeaConnexion CEO's name, Morosco hung his head and let out a groan. "Staller again." Then he looked up and sighed as he pulled another manila folder out of his bag and opened it. "I know, I know. You still got a feeling about this guy. What is it . . . he making too much dough?"

"That's not it," Thurgren replied thoughtfully, as if trying to explain his suspicions to himself as well as Morosco. "Lot of people make a lot of money. There's just something bothers me about this guy, like I'm staring right at a sign, except it's in Greek."

"Well, here's the latest scheme from the diabolical Mr. Staller." Despite his sarcastic protestations of frustration, Morosco had learned to respect Thurgren's hunches as something more than just vague intuition, which didn't stop him from poking fun at his boss whenever the topic came up. "He took a pretty good-size position in *TillYouDrop.net*."

Thurgren raised his eyebrows questioningly. *TillYouDrop.net* had been one of the early entrants into the world of on-line retailing, but, as had happened so often in that sector, had gotten left in the dust by others who had seized upon its innovative concept and improved on it while the original wallowed in the stagnant waters of its former creativity. "How big a position?"

"Four and a half percent."

Thurgren snorted and shook his head: It was just under the 5 percent threshold that would have required Staller to file forms with the SEC to alert the investing public that someone was taking a significant position in the company. "What do you suppose he wants with that junkyard dog of an e-tailer?"

"My guess? He wants to combine it with something else he owns."

"Aren't they based in New Mexico? What else has Staller got in New Mexico?"

"Not a thing, but so what? All this modern technology, it could be in Kuala Lumpur for all the difference it'd make. Anyways, why I'm telling you this, it's because you wanted to know everything the guy does, so there it is, but don't expect me to come up with a good conspiracy theory for you, too."

"What's it doing?" Thurgren asked, referring to the price of *Till-YouDrop.net* stock.

"Let's just say the Staller effect is taking hold."

Thurgren easily interpreted the cryptic remark: People who had never even heard of the company would start buying it just because Staller had. Then everybody would think Staller was a genius for latching on to an obscure stock that was poised to rise, none of them realizing that his interest was the only reason for the boost in share price, so the next time he bought something else it, too, would go up for the same reason, making him look like even more of a genius, and so on, *ad delirium*.

Thurgren nodded knowingly. "Is that all of it?"

"I sincerely doubt there's anything more."

"Well you keep an eye on this, y'hear me, Lewis?"

"Like a hawk, Jubal. Really, I'm all over it. Now can we talk about *Artemis-5.com*?"

"Sure. What's new?"

"Not a damned thing. There's no indication anything's out of line, and I'm starting to think if we don't get aggressive, this one might be a dead end, too." Thurgren frowned but didn't respond, so Morosco continued. "You still want me to get close?"

Thurgren nodded. "As close to James Hanley himself as you can get."

"Not gonna be easy. Can't be just a one-way street or else we're not gonna get anything."

"What are you telling me?"

Morosco dropped the folder on the desk. "Let's get this thing started off right, Jubal. Let's toss them a giant bone right from the get-go."

SEPTEMBER 18

THEY'D BEEN HOLED UP IN A SMALL CON-
ference room all morning, Jim Hanley and Lance
Muldowney, engaged in what (very) old computer
programmers used to call "core dumping." In trying to understand how they were going to work
together, they shared as much background data,
business philosophy, relevant experience and contact information as they could dredge up in the
marathon stream-of-consciousness conversation.

They'd easily fallen into a rhythm of can-
dor normally not seen in a commercial setting
since, well, forever. In the hell-bent-for-leather,
breakneck paced world of high technology, where
today's supercomputer was next week's tie clip,
there was no time to dance warily around each
other hiding weaknesses that would eventually
emerge, anyway.

CHAPTER FIVE

Hanley made it clear that he was a big-picture guy, a deal maker unwilling to get crowded by details best left to people who were good at those sorts of things. He didn't understand the physics of technology, and didn't much care about it. What he was interested in—what every visionary entrepreneur was interested in—was the application aspect: What could it do, and to whom can we sell it? Tell him that a handheld satellite phone used time-division multiplexing in the gigahertz range and his eyes were likely to cross. Tell him instead that a geologist in a remote corner of Namibia could phone his company in Nebraska the instant his tests disclosed an underground pocket of oil, and Hanley got interested. Tell him that the company in Nebraska couldn't care less what that phone call cost and he got very interested.

Muldowney was also relatively uninterested in razzle-dazzle technology for its own sake. As a matter of fact, he wasn't even much interested in the application side, either. What twanged his heartstrings was corporate finance, the administrative compartment that cared not a fig what a company actually did, or how it was run, but only how it managed its money. Muldowney knew all too well that the best operations people in the world could bankrupt a corporation if the real businessmen, the ones who handled the dough, didn't do their jobs right.

When a company got into trouble and needed to get rescued in a hurry, the board never brought in an engineer or a scientist or a project manager. They brought in a finance guy, someone who knew how to swing the axe and could lop off heads or entire divisions with little regard to operational consequences. When a maverick personal computer maker predictably got into serious trouble because it got too big for its founders to manage, the board didn't go out and find a computer jock to set things right; it found someone who'd been running a soda pop company. As far as that board was concerned, it didn't matter what kind of outfit he was running, as long as he understood numbers. They knew perfectly well that the investment community gauged the health of a company by a set of figures that could fit on an index card but was almost wholly unconcerned with how those numbers got there.

Muldowney had watched, stunned at first, then aghast, then mesmerized, as giant corporations whose stocks were sinking like torpedoed rowboats lit fuses under their share prices and watched them soar by doing nothing more than changing the method by which they determined the value of inventory. Same employees, same factories, same sales . . . the only thing that was different was ten lines in a computer program that calculated how much the stuff in the warehouse was worth, but it was often enough to turn the company from a dying dog into a financial superstar.

To be sure, the first reaction was generally a drop in share price because of suspicion that the company was cooking its books, but after that minor tremor they simply didn't care. The reason was, they knew nobody else would care. And since the only thing investors do care about is the share price of their stock, the only thing they were really interested in was what everybody else thought those shares were worth. So, if the new corporate savior shut down a division just so he could announce he'd reduced costs by half a billion a year, who cared if that division was the company's only real hope for a future? Drastically reducing costs was the only sure-fire way to kick up the stock price, which was why the legendary hatchet men who waltzed in and fired thousands of employees may have been detested and reviled by workers for their disregard of tragic human consequences, but they were revered by the investment community, which applauded them for their bold vision, awe-inspiring decisiveness and square-jawed resolution in the face of a distasteful task that simply had to be done.

But no one ever wanted to put himself in a situation like that, which was why smart executives tried to preempt it by making sure they always had good finance people around who could advise them on how to keep those stock prices rising, which translated directly into keeping investors off their backs so they could concentrate on managing the business rather than just its image.

In the case of *Artemis-5.com*, there were no investors yet, other than Caruthers & Osborne, so it was Muldowney's job to see to it that, when shares in the company were at last sold via an initial public offering, the maximum number of dollars flowed back into the corporate coffers. Traditionally, an IPO occurred after several decades of solid operational experience, steady profits and a rosy future. These days, it sometimes happened before the phones were even installed, little or no revenue had ever been generated, and the future was clouded in the impenetrable murk of technology changing so fast that equipment could become obsolete even before the warranty expired.

Since a start-up technology company was likely to be sold off well in advance of proving itself in the marketplace, the corporate finance department was often more important than the people actually trying to produce a profit.

"FIRST THING WE GOTTA DO," MULDOWNEY SAID, "WE GOTTA raise more money. As much as we can. Last thing we need is to run short of cash just when you're trying to do something important that costs money."

"My feeling is that we've pretty much exhausted traditional avenues with respect to replenishing liquid resources."

It took Muldowney a while to unravel the words and get to the meaning. "You're tapped out on venture capital?"

"In a nutshell."

"Bullshit." Muldowney waved a hand in the air. "You haven't even started. Hell, you got thirty mill practically just for showing up. Do some real shit, you'll get a lot more."

"Like what? Our midterm strategic thrust isn't based on a product-oriented paradigm, so directly addressing the market isn't a mission-critical priority yet."

Muldowney did a double take. "I'm not a potential investor, Jim," he said with a grin. "You don't have to talk like that, just two of us in the room."

"Talk like what?"

The grin disappeared and Muldowney shook his head to clear it. "Got nothing to do with nuts and bolts, anyway. Got to do with perception. We need to talk about the board of directors. Where do you stand so far on—"

There was a knock on the door and Hanley's secretary Beth stuck her head in. "You moguls too busy being important or are you hungry?"

They fussed about ordering sandwiches and then Beth left. "I was asking about your board," Muldowney said as he stood up and walked over to a pot of coffee resting on a burner. "Heard you're lining up some pretty heavy hitters."

"It's a real dilemma," Hanley said as Muldowney dumped the remains of his last cup and poured a new one. "Tell you the truth, I'm not sure I want a heavy board. I know just how I want to run this place, how to focus in on the main priorities and not lose sight of the strategic objective, and I don't want a gaggle of outsiders zooming in to tell me what to do before they head back out of town."

Muldowney took a sip of coffee and stuck his tongue out. "Could fill my pen with this shit. I know how you feel, but it's the first step in attracting serious bucks. Gather yourself an A-list bunch, the world comes by to throw money at you."

"Gee . . . you planning to teach me Business 101? Besides, I've been sniffing around for weeks, and most of the top dogs are already sitting on boards."

"But here's the thing, Jim: These super hotshots, sitting on boards is what they do for a living. Two, three meetings a year they sit there and act wise, they collect big fees, they don't really give a shit what you do afterward."

"Then of what use are they besides as window dressing?"

"You make it sound like window dressing is a bad thing. Some of these guys, they're worth their weight in gold, it comes to public perception. Why do you think so many boards have so many people on them who don't work for a living anymore? They got successful, it's time to relax . . . they join boards."

"It's not as simple as you make it sound, Lance. They do have to attend a meeting once in a while, and there are only so many days in a year, so they can get pretty picky. Minorities and women, they're especially tough to land because everybody wants them."

"Yeah. Keeps the liberals and the 'socially responsible' mutual fund assholes out of their hair."

Hanley mulled it over for a few seconds. "So let's forget minorities and forget women," he announced suddenly.

"Why?"

"Because a board full of white males will send the message that we're serious and not distracted from our strategy by worrying about what looks right. We look serious, serious money comes our way."

"People are gonna scream."

"That's their right, as is ours to choose our own people. One thing about business, nothing gets in the way if there's a real buck to be made."

"I don't know, James."

"Well, I do. Why do you think tobacco companies are still around? Because they generate tons of revenue and profit, that's why. One of them even used to sponsor women's sporting events, for God's sake, and all those athletes who wouldn't dream of getting within fifty yards of a cigarette let them do it, and you know why?"

Muldowney nodded without answering out loud.

"Damn right. They may be killing off women by the thousands, but they poured money into tennis so all was forgiven and nobody said a word. Lord help me, I know *cancer surgeons* who have money in Phillip Morris. That Hollywood studio exec, the guy who embezzled money from one of his own actors? Right back running a studio two years later, because he always made money for the company." Hanley tapped two fingers on the table and pointed them at Muldowney. "So don't tell me investors are going to screech because we're not *diverse* enough. So long as they see their share prices go up, we could be sodomizing two-year-olds and there's no way in hell they'd interfere."

Beth knocked again and walked in carrying two bags of sandwiches, drinks and the usual accompaniments. She started to unpack everything, but Hanley politely shooed her out and took over. "Okay, Muldowney," he said as he handed over a can of soda, "as long as we're shooting for the stars here, let's start off by getting Burton Staller."

Muldowney had his finger under the pop top but stopped it there. "Staller? What for?"

"Because he's like Midas. Everything he touches turns to gold."

Muldowney set the can down without taking a drink. "You think he's some kind of genius?"

"Sure, the new Isaac Newton. Don't confuse cause and effect, Lance. Companies take off because he's interested, not the other way around. Everybody thinks he's psychic, so whatever he buys into, everybody else buys in, too. That's why the shares go up."

"So, if he's not as smart as everybody thinks, why do we want him?"

"*Because* everybody thinks he's smart. Nothing else matters."

Muldowney thought it over. "Okay, Staller, but that one's gonna cost us. He's not a professional board member, and he's going to want a chunk."

"Not a problem, if he makes money for us. Anything else?"

"Yeah," Muldowney said as he snapped open the pop-top. He took a deep drink and wiped his mouth with his hand before reaching for a sandwich. "We gotta throw something back to my guy at the SEC once in a while. Not just useless bullshit, either, or he's gonna dry up as a source."

Hanley nodded his understanding. "Agreed. Quid pro quo is the lifeblood of commerce."

"Don't have to give away the farm, but it's gotta get them excited."

Hanley bit into his ham and cheese and mulled it over. "How committed are you, Muldowney? To this company, I mean. And me."

"Honestly?" Muldowney scratched the side of his nose. "Depends how rich you're gonna make me."

It was a good response. Any proffers of personal loyalty or deep feelings for the long-range vision of *Artemis-5.com* would have made Hanley skeptical. But Muldowney was clearly all business, and he looked at this relationship as a business deal: As long as both sides benefited, he was on board 100 percent. "Your friend at the SEC," Hanley finally said as he reached for a can of soda, "tell him *Artemis-5.com* is about to put three of the best-known Internet gurus in the country on its board."

Muldowney nodded as he bit into his sandwich, pleased that Hanley had seen fit to accept his guidance. He didn't want to belabor the point, though. "Another thing. You want to start taking out patents. Right now. This week, even."

"Patents?" Hanley, surprised, stopped chewing. "On what? Who says we're manufacturing anything?"

"Doesn't matter. Just start patenting everything in sight, okay? And one other thing." Muldowney set his sandwich down, took a long drink from his can of soda and folded his hands in front of him. "I don't want to be out front in this company."

"I don't get you."

"I want to be the backroom guy, pure and simple. Don't want to be an officer, don't want to meet with analysts, none of it."

Hanley frowned in puzzlement. "Must tell you, Lance, that surprises me somewhat. I would've thought you'd want a little personal splash."

Muldowney shook his head forcefully. "James, I don't even want a title. You have to be the man here. It's all gotta get built around you."

"I've never gone in for cult of personality rubbish."

"Doesn't matter. It's what people invest in. That's why they make heroes out of cyberwonks who can barely hold a civil conversation, and why stockholders worship men who couldn't even get a date in high school. Then your share price dips two cents and the press starts printing features about how you're all washed up at the age of twenty-three and the signs were there all along and you're not really as smart as they've been telling their readers you were, but somehow it's your fault, anyway." Muldowney picked his sandwich back up. "Not for me, Jim."

"The way you make it sound, it's not for me, either."

"But you don't have a choice." He bit into the sandwich, taking a huge bite. "I do," he said around the mouthful.

SEPTEMBER 22

PROFESSOR MALLORY J. COMPTON, PRESI-dent and CEO of eConceptics, didn't even bother to read the nondisclosure agreement, just took a few seconds to see that it looked like the hundreds he'd signed before. "Okay," he said, throwing his pen down impatiently and making a show of looking at his watch. "So what's your big idea?"

Hanley took the NDA back and put it in his briefcase. "As it happens, Professor, even with this statement, I'm only going to afford you the sketchiest outline. I'm not comfortable sharing the baseline strategic imperative that defines the synergy we're attempting to achieve."

Compton sighed and nodded with undisguised boredom, then sat back and prepared to listen, as though Hanley were just another eager-beaver student who, like so many others, thought he'd have the world at his feet within weeks.

"The problem with most of the marketing that's done on the Web," Hanley began, "is that everybody thinks they're thinking big, but they're all thinking small. These companies pushing portals, their core concepts are too inside the box. They think that if they can figure out what sites you're visiting, and what pages you open once you're there, they can figure *you* out and sell that information to on-line retailers, who can then target you for advertising." Hanley knew that several of Compton's biggest ventures were along just those lines, and that he was essentially insulting the great guru in his own ashram.

"So what's wrong with that?"

"As a core concept, it's self-limiting and nonempowering." Hanley decided spur of the moment that there wasn't a business buzzword Compton hadn't himself pretty much beaten to death on the lecture circuit, and under an onslaught of more of the same he was likely to sink into a well-practiced stupor. Besides, his condescending complacency needed puncturing in order to provide a clear airway to his attention, so it was time to change linguistic gears, something the chameleon-like Hanley was able to do with ease. "And if retailers believe in it, who gives a shit if you rob them blind? Sell 'em data on a million users, and if you only get a thousand of them right, what the hell: Net advertising is cheap, and maybe a tenth of a percent hit rate is good enough."

Compton bristled visibly but said nothing, so Hanley twisted the knife a little. "Those guys can't even tell if somebody's really interested in what they're looking at or just doing it for a high school project. I mean, they don't even know what the user is doing unless they go through portals like *Whoopie!.com* in the first place, and once somebody's found what he's looking for, what the hell does he need the portal for next time, and next time is most probably when he's actually going to buy something. So just when the user is doing something you really want to know about"—Hanley spread his hands, as though it were obvious—"you've lost him. You don't know shit. You're lucky if you even get that tenth of a percent."

Compton twisted uncomfortably in his chair. He was too smart not to know Hanley was speaking the truth. He was also too smart for this to be new news. It was a problem he'd been fighting for years, not by actually doing anything but by trying to talk his way out of it. "So, what are you going to do that's so special?"

Notwithstanding Compton's irritation, Hanley had at least caught his interest. "Can't tell you, Professor. But let me ask you a hypothetical question."

"You can't tell me? I just signed your NDA!"

"I'm not telling you, anyway. Not yet. Now, you want to hear my hypothetical?"

Compton waved a hand by way of assent.

"Suppose there was a way to trap every single Internet transaction in the entire world and use them all to look right into people's souls."

Compton grew still and stared at Hanley unblinkingly for several long moments. "You're full of shit," he said, but he said it hesitantly, and licked his suddenly dry lips.

"You think so."

"I know so. You can't do that. You can't possibly tap into everybody. There are dozens of portals, and even combined they don't come up to even a thousandth of a percent of all the traffic. Besides, they won't let you come anywhere near their—"

Compton could tell by Hanley's expression that he was humoring him by letting him rag on, that this enigmatic entrepreneur had already thought of all that, and that the more Compton spoke, the stupider he was going to sound when he finally shut up and let Hanley tell him what he was planning.

But it was hard for Compton to do that, because, when you got right down to it, he was a bit scared. What Hanley had just told him was not only the ultimate net-marketing dream, it was also the ultimate privacy nightmare, depending on your point of view.

Finally, realizing he was rambling, he settled down. "How?" he asked simply.

"You've got your mind so wrapped around portals and piddling stuff like that, you're missing the bigger picture."

"Am I?" he said icily. Telling Professor Mallory J. Compton he was missing the bigger picture was like telling Einstein he'd made a mistake adding up his grocery bill.

"Yup." Hanley leaned forward and rested his elbows on the desk. "Fuck the portals, Professor: I'm going after the backbone servers."

Compton stared at Hanley, then dropped back against his chair as Hanley continued.

"Let me give you my view of things and you correct me if I'm wrong." He settled back and tried to sound like he was summarizing rather than lecturing.

"Quite literally, there is no such thing as the Internet. It doesn't actually exist, any more than 'the English-speaking world' actually exists, and is essentially just an agreement among millions of computer users to employ a common set of protocols in sending information to each other. As long as everybody uses the same standards, they can decipher what they send each other. There's no Internet you can actually put your hands on, no central office anywhere controlling things, no single entity calling the shots. As long as everybody adheres to the same standards, it all works, and even though it occasionally looks like one big, integrated system, that's just an illusion.

"It's like lumping every single English-speaking person in the world together, regardless of where they're located, and calling the result 'Englishnet.' It looks like a single entity and anybody who's a member can communicate easily with every other member. But it's purely an artificial construct, bound together by nothing more than adherence to a single standard. There is no overseer, no administration, and no dues except phone charges. And, just like with the Internet, there is absolutely no way to tell how many members there are, or who they are."

Hanley paused, as if to see if he was meeting with Compton's approval. Taking silence as tacit admission that he was making sense, he went on.

"But you can get close. With Englishnet, eventually every member is going to use the phone, and if you could get your fingers into all the phone companies and monitor every conversation, you could pick out all the ones conducted in English and, over time, get pretty close to identifying most of the members. Not only that, from the content of those conversations you could learn an awful lot about each of them.

"Backbone servers are like the Internet's phone company. They're giant computers that route messages around, taking your e-mail or your

Web query and figuring out where it's supposed to be sent, then bringing you back the reply. Eventually, nearly every Internet communication finds its way into one of those massive machines, which, taken as a group, handle billions of transactions every second."

He stopped and took a breath, then concluded. "They're the heart and soul of the system, Professor. Everything anybody ever does on the Net is in those servers. *Everything.* Get your hands on that and it's like the Rosetta stone to people's lives."

"No question about that . . ."

"Imagine consolidating just a day's worth of someone's Internet activity. Suppose you saw that he'd ordered flowers, made a reservation at some snooty restaurant, sent an e-mail telling his girlfriend about it and another to his parole officer moving his appointment, and then refilled his prescription for herpes medication. Aside from the obvious blackmail opportunity, information like this is solid gold to anybody wanting to sell him wine, jewelry, theater tickets . . ."

"Or somebody *not* wanting to sell him medical insurance or offer him a job."

"Exactly. Some artificial intelligence software picking this stuff out of the backbones," Hanley explained, "and you've got profiles of people so detailed we'd know more about them than their psychiatrists."

Compton's eyes darted back and forth frantically. "It can't be done," he said weakly. "The people running the servers won't allow it. The secure layers . . . actually identifying the users . . . even consolidating packets to reconstruct the original transactions . . . no, no, no, it can't be done!"

"Actually, it can," Hanley said, reverting to his Earl Grey mode of speech. "But, as I took pains to point out to you, I was speaking purely hypothetically." And he left it at that.

Compton stared at the top of his desk, continuing to imagine all the hurdles while chewing at a fingernail.

Hanley could see the good professor's mind shift from contemplating obstacles to calculating the value of success. "Don't think of it in terms of dollars per user," he offered helpfully. "Think of it in terms of the percentage of the gross retail product of the entire planet."

Compton went pale and tried to gulp, which was difficult considering how constricted his throat had become. "What do you want from me?" he finally managed to croak.

"I want you on my board. For that, you and the other board members share a one percent stake, which you pay for yourself at the offering price."

At that Compton frowned, talk of money being the most effective way to bring him back to earth. "We share one percent? I usually get at least that for myself. Gratis."

Spoken like a true whore, Hanley thought. "There are only going to be ten board members. Tenth of a percent? You're looking at, I don't know . . ." He let Compton do the calculation himself.

"What do I have to do?"

"Not a damned thing. Which is one of the reasons you don't get free stock, just an option." Compton knew that wasn't an ethical or business consideration, it was a legal one: Getting stock without giving anything substantial in return would constitute "illegal consideration" under SEC rules. "All I want is your name and your commitment to get Katerina Heejmstra on the board." Hers was one of the other top names in the Internet world.

"What about Pauling? Seems to me he'd be the—"

"Got him already," Hanley said, enjoying the renewed interest he saw in Compton's face.

"I don't think you can pull this off," Compton said, sobering a little.

"As you wish," Hanley answered as enigmatically as he could.

They were both thinking the same thing: Compton had little to lose. If Hanley failed, what did it cost Compton . . . one day spent at a board meeting? And if Hanley succeeded, he'd be rich as Croesus.

It was the same rationale the self-styled guru had used to lend his name to at least two hundred other companies. He was like the guy selling pencils on Forty-second Street and charging $300,000 apiece for them. Asked if he really expected to sell any at that price, he answered, "Only gotta sell one."

ONCE THEY HAD COMPTON ON BOARD, HANLEY AND MUL-downey approached one of the biggest venture capital firms in northern

California and told the money men that they had Compton and Katerina Heejmstra sewn up. They let a second firm know they had Alan Pauling and the chairman of Schumann-Dallis, and told a third they had the president of CitiTrust.

As fiercely competitive as they were, VC firms comprised a tightly knit community not unlike a multicellular organism. As soon as a bit of information became known to one, it propagated throughout the network via synapses so dimly understood that verification became largely hit or miss. Supposition could take on the appearance of fact with blinding speed, and midlevel managers, in an effort to impress their superiors with their uncanny ability to ferret out useful data, were prone to attribute the papal imprimatur to information that only minutes before had been but the vaguest rumor, lest they be denied credit should the rumor prove to be true.

When the names of the purported *Artemis-5.com* board recruits began crackling around the VC network, nobody realizing that neither Hanley nor Muldowney had ever even met any of those people except for Compton, the pressure was on and each of the VC firms tried to crawl over the other two to be the principle financier of the start-up. Caruthers Osborne knew this was going on, but it didn't matter: Hanley planned to use $36 million of the new funding to exercise his option and repay them in full, with interest, and thereby be released from his promise not to secure other financing. C&O would have no claims of ownership rights once that had been done.

Each of the three new funding sources, acutely aware of the other two, privately offered exorbitant lines of credit to Hanley in exchange for options to increase their positions once the initial public offering was in place. Hanley let himself be pressed to the wall over a period of some days, and then accepted.

All three deals.

OCTOBER 3

ON HIS WAY IN TO THE OFFICE BUILD-
ing that housed the estimable technology guru Katerina Heejmstra, Hanley reached for his chirping
cell phone with some annoyance. "What?"

"Jim, glad I caught you."

"Why? I'm just on my way up to see
Heejmstra."

"I know. Listen, don't tell her you've got
Burton Staller on board. Don't even mention
him."

"Are you mad? He's one of our strongest selling points! Wait . . . are you telling me we're not
going to get him?"

"You can probably get him easy."

"Excellent! So—"

"He's under active investigation by the SEC."

Hanley moved away from the revolving doors to the lobby and pressed himself against the wall. "Not possible."

"Wanna bet?"

"Holy Hannah, Lance!" Hanley put one hand over his free ear to block out the ambient noise. "Have you any idea how many people we've informed that he's already on the board? We're going to get caught with our—"

"No, we're not. I'll explain later, but I'm telling the *Journal* and *Business Week*, off the record, that Staller was under consideration but rejected because he didn't pass *Artemis-5.com*'s stringent sniff test."

Hanley kicked off from the wall. "Burton Staller not pass a sniff test? Why don't you also tell them Tiger Woods didn't make the cut in a miniature golf tournament!"

"There's no time to discuss this now. Go to your meeting and let me handle this."

"Lance—!"

"Trust me, James . . . I know what I'm doing."

"THE ONLY REAL ISSUE IS CUSTOMER LOYALTY, MS. Heejmstra."

When Hanley had first brought up Katerina Heejmstra's name, Muldowney's first reaction had been predictable. "I thought you said no women."

"What I meant was, no token women." Heejmstra was far from that. As publisher of the leading industry newsletter, an eight-page weekly that carried no advertising and for which she charged subscribers $2,000 a year, she was more influential than those in the business who actually produced a technology product. She was the Liz Smith of the Internet, and CEOs would tell her things they wouldn't tell their bankers, but unlike her columnist counterpart, Heejmstra had a brutal instinct for winnowing inflationary corporate hype out of the mix and publishing only real news.

"The only issue?" she said in reaction to Hanley's observation.

"I know what you're thinking: Another entrepreneur who thinks he has it all figured out. But just listen for a second. You're on the board of *Whoopie!.com*—"

"I knew that."

Hanley smiled to show he could take a little ribbing. "They're generating significant revenue, and why is that? Because the company is peopled with certified geniuses? Because they have such visionary ideas?"

Heejmstra warmed to the conversation. "I take it from your sarcastic tone that you don't think so."

"It's because they were there early. That's the only reason. And it's the reason they may not last."

"You're talking about a company with a capitalized value of ninety billion dollars, Mr. Hanley. You're telling me it's going to fade away?"

"It might. Tell me, why are people buying on the Web?"

"Lots of reasons. There's no sales tax, for instance."

"But the shipping charges wipe out that advantage. That's why all these e-tailers are so terrified of a sales tax. Charge a tax and, just like that, it's too expensive to buy on-line, and you're out of business."

"But the prices are lower to start with."

"I'll give you that, but look, there are a dozen search engines out there that locate the lowest prices on commodity items. Nobody gives a tinker's cuss if they buy an ink cartridge from *Whoopie!.com* or Joe Blow. It's a commodity, and it doesn't make a difference who sells it to you. The ducks already proved that."

He was referring to "cyberducking," a process in which people duck into a retail store, learn everything they can about a product, usually by taking up a lot of a salesman's time, then duck out and order it on the World Wide Web from whoever's got the lowest price.

"The only thing that counts is the price," he went on, "but you can't compete on price because everybody's already slicing the margins razor thin. So what competitive advantage does one Web retailer have over another?"

"Reliability," she said unconvincingly.

"There are thousands of reliable on-line vendors. There's only one reason people buy on the Web, Katerina, and that's because it's convenient, which still leaves us the problem of how to get them to use *your* site instead of the other guy's."

"And you have this figured out, do you?"

"Maybe. People buy on the Web in the first place so they can do it in a hurry. If it's a pain in the neck, they get frustrated or give up. What you have to do is make things easier, like allowing a user to enter an order with one mouse click instead of spending fifteen minutes typing in the same damned information he typed in for every other thing he ever bought on-line. We should just store the information once, and all he has to do from then on is point to what he wants and click it. Finished. Two seconds later his credit card is charged and the goods are on the way. Don't give him a chance to think, to change his mind, or to figure out that too much data entry isn't worth the benefit. Point . . . click . . . we've got his money."

Heejmstra stayed quiet. And Hanley knew why, but purposely kept it to himself. "Now that's too simple and obvious. A six-year-old could figure that one out. What we need is something better. Much better."

"Who else has agreed to serve?"

"Well, let's see: Mallory Compton, Alan Pauling . . ."

But unlike Compton, Heejmstra wouldn't be pressed into any quick decisions, and Hanley left with her interest but not her commitment.

OVER THE NEXT TWO DAYS HANLEY AND MULDOWNEY, AS A team, approached the chairman of Schumann-Dallis and the president of CitiTrust, telling each of them that the other was aboard, and that they'd gotten major money from three top venture capital firms. Upon hearing that, the two agreed to be on the *Artemis-5.com* board, and to accept the same deal as everybody else: They'd serve for a dollar a year, plus the opportunity to buy into the company at the initial offering price.

Hanley started spending his $54 million in new venture capital money immediately. A big chunk went toward advance payments on technology transfer agreements he struck with prestigious universities, all of whom were eager to accept large amounts of cash in exchange for only vaguely worded commitments and strongly worded nondisclosure agreements.

Hanley promised each of his contract partners a share of the gross revenue to be realized. While the percentages seemed relatively modest, these people were smart enough to know that, quite often, net proceeds could be manipulated all the way down to zero even on products that were in fact wildly profitable. As Hanley liked to point out, even though

Batman was one of the highest-grossing films in history, no net profit participant ever received a dime because the studio loaded the film's books with so many totally unrelated expenses they made it look like the film lost money. The only way to cheat on gross revenue, however, was to actually fake the books, and since manufacturers lived on the bragging rights afforded by high sales, that was next to impossible to do at any significant level.

Another chunk of start-up funding went to down payments on open-ended development contracts with companies such as Microsoft, Sun, Cisco, and Qualcomm, as well as a host of respected overseas firms. Again, the agreements didn't commit the subcontractors to anything specific. What they did do, however, was prevent every one of those companies from competing directly with *Artemis-5.com* or cooperating with any other companies that did.

OCTOBER 13

HANLEY HAD SLEPT LIKE A HIBERNATING bear following his flight to California. Because of the time difference, he'd fallen fast asleep at eight in the evening and had been wide awake and raring to go at four the next morning.

Dr. Alan Pauling, head of the Artificial Intelligence Laboratory at the California Institute of Technology, looked like he hadn't slept in two days. He was used to working in the lab until very late and not rising until mid-morning, but when he'd jokingly told Hanley by phone that he simply didn't have time to meet unless Hanley was prepared to fly to Pasadena and do it at six in the morning, he hadn't been prepared to hear that this was a perfectly acceptable arrangement.

That he'd hardly slept the night before due to his anxiety at having to get up so early was not at all a problem for Hanley. "Dr. Pauling, imagine a piece of computing hardware so powerful it makes a Cray supercomputer look like an abacus, yet it runs on a nine-volt battery."

Pauling smiled indulgently and groped for his coffee without turning his head to locate it first. "There's only one technology in existence that could hope to make that claim, and I doubt very much you're even aware of—"

"Quantum computing. That pretty much sum it up, Doctor?"

"So you read science magazines. Then you also know that a practical computer based on the principles of quantum mechanics is at least thirty years away."

"No, it isn't."

"Young man, you're wasting my time." Pauling rubbed uselessly at his uncooperative eyes. "There's only so much of me to go around and I don't join the boards of frivolous corporations headed by pipe-dreaming children who—"

"Russell McDiver doesn't think it's thirty years away."

"McDiver?" Pauling's supercilious smirk disappeared at the mention of that name. Russell McDiver was the Bobby Fischer of science. A borderline schizophrenic who was the only person ever to win two Nobel prizes in physics, he'd stormed out of the second ceremony in Stockholm after announcing that he was sick of being hounded by reporters and talk show hosts who confused him with Madonna. He was, as he'd put it, "getting the hell off this planet to do some thinking."

"Spoke to him just this morning."

"Where is he?" The note of hopefulness in the scientist's voice was heartbreaking.

Hanley patted the small metal attaché on the floor by his feet. "At the other end of this satellite phone. Can I call him and tell him you're joining us?"

Pauling gulped, suddenly wide awake. "Who else is on your board?"

"Well, let's see: Murray Compton, Katerina Heejmstra . . ."

It wasn't lost on Pauling that Hanley had referred to Compton by a nickname used only by the great man's intimates. "And you're going to make a quantum computer."

Hanley eyed him carefully, for several long moments, then slowly turned his head to one side, then the other, then back again. "No. We're not." His eyes bore into Pauling's.

The scientist nodded back in understanding.

Hanley caught the 9:00 A.M. American flight back to New York.

OCTOBER 14

"We're behind the eight-ball here, Jim," Muldowney said. "Takes a lot of bodies to go public, but here we are, a couple of guys and a secretary, and there's nobody to do the work."

"What work?" The reverse jet lag had caught Hanley by surprise, but at least now he had a little empathy for how Dr. Pauling had been feeling the day before.

"Going public, it's like launching a damned battleship. It's a wonder companies don't go broke just trying to get it done. It's got more rules than golf and if you break one of them, guys like Jubal Thurgren are standing inches away ready to bring the hammer down. So we gotta—"

"I don't want any more employees."

"You don't—what? Whaddaya mean, you don't want any more employees!"

"Just what I said. What's the point of loading up the payroll with a lot of mouths to feed? Before you know it, we'll have people bringing their dogs to work and organizing football pools and lunchtime volleyball games. I'll have people in here nine times a day grousing that somebody made them *uncomfortable*, which I understand is now a crime, and filing worker's comp claims for their past-lives therapy sessions because of some lunkhead downloading porn on his computer terminal, which, not incidentally, *we'd* be paying for. I'll spend more time worrying about medical benefits and assigning parking spaces than I will about running the business, and I'll not have that."

"James—"

"You had me hire a *compliance officer*, Lance. Now, what in blazes is that? We're only going public once, not doing it forever, so what the hell do we do with all of these employees once that's done and we've already turned into a giant day-care center?"

Hanley knew the question would throw Muldowney. Traditionally, companies going public were already well-established, thriving enterprises, selling shares based on a solid business foundation and a long history of excellent performance. Many, like UPS when it was offered up in 1999, had been around since the Earth cooled and had many thousands of employees, so they could easily funnel a few into the IPO effort.

But things were different in the technology game. IPOs were being undertaken by outfits so small the CEO could have the entire company over for Christmas dinner, and so new that their names weren't even up on the tenant listings of their office buildings yet.

"So, what do you want to do?" Muldowney asked.

"You know, Lanny, the trouble with you is, you placed money for years but you have no idea how things really work in a company."

"So enlighten me."

"We're going to outsource everything," Hanley announced. "We find people, good people, we hire them on as outside consultants, not employees. They work for themselves, and we contract for their services. We don't have to provide health coverage, we don't pay workman's comp, we don't do any personnel administration at all. We don't even have to have a personnel *department*, or whatever the hell they're calling it these days."

"Human resources, Lord help us," a voice said from the doorway.

Jackie Toland was a stereotypically severe-looking female attorney whose tightly pulled-back hair, edge-defining makeup and thick, multi-layered clothing instantly transmitted an attitude ten degrees beyond no-nonsense. Even the way she stood or sat announced a belligerence that made you hope she was on your side instead of your opponent's, and she tended to speak with great authority regardless of the topic or her level of expertise, as though doing anything less might be taken for weakness.

She sat down as Muldowney said, "Gonna be hard to control people."

"Hard?" Hanley shook his head. "Easiest thing in the world. If somebody fails to perform, he's out, and we don't have to worry about wrongful termination lawsuits or unions or bureaucratic storm troopers telling us what we can't do and what we have to do. We don't have to fol-low any labor laws, either."

"We can do that?" Muldowney asked.

"Look at me," Toland said. "I don't work for the company. I'm an outside contractor."

"But you're a lawyer!" Muldowney exclaimed.

"So what? All that means, I'm a temporary. You can do the same thing with bookkeepers, engineers, programmers . . . even secretaries."

"I heard that!" Beth yelled through the half-open door.

"You pipe down!" Hanley called back. "You're already on the pay-roll, remember?"

"Only thing is," Toland said, scratching at her ear, "that's how Microsoft started out, and the labor department nailed them for it. Said the contractors were employees in every sense of the word and had to be on the books as such."

Hanley had already thought about that. "Easily remedied. Nobody works more than twenty-five hours a week. That way, nobody can make the case they're really full-time."

"But they won't make enough money," Muldowney protested, "and we won't get enough done."

"Sure we will. We'll assign deadlines that can't be completed with less than forty hours a week—or eighty—even though we'll only let them report twenty."

"Now, why would they do that?"

"Because we'll pay them a hundred dollars an hour, and keep pay-ing them that as long as they get the work out."

"That's a lot of money."

"It's less than they'd end up costing us if we had them on the pay-roll, especially when you roll in the administrative overhead and all the compliance folderol."

"Still," Toland said, "at some point the labor department's going to put its foot down."

"Think outside the box here, Jackie. As soon as the feds tell me I've got to hire all of them, I tell them, sure, no problem. Then we cut every-body's compensation in half, and sit back as they wear a groove into I-95 rushing down to D.C. to tell those regulators to mind their own bloody business."

"That still won't do it."

"I know. But by that time, the IPO is done."

"And then?" Muldowney asked.

"We fire everybody."

"We fire them. Good plan."

"Then we advance a couple of them the funding to start their own consulting firm, they'll hire back everybody we got rid of, and the next morning everything's back to normal."

Toland pursed her lips and moved them back and forth, like she always did when she was thinking. "This I like," she said at last.

Beth appeared at the door and said, "Lawyer here to see you, James."

"From where?"

"From *Whoopie!.com*," said a strong voice as a young man stepped up behind Beth.

"Still don't know how anybody can say that with a straight face," Toland said as she stood up. "I'm next door if you need me, James."

"NAME'S SIMONSON," THE ATTORNEY SAID BRUSQUELY, OFfering a perfunctory handshake. He was all business and brimming with self-confident bravado. He had his briefcase open before his rear end even hit the chair. "I'll come right to the point, Mr. Hanley. The—"

"Have you a first name?"

Hanley had him read already. A nouveau bar admittee, his first major corporate client, finally made the big time, his first experience on a solo assignment with no partner breathing down his neck, sent out on a simple matter and determined to smirk his way back to the office with a signed consent agreement from an adversary he'd thoroughly cowed by virtue of his legal acumen, airtight argument and the awesome power of his mere presence, by God. "Pardon?"

"A first name. You know, like Sam, Willy, Billy Bob . . ."

"Yes. Of course. It's, uh, Nicholas."

"Nicholas." Not Nick. Nicholas. 'Nick' smacked of stealing apples from pushcarts on your way up to *capo* in the local subfamily, your Uncle Nunzio getting you into law school via "a little something" to ensure the dean's financial security in his dotage or a threat to break his legs, whichever he responded to better. 'Nicholas' was old money, an ambassador, J. P. Morgan's right-hand man. "Mind if I call you Nicholas?"

"No. What I—"

"And I'm just James, okay?"

"Certainly. The thing—"

"Or Jim, when we become friends. Well, okay, Nicholas. How may I be of service? You say you're a staff attorney for *Whoopie!.com*?"

"That's correct. And you, *James*, are in violation of our 'One-Shot' patent."

Having delivered his death spear, Simonson watched with satisfaction as it lanced its way into Hanley's heart and shook him so badly that the heretofore arrogant head honcho of *Artemis-5.com* crumbled right in front of his eyes, turning into a blithering wretch who wanted nothing more than to make peace at any price and somehow get out of this with at least some small shred of his dignity intact.

At least that was the plan. "What in the flaming hell is a 'one-shot'?" Hanley asked.

"Not *a* 'one-shot.' Just 'One-Shot.' "

"Ah. Well, that clears up everything, Nicholas. Thanks so very much for coming."

"You know perfectly well what it is, Mr. Hanley. I didn't come here to play games." This accompanied by a withering stare that could freeze a Mongol warrior's blood.

Hanley scratched his ear. "I've certainly no wish to play games either, Nicholas, so just tell me what it is."

Simonson sighed, the deeply bone-weary sigh of a man about to indulge a superfluous query purely for the sake of civility. "It's a process that allows an on-line shopper to enter all his identification, address and credit card information once and not have to do it again for subsequent purchases. The information is stored securely and recalled when needed."

Hanley nodded in understanding as Simonson spoke, then said, "And . . . ?"

"And what?"

"And what else?"

Simonson blinked a few times. "And then, nothing. That's it."

"That's it? That's what you patented?"

"We most certainly did."

It was the exact same process Hanley had cited to Katerina Heejmstra as an example of how to make the Internet more convenient to shoppers. "Tell me you're just having a go at me, Nicholas. That'd be like getting a patent on a spoon."

"It's a novel business practice, Mr. Hanley."

"Novel? It's absurdly obvious! Doesn't something have to be—what is it now—'nonobvious to a practitioner skilled in the art' or something like that?" It was exactly like that.

Simonson bristled visibly but, to his credit, didn't allow himself to be drawn into an irrelevant debate. "We can argue about it all day, but the fact is, *Whoopie!.com* has a patent on it and therefore *Artemis-5.com* is in violation of our rights, and if you use it, we'll sue you so fast and so hard it'll melt all your hard drives. At the very least, we'll tie your whole damned company up in court for years."

Hanley could smell the fear surrounding Simonson, who'd made the mistake of firing his guns before he thoroughly understood the target and was now praying fervently that it wouldn't backfire on him. There was no advantage to be gained by exploiting that situation prematurely, so Hanley played it out as Simonson had scripted it, adding a faintly pleading tone to his voice. "How can you sue us when we haven't done anything yet?"

"I have it on good authority that you plan to," Simonson countered with what he hoped was just the right touch of I-know-a-lot-more-than-I'm-letting-on mystery.

Hanley put his hands up in the air, as if to ward off any implication that he was other than a straight shooter. "Let me assure you, Nick— may I call you Nick? Let me assure you that I have no intention of violating anybody else's legitimate rights. For one thing, I don't have the time. My thrust right now is implementing vision-oriented, needs-based logistical enhancements, and my chief concern is competitive threats to our value proposition, you see?"

"Uh, yes. I do."

"Well, there you go! *Synchronicity,* Nick, that's the key!" Hanley leaned in close. "But let's keep that strictly *entre nous,* know what I mean? On the QT, as it were. Hate like the dickens to let our core strategy leak." As Simonson nodded his assent, Hanley straightened up again. "Anyway, that's pretty much all I can manage to squeeze in on the old DayTimer, so violating your patent isn't on the table."

"Fine." The lawyer whipped a piece of paper out of his briefcase. "Then sign this."

"What is it?"

"Nothing more than you just agreed to, Mr. Hanley. It's an agreement stating that *Artemis-5.com* won't violate the *Whoopie!.com* 'One-Shot' patent."

Hanley nodded vigorously. "Certainly. No problem at all with that." He saw Simonson's eyes go wide as the imminent victory hovered and visions of the fast track to partnership danced so close to his face the tightly wound lawyer almost got dizzy. Hanley gave it another second, and just as Simonson wetted his lips, he leaned over and hit a button on his intercom. "Jackie, come on in here a second, will you?"

To Simonson's inquisitive stare Hanley said, "No big deal, Nick. Just going to have my lawyer give it a quick look. You'll be out of here in five minutes. Got a pen?"

Simonson almost dropped his briefcase in his mad scramble to locate one, and had it out and waiting for Hanley when Toland walked in.

Hanley handed her the agreement. "Just going to sign this and thought you should have a glance."

Toland took a few seconds to read it. "Looks straightforward enough."

It was all Simonson could do to keep from gasping. He began fiddling with his briefcase to cover his anxiety, half rising in anticipation of grabbing the signed document and getting the hell out of there.

Toland turned the piece of paper over, looked at the back, then turned it over and looked at the front again. "Where's the other piece?"

Simonson went as rigid as the great stone heads on Easter Island. "What other piece?" he managed to gurgle.

Toland shrugged, as if it were obvious. "The one that says what *Artemis-5.com* is going to get."

"What's the matter, Nick?" Hanley asked with great care and concern.

"I, uh—What are you talking about, Miss Toland?"

"This is a one-way deal," she answered, holding the piece of paper up, "for *Whoopie!.com*'s benefit only. What's in it for our company? Well, *his* company," she added pointedly, the issue of her eventual position in *Artemis-5.com* still a sore point between her and Hanley.

"It's not a business deal. It's just an agreement that you won't—"

"So why should he sign it?"

"It's a written promise not to infringe our patents!"

"Oh, sorry. Must have misunderstood." Toland turned to Hanley. "James, you plan to infringe any of their patents?"

"Nope."

Toland handed the paper back to the lawyer with a shrug.

"But he didn't put it in writing!" he protested. It came out as a whine.

"Why should he?"

"To make it legal!"

"What's in it for us?"

"There's nothing in it for you! You can't violate our patents!"

"Agreed. So what else is new?" Unwilling to torture the poor schnook any further, Toland said, "Look, let me put it to you this way: If James doesn't sign it, what happens?"

"If he doesn't infringe our patents, nothing. If he does, we sue."

"Okay. And if he does sign it, then what happens?"

"Same thing."

"So there's no difference if he signs it or not?"

"Sure there is. We'd have his promise in writing."

"Which you already said doesn't make any difference, except it strengthens your position in court and weakens ours." Toland dropped the paper in front of him. "By the way, Mr. Hanley also promises not to drive through any red lights and not to kill the President. You want him to sign papers to that effect as well?" She turned to Hanley. "What patent, anyway?"

Hanley explained, and Toland snorted before he finished. "Pile'a bullshit. You can't get a patent on something like that. For one thing, it needs to be nonobvious to someone skilled in the art, and anybody with half a brain could figure this one out. Hell, I've had a charge account at Bloomie's since I was fourteen that does essentially the same thing.

Anyway"—she turned to go—"you take care, there, uh, whadja say your name was?"

"Nick," Hanley answered for him.

"Nick. Okay, you take care, Nick." She waved and was gone.

Simonson sat back down shakily. He needed to go back to his company with a victory, not a vague oral promise. "Listen, Jim," he said, inexpertly disguised desperation lacing his voice. "Let's work this out like reasonable men, okay?"

"Reasonable men." Hanley had already made his point, and there was nothing left of Simonson's former swagger, but there was one last task to accomplish, and that was to purposely piss the lawyer off as much as possible. "You storm in here and threaten to sink my company under a lawsuit and now you want to be reasonable?"

Hanley retrieved the agreement from in front of Simonson and carefully tore it in half, then in quarters. "Well, you can take your bullshit patent and One-Shot it right up your ass," he said as he dropped the pieces into the lawyer's briefcase. "And the next time you try to strongarm me, you'll wish you'd gone into forestry instead of law. Now get your bony ass out of my office!"

Simonson barely felt the insult, because by the time he found himself out in the hall uselessly but desperately jabbing at the elevator button, he was already too busy composing his résumé in his head.

HANLEY STEPPED OVER TO JACKIE TOLAND'S OFFICE. SHE was printing something and staring intently at it as it came out. Muldowney was reading it over her shoulder.

"You won't believe this, James," she said without turning around when she heard Hanley's footsteps, "but they really do have a patent on it."

"I don't believe it."

Toland grabbed several sheets of paper from the exit tray and held them up. "Told you so," Muldowney said.

"Do you mean to tell me somebody can actually get a patent on something as—it doesn't make sense!"

"Yo, Jim." Muldowney rapped a knuckle on Hanley's head.

"Doesn't matter!" he said with exaggerated enunciation. "It is the way it is, not the way you think makes sense. So deal with it and let's start taking out our own."

Hanley nodded in resignation, then said to Toland, "I want you to go see Katerina Heejmstra."

"And do what when I arrive?"

"Sign her up to the board."

"Has she agreed?"

"She will by the time you get there."

HANLEY WENT BACK INTO HIS OWN OFFICE AND PICKED UP the phone, then sensed movement behind him and turned to see that it was Toland. He hung up as she closed the door.

"I'm getting a little tired of working on an hourly basis, James. You and Lanny are sitting on a uranium mine here and I've got to believe I've been as valuable as him."

"You've been nowhere near as valuable as him."

That was the last thing she'd expected to hear, and she was unable to form a quick reply.

Hanley let it hang there for a few seconds, but before the hurt and disappointment on her face deepened, he added, "Which doesn't mean you're not very valuable. Just don't throw offhand analyses like that in my face and expect me to roll over and automatically agree."

"I've kept you out of a lot of trouble," she said, recovering. "Half a dozen times I—"

"And I appreciate it. I like you, you're good for this company, but don't kid yourself that there aren't five thousand lawyers within three miles of this building who are every bit as competent as you."

"What the hell, James!"

"What do you want me to do . . . stand here and drip praise all over you while you ask me for more money? You started a negotiation and I'm negotiating. It's called *business*, Jackie."

"Okay, fine. Business then. So what's my end?"

"I've told you before: There's going to be enough for everybody, and we'll take care of you."

"You're asking me to take a lot on faith. I'm a lawyer, and faith isn't in my playbook."

"It's *because* you're a lawyer that we don't want you holding an equity position just yet. You have to act as outside counsel. Jesus, you're the one who told *me* that!"

"I know. It's just that—"

"And don't try to tell me you're not pocketing some pretty fancy lucre in the meantime, either. Not exactly a painful wait, is it?"

She relaxed her face and folded her arms across her chest. "Not exactly."

"Alright, then." His voice grew softer and he smiled at her, the rancor in the air evaporating rapidly. "Will you trust me, Jackie? I'm not planning to forget my friends. Now please get on down to Heejmstra's office before she leaves and try not to fret more than you have to."

"Hang on a second."

Hanley picked up the phone. "Jackie, I really need to—"

"Only a second!" She went back to her office and returned immediately carrying a manila folder. Hanley sighed as he spotted the papers sticking out and returned the phone to its cradle. "Now what?"

"I want you to give me power of attorney so we can expedite all the paperwork flowing in and around this place." She set the folder down and withdrew the first sheet. "Now this one here, this is a codicil granting a corollary estoppel in the event that—"

"Yes, yes . . ." Hanley yanked a pen out of his shirt pocket and scrawled his signature at the bottom. "What else?"

Before she could explain the next one, Hanley jumped to the signature line and signed once again, as he did for all the sheets she handed him. "See? You shove a bunch of papers at me and I sign them. Trust, right? The new human resources paradigm, managing your people as a strategic asset. Now get going."

As Toland left, mollified at least for the moment, Hanley finally placed his call to Katerina Heejmstra and was put through immediately. "I'm faxing over a copy of the nondisclosure agreement you signed," he said after the pleasantries were quickly dispensed with.

"Why are you doing that?"

"I'll tell you why. I just had a visit from a *Whoopie!.com* attorney who threatened to sue me if I violated their preposterous 'One-Shot' patent, that's why."

"And . . . ?"

"Tell me, Katerina: Do you have any idea where he might have gotten the notion that I was planning to do any such thing?" He paused, then into the ensuing silence added, "Because sure as the dickens *I* wasn't the one who told him."

OCTOBER 27

JUBAL THURGREN LOOKED AT THE NEWS-
paper Lewis Morosco had just tossed on his desk.
As his eye roved at random over the page, Morosco
tapped a finger on one article above the fold. The
headline read, "Aggressive start-up hits for the
upper deck in choosing board."

Thurgren began reading the story but looked
up two paragraphs into it. "Heejmstra, Pauling
and Compton? He got all of them?"

Morosco touched the side of his nose.

"I'll be dipped in poop," Thurgren said as he
returned to the article. As Morosco well knew,
Thurgren's admiring expression was not because
James Hanley landed three of the heaviest-hitting
superstars in the Internet world, but because Morosco had correctly ferreted out that piece of intelligence a full two weeks ago. It strengthened

their confidence in the fact that, should Thurgren's suspicions about *Artemis-5.com* prove justified, they'd have an inside track on proving it.

Jubal Thurgren was not anything like the kinds of personalities who typically populated the federal government's policing divisions, especially the self-important, superannuated nebbishes over in DoJ antitrust who were so intent on bringing down the giants of the new world order. Thurgren maintained the proper perspective, that of ensuring no repetition of the kind of uncontrolled excess that presaged a plunge into years of darkness in the thirties. But he was smart enough to know that this was insufficiently motivating to the kind of young, smart, ambitious people required to get the job done. For them, something else was required, and there it was once again, as he saw Lewis Morosco get caught up in the self-righteous zeal of the enforcers, the kind of people who charted their career progress by how many of the rich and famous they could bring crashing to Earth.

Thurgren read enough of the article to know everything past the first few paragraphs was filler, then pushed the paper away. "Why'd he call it *Artemis-5.com*, anyway?"

"Beats me. Something about Artemis being Apollo-somebody's sister."

"Not Apollo-somebody. Just Apollo. A Greek god."

"What, you mean like Jupiter?"

"Yeah, like Jupiter, only not Jupiter. For one thing, Jupiter was Roman. Apollo was Greek."

"They're different?"

Thurgren regarded Morosco for a long moment, wondering if his leg was being pulled in response to what might have been his condescending explanation of mythological diversity. Then he decided it was no such thing. "Not really," he said, which seemed to satisfy Morosco, who forgot about it as soon as he heard it and moved on to the next topic.

IT WAS LIKE WALKING INTO THE "FUNCTIONAL LOONIES" ward of a nuthouse. Leon Loudermilch's office, or at least what Hanley could see of it through a thick haze of acrid cigarette smoke, was an avalanche of paper covering nearly every square inch of horizontal space. His filing cabinets, credenzas, bookshelves, chairs, windowsills—even the planter holding a thoroughly desiccated palm had a loose-leaf binder resting right on the soil that hadn't been watered in months. The only reason Hanley could even tell where the man's desk was positioned was because of the fresh smoke rising up from behind precipitously high stacks of papers.

"Mr. Loudermilch?" he ventured cautiously.

There was a great clatter and a head popped up from behind the stacks, eyes staring at Hanley in wide surprise, like those of a deer trapped in headlights. A cigarette dangled from Loudermilch's mouth, a stream of smoke rising from it, and Hanley could see a separate column of smoke still coming up from somewhere on the desk. For a second he thought maybe some papers had caught fire, then he realized the smoke was from a second cigarette Loudermilch had apparently forgotten about when he'd lit a new one.

"What," the attorney said perfunctorily.

Suppressing a cough, and trying not to wave the smoke from in front of his face—where was it going to go, anyway?—Hanley gave his name and said, "I'm from *Artemis-5.com.* I phoned earlier . . . ?"

Loudermilch continued to stare at him for a few seconds, then snapped his head to the side and back again. "Whatever. Siddown."

He had to be kidding. It would take a week of excavation to uncover a chair. Hanley remained standing, and Loudermilch didn't seem to notice anyway. "So what do you—" he began, but just then a secretary came through the door holding a sheaf of papers.

"Filing's due for *briss.com,*" she said, waving the papers.

Loudermilch turned his stare from Hanley to her, not saying a word.

"Give them to Swenson?" she asked.

"Yes!" Loudermilch exclaimed, relieved, his cigarette bobbing up and down as he spoke. "Give them to Swenson!"

"Got it." She turned and left, and Hanley looked at Loudermilch inquisitively.

"I have no idea who the hell Swenson is," the attorney said disconsolately.

"She seemed to think he was the right guy," Hanley offered with what he hoped was a degree of comfort.

Loudermilch nodded and looked down at where his desk was supposed to be. "I have no idea who the hell *she* was, either." He drew in a great lungful of smoke without touching his cigarette with his hands.

"I have this idea for the Internet," Hanley said, "and I want to know if I can patent it."

There was a second's hesitation, then Loudermilch exploded. A huge cloud of blue smoke burst out of his mouth as he began laughing uncontrollably, and only when he realized that his cigarette had shot out as well did he grab hold of himself long enough to scrabble around trying to find it before it ignited all the kindling on his desk.

"Guess you heard that one before," Hanley said, embarrassed.

Loudermilch waved it off. "It's not that." He lifted the cigarette into the air with one hand and smacked at a smoldering spot on some papers with the other, noticing for the first time the second cigarette still burning in the ashtray. "You want to know if you can patent it, I mean Christ, Harry—"

"Hanley. My first name's—"

"You can patent damned near anything!" Loudermilch finally figured out that he could put the newly located cigarette out in the ashtray and still have the other one to smoke.

He came out from behind his desk. His clothes looked like he'd dressed for the week rather than the day, and this was Thursday already.

"Time was," he said absently, "getting a patent was like sitting through orals for a PhD. Buncha guys crawling all over you, making sure your idea was new, that it really worked, that all the rules and regulations were strictly adhered to." He walked to the window and looked out. "Steam engines, radio, the transistor . . ." he mused wistfully. "Boy, those old guys really came up with some serious shit!"

He'd gone quiet and distant. "And now . . . ?" Hanley prompted gently.

Loudermilch awoke with a spasmodic jerk of his body, turning to look at his visitor. "Now?" He stepped over to the potted plant and yanked the loose-leaf out of the soil. Bits of dirt flew off the cover as he waggled it back and forth in front of Hanley. "This guy's got a brainstorm. I'm talking a world-class technical revolution right here, brother."

"Which is . . . ?"

"He sells apples over the Web, see?" Loudermilch stepped closer and squinted at Hanley. "Yeah, apples. Now this patent application here, what this is for, you can order a bushel of any type you want—McIntosh, golden delicious, fujis, what-the-fuck-evers—and this here cybernetic marvel will figure out the weight, on account of it knows how big each type is and how many can fit into a bushel, and how much each one weighs, and therefore what it's going to cost you and how big a box it'll take to ship it."

Hanley nodded his understanding. "And . . . ?"

Loudermilch smiled. "And nothing."

"That's it? That's all of it?"

"Uh-huh."

Hanley had trouble believing it. "But any high school kid could write a program like that on his calculator! What the hell is the big deal?"

"The big deal," Loudermilch said, dumping the binder back into the pot and raising a fresh puff of dirt, "is that nobody else can do it on account of he's got a *patent*!"

"On the software?"

"No." The lawyer shook his head and went back to his desk. "On a novel business practice."

Hanley guffawed his disbelief, but Loudermilch seemed to take no offense. "There are guys got patents on pieces of shit you wouldn't believe," he explained. "Place an order with one mouse click, that's right up there with the television in the Patent Hall of Fame. Automatic auction bidding? High school kid wrote it in a week and it's worth more than the laser printer."

Loudermilch sat down. At least Hanley assumed he had, because his head disappeared. "Now whatever it is you got—"

"It's an idea for gathering—"

"Yeah, whatever. Patents cost you five grand each if they're uncontested. You write it up, we take it from there." Loudermilch was on autopilot now; Hanley could hear the sounds of computer keys being tapped as he moved on to whatever he'd been doing when he interrupted. "Detailed technical review prior to submission, that's another five grand per. How many you got altogether?"

"Um, I figure about ten, maybe a dozen . . ."

"Fine. We get paid prior to submission." The clicking increased in frequency and intensity. This meeting was clearly over.

"Is there someone here who can help me write it up?" Hanley asked.

The clicking stopped, and there was silence as Loudermilch stood up and looked at Hanley vacantly. Suddenly he cried, "Absolutely!" and leaned over to jab a finger at something on his desk.

"Get Swenson in here!" he barked happily into his intercom.

OCTOBER 28

"DON'T KNOW HOW YOU GOT HER TO DO it, James," Toland said to Hanley over the cell phone.

"Who?"

"Katerina Heejmstra, who do you think?"

"Oh, that. Just another business whore at heart, Jackie. She joins the board, all it costs her is the time it takes to sign the papers."

"I'm not talking about her joining *our* board, dummy. I'm talking about her quitting *Whoopie!.com*'s."

"Quitting—what?"

Hanley asked some question, then hung up and called Heejmstra. "You didn't have to do that, Katerina," he said when she came on the line, not bothering to preface it with any explanation of what he meant.

"It wasn't my idea. The rest of the board told me it was yours or theirs, so I quit theirs."

Hanley hesitated before replying, thinking Heejmstra would read it as remorse, however slight. "Just so you know," he then said, "that business about how their attorney found out you and I had spoken about the 'One-Shot' thing? I never would have said anything about that to anybody, about how you violated the nondisclosure agreement. I just wanted you to know I was annoyed."

Heejmstra laughed. "You think you scared me? No way you could prove I ever told him anything."

"Then how come you—"

"Because I think your company is going to blow *Whoopie!.com* out of the water, that's why."

"What makes you so sure?"

"To be completely candid? Wait until John Q. Investor finds out I left their board to join yours. And don't try to tell me you recruited me for my deep insights into modern management, either."

"Then I imagine we understand each other."

"Perfectly. I didn't get into this business to be a nice person, Hanley."

OCTOBER 29

She was right. When the *Wall Street Journal* hit the stands the next day announcing that so formidable a personage as Katerina Heejmstra quit the *Whoopie!.com* board to sign up with *Artemis-5.com*, the buzz on the Street became a scream. *Whoopie!.com*'s stock lost $18 billion in value before the NYSE invoked one of its "circuit breakers" just before noon and called an emergency halt in trading to stop the hemorrhaging.

But they couldn't stop the ripple effect throughout the rest of the market.

"The Dow dropped over four hundred points," Toland said as the late-fall light died outside.

"The Dow is the biggest bullshit indicator on the Street," Muldowney opined. "Doesn't mean a damned thing."

"Okay, smarty-pants, try this: The NASDAQ plunged two fifty."

"Now you're talking!" Muldowney exclaimed with a smile.

Hanley shook his head in disbelief, then said, "Everybody out. I've got to figure out how to spread more of our venture funding around."

NOVEMBER 1

The biggest slice of the *Artemis-5.com* venture capital pie, the part that was left after Hanley paid off Caruthers & Osborne, was spent on marketing, a campaign modeled on an old PR strategy once used by a well-known movie actor. Hanley directed his publicists to relentlessly hype his privacy, driving home the fact that he wouldn't give interviews or disclose any details about the company. There was no official word on whether it would even go public. All of this was purportedly premised on the company's determination to maintain the highest levels of integrity and not exploit the feverishness that had overtaken the rest of this market segment. The public, of course, read it as Hanley protecting an earth-shattering breakthrough, but he himself couldn't be faulted for propagating those kinds of rumors. After all, he hadn't said a word in public.

Over the next few weeks, the public perception Hanley had been trying to perpetuate began to pay off.

Schoolchildren could name members of his board. Internet backbone providers ordered additional equipment to handle the anticipated increases in network traffic. Blue-collar workers played hooky to plant themselves at brokerage offices to try to get wind of any IPO. Housewives skimmed from the food money in anticipation, and a reservation on the buy list became a hotter commodity than a ticket to the Oscars, even though nobody had any idea at all which brokerages would be blessed with the right to divvy up the paltry number of shares that would be left over once the underwriters and big institutional investors had sucked up the bulk of them.

Five months after it was conceived, *Artemis-5.com* was finally making its presence felt.

NOVEMBER 21

"SOMEONE HERE TO SEE YOU, JAMES," BETH said over the intercom.

"Who?"

Hanley's voice came through Beth's lightweight headset rather than a speaker. The visitor couldn't hear the other end of the conversation. "A Mr. Paul Steffen."

"No."

"Certainly. Just a second."

"Just a second what?"

Beth smiled at Mr. Steffen and pulled the headset cord out of the intercom as she stood up. Once inside Hanley's office, she closed the door behind her. "He looks serious," she said.

"They all look serious," Hanley said impatiently. "Since when do you—"

"And scary, too."

"What do you mean, 'scary'?"

Beth shifted uncomfortably and looked away. "I'm not sure. It's just that—Jim, I don't want to have to tell this guy to go away empty-handed."

Hanley grew still and regarded her carefully, deciding she wasn't kidding around. "Okay, let's get it over with. Bring him in."

"He wants to take you to lunch."

"Beth!"

"He suggested the Bangkok Bistro."

She watched as Hanley's eyes widened. He ate there at least twice a week, and he didn't have to ask to know that Beth hadn't mentioned that to the man waiting outside. "Okay," he said at last. "Tell him twelve-fifteen. And tell him I've got a one o'clock to get back for."

HANLEY ARRIVED AT THE DECIDEDLY UNFANCY THAI RES-taurant on Fiftieth and Eighth on time. Paul Steffen was not hard to spot. Even in the crowded room his very presence seemed to rearrange everything in his vicinity into a sphere with himself at its locus. The fabric of his suit was understated, but the tailoring was the kind designed to show not only the physique beneath but the checking account that had paid for it. Hanley couldn't imagine any dishevelment about this guy even at the end of an eighteen-hour day.

Steffen spotted him and rose without hurrying, the simple action conveying both supreme self-confidence and the kind of faint arrogance a mountain would radiate if it deigned to come to Mohammed.

His handshake was too firm but Hanley got the definite impression the man had eased up for his benefit. "Mr. Hanley, a pleasure."

A waitress had spring rolls and a diet soda with a wedge of lemon in front of Hanley before he'd even touched down on the chair. "You, too."

Steffen looked around with an amused expression as the waitress set down some appetizers and left. "Elegant place."

It was in keeping with Hanley's purposefully restrained lifestyle, determined as he was to be the picture of fiscal responsibility to potential investors. "Food's good. Try the *mee krob*. So what's on your mind, Mr. Steffen?"

"Business proposition."

"Truly." Hanley reached for a spring roll and glanced at his watch as he brought his hand back.

"Yes." If Steffen was insulted by the ostentatious demonstration of bored impatience, he didn't show it. "You're heading toward a public offering and have quite a bit of excitement whipped up, not just on Wall Street but Main Street as well."

"So I hear." Hanley leaned back as another waitress brought a pot of tea.

"You got thirty million from Caruthers and Osborne, which you paid back out of another round of financing. Hired yourself a lawyer and a crackerjack corporate finance whiz kid, made a lot of contacts, have a few technology contracts in the works . . ."

All of that was available from sources not too difficult to tap into. "See here," Hanley said as he poured some tea into Steffen's cup. "I appreciate your buying me lunch, but I really—"

"And you're being looked at very carefully by the Securities and Exchange Commission. That's the expression, isn't it? Looked at? When they're getting ready to start a formal investigation but don't want to blow their hand just yet?"

Hanley hesitated for only a second before bringing the spout of the pot above his own cup. "How would I know?" he said as he began to pour. "Like you said, they keep it to themselves as long as they can. Until a formal order is issued, they don't have to say a word."

"Fella named Jubal Thurgren is taking the lead." Steffen picked up the tea and took a sip. "Tough guy, Thurgren. Used to be in public accounting."

"Is that so."

"Uh-huh. Got religion and jumped the wall, and now he's looking to make an example of some Internet start-up, bring it crashing down as a way of putting the brakes on all this IPO craziness. Kind of a sore point with him."

The part of Hanley that wasn't currently preoccupied with the breadth of Steffen's knowledge about his business noticed that his mode of speech didn't comport so well with his appearance. This man had not been born into money, but had come up to it from someplace else.

What he'd just described was more than Hanley himself knew, but not by much. "What's any of that to do with you?"

"With me? Nothing." Steffen took another sip of tea. "But the people I represent would like to buy a hundred thousand shares of *Artemis-5.com*."

"So what's stopping them? It's called a *public* offering for a reason."

Steffen smiled. "Are you testing me, James, is that it? See if I know what I'm talking about?"

The worst-kept secret in the IPO world was that the public at large had essentially no opportunity to buy shares in a new company at the initial offering price. The standard line was that if you got the shares you asked for, you'd better not take them because it means nobody else wanted them.

The underwriting syndicate—the primary investment banking firm undertaking the sale and other firms invited in to help spread the responsibility—would sell about 85 percent of the new *Artemis-5.com* shares to big institutions that managed mutual and pension funds. A select group of brokerage houses would split the rest and make them available to their best customers, people who maintained account balances of upward of a million dollars. The retirees who hung around the retail brokerages watching the tickers all day and who traded a few hundred shares here and there had about as much chance of getting in on an IPO as they did of winning the lottery and being hit by an asteroid on the same day.

"They want a guarantee from your underwriters that they can buy a hundred thousand on opening day," Steffen repeated.

"And why on earth would I want to give them that? What's it got to do with the Thurgren problem?"

"Maybe I can help."

"Because your cousin's brother-in-law's chiropractor's aunt is a secretary at the SEC?" Hanley sneered and called the waitress over. "Just what I need . . . a bunch of random tips I have no way to verify and probably couldn't do anything about anyway, and a prison stretch if I'm caught." The waitress came to the table, pad at the ready, already tapping her pencil impatiently on it before she'd barely stopped walking.

Hanley pointed to something on the menu and was about to speak. Steffen, without taking his eyes off of him, said, "He hasn't decided yet."

When the waitress made no immediate move to leave, Steffen shifted his gaze to her, which was all it took to send her skittering away, no questions asked.

"Hey!" Hanley set the menu down and glared at Steffen. "What the—"

"Listen to me." Hanley stopped talking instantly. "Jubal Thurgren is a problem for your little enterprise."

"I already—"

"And I happen to be in the business of making problems disappear."

HANLEY TRIED AS HARD AS HE COULD TO REMAIN OUT-wardly calm, but his stomach was suddenly seized with a nameless dread that paralyzed him. In less time than it took to blink, this wasn't fun anymore. Steffen's gaze was steady and patient, and seemed to say he knew exactly what was going on inside Hanley's head, that he'd been here many times before.

Hanley was starting to feel uncomfortable just sitting there and not saying anything, but he didn't trust himself to speak. He didn't know the right words, and he wasn't sure he could manage more than a croak even if he could think of something to say. He didn't want to look weak, not at a time like this. Maybe he should just—

"Why don't you have a sip of water," Steffen said. It came out as a command rather than a suggestion.

Hanley nodded dumbly and reached for the glass, but it was empty. Steffen raised his hand without taking his eyes off of Hanley. Although the restaurant was crowded and noisy and the four harried waitresses could barely keep up with the workload no matter how they scurried about, two of them were instantly upon them with pitchers of water before Steffen's hand had gotten more than a few inches off the table. Hanley hadn't realized quite how dry he'd gone until the cool water re-moisturized the back of his throat.

The woman obviously in charge approached with another plate of spring rolls, and the other two skittered away. "You ready order now, Missa Hanley?"

"Sure," Steffen replied when Hanley didn't. His menu remained unopened at his elbow.

"Okay fine." She set the spring rolls down. "Shoot."

Steffen held a hand out toward Hanley, who said, "Some, uh, some—"

"*Mee krob?*" the head waitress prompted.

"Yeah. Thanks, Trinh."

"Okay fine. Same for you?"

Steffen shook his head. "Do you have *stirply kamurgle*?" At least that's how it sounded to Hanley.

"Not on menu, but we have. You want some *whong nikldrk* widdat?"

"Can you make it with *smifpiktik*?"

"Sure you bet," she said with a smile, Hanley completely lost as he listened uncomprehendingly. He'd eaten in this restaurant two or three days a week for four months and had never heard of any of that stuff. "My sister make. Okay fine." And until this moment, he hadn't known Trinh was capable of smiling, either.

When in doubt, start asking questions. "How am I to know you'll do it?" Hanley asked when Trinh had gone off.

Hanley purposely avoided the subject of exactly what "it" was. Steffen had worded his offer ambiguously. It could mean everything from providing him with advice on how to deal with arcane regulatory issues to . . . whatever.

Hanley thought he saw Steffen nod imperceptibly, as though approving of the implicit consideration of his proposal. "It'll be kind of obvious, don't you think? Besides, if you don't think we held up our end, you can always withdraw our reserved shares."

"How do you know I'll hold up *my* end?"

Steffen smiled indulgently. "You don't really want me to answer that, now do you?"

Damned right I don't. "Merely ascertaining the ground rules."

"There aren't any ground rules, Hanley, but the first one is this: *Don't fuck with me.* Are you going to eat that spring roll?"

Hanley wasn't sure if he'd ever be able to eat anything else again. How could Steffen be thinking about food when the entire room was spinning crazily, and everything else in the universe along with it? "I don't know how I can get you on the list for that many shares. There are people out there who are ready to sell a kidney just to have a crack at five hundred."

"Ten thousand to each of ten corporations," Steffen said.

"Still going to look suspicious."

Steffen's eyes froze over. "Without us, you may not even have a company, so let's not waste each other's time discussing piddling details. Just handle it."

"I didn't say I was going to do it."

Hanley regretted it the instant the words hit the air. Not the words themselves, but the note of defiance. He thought he sensed some wire in the man's body start to quiver, but Steffen seemed to consciously will it away. "You want to think about it."

"Yes. I mean . . . yes, I'd like to mull it over."

Steffen bit into the spring roll as he nodded. "Fair enough," he said around the mouthful. "Forty-eight hours enough?"

"How will we get back in touch?"

"Just meet me right here," Steffen answered. "Ah, now this looks good."

Trinh was proudly carrying a plate of something Hanley had never seen in the Bangkok Bistro before and placed it gently in front of Steffen. "Good stuff," she said proudly.

"Smells like it," Steffen confirmed as the heady steam swirled up into his face. Trinh barely looked at Hanley as she directed one of the other waitresses to set his plate in front of him.

When all the bustling was done and the waitresses had withdrawn, Steffen expertly deployed a set of chopsticks and began eating, closing his eyes for a second in delight. "You were right, Hanley," he said when he'd swallowed. "This is excellent." He took another bite, the substance of the meeting clearly having been concluded.

"I have to—" Hanley cleared his throat. "I have to get back."

Steffen nodded as he chewed, and waved toward the door with his chopsticks without looking up. He didn't bother to ask Hanley why he was leaving before he'd eaten a single bite.

· · ·

First words out of Beth's mouth when Hanley walked back into the office, and he hadn't yet said a word himself. "Of course I'm okay. Lanny around?"

"In your office."

"Did you tell him where I was?"

"Just at lunch. Why?"

"No reason." It was a dumb question to have asked her. He needed to get hold of himself. Now that he was back in the safe confines of the "suite," what had happened over lunch seemed surreal and far away. Would it sound in the retelling as it had when it had occurred? On the other hand, he wasn't planning on telling anybody. He wasn't sure *what* he was planning.

"Hey." Muldowney looked up from his seat near a bookshelf when the door opened. "S'matter with you?"

"What do you mean, what's—what the hell is going on around here, anyway! Do I have blood on my face?"

"Looks like you have no blood at all, James. You're white."

"Should I require a nurse, I'll go out and buy one." He turned to close the door and shrugged off his jacket. "What do you want?" he asked as he hung it up and turned toward his desk. His head was still reeling and he needed some quiet moments to sort things out.

"Not sure which of these filings we should make public at this point," Muldowney said, waving a handful of loose papers in the air. "The rules are a little ambiguous and it seems, uh, seems a herd of red elephants in the Congo recently opened up a coffee shop for chimpanzees."

Hanley nodded absently, annoyed at the intrusion on his thoughts. Steffen's appearance on the scene complicated matters beyond imagining. Hanley had plans, he had it all mapped out . . . *wait a minute*: "Elephants? What elephants?"

Lanny rolled his eyes at the ceiling. "You haven't heard a word I said."

"Uh, filings. Indeed. So let Jackie *esquire* handle it. It's what we compensate the overpriced shyster for, isn't it?"

Lanny stared at him, then dropped the papers to the floor, sat back and folded his hands. Hanley really hadn't heard a word he'd said. "Jim, what's going on?"

Hanley was standing next to his desk, staring out the window. "Had lunch with someone."

"Who?"

Hanley sat down, and seemed to shrink in his chair. "Scary fellow."

He recounted for Muldowney, nearly word for word, his lunchtime conversation with Paul Steffen. If he'd harbored any illusions at all about the true nature of what Steffen was offering to do, they evaporated as he played it all back. Steffen's meaning was unambiguous.

"But it's nothing for you to worry about," Hanley assured Muldowney when he'd finished. "It's got nothing to do with you."

Muldowney didn't seem to hear that last part, or to care. "What're you gonna do?"

Hanley realized that, in his disorientation, he'd not given much thought to what he was going to do. "I don't know."

"You don't know," Muldowney echoed without affect, continuing to stare at Hanley, who shook his head.

Another second or two passed and then Muldowney was out of his chair and in Hanley's face so fast an onlooker would have sworn he'd teleported himself across the room. "Are you out of your fucking mind!" he demanded, heedless of whether his voice might carry outside the room.

"Will you take it—what's the matter with you?" Muldowney's abrupt reaction seemed to have snapped Hanley out of a half-trance.

Muldowney's hands were shaking and his face was turning red as he hovered threateningly over the desk. "I'm asking you, are you completely nuts or what?"

"For pity's sake, Lanny . . . I didn't say it was my intention to go along with the man."

"But you're thinking about it!" Muldowney nearly shouted. "You're sitting there and it's running through your mind! Tell me I'm wrong!"

"Really, Lance, don't get so—"

"Tell me I'm wrong!"

"Now, see here!" Hanley slammed his hand on the desk and jumped to his feet, but neither the sound nor his sudden movement had any effect on Muldowney at all. "Calm yourself!" he said in his most authoritative voice.

But still Muldowney wouldn't back away. "You can't do this, James," he said, his voice at a lower volume but no less intense. "You can't, you hear me? You'll throw it away, all of it, and you'll end up in jail. *I'll* end up in jail! You can't do that to me! You can't do that to the company!"

"I told you, this hasn't got anything to do with you."

"It's got everything to do with me!"

"How do you figure that?"

The question seemed to stop Muldowney short and make him think. "I'm your second-in-command, James. Everybody knows that. Beth out there knows I'm the first person you saw when you got back from meeting with that guy. And if a hundred thousand shares get special reserved, there's no way in hell that can happen without me being involved."

He was right. A bit self-centered, but right. "Nobody's going to jail, Lanny. You have to get caught first, remember?"

"They always get caught! Sooner or later it surfaces and everybody involved gets nailed!"

"In actual point of fact, hardly anybody ever gets caught. That's why corporations can wreak so much carnage."

"Don't joke, James!"

"I told you, Lanny, I didn't agree to anything, so why are you getting so exercised?"

Muldowney finally backed off and ran a hand through his hair. Trembling, he dropped back onto the seat by the bookshelf, abandoning his hair and wringing his hands instead. "Tell him you're not going to do it." He said it with such raw, pleading misery in his voice Hanley thought he was going to cry. "Who're you kidding? You know exactly what he has in mind, and if you think you'll be able to rationalize it away later as a semantic misunderstanding, we'll never get away with it."

Hanley had already shifted his thoughts before Muldowney was half-finished. "Okay, Lanny. I'll turn him down."

Muldowney went still. "You mean it? You're not just saying that?"

"I mean it. Trust me."

Waves of relief washed over Muldowney, and he needed a few seconds to let the last of the adrenaline dissipate. "What was the next move going to be?" he asked at last.

"Another lunch."

"When?"

"Two days."

"Okay." Muldowney nodded, cleared his throat and looked at his watch. "I gotta go meet with Jackie on these papers before she leaves."

He stood up, flexed his knees a few times to make sure his legs still worked, and headed for the door. Hand on the knob, he hesitated.

"Now what's the problem?" Hanley asked him.

"Not problem. Opportunity. Luckily, we're still in good shape."

"What do you mean?"

Muldowney looked at his watch. "Not too much time has passed."

"So?"

"You're going to call the SEC and report what happened. All of it."

"The hell I am."

"The hell you're not!"

"DR. COMPTON ON THE LINE," BETH SAID OVER THE intercom.

Hanley looked at his watch: seven o'clock. He was tired, hungry, and more than a little shook up. He sat down heavily and picked up the phone. "Murray, how are you?"

"Good. I may have something for you. I want you to meet a couple of students of mine."

Hanley closed his eyes and rubbed them wearily. "Rather not, Murray. I've spent more time discussing more useless crap than you could possibly—"

"Trust me on this one, James. Unless you came after me for your board because you thought I was a good tennis player."

No, I came after you for your name. "So what's the proposition?"

"I'll tell you later. You heading home?"

"I am."

"Okay. I'll call you tonight."

"HE ACTUALLY REPORTED IT," LEWIS Morosco said, shaking his head in disbelief.

It was the fourth time he'd uttered the same phrase since walking into Jubal Thurgren's temporary office at the SEC's New York field bureau some twenty minutes earlier, but rather than get annoyed, Thurgren shook his own head and said, "Yep," also for the fourth time.

"Does this change your thinking on the guy?" Morosco asked.

Thurgren pressed his lips together and swiveled his chair around. Outside, the towering office buildings of lower Manhattan took on a surrealistic isolation as the early winter sun elongated their shadows, but Thurgren was staring *at* the window rather than through it. "Not sure what it does. Perfect opportunity to make his SEC problems evaporate. . . . I'd have bet any amount of money against him doing the right thing."

"I don't know, Jubal." Morosco slumped down on his chair and folded his arms across his chest. "Monkey business, a little slippin' and slidin' here and there, that's one thing. But contract killing?" Thurgren winced at the term. "Even if Hanley's a baddie, doesn't mean he'd go that far."

"Guess not. Course, I've never met the guy." Thurgren went quiet. "Jubal . . . ?"

"Maybe it's time I did."

Morosco unfolded his hands and sat up. "You're not serious!"

"Why the heck not?"

"Face to face?" Morosco stood up and put his hands on the front edge of Thurgren's desk.

Thurgren swiveled back around. "Size him up a little, get the cut of his jib? Good police work, is all. Maybe I can shake him up some while I'm at it."

"That's insane!"

"What are you getting so—"

"What do you want to shake him up for . . . so he gets more careful? I thought you were trying to nail this guy!"

"I am. If he's a bad guy."

"You *know* he's a bad guy. Why confront him this early and tip your hand?"

"How can I tip it any more than it already is? He talks to Muldowney about it, you said."

"Mentions it." Morosco stood up straight and backed away from the desk, hands in his pockets. "But he's not convinced you're either serious or have the goods on him."

"But now Steffen shows up and offers to take me out, so if Hanley was suspicious before, he's got to be certain now."

Morosco had to agree. Steffen gave the impression that he knew more about what was going on in the SEC than Hanley did, which he'd used to bolster his credibility. So if he said that Thurgren was a serious problem, then Hanley had to believe that was true. "What we don't want to do, we don't want to give Hanley any more about the specifics of the investigation than we're feeding him now. We don't even want him to know that it's officially under way."

"No problem," Thurgren agreed. "And this is a perfect way to meet him without doing that. If I stick entirely to the subject of Steffen, it might make Hanley relax a little about whatever else he thinks is going on. Might even make him careless in the process."

Seeing that his boss was determined, Morosco relented and played the good soldier. "I'll set it up. How do we explain that it's the SEC gonna see him, not the FBI?"

"Because it involves potential violation of securities laws. Set it up for tomorrow, Lewis. Morning, not evening."

"Yeah, I know: It's your bowling night."

NOVEMBER 22

Compared with Lance Muldowney, Hanley's behavior was positively serene as he ran down every last detail he could think of while Thurgren took notes. "Are we doing some good here, Mr. Thurgren?" he asked when they were nearly finished.

"You bet!"

"Are you sure?"

Thurgren looked up in surprise. "Why do you ask?"

"Because I would have expected the FBI to show up." Hanley shrugged and inclined his chin toward Thurgren's notepad. "And I can't seem to discern a pattern to your notes."

"I don't get you."

"What you write down and what you don't. What you consider important."

"Ah." Thurgren's look of confusion became a smile, and he scratched self-consciously at his ear. "Tell you the truth, Mr. Hanley, importance has nothing to do with it. It's more a question of what I think I can remember." As the idle chitchat went nowhere, he noticed Muldowney fidgeting off to the side as though he'd been set upon by insects. "Some things just stick in my mind more than others."

"Well, that explains it. Except you wrote down what he was wearing but not my estimates of what time things happened."

"That's because I'm real good with numbers but lucky if I can match my socks up in the morning. As to the FBI, well, the mortal threat was ambiguous, even, uh, let's say—"

"Vague. And I'm paranoid, is that it?"

"No, no, not at all," Thurgren protested vigorously. "Threat like that is just difficult to assess, was all I meant, but the potential violation of securities law isn't. Since I'm a sworn peace officer as well as an accountant, you kind of get a two-for-one special."

"I see. So what do you think?"

"About what?"

"Is this fellow for real, and what do you intend to do about it?"

"Well . . ." Thurgren flipped his notebook shut and put an elbow on the armrest of his chair, resting his chin on his hand. He enjoyed the increase in Muldowney's discomfiture as he took his time. "FBI guys think it likely he's just scamming you somehow, but we have to take the threat seriously."

"And that means . . . ?"

"Go meet him for lunch and we'll nab him."

"Splendid!" Hanley nodded his head vigorously and turned to Muldowney, as though soliciting his affirmation that this was a good plan, that it would end the situation definitively. "I want to wear a wire."

"No damn way in the world. Why would you want to do that?"

"For my own protection."

Thurgren caught Muldowney's foot pumping up and down and wondered how he could do that so fast. "Mr. Hanley . . ."

Hanley jumped up and folded his arms tightly across his chest. "I'm not an idiot, Thurgren," he said as he began pacing nervously. "You arrest Steffen and it's his word against mine. Should he manage to avoid prosecution, he's back out on the street, and I'm, as you put it, in mortal danger."

Hanley's affected speaking style was beginning to grate on Thurgren. "That's a little dramatic. A wire, I mean, heck, that's a major operation. We need a truck, a technician, backup people . . ."

"Of what moment is that, Thurgren? *You're* the one he threatened to kill!"

"I'm not worried about it. You ask me, he's probably just some lowlife grifter trying to put the squeeze on you."

"No." Hanley shook his head forcefully. "I know people, and this was no ordinary thug. This was a serious player. I can fling the *merde* with the best of them and I know it when I see it."

"So I've heard."

Hanley came to a halt. "What's that supposed to mean?"

"Nothing. Forget it. What I'm trying—"

"Is my company under investigation?"

Their eyes locked. Muldowney's foot stopped pumping, and for all Thurgren knew, his heart might have stopped right along with it. "Of course it's under investigation."

Hanley, taken aback, blinked but didn't reply.

"Far as I'm concerned," Thurgren continued, "every public company and every one thinking about going public is under investigation."

Hanley relaxed, but only slightly. "I see that you, too, have a certain facility for deception. Is there a formal investigation of *Artemis-5.com* under way?"

"You mean, into alleged wrongdoing?"

"That's what I mean."

Thurgren let him hang for a second. "Heck, no. Why? Should there be?"

Hanley started, but recovered quickly. "No. Just heard some things, here and there."

"Well, I can't be responsible for rumors. But you are, you know."

"How's that?"

"If you're really contemplating going public, you've got an obligation to squelch rumors and misinformation that get out about your company. Keep everything clean, know what I mean? Everything on the up and up. I assume you've got a lawyer helping you with those kinds of things."

"Yeah. I mean, yes, I do. And Lance here, he knows the ropes."

Thurgren turned toward the young man. "Nothing more valuable than having a guy's been through it before," he said, nodding his approval. "So. I think I've got everything I—"

"But we're not done, Thurgren. I did the right thing. I reported it right away and that in itself involved a good deal of risk. I was a good citizen, so kindly refrain from telling me you're going to make a useless arrest and hang me out to dry when that criminal posts bail!"

"But a wire, jeez . . ."

"If you don't convict him," Muldowney said, "then he's still out there."

Hanley held a hand out toward him as he addressed Thurgren. "You think he's likely to simply walk away when he gets out?"

"Then don't go back to meet with him at all."

"Even worse. If he's for real—if the people who sent him don't appreciate bad news—what do you think is likely to occur when he goes back and says, 'Well, I tried, but Mr. Hanley didn't show up'?"

Thurgren inhaled deeply, then let it out noisily. "You've got a point there."

"Quite right." Relieved, Hanley suddenly found himself out of fight. "So, what happens now? How does this work?"

"YOU GONNA RUN IT YOURSELF?"

"No choice." Thurgren shifted the cell phone to his other ear as he raised his right hand to try to flag down a cab. "It's bull, so who am I going to flip it to?"

"You're gonna miss your bowling night," Morosco said, unable to keep the mirth out of his voice. "Want me to book you a hotel?"

Two cabs had already passed him by. Now a third one did the same. "No, my sister's in New Rochelle. Might as well visit. Hang on a second."

Thurgren pulled his wallet out of his pocket and opened it so his brightly polished badge was visible. He stepped into the street and held it up as another cab approached, and waved the driver down. "Seven World Trade Center," he said as he got in. The SEC's Northeast Regional Office was on the thirteenth floor. "Lewis, you still there?"

"Yeah. New Rochelle? Better leave real early coming back tomorrow. Traffic's gonna be murder. So, what did you think?"

"About what?"

"Hanley. How'd he strike you?"

Thurgren thought about it, trying to aggregate the various impressions he'd garnered into some kind of cohesive assessment. "I think he's full of it."

"You think?"

"Whole operation smells fishy, but not much I can put my finger on. We'll talk more tomorrow."

"Okay. What time will you get in? Remember rush hour."

"Then I won't leave until later, like maybe ten."

HANLEY WALKED INTO MULDOWNEY'S OFFICE JUST AS HE WAS finishing off a call, and took a seat opposite his desk.

Muldowney hung up and leaned back on his chair. "Hope you know what you're doing, Jim."

"I have no idea what I'm doing. This wasn't on the syllabus in business school." Hanley nervously rubbed his chin with the back of his thumb. "One thing I do know is that protecting me isn't Thurgren's number-one priority."

Muldowney looked off to the side as he considered it. "I don't know," he said, bringing his eyes back to Hanley. "These days, a public official gets negligent with a citizen's safety—especially one who came in and did the right thing—anything happens to you, he'll feel some serious heat."

"Maybe. Do you think he takes this Steffen business seriously?"

"You ask me, only reason he came up here was to see you face to face. He coulda interviewed you by phone."

"I got the same impression. It wasn't lost on me that I got some SEC bean counter to investigate when it should've been an FBI matter."

"Which probably means he's not too worried about Steffen taking out after you. Tell you the truth?"

"You don't think he will, either. I know." Hanley reached into his jacket pocket and withdrew an envelope. He tapped a corner of it against his cheek, as if trying to come to a decision about something.

"Whatcha got there?"

"Cashier's check for ten million dollars." Hanley tossed it onto the desk. "From the start-up money."

"Where's it going?"

"With you. To Switzerland."

Muldowney picked up the envelope and opened it, withdrawing the check and verifying that it was, indeed, for $10 million. "I don't get it."

"I've a bad feeling about all of this, Lance. Not just about Steffen, but about Thurgren, too." He pointed to the check. "I want you to fly to Switzerland, tonight, and deposit it in a numbered account."

Muldowney frowned. "What's this all about, Jim?"

"It's contingency money. Money to buy my way out of a bad spot if I need to. I want it isolated and distant, but where I can get my hands on it should I need it."

"I'm not sure our backers are gonna approve of you offshoring their dough in your own private account."

"Then open the account in your own name, Lanny. You're the corporate finance man. It's none of their business, anyway. We're not spending it, we're banking it, and we don't require their approval for which bank is the custodian. You're going to need a ticket."

Hanley stood up and turned to call to Beth, but Muldowney stopped him. "Tomorrow night. I'm not leaving until after your meeting with Steffen."

"Lance . . ."

"No way I'm leaving you to do that alone, James. Besides, maybe Thurgren will let me hang with him, surveilling or what the hell ever. Gives me a chance to schmooze him a little, make him understand he's got no reason to stay on our case."

"Good thinking." Hanley resumed his seat. "Don't mind telling you, I'm not relishing another tête-à-tête with Steffen."

"*Fuck* Steffen," Muldowney said angrily. "He thinks he's got the upper hand here on accounta he shook you up? *Fuck* him! Show him who's boss and you'll scare him off, I guarantee it."

"What do you want me to do?" Hanley said, laughing at Muldowney's display of bravado. "Bring a shotgun?"

"No. Just talk tough right back to him. Show up late, make him stew for a while, like you don't give a shit. Hell, don't even order anything to eat. Get him on tape, tell him to stick it in his ear, and get the hell out."

"Ah yes." Hanley stood up, still smiling, Muldowney's indignant tirade having mollified his fears somewhat. "Maybe I'll smack him around a little, too."

"That's the spirit," Muldowney said with self-deprecating good humor, mildly embarrassed at his theatrical harangue. "You free for dinner?"

Hanley shook his head. "Meeting with a couple of college kids."

"Another deal. Who you taking with you?"

"Nobody."

"Don't you think you should take one of the tech guys?"

Hanley shook his head. "I'm getting pretty good at this. Why do I need to suffer through the tedium of some engineer asking three thousand questions I could care less about? The big picture, that's what counts."

"You're sure about this."

"I've got it covered."

CHAPTER THIRTEEN

BARRY ROTHMAN, THE SLIGHTLY LESS
geeky of the two, extended a hand. "Nice to meet
you."

"Likewise," Hanley said as he accepted the
handshake, which felt somewhat like a dead or dying carp. Yoshi Noruyaki's wasn't much better.
Hanley lifted his eyebrows toward Professor
Compton: *So?*

"Sit down, boys," Compton urged the students. As Noruyaki did so, he placed the smaller
of the two metal suitcases he was holding on Hanley's desk. It was about the size of a personal computer tower, and Hanley looked at it impassively,
and with not much hope. He'd seen more hare-
brained technological marvels in the last two
months than any human being ought to have been
subjected to: incredible science housed in utterly

useless products, great ideas with inventors clueless as to how to implement them . . . He'd pretty much had his fill.

Rothman had opened the box and was withdrawing a contraption consisting of a plastic enclosure from which wires poured out in seemingly random fashion. It looked something like a large radio that had fallen off a high shelf.

Meanwhile, Noruyaki opened the larger suitcase, which contained a much more sophisticated-looking device. As Hanley watched him he failed to notice Rothman, screwdriver in hand, busily attacking his computer, until it was too late. "What's he doing?" Hanley asked, just as the cable running to his monitor came off.

"Fomenting revolution," Compton replied, as Noruyaki flipped open the top of the first gadget, revealing a cupped enclosure with a curved edge.

The student positioned the device so it faced Hanley, then connected a cable from it to the socket on Hanley's computer from which he'd disconnected the monitor. By that time Noruyaki had stopped fiddling with the larger machine and waited, sitting cross-legged on the floor.

Rothman put his face to the cupped enclosure and hit a few keys on the keyboard sticking out of Hanley's desk drawer. "Bump the refresh two ticks, tone down the red chroma, and muffle the midrange contrast a touch," he said without looking up.

Noruyaki nodded and tweaked some dials. "Up the green?"

"Just a hair," Rothman replied. "Whoa, hold it . . . back off . . . there!"

He stood up, grinning, and held his hand out for Hanley to put his eyes to the viewer and have a look.

As Rothman took a step back and folded his arms across his chest, Hanley, trying not to appear prematurely dismissive, did as instructed.

"Holy shit!" he yelped involuntarily, jerking his head back.

Noruyaki giggled and swiped at his nose, then handed a compact disc to Rothman, who inserted it into the computer but didn't do anything to start it up just yet.

Hanley once again pressed his face to the cupped enclosure, and this time kept it there as he drank in the sight before him.

It was just his computer screen, as he'd always known it, a handful of icons and several running programs displayed in small windows. Except that it was completely different.

The screen looked as if it were twenty feet away and the size of an entire wall of his office. The colors were brilliant, and every graphic and character looked as sharp as if it had been chiseled into rock. It was as if he were sitting in a movie theater seeing his monitor across the entire screen, and because of the illusion that the screen was so far away, his eyes were focused at infinity and therefore completely relaxed.

"We can adjust the diopter," he heard Rothman say. "People who wear glasses won't need them when they're using it. Try your mouse."

Hanley, unwilling to tear his eyes away from the viewer, fumbled for the mouse and saw the cursor on the screen jiggle as he touched it. "Can I use one of my programs?"

"We haven't touched your computer, Mr. Hanley," Noruyaki said. "It'll work completely normal."

Hanley double-clicked a graphics application and brought up the presentation he'd made to the venture capital firms. He caught his breath as the first illustration flashed into view, looking for all the world like a Disney extravaganza rather than something he'd casually cooked up himself in just a couple of hours.

"Oh, and here's another thing," Rothman said. "May I?"

Hanley reluctantly tore himself away when he felt a tentative nudge on his shoulder. The student settled his hands on the keyboard and took over the viewer, his fingers soon flashing at a speed impossible to follow. "What're you doing?"

"Changing your screen resolution," Rothman said without looking up. "It's such a huge viewing area, you can cram lots more stuff on it and still see everything clearly. Here." He stood up and backed away again.

Hanley marveled at the complexity that quickly resolved itself into utter simplicity. His word processor was running in the upper left, and even though it took barely an eighth of the display area, he could see it more clearly than when it had been the sole occupant of his ordinary monitor. The presentation was still up, along with his phone contact list, two separate Web-site displays and his e-mail program. In the middle of the screen, his entire desktop was still visible.

"So what do you think, James?"

The subliminal twang of commerce in Compton's voice jarred him out of his semitrance. "Nice machine," he said as he finally pulled back from the viewer. "But who the hell is going to want to keep his face glued to this huge thing for more than five minutes at a time?"

The students and their professor fell all over themselves to respond. "No . . . wait . . . that's not . . ." they said simultaneously.

"Boys, boys," Compton admonished gently, and the students fell silent. "James, the idea here is to get the whole thing into a lightweight pair of goggles you can slip on and off easily, eventually without wires, too. What you're seeing here is just a very crude prototype. Just think of the applications . . ."

Hanley could, easily: Laptop computers that could run for days on a single charge, for starters, because the high-power drain screens could be eliminated. For the visually impaired, the gadget could make individual letters look three feet tall and bright as the noonday sun.

Hanley tapped the side of his chin with a finger for a few seconds, then said, "What're we looking at for unit cost?"

"We figure, ah, we figure maybe around three hundred dollars," Rothman said.

"Could be less," Noruyaki added. "With enough volume, do it overseas . . ."

"So we could wholesale it for four hundred. Patents?"

"Applications are being prepared," Compton answered. "University's tech transfer department is handling it."

Hanley nodded, then looked from Rothman to Noruyaki and back again, trying to figure out which one was the businessman. "What do you need to scale up?" he finally said, looking at the gadget.

Rothman looked uncomfortable, and shifted nervously on his seat. "If we contract out the manufacturing, we figure, I don't know . . ."

Noruyaki's knee was waggling back and forth rapidly. "We were thinking, maybe six hundred thousand, we could get the production going, but channels of distribution, marketing, that might be—"

"I'll give you a million dollars for it up front."

Rothman gagged, but there weren't enough neurons left in Noruyaki's brain that hadn't snapped for him even to mount that basic reflex.

"You sign the gadget over to *Artemis-5.com*," Hanley went on, "which owns it outright. Murray, I'll handle the patent applications myself, and give the school fifty thousand in grants for its trouble." He turned back to the two students. "Once we're in production, you two get ten percent of the gross margin on every unit shipped."

Rothman gulped and gripped the arms of the chair, trying to keep himself under some kind of control. Noruyaki was flashing him telepathic signals so powerful even Hanley could read them.

Hanley leaned back and smiled. "In your wildest dreams you never imagined a deal like this, and now you don't know what to do because all those negotiating classes you've been taking warned you never to take the first offer, am I right?"

The two of them nodded dumbly. It was hard not to when somebody else had just voiced out loud your very thoughts, and done so nearly word for word.

"Okay, then let me make this easy: I'll give you fifty thousand for it."

Rothman frowned in confusion.

"No? Okay, a hundred thousand. No? My word, okay, two hundred grand, how does that strike you? Still no? Boy, you fellows are tough! Okay, my final offer: a million up front and ten percent on the back end. Take it or leave it. You've got three seconds."

The only thing that stopped Rothman from flying across Hanley's desk and knocking him back into the wall was Noruyaki simultaneously trying to do the same thing. This time their handshakes felt like Schwarzenegger's might if he'd had too much coffee.

NOVEMBER 23

Thoroughly sated with the lavish breakfast his sister had prepared for him, and which he could almost feel wrapping itself around his arteries, Thurgren made his way down the Cross Bronx Expressway, steering wheel in one hand, toothpick in the other.

He saw someone on an upcoming overpass leaning on the railing observing the relatively sparse flow of fast-moving traffic below, and casually took note of the figure straightening up and stepping back out of his sightline. As Thurgren started to pass beneath, he saw something falling on the other side, but by the time his brain integrated the data and telegraphed back that it was about to hit him, there was no time left to take any evasive action.

Abandoning the steering wheel, Thurgren managed to raise his arms and get them across his face. He had his eyes squeezed tightly shut just as a sickeningly loud double bang exploded in the car, followed immediately by the sound of raining glass.

It was over, and all that remained was the rush of wind blowing past him. Thurgren opened his eyes, squinting against the oncoming air but seeing enough to regain control of his car. As it slowed, he noticed that the cars around him were slowing down, the drivers staring at him with mouths agape. The hood of his car was depressed in the middle, the edges sticking up into the air. The entire windshield was gone, and there were a thousand marbles of safety glass covering the interior. On the passenger seat next to him sat the cinder block that had caused all the damage when it was thrown from the overpass. The double bang he'd heard was from the block first hitting the hood and then slamming into the windshield.

That's when he noticed that the sleeves of his coat were torn practically into strips, little rivulets of blood trickling from behind the fabric. Had he not instinctively let go of the wheel and thrown his hands up, it would have been his face that had been shredded.

He pulled over to the side of the road and shut off the engine, and although he had enough presence of mind to look back at the overpass, there was no sign of the person who had tossed the cinder block at him. Shaken and disoriented, he wasn't aware of how he'd been responding to the half dozen other drivers who pulled over to offer assistance, or how much time had passed before a police cruiser pulled up. The sight of the flashing lights and the two cops getting out of their car sobered him up a little, and he managed to climb out of his car on numb legs.

Thurgren explained what happened as best he could, the cops nodding sympathetically but knowingly. "Used to be we put fences up there," the older one said, his eyes deadened beyond the ability to be surprised by anything anymore, "but after a while nobody was t'rowin' shit anymore, people figured, well, guess we don't need 'em now. Assholes! What th' fuck did they think was stoppin' the creeps but the fences!"

They offered to call an ambulance. Looking at his watch and realizing how late he was, Thurgren showed his badge and promised to come to the station house to give a statement later.

Back in the car his cell phone was ringing, and he excused himself to go answer it. The cops waved him away and turned back to their squad car as Thurgren reached for the phone, wiping glass from the driver's seat at the same time.

"Jubal! Where the hell are you?"

"Don't ask, Lewis." He got in and started the engine.

"I didn't hear anything, so I called the surveillance van outside the restaurant and they said you hadn't even shown up there yet."

Driving slowly because of the wind whipping in where the windshield used to be, Thurgren gave him the short version and told him he was on the way.

"Might's well take your time," Morosco said. "According to the van guy, Hanley hasn't shown yet, either."

THURGREN ARRIVED OUTSIDE THE BANGKOK BISTRO FORTY minutes late. In the van an assistant, reading a newspaper, his headphones on the wall peg behind him, told Thurgren that Hanley was now inside the restaurant. "Says he was late on purpose because he didn't want Steffen thinking he was scared."

Thurgren walked out of the van and straight into the restaurant. Hanley looked up, horrified, as he watched Thurgren cross the crowded room and then veer off toward the entrance to the kitchen.

"Can I get a cup of coffee?" Thurgren said to a waitress as he walked past the kitchen without slowing down.

"Are you crazy?" Hanley managed to hiss as Thurgren approached the table. "He could show up any second!"

Thurgren shook his head and sat down. "He's not coming, Hanley. Like I told you, just a scam artist trying to worm his way into some easy money."

"You don't know that!"

"Yeah. Well, he's not here, is he?"

Hanley pointed at Thurgren's arm. "What the hell happened?"

Thurgren looked down at his ruined coat, dried blood visible on the sleeves. "Just some disenfranchised youth in a high-risk environment expressing his anger." He hadn't paid much attention to it, but now noticed some stinging sensations on his arms from the minor cuts caused by bits of glass penetrating the coat fabric.

"So what happens now?" Hanley asked, ignoring the sarcastic social observation, what little sympathy or curiosity he had for Thurgren's condition apparently fully spent.

"Go back to work and try to forget about it."

"Try to . . . listen, are you telling—"

"It's over, Hanley." The coffee arrived and Thurgren took several deep gulps. "We're not spending any more time or manpower on it."

ANGERED BY THURGREN'S CASUAL DISMISSIVENESS, HANLEY stomped back to his office without having eaten. "Where's Muldowney?" he said to Beth as he swooped through the anteroom without pausing.

"Don't know," Beth replied. "He's not around half the time."

Hanley slammed his door and dropped onto his chair. Looking around for a way to distract himself, his eyes fell on the prototype gadget still sitting at a corner of his desk. Smiling, he picked up his phone and called patent attorney Leon Loudermilch.

"Hanley, Jesus, what the hell piece of shit you got for me this time?" Loudermilch's voice was slightly garbled because of the effort required to keep his cigarette from flying out of his mouth as he spoke.

"No time to tell you right now. I'll come see you—" His intercom buzzed. "Call you later, Leon."

"Rick Bressler on three," Beth announced.

"Yeah?" Hanley said into the speakerphone as soon as he'd hit the button.

" *Yeah?* ' That's how you answer a phone?"

The public relations expert's amiable voice had a calming effect on Hanley. "Sorry, Rick. Not in too good a mood."

"Whyzzat?"

Frustrated and still angry, Hanley told him. When he'd dumped it all, there was a pause, then Bressler said, "Holy shit."

"Indeed. That's exactly how I feel."

"No, Jim. I mean, *holy shit!*"

· · ·

turned out to have been a brilliant triple whammy.

For one thing, Hanley and Thurgren finally had a chance to meet. A debatable benefit to Hanley, perhaps, but Muldowney's feeling was that it would be harder for Thurgren to harass them once they'd gone face to face and assessed each other as human beings, especially considering how responsibly Hanley had behaved.

Second, making that call to the FBI was a clear-cut demonstration that Hanley was a good citizen. Not only did he turn down the offer for mysterious persons unknown to intervene on his behalf, he reported the felonious solicitation at considerable risk to himself, if Steffen's thinly veiled threats were to be believed. He'd done it within minutes of meeting with Steffen, too, betraying no hesitation in doing his duty. Having spoken with Steffen only long enough to trick him into revealing his reprehensible intent and memorized enough details for a solid identification, he'd marched straight back to his office and made the call.

Finally, and most critically, PR-meister Bressler had gone to work swiftly and with a vengeance.

The highly publicized story of the incident thrust *Artemis-5.com* even farther into the public spotlight. Cynical suggestions that this might have been a publicity stunt on the company's part were laid to immediate rest when Jubal Thurgren flatly refused to appear at a press conference. Hanley had insisted that he appear, but Thurgren was adamant. Nobody else from the SEC or the FBI would, either. All any of them would say was that the FBI took all threats seriously.

Hanley was initially enraged, but after Muldowney calmed him down he realized that, in the eyes of a skeptical public already wary of federal law enforcement, that refusal to make any comment was taken as proof positive that Hanley was telling the truth.

News reporters ran out of words trying to give their readers a feeling for the kind of frenzy that ensued once it got out that people were literally willing to kill to get in on a stock offering that hadn't even been announced yet.

"Where the hell have you been, Lance?" There was no malice in Hanley's voice; he was just overexcited. "Think it might be nice to visit the office once in a while?"

"Don't give me any shit, James. I do the job, you stay outta my face. What're you so amped about?"

"I'm thinking seriously of naming my first born after Paul Steffen," Hanley said as he fondled a sheaf of clippings from the morning papers.

Muldowney was looking at the prototype gadget lying on the floor in a corner of Hanley's office. "What the hell is that?"

"It's the future."

"Looks like the future of my breakfast. What's it do?"

Hanley explained.

"So how do you use your keyboard?" Muldowney asked.

"What?"

"If you're not a touch typist, how do you use the keyboard when you can't see it?"

"They're working on it. But forget that." Hanley picked up the clippings and shook them at Muldowney. "So, Lance . . . what do you think?"

Muldowney looked at the clippings and nodded. "I think it's time, Jim."

CHAPTER FOURTEEN

ON DECEMBER 19, ARTEMIS-5.COM AN-
nounced its intention to transform itself into a
public company by offering stock for sale on the
open market.

There was no word of when that was scheduled to take place, nor who the underwriters would
be. The number of shares to be offered, what percentage of the company they would represent,
what the opening price might be, and how shares
would be allocated were never mentioned. The
discreet notice in the *Wall Street Journal* said only
that the company's principals had notified the Securities and Exchange Commission of their intent
"in order to facilitate the process of full disclosure
by giving public notice to all parties with a potential interest in the transaction."

Although no one would have thought it

possible given the almost complete lack of details, the tumult surrounding *Artemis-5.com* increased even farther. Or perhaps it was *because* of the lack of useful information. The announcement in the *Journal* had been so small and hidden away as to invite suspicion that it had been deliberately buried, even though the company had assured the public that the only purpose was to avoid the reckless spending of investors' money. The suspicion, however, was that *Artemis-5.com* was trying to keep the lowest profile possible in order not to call attention to the fact that very few shares would be made available to the general public. It also hadn't gone unnoticed that there was no record of James Hanley having obtained any mezzanine financing to see the company through to the IPO, which most took as a sign of the company's unusually sound financial health.

It took nearly a month for the company to work its way through all the paperwork and regulatory procedures, and that was with the twelve "contractors" hired by Lance Muldowney working full-time to get it done.

On January 14, Hanley filed the formal S-1 registration statement, which showed an expected price range centered around $50 a share, and a new storm broke out.

A junior compliance watchdog within the SEC, based solely on his understanding of precedent and apparently without having given much thought to the public relations implications, casually mentioned to a financial reporter from *Barron's* that, given the number of shares to be offered, $50 per was an inappropriate figure for a start-up company because it bore little relation to the tangible worth of the company and would never wash. (His exact words were that this figure "still had brown stains all over it," but the reporter, a day-trading lay minister and chairman of the Greenwich Family Values Brigade, wisely saw fit to euphemize.)

An unnamed *Artemis-5.com* official took up the gauntlet, saying that it was a simple matter to demonstrate, using other corporations as an example, that the worth of the company was so subjective as to defy traditional analysis. "Besides," James Vincent Hanley told *Forbes* on the record but not for attribution, "if the public at large doesn't think it's worth that, they won't pay it, and isn't that what a free market is all about?"

He'd phrased it somewhat differently to Lance Muldowney the week before. "We go high or we go home. Anything less than five billion in the door and we are but grazers at the IPO banquet."

Predictably, Hanley was backed up in his position by nearly every free market–advocating television talking head, newspaper editorialist, political pundit and Internet newsgroup in existence. Less predictably, and quite inexplicably, he also received very vocal support from some of the most prestigious charities in the country, including those traditionally loath to get involved in controversies that might risk alienating segments of their broad contributor bases.

Much to his surprise, SEC enforcer Jubal Thurgren suddenly found himself, if not in the center of the storm, then certainly close to its fiercest winds. The hurricane of vilification began shortly after his informal noninvestigation of *Artemis-5.com* became known, most likely from the unnamed *Artemis-5.com* spokesperson who, when asked why it took so long to get from the IPO intent announcement to the estimate of an opening price, let it slip to the Internet-based *Grunge Report* newsletter that "some lowlife sonofabitch in the SEC is taking it upon himself to bust the balls of a solid citizen who risked his own neck to do the right thing and is now being punished for his good deed."

It never occurred to the *Grunge Report* correspondent, whose only known prior affiliation with any financial organization was his position as treasurer and sergeant-at-arms of the Back Bay Harley Club, to entertain any misgivings about quoting the anonymous source verbatim.

"THE WAY THIS WORKS," MULDOWNEY WAS EXPLAINING, "you've got to strike a balance between painting a blue-sky picture and misleading potential investors."

The draft of the *Artemis-5.com* IPO prospectus lay on the table between them like a dying albatross. Hanley and Muldowney had spent more time noodling the placement of commas than they had about spending the $54 million in new start-up funding, and they were just now getting around to the difficult part.

They were working on the "Risks" section and, thus far, Muldowney had been doing all the talking. "It's a sales document, sure, except that you've got to make sure you tell them everything. Full disclosure, almost like you're trying to talk them out of it."

He stood up, stretched, and walked around the conference room kneading the small of his back. "Management is aware of the many risks inherent in the business sector the Company occupies," he said, as if giving dictation, "including technological obstacles, the entrance of new competitors, uncertainties arising as a result of bibbity-bee, bibbity-bah . . ."

Muldowney's concerns were traditional, that of making the offer attractive while candidly outlining the risks in a manner that wouldn't open them up to an SEC challenge or class-action lawsuit later. He'd spent most of the last hour experimenting with endless combinations of weasel words designed to soothe fears without devolving into regulatory noncompliance. "Recent experience has shown that, despite the apparent paucity of barriers to entry, those companies that have aggressively pursued primacy in niche markets—"

Hanley grabbed a yellow legal pad, scratched at it for less than two minutes and tossed it to Muldowney, who stumbled awkwardly but caught it. "Print it as is, word for word."

Muldowney began to read, but stopped in the middle of the third sentence. "Very funny, James. Now whaddaya say we get down to—"

"Word for word, Lance. Exactly the way I wrote it."

"Jim—"

"Conversation's over."

Muldowney saw that it was. Resigned to it, he reached into his attaché, pulled out a deposit confirmation slip, and held it up. "What about the ten million in the Swiss bank? Think we ought to pull that back now?"

Hanley shook his head. "One thing Burton Staller once told me, he said, 'Son, always keep a little "fuck you" money in your back pocket, just enough so if somebody thinks he's got you up against a wall, you can tell him "Fuck you," because you don't need his dough, see?' " He took the confirmation slip and put it in his pocket. "That was good advice."

"Good possibility Staller's a crook, Jim."

"Doesn't mean he hasn't got his good points."

. . .

IN A CONFERENCE ROOM AT SEC HEADQUARTERS IN WASH-
ington, Lewis Morosco finished reading out loud from a document, then
tossed it onto the table.

A distinctly unhappy and thoroughly frustrated Jubal Thurgren eyed
it but made no move to pick it up. "Sonofa—He's even smarter than I
thought, and I thought he was pretty gosh-darned smart to begin with."

"Hell's a matter with you, Jubal?"

Thurgren turned around to see FBI assistant director Harry Friedenthal walking in. Morosco pointed to the document on the table. "*Artemis-
5.com* prospectus," he said.

"Ah." Friedenthal nodding knowingly, traces of a poorly suppressed
smile playing about his mouth. "You still badgering that poor bastard?"

Thurgren sighed and slumped back on his chair. "Thought for sure
I'd be able to find a couple three hundred defects in the prospectus."

"But Hanley thought of everything, right?" Friedenthal sat down
heavily and pulled a piece of quit-smoking gum out of his shirt pocket.
"Lewis, you mind if I have a couple minutes with Eliot Ness here?"

"He's all yours," Morosco said eagerly, and began gathering up the
papers. "Too damned morose for my blood."

"Leave those," Friedenthal directed. "Only be a few minutes."

He wrestled with the foil wrapper on the gum as Morosco made his
way out of the conference room. "Jubal, the SEC's got enough to do just
trying to get everything shifted over to the decimal system. You're not
doing yourself any favors by wasting their time."

"You giving me career advice now, Harry?"

"Call it what you want, but you're not going to be getting any more
Bureau resources."

"Harry—"

"I'm sorry, Jubal."

"What, it's out of your hands?" Thurgren sat bolt upright. "That it?"

"Nope." Friedenthal popped the gum into his mouth and made a
face at the taste. "It's right in my hands, and that's the call I'm making."

Thurgren wasn't prepared for that, and had nothing to say. He might
doubt Friedenthal's judgment, but never his motivation, so there was no
sense appealing to him on a personal level.

"This guy you're after," Friedenthal said, "Hanley. He reported an
approach from someone who could have helped him out. Didn't hesitate,

either, just walked back to his office and picked up the phone. Doesn't strike me as a guy I should be wasting agents on."

"You're missing the point, Harry. Just because he didn't go in for having me killed doesn't mean he's still not a con artist of some kind."

"But you have no proof! What are you going to go to the U.S. attorney with?"

"Jeez, Harry, I wish you'd go back to smoking. It's an *investigation*, for cryin' out loud! You investigate, and *then* you press charges. What are you telling me—that if we come up short one time, we call it off?"

"You got to have some kind of basis to be suspicious in the first place, something that justifies the resource expenditure."

"I know this guy is wrong."

"A hunch?"

"More than a hunch. And don't give me that look. Some of your biggest successes started with hunches from experienced agents."

"True. And while we're on the subject of waste . . ." Thurgren knew what was coming, but wasn't about to help Friedenthal out. "I think a guy with Morosco's talents is wasted on an operation like this."

"Wasted? You don't think enforcing securities regulations is—"

"Come on, Jubal, who're we kidding here? Yes, it's important, but it's a war waged by accountants using laptops. There's no room for somebody like Morosco to stretch."

"So what you're telling me—"

"Let me sound him out about coming to work for us."

Thurgren tried not to betray his frustration. He was not about to stand in Morosco's way, or deny the FBI an opportunity to recruit someone whose talents and temperament seemed well suited to their mission, but he was getting damned tired of losing good people this way.

Fact was, Thurgren's livelihood, like everybody else's in the division and in the whole commission, for that matter, was entirely dependent on keeping the straps tightened down on people who were out on the front lines of American business. Nothing he or his colleagues did was of an "enabling" nature. There was no service they performed to businesses to help them succeed or grow, unless you counted keeping investors assured of fair dealing so they'd put money into the capital markets, or keeping the playing field level to ensure fair competition, but hardly anybody ever took those services into account. Their function was just to make the titans of industry, entrepreneurs and old school alike, toe the line.

It wasn't conceptually different from a police function, and even though the criminals Thurgren dealt with usually had ink on their hands rather than gunshot residue, it was still a critical area of law enforcement. The temptations for corruption were so huge that, without Thurgren and his ilk, entrepreneurs like Hanley, the short-thinking venture capital community and CEOs staggering under stockholder pressure to increase the value of their shares would run rampant over the entire process and likely destroy it while doing so. It was that thoughtful sense of responsibility that kept Thurgren going, and which he tried with only partial success to instill in the minds of the young Turks in the division who had to deal with the double whammy of not only being official party poopers but being so in an unexciting environment to boot. It was inevitable that, when somebody like Morosco came along, he'd likely be snapped up by the far more glamorous FBI.

"I won't stand in his way," Thurgren said. "You know that already. But don't start planting ideas in his head until after the *Artemis* matter is closed. Then you can sound him out all you like."

"That could be forever."

"Then give me those Bureau resources."

Friedenthal had risen and was walking toward the door. "Not gonna do it, Jubal."

"Then it could be next week," Thurgren threw back. "We're letting the IPO proceed."

Friedenthal paused with his hand on the doorknob and looked back. "Really?"

"Got no reason to stop it."

Friedenthal turned the knob and pushed the door open slightly, then said in a voice low enough so the waiting Morosco couldn't hear, "Even a snapping turtle lets go at sunset, Jubal."

CHAPTER TWELVE

FEBRUARY 2

THE FINAL IPO FILINGS WERE DONE AND would be presented the next morning, which was when the "quiet period" would begin.

"Always sounded like an infringement on one's right of free speech," Hanley had complained to Jackie Toland.

"There're a lot of things you can't say, so why let this one bother you?"

"Like what?"

"Like, I'm going to kill the President, or Senator Schnookhead shot heroin in high school, or I saw my neighbor strangle his wife, when he did no such thing."

"This is different, and I don't buy it."

According to the Securities Act of 1933, any company that wanted to sell shares of itself to the public had to base its offer solely on a written prospectus that served as the company's official position on the matter. "If anybody in the company opens a mouth," Toland had said, "and says something that might be seen as amending that prospectus, or God forbid contradicting it, you're in a shitpot of trouble. And if you seem to be stimulating the market, that's even worse."

"I already knew that, Jackie. But I can tell them we're planning to build a new office building, right?"

"If that's in the prospectus, and you state it as a simple fact, yes, you can say that. But the best thing is, just shut the hell up."

"Stimulate the market," he'd mused.

"You got it."

"That's bad."

"Worse than bad."

He'd thought about that, then said, "We're going to do it, Jackie."

"It" meant Muldowney appearing on the *Prime Time with Billy O'Malley* talk show.

"FORGET IT."

Hanley looked at Muldowney in surprise. "What do you mean, 'Forget it'? This is important, Lance. You know that."

"I'm not doing it."

Hanley sighed and dropped onto one of the visitors' chairs in Muldowney's office. "See here, it's no big deal. We retain one of those—what are they called?—one of these *media image* specialists or somesuch. By the time he's through with you, there's nothing to be nervous about."

"You're not listening, James," Muldowney said forcefully. "We had a deal. I stay in the background, keep a low profile, you do all the front work."

"I don't get this, Lance. How come—"

"It doesn't matter. I'm not gonna get into a debate about it because we already had an understanding and I'm not renegotiating."

Hanley eyed Muldowney carefully. "You know, you don't even have an official position in this company. Didn't want a title, you said. You're kind of serving at the head man's pleasure, if you catch my drift, and I'm the head man."

"You want to fire me, James?"

"No. I want you to go on that show."

"We can talk about it all you want, but I won't do it, so if you plan on threatening my job, don't fuck around like a candy-ass, just tell me. Two seconds and I'm out of here."

Hanley stared at Muldowney for a few seconds, then screwed up his face and flapped his hands at him. "God's sake, Lance! What are you getting so worked up about? Two fellows can't even have a civil debate without throwing down ultimatums?"

He stood up and walked toward the door. "You don't want to do the show, don't do it. I'll do it myself."

"Good."

"But the spotlight's coming down, Lance. Don't see how someone as up to his elbows in it as you are can escape some of the glare."

TOLAND WAS SENT TO DO THE PREINTERVIEW WITH O'MALLEY a week in advance. When she took a tough stand regarding the form and nature of questions to be asked, O'Malley snidely told her to take a hike. Toland replied that Hanley wouldn't show up unless they had agreement on a few matters, in writing.

"Bullshit," O'Malley had remarked, forgetting that CBN had jumped the gun and already begun wide-scale advertising of the upcoming show. So Toland turned on her heels and left, then refused his phone calls for three days. Rumors spread about Hanley appearing on a different show.

On the fourth day, she took O'Malley's call and reminded him that Hanley was agreeing to appear despite several hundred SEC regulations that made that risky, and if they started to touch on any topics that could put the IPO in jeopardy or reveal trade secrets, Hanley would brusquely decline to answer, and if O'Malley persisted anyway, he'd get up and leave the set.

"Fine," O'Malley replied.

Fine? Toland suppressed her surprise at the sudden attitude readjustment and proposed an agreement as to what was to be avoided, such as pesky little questions about what the company actually did. Toland assumed that O'Malley's easy acquiescing was due to his eagerness to get Hanley on the show now that he'd already advertised it. Realizing that he would now have to agree to damned near anything, she pressed the advantage.

Not that it mattered for her purposes, but O'Malley had other reasons for rolling over.

"So this is the famous 'green room,' " Hanley said on the night of the broadcast.

"This is it." O'Malley sat down and slapped Hanley on the knee. "Nervous?"

"A little."

"Ahhh . . ." O'Malley waved a dismissive hand toward the door, as if implying that his forty million regular viewers weren't worth worrying about. "Nothin' to it. Be yourself, don't think about the cameras . . . piece'a cake."

"Sound advice, Bill. Thanks."

"So lemme ask you something, James." O'Malley hitched himself closer to Hanley and lowered his voice. "I mean, we can get into this on the show, but just so I don't walk into anything that'll make you uncomfortable, you know what I mean?"

"Certainly. I appreciate that."

"Absolutely. You bet. So what I'm wondering"—He made his voice even lower and leaned forward—"is there any way, uh, you know . . . any way an ordinary mortal can get in on the offering? On accounta my viewers would want to know that, see what I'm sayin' here?"

"Sure. I understand. Except, I don't know . . ." Hanley scratched at his ear as he thought about it, real hard. "Might be a bit dicey getting into that, what with the quiet period and all."

"Yeah, the quiet period." O'Malley nodded sympathetically, and thought back to a rushed conversation he'd had with one of his staff researchers barely an hour before. Still angry at having lost a testosterone battle to Jackie Toland, O'Malley had directed his people to see if there were any loopholes in the seemingly airtight story she'd spun to excuse Hanley's refusal to discuss certain specific matters.

The researcher had reported that, at least according to the regs, there *was* no quiet period.

"What's that supposed to mean?" O'Malley had demanded.

"Just what I said, Bill." It wasn't mandated by SEC regulation, at least not directly. Rather, the quiet period was a self-imposed moratorium on promotion of the company, or on any other kind of behavior that could even remotely be construed as "conditioning" the market following the initial registration of securities and prior to their actually going on sale.

Fact was, the SEC regulations on the topic were so broadly drawn, so ambiguous and so vulnerable to wildly differing interpretations, that securities lawyers uniformly counseled their clients to simply shut the hell up rather than risk incurring the wrath of some overzealous SEC official with too much leisure time on his hands and a bone up a different place.

Now O'Malley had Hanley dead to rights. "Yeah. Well, I understand, you gotta worry about stuff like that." He went quiet.

Hanley waited a beat, then said, "But let's you and I talk about it after the show, off the record. Just the two of us, what do you think . . . that be okay?" He put a slightly pleading note in his voice, as if hoping that O'Malley wouldn't be mad at him and would agree to accept this woefully inadequate concession as recompense for making him disappoint his faithful viewers.

A thousand-watt light bloomed behind O'Malley's eyes and seemed to fill his entire body with its warm glow. "Perfect, James! Yeah, that'd be just perfect, yessiree."

He jumped up out of the chair and rubbed his hands together, looking much like a twelve-year-old with a rare disease who'd just been told he would survive only if he ate at least a pint a day of Häagen-Dazs for the rest of his life. "So let's go do us a show, whaddaya say there, Jim?"

"You bet, Bill."

"JAMES, FIRST THING I GOTTA ASK YA, SO HOW COME A famously reclusive CEO suddenly decides to go on national television? I mean, you haven't said word one to the media, and now you're facing my forty million viewers. What's up with that?"

Hanley started nodding halfway through O'Malley's question. "I felt an obligation, Billy. An obligation to clear things up and put to rest some of the distortions that have been promulgated about our company."

"And that company is, of course, *Artemis-5.com*, about which there's been more hype and buzz than maybe in the entire history of Wall Street, am I right? That's true, isn't it?"

"Well . . ." Hanley smiled shyly. "There's been some talk, sure."

"I mean, come on, who you kiddin'? People are gonna line up like they do for Metallica tickets."

Hanley brushed it off modestly. "Who can really say? But what's important right now, I just want to make sure your viewers know the enormous risks involved in a venture like this. Any company that springs up overnight can be put out of business overnight."

"What you're saying—"

"That's exactly right, Billy. If it's that easy to get that big that fast, the opposite is also true, because if it's that easy, other people can do it, too."

"How do you figure, James?"

"It's all about barriers to entry, Billy. The best protection a company has against imitators is how difficult it is for somebody else to do the same thing. That's why patents and copyrights are so important."

"Absolutely. *I* understand, but expand on that a little for our viewers."

"Look at it this way: Why do you think all of these Internet providers and entertainment companies and retailers are in such a hurry to form strategic alliances? Sure, there's a lot of opportunity for synergistically responsive penetrative capability, but the main reason is to make sure nobody else beats them to it!"

"Ah-ha!"

"What with all the merger mania of the last decade, there's a dwindling number of huge retailers with global reach, so if you get all those outfits sewn up early, there's no room for anybody new to come in. Same thing's true of book publishers. There's really only a couple of separate companies out there and they own everybody else. That's how you erect barriers to entry, and it's the only way that companies who don't necessarily have any real innovation to offer can lock up entire markets."

"Well, then, how does an *Artemis-5.com* get started?"

An insightful question, actually. "Simple, Billy. What we're doing has never been done before. But do you think I delude myself that this is it, the end of the line in innovation?"

"Sure you're not being overly modest there, James?"

"Just learning from history, Billy. It seems that every time somebody comes along with a breakthrough, something really new, it isn't too long before somebody improves on it by effectuating a heuristics-based paradigmatic shift. Stated a little more simply, it's really nothing more than integrated, n-level synchronicity."

"I agree a hunnerd percent. Give the viewers an example."

"Take the lightbulb. A true marvel, but how long was it before the neon bulb came along, using a totally different approach to the same problem?"

"I get you."

"Edison also invented the phonograph, and vinyl records lasted a good long time, but then along came tape, and then the CD, and you can hardly even buy a record now. Watt changed the world with steam engines, and they don't even *exist* anymore."

"That's true, now you mention it. And that's what you meant by, uh, interpretive simultaneity, right?"

"You hit it right on the head. Now we have the Internet and nobody can see much past that, but you know what? The fact is, the World Wide Web is a worldwide pain in the ass. Oh my, can I say that on television?"

"Whaddaya mean? What could replace it?"

"How should I know? Doesn't matter. Point is, the Internet's too unreliable, it's slow as heck, it's unwieldy, and it's too difficult for a lot of people to use."

"But it's still young, right?"

"It's getting real old, real fast. At least in its present form. Development is completely uncontrolled, and despite a lot of romantic nonsense about its being the last great outpost of the people, the fact is that there are so many companies falling all over themselves to look different from all the other companies who are trying just as hard, the whole thing is one giant swamp that never looks the same two days in a row."

"But people sure are using it."

"Yes they are, but how long do you think it's going to be before they start resisting some aspects of it? Just as an example, the biggest on-line service in the world bombards you with so much advertising there's hardly room for the stuff you logged on to see. Now when network television began, you had plenty of commercials, too, but the service was completely *free*. These on-line guys are charging twenty-two bucks a month! The thing is, the novelty really hasn't worn off, see, so people put up with it, but the day isn't too far off when they say, 'Hey, I don't need to shell out twenty-two bucks a month so these guys can drown me in ads,' and somebody else will come along and give it to them the way they want it."

"That's a point."

"Sure. Right now there are trillions of dollars worth of companies surviving on a business model based on advertising. You can use their Web services for free, because they're subsidized by all those companies advertising on their sites. Right now consumers are feeling rich and those advertisers are happy to pay, but what's going to happen when the economy cools down and people stop buying all that worthless junk?" It was a thinly veiled reference to *Whoopie!.com*, whose sole source of income was from advertisers running banner ads.

"Gotta give you that there, James. So you think there's a better answer?"

"I absolutely guarantee it. In ten years—probably less—the Internet won't look a thing like it does today. It'll be so different as to be unrecognizable, and what we have right now will look like a slide rule by comparison. Billy"—Hanley held up his wrist—"there's more power in this wristwatch than there was in the biggest IBM computer in the world when you first went on the air."

"Boy, that must be some kinda watch!"

Hanley took it off and tossed it to him, smiling as O'Malley fumbled around trying not to damage such an awesome piece of technology. "It's yours."

"You're kidding!" O'Malley exclaimed when he finally settled down.

"Cost me twenty bucks at Wal-Mart. Next year it'll come free in a box of Cracker Jack. See, there's no telling whether the big players today will be the big players tomorrow, because a lot of yesterday's big players are barely even in today's game, and some of them don't even exist anymore. It's just not all that hard to jump in with new ideas and blow the other fellow out of the water. IBM pioneered the personal computer, and now they're sucking hind—they're way down the list. VisiCalc gave us the first spreadsheet, then Lotus grabbed the whole market, and now they've been ridden over by someone else. Where's the Pulsar watch?

Where's the Osborne computer or the Wang calculator?" He shook his head. "Edsels, every one of them."

"*Including* the Edsel!"

Hanley laughed heartily at O'Malley's hysterically funny ad-lib. "Yes, even the Edsel!"

O'Malley was still fiddling with the watch. "You're painting a pretty bleak picture there. Everybody else in the world seems to feel differently."

"They've always thought like that, and they've always been wrong. If somebody comes along with an innovation different enough to get people's attention and some funding to back it up, what looks like a hundred-billion-dollar powerhouse right now could turn out to be a dog's breakfast by morning, and an awful lot of nest eggs are going to go missing."

"So even after you get started and make a big splash, you're vulnerable."

"Even more so! Once you demonstrate that something new can make money, others will come along to copy your idea and try to throw you out in the cold in the process."

"Like they're after *Whoopie!.com*, right? Except I suppose you don't want to discuss your competitors specifically."

"That last part's true, Billy, but let me make one thing a hundred percent clear: *Whoopie!.com* is *not* my competitor."

O'Malley could sense several million sphincters suddenly go tight around the country. "Then how come their stock dropped when that woman jumped to your board?"

"I haven't the slightest idea."

"So, you really think the Internet will change all that much in just ten years?"

"No question about it. And ten years is an outside estimate. Billy, the cell phone I bought exactly one year ago when it was state of the art is so obsolete the phone company that sold it to me won't even let me use it on their system anymore."

O'Malley let loose with a zinger. "But from what you're saying, *Artemis-5.com* is just as vulnerable, right?"

Hanley grabbed it, sharpened the tip, and threw it right back. "Absolutely! And I'll even go you one step further, Billy: We're the fellows who are going to provide the funding for people trying to blow us out of the water!"

"What!"

"You heard me. It's a simple case of prospective competitive reflex back pressure. Our basic assumption from day one has been that we're going to be obsolete any second and we'd better get prepared for it. We're the exact opposite of arrogant: We're downright self-loathing. We *want* to become obsolete, because we're going to own a big chunk of whoever comes along to *make* us obsolete. That's the reflexive back pressure component of the overall paradigm."

"This is crazy talk," O'Malley said amiably.

"Let me see if I can put this in some larger perspective."

"That's important."

"It's critical, because an awful lot of people are putting an awful lot of money into something they don't really understand. The Internet, young as it might be, is nevertheless already undergoing a profound metamorphosis. It used to be fun; now it's business. Very, very serious business, involving very serious players and hundreds of billions in very serious money. And whenever that happens, the one thing you can count on with one-hundred-percent certainty is that the cowboy days are over."

Hanley leaned forward, gesturing with his hands. "When big companies start pouring money into something, it's going to be run their way, whether they created it in the first place or not, and there's no force on Earth that can stop them. A corporation willing to pay a million dollars to a copyright-infringing extortionist just to ransom a domain name that should have been theirs in the first place is capable of all manner of irrational juggernauting."

"You're so right, James. Any thoughts before we take some calls?"

"Just this: I want to make it absolutely clear that there is a very real possibility that anybody who invests in my company will probably not only fail to make any money, he'll probably lose everything he invested. I'm telling everybody, no baloney, that we're going to be sinking all our money into things whose success nobody can predict. A month from now two college kids could pop up on the other side of the world and put us out of business."

Hanley looked away from O'Malley and directly into the camera.

"This is no place for amateurs. Don't put a dime into this company that you're not prepared to lose."

"Okay, let's go to your phone calls. Topeka, you're on the line. Hello?"

"Hello?" It was a woman's voice.

"Yeah, Topeka, you're on the line. Go ahead."

"Yes, um, uh, a question for Mr. Hanley?"

"Go ahead, Topeka."

"Mr. Hanley, isn't it a fact that the only reason you're trying to discourage people from buying in is to reduce public demand because all the shares have already been spoken for by your cronies and Wall Street big shots? It's the old-boy network all over again, isn't it? So, do you really expect people to believe that you're actually trying to talk them out of—"

O'Malley hit the kill button and, with the keen investigative journalistic sense for which he was justly famous, homed right in for the kill. "There's absolutely not a single shred of truth in that ridiculous accusation, is there, James?"

"Absolutely not, Billy!"

"Course not. Let's go to a break."

"And . . . we're clear!" a production assistant announced.

Hanley tore his earpiece out and held it up. "This is what I have to listen to?"

O'Malley shrugged apologetically. "Sometimes we—"

"I don't want anymore phone-ins if that's what I can expect to be subjected to!" Hanley said, sweating and visibly disturbed. "What's next . . . did I mind-meld with Howard Stern's penis?"

O'Malley winced at the barbed reference to a different, more infamous on-air interview with a former First Lady, then hit the intercom and treated his call screener to a stream of withering invective for his unforgivable incompetence.

"The broad said she wanted to wish him a happy birthday and good luck!" the thoroughly cowed screener replied.

MULDOWNEY AND TOLAND CACKLED WITH GLEE. "THE SON-ofabitch cut me off!" Toland howled in mock pain.

Muldowney had a satellite dish and, like thousands of other dish owners watching *Prime Time with Billy O'Malley*, he got a continuous feed direct from the studio, uninterrupted by commercials. "Watch this! Watch this!" he shouted, pointing to the screen. Hanley discreetly tugged at an ear, scratched his chin, and tugged at the ear again. Toland and Muldowney high-fived each other triumphantly, then watched as the broadcast resumed and Hanley spent several more minutes doing everything he could to denigrate the value of the stock to be offered.

"Understand you're putting up your own office building, that right?"

"Yes, Billy. I know there's office space available in New York, but you know what? What we're interested in is a caring, nurturing environment for our people, a place where they can feel like they're part of a family, where they're empowered to be all they can be, in an unstructured, noncompartmentalized, functionally cohesive and task-facilitating capsulation that is one hundred percent needs based from an individual perspective." Hanley smiled conspiratorially and leaned in slightly. "Know what we've got printed on our ID tags?"

"What's that?"

"PEOPLE ARE OUR GREATEST ASSET."

"Oh, I like that! You think that up yourself?"

Hanley brushed it aside modestly. "And it's tightly integrated with our strategic vision. I think we have a real edge there. Whoops, there I go again. Must remember the quiet period."

MULDOWNEY AND TOLAND SIPPED CHAMPAGNE AS THE SHOW wound down. One caller wanted to know if Hanley considered God to be on his board and, if so, would he be tithing the church out of *Artemis-5.com*'s profits.

Muldowney reached for the remote and muted the television as O'Malley announced another commercial, then picked up his pager and clicked a button to see the count of messages waiting.

"How many?" Toland asked.

"Forty-three," he answered. He kept his eyes on the readout for another few seconds. "Forty-four, -five, -six . . ."

"Since . . . ?"

"Last twenty minutes. Jim done good."

Toland didn't respond, but stared at the dead television screen and idly twirled a strand of hair. "S'matter with you?" Muldowney asked.

Toland took a sip of champagne. "Glad you're happy the deal is going to go down big."

"Aren't you?"

"What do I care? I get the same hourly rate, regardless. I'm supposed to applaud because you and he are going to get rich?"

"I can't speak for James. It's still his company. But what I understand, you'll be in the picture."

"Don't see much sign of it."

"Didn't he tell you he'll take care of you?"

"No specifics. Doesn't mean anything."

"There's a good reason for that, and you know it. It was your idea for corporate counsel to stay at arm's length."

"Do you trust him, Lance? Just because he talks with that bullshit faux-British affectation doesn't mean he's a knight. Should *I* trust him?"

"Not a doubt about it, Jackie, but you want some advice?"

She shrugged. "Advice is about all I'm getting lately."

"Well, this may be better than you've been getting." Muldowney shifted on the couch so he could face her. "Quit bitching. Starting right now. Don't be a pain in the ass, be a team player. Pretend you already own fifty percent and behave that way every second. Prove how indispensable you are, how enthusiastic, and don't keep whining for your piece of the pie, because instead of a valuable resource to take a load off James, you become just another problem he has to handle, and why would he want to lay points on a fucking problem?"

Toland stared at him in wonder. "That seems a little harsh. I thought we were friends."

"It's *because* we're friends."

Toland looked away. "Easy enough for you to say. You're already getting yours."

"Fine." Muldowney grabbed for the remote and unmuted the television. "Keep hounding him, and see if he cuts you in, makes you a key inside player, just to get you to shut up. I've heard that's worked before."

．　．　．

"Y' KNOW, JAMES," O'MALLEY SAID WITH A SLY GRIN, "regardless of what happens, you stand to make a fortune, am I right?"

"I'm going to make some money, yes. But I'm not going to take advantage of a run-up in price on the first day. I've already committed to not selling a single one of my shares for at least six months after the public offering. Furthermore, well . . . ." Hanley's voice trailed off as he appeared to grow nervous.

"What's that, James?"

"Well, since this is a purely factual statement, I suppose I can—" Hanley looked off camera, reading a NO SMOKING sign behind the cameras. On screen, it looked as if he were seeking approval from an aide. "Okay, here it is, Billy: I've decided to retain only twenty percent of the company's shares rather than the more traditional controlling interest of seventy or eighty percent."

"What!" O'Malley sat upright and quickly turned to the cameras. "What's this all—you're selling off a *majority* interest in the company?"

"You heard me right. And all of the money we raise through the IPO is going to be plowed right back into the company to fund the only proper pursuit of a publicly held corporation." Hanley held up a finger. "Increasing shareholder value."

O'Malley suddenly remembered his viewers and looked directly into the camera. "You're hearing this for the first time on our show!" he said, then turned back toward his guest. "What's this all about, James?"

"Just what it sounds like, Billy, and there's more. I plan to make an additional fifteen percent of the offered shares available for sale during the first week of trading, at the opening price."

"But that's unprecedented, James!" O'Malley exclaimed with authority. "Isn't it?"

"I don't really know, to tell you the truth. I just feel it's right. Finally, I've directed the underwriters to reserve five percent of the entire offering as a gift to a slate of charities we've selected."

"This is unbelievable!" O'Malley gushed, slamming his open palm onto the desktop. "Absolutely unbelievable!"

UNBELIEVABLE WASN'T EXACTLY AN APT DESCRIPTION. Jackie Toland shook her head and smiled at Muldowney, who was too engrossed to notice and only snapped out of his trance when O'Malley thanked Hanley prior to ending the broadcast and announcing that they'd be revisiting the OJ trial on the next show.

"He's very good," Toland said with sincere admiration.

Just as he was about to respond in the affirmative, Muldowney was distracted by the insistent and continuous beeping of his pager.

FEBRUARY 4

THE ARTEMIS-5.COM OFFERING WAS THE biggest smash in Street history. There were near riots in Chicago, Los Angeles, Dallas and Boston, instigated by people who had watched Hanley on television and thought there would be plenty of shares available, and who were unfamiliar with the time-honored system that had every first-day share allocated in advance.

In fact, fifteen times more shares than were available were spoken for before the opening bell. While that oversubscription rate was high in itself, it was even more so considering that nearly 80 percent of the company was being sold off. And far from being considered a greedy mercenary like many of his contemporaries, James Hanley was being hailed as the very picture of modern enlightenment.

At least in the eyes of the general public; the professionals knew better. Hanley's rapturous commitment not to immediately sell off his shares didn't stem from a caring and sensitive heart but from the fact that the underwriters would be locking up those shares to prevent "flipping," a derogatory term referring to selling out early and potentially damaging the stock. Corporate officers were strictly forbidden from selling any of their shares for six months following an IPO in order to prevent price destabilization as insiders rushed to cash out, and also to ensure that they kept focused on running the company rather than abandoning it and turning the whole offering into a destructive get-rich-quick scheme.

As for the additional 15 percent he would so graciously be putting into the market during the first week, that was equally misleading. Known as the "green shoe," those additional shares were an overallotment option given to the underwriters in case demand exceeded supply on the first day. That they would be offered at the initial price was not magnanimity on Hanley's part but a key provision of the standard deal, and all of those shares would go to the underwriters and thereafter to their best customers. The public at large would be no closer to getting its hands on them than when they'd tried to storm the doors of their local brokerages.

But even the professionals shook their heads in wonder at Hanley's willingness to give up absolute control of his company by selling off most of it and retaining only a minority interest. There were various speculations about that, but as for the truly shocking gift of 5 percent to charities, nobody even had a starting point from which to construct a plausible rationale. The huge number of messages stacked up on Muldowney's pager had not been congratulatory, but were frantic inquiries into whether Hanley was enjoying his first trip to this galaxy.

Those were the professionals. They could talk and guess all they wanted, but none of it prevented Hanley from being instantly catapulted to the top of the list of supremely ungreedy corporate leaders whose only concern was for his employees and his investors.

By noon on the first day the price skyrocketed to nearly $500, settling down to about $380 by the end of trading. By the time the underwriters had "taken down the green shoe" on the additional shares a few days later, Hanley was personally worth well over $1 billion.

The single largest shareholder was SCalERS, the stodgy State of California Employees' Retirement System, which had been criticized by its members for its reliance on traditional, bricks-and-mortar investments. Muldowney had argued strenuously not to let such a large block get into a single entity's hands, but Hanley had insisted, and now it was done.

JUBAL THURGREN WAS BESIDE HIMSELF AS HE WATCHED *Artemis-5.com* push ahead into uncharted waters. Here was a company worth $35 billion that had never had a dime of income, no hard assets listed on its filings, didn't even have a Web site unless you counted the blinking UNDER CONSTRUCTION notice, hadn't even *existed* a year ago, and there wasn't anybody who could quite explain what it would be doing once whatever it was supposed to be doing was up and running.

The only thing listed in the vague and ambiguous registration that made any sense at all was the "*Artemis-5.com* Foundation for the Advancement of the Internet," a not-for-profit dedicated to identifying bright college students with practical ideas and then funding those ventures in association with *Artemis-5.com* itself.

And James Vincent Hanley was still playing things close to the vest. His publicists no longer needed to plant items in the media. Their main job now was simply managing the flood of inquiries pouring into the company, not to mention the overwhelming number of applications to the foundation for new venture money.

Thurgren directed Morosco to get him a list of the companies and schools with which *Artemis-5.com* had entered into development contracts.

"Some of 'em aren't companies," Morosco reminded him. "Just some guys."

"Then get me their names."

"Could be tough."

"I *know* it's tough. If it was easy I would've asked the gosh-darned receptionist."

NOW THAT THE DEAL WAS DONE, LANCE MULDOWNEY INDULGED himself freely. While his actual equity percentage of *Artemis-5.com* was small, a small piece of something gigantic was still quite substantial. Because of the SEC's antiflipping provisions, however, he couldn't cash in any of that equity, but there was nothing to motivate the creativity of a clever money man quite like self-interest.

The first thing was a 4,000-square-foot triplex on East Sixty-second, purchased by *Artemis-5.com* and listed as an "unassigned corporate perquisite," with the unwritten understanding that it was for Muldowney's personal use. It would be reported on the up-and-up to the IRS as having a value to him of $1,500 of rent he didn't have to pay, which Muldowney would dutifully report on his return as income, and on which he would have to pay taxes. That the actual value was more like ten times that amount was evaded by the convenient existence of a small, one-bedroom servant's apartment completely separate from the main unit. It didn't have a common wall with Muldowney's residence, nor was it actually on the same floor, but the combination of the two apartments, which was only a single location on the books, was officially for the use of visitors to the company, and unless the IRS decided to come sniffing around and examine firsthand who was sleeping where, those niggling little details were quite beside the point.

Hanley himself chose to remain where he was for the time being. He would be the one coming under the most personal scrutiny, the rest of the world barely aware that Lance Muldowney even existed. Both of them naturally had access to the company's round-the-clock limousine service, and although neither officially had his own assigned chauffeur or vehicle, which would have been too showy a perk to risk, the company only had two of each, and Hanley and Muldowney were the only two officers entitled to them.

Expensive restaurants were paid for with corporate credit cards, which the general ledger automatically assigned to the "Marketing: general:incidental" expense account. Negotiations for a modest jet were under way, justified by the global reach *Artemis-5.com* was trying to achieve by entering into technology transfer agreements in as many countries as it could.

Muldowney, despite his sincere attempt at staying hidden away, nevertheless managed to discover the world of "cybergroupies." These were surprisingly well-educated and self-sufficient women nevertheless irresistibly attracted to the tidal waves of money and power that washed over the heretofore great *un*washed. Muldowney could be seen, by anyone who cared to notice, in some of the poshest watering holes in town, accompanied by some of the classiest-looking ladies, many of whom had decided that some of the more venerable methods for ascending the ladder were a lot quicker than that antiquated, overrated fad of doing it on your own. The appearance on the scene of Lance Muldowney, who didn't look anything at all like a pencil-necked stalwart of the high school computer society, made that avenue a good deal less painful.

Hanley, on the other hand, elected to keep a relatively low public profile. He didn't much care what the masses thought of him, since his particular ambition, whether he was aware of it or not, was to strut his stuff among the titans of industry who, until recently, he could only envy from a distance. He knew all too well that public perception didn't matter one whit to the people who did matter, since they were acutely aware that all it took to manipulate that perception was a great deal of money, and the will to use it.

Their scorecard was money and influence. There was no way on Earth that a titan of industry with a personal net worth already comfortably into nine figures could rationally justify the need to tack on another billion or two. That's why PR firms had labored for years to come up with alternative explanations for the continuing amassing of wealth. "I can't stand to see a badly run company," one legendary accumulator of corporations maintained for years. "The more I have, the more I can give away," boasted another. "I have an obligation to my shareholders to generate wealth. The more I own, the better I'm able to enhance my employees' lives."

And on and on. Hanley knew that all that vaunting and self-aggrandizing pursuit of ever more had only one real purpose, and that came at the annual Wrecker's Ball, a costume extravaganza that was one of the few social occasions in which none of the real players felt it necessary to euphemize his way out of what it was they were all trying to achieve, male and female alike, which was to lay claim to the biggest swinging dick in the entire capitalist world.

And if nobody could claim clear title, the situation was easily remedied. It was at the last ball, for example, that the heads of the two largest entertainment firms in the world agreed to merge their companies, leaving the details to be worked out by their armies of underlings, and flipping a coin to see which of them would be the recipient of the resultant pecker graft known as the CEO's job.

AT THE SAME TIME THAT LANCE MULDOWNEY WAS LEAVING the hippest saloon in New York, a bowling ball was hurtling down an alley in Arlington, Virginia, as though it had been shot out of a cannon.

"Criminy," assistant FBI director Harry Friedenthal muttered from his seat at the scoring table as the ball missed the pocket, missed the headpin altogether, but slammed into the rest of the pins so hard that the wild ricocheting knocked all ten down anyway.

They'd hardly stopped bouncing before Jubal Thurgren spun on his heel and walked back toward the table.

"You break the machine, you pay for it," Friedenthal said, even as he kept up rapid-fire chewing of his quit-smoking gum.

"Got the gosh-darned strike, didn't I? Wish you'd start smoking again."

"Why? Make me less antsy?"

"No. So you'll die sooner."

Now that *Artemis-5.com* was a publicly held company, Thurgren had a clearer investigative mandate and thus more latitude in his probing of its operations. He'd made the decision to devote more division resources to it despite harsh warnings from colleagues and superiors who intimated that he was undertaking a personal vendetta, fueled by animosity toward James Vincent Hanley, who thus far had beaten him at every turn. They also pointed out how much good Hanley was doing with the *Artemis-5.com* Foundation for the Advancement of the Internet, to which Thurgren had responded, "Gates gives away billions, and that didn't stop us from pushing an antitrust case." Having it pointed out that the case against Microsoft was DOJ, not SEC, didn't make Thurgren feel any differently about it. "It's still the federal government, isn't it?"

Friedenthal exhaled loudly and shook his head. "Don't know what's gonna wreck your career first, Jubal: pursuing this dog of a case or having a nervous breakdown."

"Gonna come to a head soon."

"Financial report, I know. Heard they got good auditors."

"Depends what you mean by good."

The *Artemis-5.com* board of directors audit committee had hired Highland & Harwick, the most prestigious public accounting firm in the industry, to examine the books and records of the firm on behalf of the shareholders. "Aren't they the best?" Friedenthal asked. "Heard some line partners there are dragging down a million a year."

"Certainly the most aggressive," Thurgren answered. "Doesn't necessarily mean the best."

"So what do you mean, it's 'gonna come to a head'?"

Thurgren picked up a small towel, wiped his hands, and threw it back onto the ball return rack. "Means that if there's still no profit or revenue, I'm sending in the cavalry."

"Ah, come on now . . . Don't you think you're being just a little—"

"Harry," Thurgren growled from between clenched teeth, "the bleepin' company's worth over thirty-five billion dollars and *nobody knows what it does!*"

Friedenthal stepped up and picked his ball off the rack. "So what's the next step?" he asked as he hefted it a few times to get the feel.

"Nothing," Thurgren replied as he sat. "Nothing until we get some audited financials."

Friedenthal turned and stepped onto the polished wood fronting the lane. "Which is when?"

"Couple months."

"What are you gonna do in the meantime?"

Thurgren closed his eyes and tilted his head back against the hard plastic of the bolted-down chair. "Work full-time on my ulcer."

PART TWO

So this guy in Vegas loses a bundle. All pissed off, he goes back up to his hotel room and asks his wife what she's been up to, and she says she played the slots and lost fifty bucks. He starts screaming at her and she yells back, "What are you shouting about? *You* just lost over a thousand dollars playing craps!" And he says, "Yeah . . . but *I* know how to gamble!"

—BURTON STALLER

CHAPTER SEVENTEEN

MAY 7

THE MORNING FINANCIAL REPORT HADN'T even finished displaying on FBI Assistant Director Harry Friedenthal's desktop computer before he grabbed the phone and dialed Jubal Thurgren's number. He reached for his cigarettes but his hand closed around his nicotine gum instead, and he had to resist the impulse to crush the damned things into powder.

"Let's put it this way," Thurgren's secretary warned him. "Unless you're the Pope or you're carrying Xanax samples, this might not be the best time to speak with him."

"What's going on, Nan?"

"Can't tell for sure, but I've heard the *F* word a few times."

"Jubal doesn't use the *F* word."

"Wanna bet?"

. . .

MULDOWNEY HAD NEVER SEEN HANLEY THIS ANGRY. IT WAS doubtful anybody ever had. He carefully removed a newsletter report from Hanley's clenched fist and smoothed it open to the column headed "Seen at ElectroComm."

"Rock 'em sock 'em CyberSpex knocked out more than a few onlookers at the IdeaConnexion booth," the piece began. "These eye-boggling goggles replace your computer screen with a mind-blowing, fully three-dimensional display so realistic this reporter got a lot of giggles watching people reaching out into thin air trying to grab things. The best part is that the goggles are transparent, so you can still use your keyboard; the screen contents are simply projected on to whatever you happen to be looking at. And did we mention the stereophonic ear-pieces? A couple of geeks got so engrossed playing their favorite games with this thing security had to be called before some harsh words turned into fistfights, we kid you not. Just think of the applications, starting with field maintenance of military hardware, where a technician can get a fully stereoscopic view of any tank or jet engine he's working on. Battle-field simulations, combat arena displays, remotely controlled bomb-disarming robots, you name it. It can completely transform the way surgery is performed; laptops will run for a week on a single charge. And let's face it, folks: The porn industry alone could turn this thing into a cash generator that would dwarf the mainstream movie industry virtually overnight, and I do mean *virtually* . . ."

Muldowney set the newsletter down on Hanley's desk. "Three-D?"

Hanley only glowered by way of response.

"And a solution to the keyboard problem, too. Well, at least you've got all the signed noncompete forms and the other protective stuff."

Hanley's glowering deepened.

"Jim? Oh, shit . . ."

Hanley finally roused himself and stabbed at his intercom. "Get Toland in here!"

Muldowney dropped into a visitor's chair. "What'd you pay for that thing?" he said, pointing to the prototype sitting proudly on a shelf.

"Doesn't matter."

The door opened. "What's up?" Toland asked as she came in.

"We got fucked, that's what's up."

She listened carefully as Hanley laid it out. "They didn't sign any noncompete agreements," he said in conclusion.

"You're kidding! What idiot let them get away with that?"

"Doesn't matter," he said for the second time in ten minutes. "What matters is, you're to go see Burton Staller and tell him I'll spend my last dime litigating his sorry ass into the ground if he doesn't make this right."

"Let's not make threats we're not prepared to follow through on," Muldowney said.

Hanley turned toward him. "Do you think for one second," he said, slowly and deliberately, his eyes smoldering, "that there is anything I won't do to protect this company?"

Surprised at Hanley's uncharacteristically naked passion and sensing trouble if Muldowney didn't respond appropriately, Toland sought to head it off and get them back on track. "Are you sure he even knows there was an earlier prototype?"

It was something Hanley hadn't considered, but he did so now. "He knows. This is his way of getting back at us for snubbing him when we were picking a board."

"Ah, yes. The sniff test episode."

"But here's the thing." Muldowney pointed toward the prototype. "How different is their new gadget from the one Jim bought?"

"I doubt it's relevant," Toland answered. "The concept is essentially identical, and those two students didn't just sell us a device, they entered into a development contract. There are some serious good faith issues here. What'd you pay for it, Jim?"

"A million up front, plus development costs, plus royalties on sales. I want you to go see him immediately. I want you to make him understand that I'll sink this entire company before I let him get away with this."

"I'll do it, but remember that it's Burton Staller we're dealing with."

"I don't give a damn. He's still not above the law, is he?"

"Interesting question, but we'll debate it another time."

. . .

you didn't know about this in advance," Thurgren was saying to Lewis Morosco. "I'm just postponing it so I don't blow a coronary artery altogether."

Morosco, who had read the summary page of the document he was holding twenty or thirty times already, read it yet again, then threw it onto Thurgren's desk facedown. "Keep trying to tell you, Jubal. There's no two people in that entire outfit who know a quarter of how it works or what Hanley's doing."

"Not even Lance Muldowney?" Thurgren said with a sneer. "His strong right arm, the go-to guy?"

Morosco shrugged helplessly. "What can I tell you? You want miracles, hire a goddamned sorcerer."

"What!" Thurgren thundered at the door as Nan's face poked tentatively from behind it.

"Are we learning to play nicely with our neighbors?"

"Nan, how do you plan to get another job if I kill you?"

"Harry's on his way over."

"What for?"

"Game of gin and some polite conversation. How the hell should I know? He's FBI, doesn't tell anybody anything."

"I need a cup of coffee."

"You need a tranquilizer. I'll get you some decaf. Lewis?"

"Strongest stuff you got."

"And the chairman's on the phone, Jubal."

"Tell him I'm not here."

"He already knows that, but he wants to speak with you anyway. Lewis, might be a good idea to step away from ground zero right about now."

LESS THAN TWENTY MINUTES LATER, FRIEDENTHAL CAME hurtling down the corridor carrying a single sheet of paper and turned into Thurgren's office suite. He looked at Morosco without breaking stride, nodded for him to follow, and knocked on Thurgren's door. The sound of a phone being hung up came through from inside, and Nan motioned for them to go in.

Friedenthal didn't bother with the usual pleasantries but thrust the piece of paper in Thurgren's direction and let it flutter to the desk.

"Somebody want to tell me," he said, "how in the flaming hell some little pissant company goes from zero revenue to half a billion dollars in three months?"

Thurgren thought it best at this point not to mention to the FBI assistant director that *Artemis-5.com* had just replaced Hewlett-Packard on the Dow Jones list of industrials. If he did, Friedenthal might ask how the Dow people had even figured out that the "little pissant company" *was* an industrial, and Thurgren had no answer for that, either. "I don't know, Harry," Thurgren said, "but I'll find out. One thing I do know—"

"And that is . . . ?"

Thurgren tapped his fingers on the report, then looked up. "Hanley's gonna flip his shares as soon as he can."

"Flip his—you mean he's gonna cash out?"

"Soon as the restriction is up."

As Friedenthal thought that over, Morosco said, "Guess this kinda overshadows my news." He adopted a pained expression in anticipation of Thurgren's reaction. "Burton Staller filed a Thirteen-D on *TillYouDrop.net*."

"A-*ha!*" Thurgren banged his fist onto his desktop. "I knew it! See, Lewis? What'd I tell you!"

"See what?" Morosco shot back, then waited as Thurgren looked at him blankly, not helping him out at all.

"What's a Thirteen-D?" Friedenthal asked.

"It's a form you have to submit if you plan to buy up more than five percent of a company," Morosco said. "Lets everybody know what's going on so you can't do it sneaky. Jubal thinks Burton Staller is a crook."

"He's up to something," Thurgren said, leaving the 'but I don't know what' part out. "What's the stock price doing?"

"Still rising. And no, I don't know why, other than the Staller effect."

"You're going after Burton Staller?" Friedenthal asked.

"You bet your—"

Thurgren stopped as Friedenthal held up his hands. "I *do not* want to hear this, Jubal. Let's get back to Hanley. When can he flip his shares?"

"Six months from the IPO." Thurgren stood up and walked over to a wall calendar hanging near the door. He tapped the square denoting February 4, the day of the *Artemis-5.com* IPO, and then tapped six more times as he ran his hand to the right. "On August fourth."

Friedenthal walked over and pointed to the calendar. "Then that's your deadline, Jubal."

"Why?"

The assistant director opened the door and stepped through, then turned around. "Because even if you have a solid case, once he has all that cash in his hands you're not even gonna be able to find the slippery bastard."

WITHIN TEN MINUTES OF THE RELEASE OF THE ARTEMIS-5 first-quarter financials, industry newsletters had shifted their focus from intense Staller-watching to noting where James Hanley was investing his new capital infusion. Pundits, who couldn't make a dollar actually investing and therefore made it by advising others where to invest, tried to guess the company's direction based on where it put its money. Since nobody ever followed up on pundit predictions anyway, this approach was quite safe from criticism and made for great fun, an amusing distraction for people who actually produced something for a living but somehow weren't at all put off by those who didn't.

For struggling companies and institutions, receiving investment dollars from *Artemis-5.com* was like being blessed by the Pope, and the manna fell on everybody from Israeli makers of exotic computer chips to Indian subcontinent software designers to university artificial intelligence labs. The mildest interest expressed by *Artemis-5.com* was enough to cause discernible spikes in stock prices, and before long it became clear that the company had vaulted itself into that rarefied level of capitalism in which its actions had ripple effects throughout the entire market.

And still James Hanley kept a low profile. He met with many business leaders and other people of influence but, contrary to Lance Muldowney's notions of visible moguldom, gave no speeches, granted no interviews and never attended symposia or other traditional haunts of the newly guru-fied. Speculation as to when *Artemis-5.com* was to hit the marketplace with a product offering became a national obsession, and world markets ticked up or down depending on such absurd signs as whether Hanley was seen at the airport with a bulging briefcase or a skinny one.

MAY 15

"YOU SCARED THE SHIT OUT OF BURTON Staller," Hanley said, skeptically repeating what he'd just heard.

"I most certainly did," Jackie Toland answered.

Hanley sat back and decided—for the moment—to give her the benefit of the doubt. "So, he's backing off the three-D goggles?"

"No." As Hanley started forward, she quickly added, "He can't, Jim. Think about it."

She explained that Staller had already made a big splash at the electronics show and now the whole enterprise was too visible. "A guy like that doesn't publicly put his tail between his legs and scurry away. Back him into a corner and you force him to do everything in his power to grind you into dust."

"I've got resources, too, you know," Hanley said with childlike petulance.

"What you don't have is the law. We could make a case for usual and customary business practices, good faith understanding with the inventors, tortious interference with contract, blabbity-blah, but you could still lose. And I've got to tell you, James: Staller does not want a fight. He swears he had no idea you already owned the rights to an earlier version."

"What'd he pay them?"

"Two million."

"Exactly twice what I did." Hanley snorted and looked at her snidely. "And you think he didn't know?"

There was a knock at the door, and Muldowney walked in. "Hi, Jackie. Did you spank bad Burton?"

"We were just talking about that. Jackie was going to tell me how she one-upped Staller. So? What makes you think you scared him?"

Toland pulled a pad of paper from her attaché. "He's going to make it up to you by letting you in on something."

"Don't even think about telling me he's going to let me buy a piece of his contraption!"

Toland shook her head. "He's giving you a stock tip."

Hanley stared at her incredulously, then laughed. "A stock tip?"

"Yeah." She waited for him to settle down, then said, "He wants you to sell *TillYouDrop.net* short."

Hanley sobered up instantly. "Sell it short?"

"That's it. He says it's going to drop like a rock. Sell it short and you'll clean up when it tanks."

"What makes him so sure?"

"I have no idea. But I believe him."

"Hold it a second!" Muldowney exclaimed. "Jackie . . . Staller owns nearly five percent of *TillYouDrop* and he's planning to buy even more!"

Hanley's eyebrows drew up slowly as he sat forward. "Are you telling me Burton Staller is going to nuke his own company?"

"I have no idea," Toland answered, "and I don't want to know."

Hanley eyed Muldowney questioningly, then dropped back against his chair. "Well, I'm not going to do it."

"Why the hell not?" Toland demanded.

"Because it's against the law."

It was the one thing Toland hadn't considered, and Hanley's simple declaration shut the conversation down instantly.

But only temporarily. "No it isn't, Jim," Muldowney said.

"Don't start playing games, Lance. Trading on inside information is—"

"What inside information?" Muldowney stood up and leaned against the wall, arms folded across his chest, and waited.

Hanley frowned and glanced at Toland. "Is he kidding, or what?"

"I don't know. Lance, are you kidding? Or is this part of an I-never-heard-you strategy?"

"What I'm asking," Muldowney said patiently, "exactly what is it that we know about this company that isn't available to the investing public at large?"

"Well, let's see," Hanley said sarcastically. "The guy who's buying up *TillYouDrop* just told us to sell the stock short."

"Okay. Why did he tell you that, Jackie?"

"I have no idea."

"So I repeat: What is it we know about *TillYouDrop* that nobody else does? Where's your inside information?"

"Come on, Lance," Toland said after a few seconds of silence. "The biggest insider of all told us he thinks the price of the stock is going to fall!"

"So what?" Muldowney said as he kicked away from the wall. "He tells you it's going to fall, but at the same time he's buying in to the company? Completely mixed signals, one man's opinion and no hard data. Somebody think we're gonna get indicted for that? And I'll tell you another thing"—Muldowney dropped into a chair and leaned forward with his elbows on his knees—"James, you're the guy on the record as having snubbed Staller," he said quietly. "Didn't pass the *Artemis-5.com* sniff test, remember?"

Toland picked up the thread. "So what would be more natural than *Artemis-5* selling short whatever Staller takes an interest in?"

"Exactly," Muldowney said as he straightened up and then leaned back. "Staller's buying into some company, Hanley thinks the guy is due for a fall . . . ?"

"I sell his stock short and bet on him failing," Hanley concluded.

But as his colleagues broke into self-satisfied smiles, he added, "Except for one thing."

"And that is?" Toland asked.

"The tip to sell *TillYouDrop* short came from Staller himself. What kind of sense does that make?"

"Beats me," Muldowney said. "For all we know the cagey sonofabitch is selling it short himself somewhere. Who knows? But whatever scam he's pulling—sorry, I mean, whatever strategy he's contemplating—he's giving you a free pass to the feast so you won't sue him."

Hanley scratched at his chin. "Jackie?"

The attorney shrugged. "One thing I know, he was definitely scared of a lawsuit over those goggles, knowing we had a reasonable case. Even if we lose, he'd look bad, so he knows that if he screws us over somehow, we can still come after him. Seems that letting us in on whatever he's planning is a cheap way for him to get out from under."

Hanley mulled it over, then tapped a few keys on his computer. "Selling around fifty a share right now. But it's been going up."

"Staller effect," Muldowney offered. "Anything he touches, that's what people buy."

"Okay," Hanley said after a few more seconds, slapping the arm of his chair. "Muldowney, call Dallis-Schumann and sell two hundred thousand shares short."

"Hey, wait a minute!" Toland yelped.

"Don't back-pedal on me, Jackie. I was looking at a major return from those goggles, so anything less on Staller's deal and I'm not interested. Lance, keep an eye on movement and we may do more if it keeps going up."

"You think we're going to find buyers for that many shares?"

"What do you mean?"

"That much being offered, people are going to start to wonder."

"No they won't. Not if Staller is buying."

"He's right, Lance," Toland said, trying to sound confident. "Hell, most people will snap them up without even bothering to find out what the hell *TillYouDrop.net* does for a living."

"What do they do?" Hanley asked.

As Muldowney laughed, Toland said, "On-line retailer."

"Where?"

"Beats me. What difference does it make? Internet's everywhere."

"New Mexico," Muldowney said. "But Jackie's right. What difference could it possibly make?"

"GOTTA TELL YOU SOMETHING, JUBAL," FRIEDENTHAL SAID uncomfortably as he looked away from the computer screen. "I never really understood this business of short selling."

He steeled himself for the derision sure to come flowing his way, especially after all the lectures he'd given Thurgren on a variety of law enforcement topics, but it wasn't forthcoming.

"Confuses a lot of people," Thurgren said, still looking at the numbers dancing across the screen. "It's because it does everything backwards, but it's actually simple as heck."

"I know it's a way to make money if you think a stock is going down instead of up, but . . ." Friedenthal turned back and shrugged. "I don't know the details. What do you mean, backwards?"

"Usually you buy a stock, then sell it. In short selling, you sell it first, then you buy it."

Friedenthal's shoulders drooped. "That's the part I hate! How the hell do you sell something you don't own?"

Thurgren smiled at him. "Done all the time, Harry. Remember last year when you tried to get rid of that piano you bought for your kid?"

"You don't forget a thing like that. For two weeks we thought he was Van Cliburn, then he got bored and wanted a snowboard."

"So you gave the piano to a consignment dealer. He was going to sell it, except he didn't own it because he didn't give you any money for it."

"But he was selling it for me," Friedenthal said, confused.

"What's the difference? Only point I'm trying to make, here's a guy who was going to sell something he didn't own."

"Okay." Friedenthal replied tentatively, giving Thurgren the benefit of the doubt for the moment.

Thurgren walked over to the whiteboard hanging on a wall. He drew a box at the top and wrote 'Acme—$50' next to it. "Let's say Acme Widgets is selling for fifty a share, and you've got a pretty good notion it's going to drop." He waited for an answering nod and went on. "You want to be able to make some money on that. Essentially, what you want to do is bet somebody else who thinks it's going up."

"Bet?"

"What do you think the market is, Harry? It's a casino. You can dress it up with a thousand euphemisms but it's still about making bets. So this is what you do." Thurgren drew some more diagrams as he went on. "You borrow a hundred shares from your broker, and you sell them at fifty a share."

"You can do that?"

"Yep. So what've you got?"

"Five grand in my pocket, free for nothing."

"Sort of." Thurgren wrote Friedenthal's name at the top of the board and '$5,000' under it.

"But that's not really my money, because those weren't my own shares I sold. Don't I have to give it to my broker?"

Thurgren shook his head. "Nope. Your broker doesn't want the five grand."

"He doesn't?"

"Harry, if he wanted the five grand he would have sold those shares himself. What did he need you for?" Thurgren tapped the marker on another box he'd drawn. "What your broker wants is his hundred shares of Acme back. That's what you borrowed; that's what he wants returned."

"So, then what?"

"Then you wait for the price to drop. Meanwhile, you have to pay your broker interest on those shares you borrowed, because this is a businessman, not Robin Hood, and the only reason he loaned them to you in the first place was so he could collect that interest from you instead of letting those shares sit in a vault somewhere doing nothing."

"So, a month later it's down to forty a share. Now what?"

Thurgren wrote the figure on the board. "Now you go out and buy a hundred shares on the market. What's it cost you?"

"Four grand," Friedenthal answered.

"What's in your pocket?"

"Five grand."

"So you spend four grand to buy the hundred shares. You return them to the broker, and you're all square with him. It's called covering your shorts."

"Except I've got a grand left in my pocket, less the interest I paid."

"Correct-*o*!" Thurgren said as he set the marker down with a bang. "That's short selling, and that's how you make money if you think a stock is going down."

Friedenthal stared at the board in wonder. "That's it? That's all there is to it?"

"That's it."

"You're kidding me!"

"Child's play, Harry. Nothing complicated about it at all."

"Well, I'll be damned." Friedenthal smiled in satisfaction and began to walk away from the board.

"Uh . . ." Thurgren said.

Friedenthal stopped. "Uh . . . what?" he said suspiciously.

"There's just this one little thing."

Friedenthal pressed his lips together, then said, "I knew it! You oversimplified it, didn't you? Made it easy for the dumb cop."

"Not a bit. It's just that we forgot to talk about one itty-bitty thing."

"And that is?"

"What happens if the stock goes up instead of down?"

Friedenthal blinked at him, then turned and walked back to the board, trying to follow the implications. "Well, lessee. I sold the hundred shares for five grand."

Thurgren joined him at the board. "So, let's say it goes up to sixty."

"I have to give the shares back to my broker. So I buy them in the open market, costs me six Gs, I give them back and now I'm out a thousand bucks."

"Right. What if it goes up to seventy?"

Friedenthal raised his eyebrows slightly. "I'm out two Gs."

"And if it hits a hundred?"

"I'm out five—Hey, hold it a second!"

"What if it goes to two hundred?"

"What the hell, Jubal!" Friedenthal turned to him in shock. "A guy could get killed here!"

Thurgren looked at him and nodded soberly. "And that's the problem with selling short. If you just went out and bought a hundred of

Acme for five grand, the most you can possibly lose is your five grand."
He pointed to the board. "But if you sell it short instead, and it goes up
and continues to go up, there's no upper limit to how much it's going to
cost you. Eventually you have to give those shares back to your broker,
and if you end up paying a couple of hundred for them after you sold
them short for fifty, well . . ." He held out his hands, having made the
point. "You lose your shorts when you cover your shorts."

Friedenthal ignored the lame joke as he thought of something else.
"But supposing I just keep paying the broker interest and never return
his shares?"

"You can do that, if you want to keep paying high interest for a real
long time. But if the broker thinks things are really going sour, or sus-
pects you may not be able to cover your short sale, he can demand the
stock back right away, and then you have no choice."

Friedenthal nodded in understanding as he looked over the board.
"Guy'd have to be crazy to go in for this."

"Or very confident."

The naturally suspicious FBI man jumped immediately to the next
logical conclusion. "Or in possession of some inside information."

JUNE 1

"WAY BACK IN THE OLD DAYS, NEW YORK wasn't even a city, just a little Dutch trading post called Nieuw Amsterdam."

Lance Muldowney paused to take a sip of his Manhattan, in no hurry since the wide-eyed if somewhat big-haired thing sitting next to him wasn't about to vacate her position next to the Street's latest wunderkind. She didn't know *why* he was a wunderkind or even, for that matter, exactly what a wunderkind was, but he definitely was one, her friend at Drexel said so, and whatever it was, it sure seemed to be impressing an awful lot of women who hadn't managed to corner this lucky seat but looked like they would swoop down and grab it if she so much as stepped away to pee, which she really had to do, and awfully bad, but she'd sooner burst her bladder than let this wunder-what-the-hell-ever get away.

Muldowney licked his lips and set the glass down. *Place full of Harvard MBAs and I wind up with Miss Tractor Pull.* "They didn't even have a single kind of money. They were using all sorts of stuff, even wampum—"

"Whomp 'em?"

"Wampum." *Pupils dilated and unresponsive, Doctor.* "Native currency?" *Flatlining—We're losing her!* "Beads and shit." *Wait . . .*

"Oh."

We're getting something on the monitor!

"Except some wise guy built a machine to make fake wampum so they stopped using it. Mostly what they used was the Spanish *real*. It was made out of real silver, and what they'd do, they'd cut it up into quarters or eighths to make smaller change. And that's where the expression 'pieces of eight' came from, and why 'two bits' is a quarter."

"A quarter of what?"

Muldowney drummed his fingers on the bar and contemplated the advisability of continued discourse. His eyes wandered to the lintel above the bar, which was festooned with campaign posters for the hotly contested and widely publicized special election for the district's recently vacated congressional seat. "Of a dollar. A quarter is called 'two bits.'"

"Oh. Like, shave and a haircut . . . six bits?"

"Yeah, like that. And that's also the reason the stock exchange uses eighths of a dollar instead of tenths, which would make a helluva lot more sense, and that's what they're trying to fix right now."

"Aha! I get it." *Christ. Ask this guy what time it is and he tells you how to build a watch.*

"Lance . . ."

Muldowney whirled at the sound of the familiar voice. "James! The hell are you doing in here?"

"Looking for you. Busy?"

"Not a bit," Muldowney answered, waving his hand to shoo whatshername away without even looking at her.

"Hey, who do you think—"

"My fault, Miss," Hanley said with an ingratiating smile. "And I apologize. Something's come up and I need to borrow this fellow for a few minutes. Would you mind terribly?"

"Uh, I guess not, but I was—"

"You keep your seat. We'll just step away."

"That's not what I—"

"Yeah, yeah," Muldowney said dismissively. He called the bartender over, pulled a money clip out of his pocket and peeled off a hundred dollar bill. "Keep 'em on ice," he said as he handed over the bill, meaning both the girl and his seat. He hoped she hadn't noticed the very obvious boss-underling relationship that existed between him and Hanley as they walked off.

"So what is he up to now?" Hanley asked when they'd moved off to a corner. He dismissed a brightly smiling roving drink waiter with a curt shake of his head.

"Thurgren?" Muldowney leaned in and lowered his voice. "He's talking to some of our board members," he said ominously. "Nothing formal, just little chats."

Hanley appeared to be waiting for more, and looked up when it seemed nothing more was forthcoming. "That's it?"

"Yeah. Nothing heavy, just some talks."

"That's not what I meant. That's all you have for me? That's the big G-2 for the day?"

"Hey, it's not like they're faxing me the meeting notes, Jim! I get what I can."

"But I already knew he was talking to the board. That's not news, Lanny!"

Muldowney looked down and twisted the point of his shoe against the floor. Hanley let it go on for a few seconds, then said, "What else?"

"Well . . ." Muldowney looked up at the ceiling and all around the room before returning his gaze to Hanley. "He needs—my guy at the SEC, he needs, um . . ." He inhaled a deep breath and let it out with a puff. "He needs a list of all the companies you've entered into contracts with." Muldowney grimaced, as if expecting a blow.

Hanley didn't move, but his glance seemed to grow more penetrating by the second. "Rather becoming a one-way street, isn't it," he said at last, "this rich resource of yours?"

Muldowney shrugged. "My guess, we get him the list, he'll come back at us with some good stuff that we need."

Hanley continued to stare at him, and Muldowney had no idea how he was supposed to be reacting to that withering glare: Throw it right back? Look obsequious and apologetic? Look perfectly neutral?

"I'll give you the list," Hanley said at last. "Some of it."

"But—"

"But what? Perhaps he'd like us to give him his own secretary and an office, too? He gets what he gets."

"But he may not come back with—"

"I'll live with it! And if he doesn't start making this worthwhile again, we cut him off." Hanley stepped closer to Muldowney. "You do remember that the whole idea here is for us to get more out of the SEC than we give, don't you? Otherwise, what's the bloody point, right?"

"What are you, kidding me, Jim?"

"Just making sure you're keeping the proper perspective here. *I'm* the guy you want to suck up to, not some bloated goddamned bureaucrat trying to shut us down." He looked back toward where the future Nobel laureate was starting to pout at the bar. "Unless you think the civil service can keep you up to your neck in more expensive pussy than I can."

"Who the hell do you—You'd still be hawking pork bellies over the phone, it wasn't for me!"

"Maybe. But a business that doesn't grow, it dies. Our shareholders didn't buy in to watch us make a nice living."

Muldowney had had about enough of this. "Don't preach business basics to me, Jim."

"Just remember why I hired you."

As Hanley turned to go, Muldowney said, "I'm gonna need that list."

Hanley paused, then continued without speaking. As he got to the door, someone called out, "Hey, Mr. Hanley! Who you backing for rep?"

"Joey Calabrese!" Hanley called back amiably, and the crowd near the door laughed upon hearing the name of a hopelessly outclassed independent candidate whose best showing in the polls thus far had been a full twenty points behind his opponent, a three-term state senator.

Muldowney waited until he could see the limo pull away from the curb, then he walked to the coat racks on the other side of the entryway. "Is he serious?" a voice said.

"He's serious about everything," Muldowney answered without looking around. He grabbed his coat and headed for the door.

The voice became a face, and said, "Listen, I'm with the *Daily News*. Did he really mean—?"

"Hey!" the girl at the bar called out.

But Muldowney had more important things on his mind, and walked out before either of them could get to him.

JUBAL THURGREN DID NOT LIKE THE WAY THIS CONVERSA-tion was going. "Ms. Heejmstra, far as I can tell, you're already on the boards of, what, more than sixty companies?"

"Do you have a problem with that, Mr. Thurgren?"

"Well, just seems a little excessive, doesn't it? How can you be of service to that many companies?"

"It's a reasonable question, and if I thought it was any of your business, I'd answer it. So unless you think I've broken any laws, why don't we—"

"Laws are fluid with respect to definition, Ms. Heejmstra, we both know that. Terms like 'reasonable' and 'fiduciary' and 'best interests of the shareholders,' they mean what judges and juries say they mean."

"So what're you telling me, you can make my life difficult even if nothing ever ends up sticking, is that about it?"

"I'm saying nothing of the sort. Nothing whatsoever. I just have a few simple questions and would appreciate your cooperation."

Heejmstra read the message clearly: *Don't answer and you're being uncooperative.* "Is *Artemis-5.com* under investigation?"

"Another fluid term. If all I do is pick up a phone, would you call that—"

"Is there a case number?"

"That's, ah, information we don't give out. Listen, let's not make this any tougher than it needs to be. I'm not asking you to reveal trade secrets or anything."

"Sure you are. Asking me what products the company plans to announce? That's the biggest trade secret they have!"

Thurgren scratched his head. Katerina Heejmstra was not a fool and would not be easily manipulated. "I'm not a competitor. I'm with the Securities and Exchange Commission, for heaven's sake!"

"And anyone working for the federal government is above corruption and irreproachable, is that it? Are you willing to sign a nondisclosure agreement?"

"You know I can't do that."

"I appreciate your honesty. I'm hanging up."

"I wouldn't," Thurgren admonished sternly. "This is a legitimate investigation and it's my intent to pursue it with the full authority of the commission. Now I don't want to go through all of that—and trust me, neither do you—so let me ask you just one question, and if you answer it truthfully, I'll defer any next steps."

Thurgren could feel her thinking it over, coming to the only rational conclusion possible: What could it hurt to listen to the question? If she then chose not to answer it, she was no worse off than she was now. "I'm listening."

"It's very simple. Without revealing to me what it is, do you even *know* what *Artemis-5.com* does?"

He waited as some shuffling, shifting and rustling sounds came over the phone. Then they went quiet. "No."

AT TEN A.M. ON JUNE 1, THE STATE LEGISLATURE OF NEW Mexico decided that sales tax would be due on any items sold by a New Mexico corporation over the Internet, regardless of where that item was ordered from or would be shipped to.

Traditional bricks-and-mortar retailers quickly swung into action, calling it the start of a return to the kind of level playing field American tradition was all about. But they didn't have the clout or money the e-tailers had. All over the country recently anointed gods of enterprise got on the phone with their lawyers, lobbyists and publicists, and the crafting of a nationwide coalition of heretofore mortal enemies began. By two o'clock that afternoon the chairman of *Whoopie!.com* was on CBN accusing the New Mexican lawmakers of "decimating American commerce as surely as if they'd dropped a thermonuclear weapon on every mall in the country." Harking back to the legislators' native roots with only thinly veiled slurs regarding why they'd failed to hold on to the New World and how this latest bit of self-destructive insanity was just another example, he hurled 'slippery slope' and 'chilling effect' epithets with the aplomb of someone who'd just been denied an NEA grant, warning consumers not to be lulled into thinking it was only an issue in New Mexico. "The virulent cancer of Internet sales taxes will spread like wildfire," he said, mindless of the mixed metaphor, and he stopped just short of predicting the death of laissez-faire capitalism altogether, despite the fact that it didn't really exist in the first place.

The most immediate casualty was *TillYouDrop.net*. Like every other e-tailer, one of its primary attractions to consumers was the absence of sales tax. In *TillYouDrop*'s case, that was about the only benefit, and before the SEC got around to halting trading that afternoon, the share price had plummeted to $28. With the kind of malicious glee normally displayed only by Hollywood studio execs when one of their close colleagues flopped spectacularly, financial columnists and television talking heads whipped themselves into sarcastic overdrive trying to describe how big an idiot Burton Staller was because, after all, the situation had been utterly predictable, although they didn't feel compelled to explain why they themselves hadn't predicted it.

JAMES HANLEY COULD HARDLY CONTAIN HIS EXCITEMENT AS he strode into Jackie Toland's office, but it metamorphosed into despair in the time it took for Toland to tell him the SEC had just halted trading in *TillYouDrop.net*.

His smile returned just as fast as she said, "Just a circuit breaker, James. They've got no reason not to reopen it tomorrow morning."

"You realize what this means to us?"

"Well, let's see: Five hundred thousand shares you sold short altogether, at an average of around, uh . . ."

"Figure seventy-five each."

"Buy 'em back for twenty-eight or so."

"Pay a little interest . . ." Hanley added.

Toland rocked her head back and forth as she mentally did the arithmetic. "A cool twenty-three mil. Not bad for making a couple of phone calls."

Even as Hanley eagerly nodded his head, he felt compelled to rain on his own parade. "Still not the hundred mil I would've made off the goggles, though."

Toland was having none of it. "Bullshit, James, and you know it. For all we know, you might've lost your shirt."

"Nonsense."

"Not nonsense. You might've sunk ten million into bringing it to market and the day before you release the product two other barely pubescent propeller heads come out with something better."

"Maybe."

"Twenty-three million in the hand is better than a risky pile of wires in the bush."

"Either way, get hold of Lance and tell him to get those buy orders in right away."

"Already on it," Muldowney said from the doorway. "What the hell do we need the exchange for? I've got two dozen phone calls in to institutional shareholders and we'll negotiate the buys in advance. Whoops—" Muldowney grabbed the pager on his belt and twisted it so he could see the display. "There's one right now. Later, folks."

Toland's phone rang. "Well," Hanley said amiably as he stood up, "guess everybody's too busy to talk to me."

Toland smiled as she reached for the phone, waving to Hanley as he walked away.

A few seconds later he heard her shout, "James! Don't go away!" She pressed a button on her intercom and summoned Muldowney back as well.

"I'm on the line, Jackie."

"Hang up, Lance!"

"What? Are you—"

"I said *hang up*!"

When the three of them were back together again, Toland stood and shut her office door, then turned to Hanley and Muldowney.

"Staller says not to close out our shorts yet. He says to be patient and wait."

JUNE 8

"You want me to *what*?"

Thurgren returned the phone to his ear, having held it an inch away in anticipation of Friedenthal's reaction. "You heard me the first time, Harry."

"You want me to bug Burton Staller."

"Yep."

"That's rich, Jubal. Say, while I'm at it, why don't I plant a video-camera in the Vatican?"

"Harry . . ."

"Jubal, I wouldn't ask a judge for a tap order on Staller unless he'd threatened to invade Canada and was already assembling an army. What the hell is wrong with you?"

"I'm telling you, this guy is *wrong*. Every instinct I've ever had tells me he's wrong."

"Even if I believed you, I still can't get a warrant based on your instincts. So what's he done that's new, anyway?"

"He filed an HSR on *TillYouDrop.net*."

"Oh my god! Oh my god, not that!"

Thurgren laughed silently, in spite of himself. "You don't even know what the hell I'm talking about, do you?"

"Not clue one."

Thurgren twisted his neck from side to side to try to relieve some of the cramping that had set in; he'd been on the phone for most of the past hour. "Hart-Scott-Rodino. It's an antitrust regulation. It means he wants to buy up more than fifteen percent of the company, but he needs approval, to make sure he's not trying to create a monopoly."

"Wait a minute. He wants to buy up more of, uh, that outfit that just . . . What was it?"

"*TillYouDrop.net*. New Mexico e-tailer. The state said it's going to start collecting sales tax, and their stock crashed into a black hole."

"Then why the hell is he buying more?"

Thurgren sighed and banged the received against his head several times before answering. "Well, if I knew that I wouldn't need a gosh-darned wiretap, now would I!"

"Jeez." Thurgren stayed quiet as Friedenthal thought it over. "He do anything illegal?"

"Not that I know of. But no way is he clean on this. It makes no sense, so he's up to something."

"What's happening on the markets?"

It was a good question. "The company was shut down from trading, but now they're back on."

"Are people dumping shares like crazy, selling in a panic?"

"Not really."

"And . . . ?"

Thurgren had no choice but to answer truthfully. "Mostly people are buying like crazy."

"Ah!" Thurgren could practically feel Friedenthal smiling smugly at the other end. "So Staller isn't alone when it comes to buying more of the stock. There's a reason people want it."

"True, but—"

"So what makes him a criminal and not the other buyers? Jubal, forget it."

"Harry, it's his own company!"

"I said forget it. You want a wire, the Bureau'll install it, but you go get your own warrant."

JUNE 10

Hanley, seething, much more menacing in his quiet anger than he might be were he more visibly enraged, watched as Lance Muldowney read, reread, then read once again the document he'd just been handed. It was a copy of a fax of a copied fax, but legible nonetheless.

A sheen of sweat broke out on Muldowney's upper lip and he swallowed dryly. "I . . . this . . ." He looked up at last. "I don't get it."

"Well, let me see if I can explain it to you," Hanley said evenly but no less venomously, as he took back the copy of Burton Staller's HSR filing. "While we're sitting on a hundred and fifty million in shorted shares, Jackie's pal is buying up a majority interest in *TillYouDrop.net*."

Muldowney frowned. "Did you say a hundred and fifty—what?"

"It's back up to nearly fifty a share. Why?" Hanley waved the document back and forth. "Because Burton Staller says he's not scared. He has faith in the future of the company."

"But how can it possibly survive!" Muldowney protested. "How can—"

"I don't know!" Hanley hissed through clenched lips. "But I'd suggest we find out." He called out to Beth and told her to find Toland and get her in.

"You don't think Jackie's scamming us, do you, James?"

"What do you think?"

Muldowney shook his head. "I don't believe it's possible. I know you've never been all that crazy about her but—"

He stopped upon hearing a knock, then rose and opened the door. "Hey, Jackie."

"Hey, yourself." Toland looked at Hanley and knew instantly that something serious was afoot. "What's going on?"

Hanley held up the document and waited as Toland stepped forward to get it, then watched her face carefully as she read it.

She sank into a chair after the first few lines, then peered at the date. "He filed this on the eighth?" she said, aghast.

Hanley nodded grimly. "Two days ago."

"And the stock is—"

"Back up to fifty a share."

"Sixty-five," Muldowney corrected him. "Just checked."

Toland rubbed the side of her head as she reread the filing, as if staring at it might make it change. "Well?" Hanley demanded.

"I don't get it," Toland said miserably. "He couldn't be pulling a fast one on us. It's too damned obvious!"

Hanley glared at Muldowney and sat down.

Toland stopped rubbing her head and went still. As Hanley and Muldowney watched, a smile began to crease the corners of her mouth, then she nodded, barely perceptibly. "I'll be goddamned," she finally said.

"What?" Muldowney pressed her.

She turned around and looked up at him. "It's an HSR filing, Lance."

"No shit."

"You, the big swinging whatsis in the world of finance!" she laughed.

Muldowney stared at her crossly. "What the hell are you talking about?" he growled.

Toland turned to Hanley. "You too, Jim. I mean, come on!" She held out the document. "Staller can't buy a single share until this gets approved, and that's still four weeks away."

"So what?" Muldowney said.

Hanley sat up straight, and saw right away what Toland was getting at. "That cagey sonofabitch . . ." he said as he, too, allowed himself to smile.

Muldowney still didn't get it, so Toland explained. "He files this thing to tell the world he's got nothing but faith in *TillYouDrop.net*, which makes everybody and his brother run out and start buying. Meanwhile, poor Burty is completely stymied, can't get any for himself for thirty days, and he just has to sit on the sidelines and watch everybody else buy it up."

"So he's got everybody thinking the company's going to survive," Hanley said, "and he's driving the price up."

"But why?" Muldowney asked, then saw it. "You mean he's selling short himself while all this is going on?"

"Oh, I'd say he is," Toland said merrily.

"But he owns nearly ten percent of the company himself!" Muldowney insisted. "If it goes down the shitter, he's—hey, wait a minute . . ."

"Do the math," Hanley said, grinning broadly now. "Figure he owns ten or fifteen million worth of shares, and meanwhile let's say he sells half a million shares short at eighty or whatever. He loses fifteen million on his stock, picks up sixty or seventy mil when the company tanks . . ." Hanley held out his hands, the rest of the explanation taking care of itself.

"By the time the HSR hold expires," Muldowney concluded, "*TillYouDrop.net* will essentially be out of business and the short sellers, including Staller, will make a fortune."

"Including us, too," Hanley reminded him. "So, what do we do?"

"You sell more shorts," Toland answered. "The stock is still going up, and the higher the price you sell short at, the more you're going to make when it craters."

"Hold it a second," Muldowney said. "How do we know it *is* going to crater?"

That answer was obvious. "Because Burton Staller is telling us it is," Hanley said.

CHAPTER TWENTY

JUNE 15

SINCE THEY'D HAD THEIR HARSH WORDS in the bar, the atmosphere between Hanley and Muldowney had changed. While neither of them might have been able to precisely define how, the easy affability that thus far had characterized their relationship had clearly been compromised in some subtle way.

Muldowney walked wordlessly into Hanley's office and dropped a newspaper on his desk. It was opened to an inside page, and Hanley read the headline: "Calabrese pulls even with Jorgensen."

"You've arrived, James," Muldowney said. Once word had spread that Hanley was supporting the hopeless underdog, Calabrese's poll numbers had risen right along with his campaign coffers.

"I was just kidding," Hanley said.

"That's my point." Muldowney stepped back

and closed the door to Hanley's office. "Burton Staller buys a pair of underwear," he said as he walked back, "Fruit of the Loom jumps three points. Trump stops in the lobby for a newspaper, somebody makes an offer to buy the whole building." He sat down facing Hanley. "You crack wise about a candidate, people start throwing money at him."

"What about it?"

Muldowney leaned forward to rest his elbows on the desk. "Means you've arrived, and there's not a damned thing Jubal Thurgren or anybody else in the world can do about it. You think you can finally relax a little?" . . . *and get off my case?*

Hanley didn't say anything for a few seconds, then he reached for a large envelope on the credenza behind him and tossed it toward Muldowney. "We've received an invitation to the Wrecker's Ball."

"About time. You gonna go?"

"*We're* going. It's for both of us."

Muldowney gulped back his excitement. "Gotta wear a costume," he said as casually as he could.

"I have someone. Owns a shop . . ." Hanley said awkwardly.

"Good. Um, we're supposed to work on some filings tonight, remember?"

"Right. I was rather hoping to get out of the city, up to my weekend place."

"No problem. I'll drive up and we can do it there instead."

"Don't you have a compliance meeting downtown?"

"Yeah. I'll take my own car and meet you up there."

THE PLODDING BUT EFFECTIVE THURGREN MANAGED TO GET four other members of Hanley's prestigious board of directors to admit that they didn't have the slightest notion of what *Artemis-5.com* was all about, but who in his right mind turned down a piece of an Internet start-up when all that was required was use of your name? Besides, the company carried the best errors and omissions insurance available, a legal suit of armor protecting directors from the consequences of their actions or, more often, their inaction. E&O was the third rail that made the cash train of corporate directorships the sweetest ride in the world.

"If you ask me," Lewis Morosco said to Thurgren, "you'd get the same answers from the rest of the directors, too."

"Five of whom are on the board because of Lance Muldowney's recommendations."

"He's just doing what he's supposed to do. What else can you expect?"

Thurgren looked out over the lower Manhattan skyline and considered the number of people represented by all the windows dotting the walls of the soaring steel monuments to commerce. "Can't help thinking, for every James Hanley we're on to, there are thousands we don't even know about. Makes you wonder about what we do. What the point is."

Morosco made a derisive, snorting sound. "Shit, Jubal; you're gonna get morose on me, I'm going across the street for some calzone. Don't you ever have any good news?"

"Yeah. I get to go back to Washington this afternoon. And then there's this." He picked up a manila folder and withdrew a large card. Hesitating teasingly, he held it out toward Morosco.

Morosco read the front of the card. "What the—"

"It's an invitation to the Wrecker's Ball. Most exclusive soiree on the planet, held every—"

"Holy Christ, Jubal, I know what it is, but what the hell are you doing with an invitation?"

"Me? Nothing. But you're going to be there."

"I am?"

"Don't think of it as a reward, Lewis. Fact is, your information flow from *Artemis-5.com* has gone pretty dry as of late. The more you press me to give stuff to them, the less they're giving back."

"Not my fault, Jubal, I told you. There're a lot of things Hanley keeps all to himself, stuff he won't even tell his attorney. But what's that got to do with the Wrecker's Ball?"

"I'll tell you." Thurgren stood up and stretched his back. "All anybody's talking about these days is that gosh-darned company. My guess, that's what they're going to be talking about at this party, and inside dope should be flowing like the champagne. Your job is to listen and drink in as much as you can. The dirt, I'm talking here, not the champagne."

Morosco looked at him in confusion. "Jubal, the heaviest-hitting execs on the planet Earth are who get invited to these things. How do you figure I'm supposed to—"

"It's a costume party, Lewis. Criminy, you're supposed to be the creative genius?"

Morosco smiled, tapping the invitation expectantly against his leg. "This is the calm before the storm, Jubal. I think we're gonna catch a real big break soon."

Thurgren sat back down and pulled some papers toward him, clearly unsmitten with Morosco's observation. "And just why is that?"

Morosco shrugged and looked up at the ceiling. "Mr. Hanley is feeling mighty secure these days, like nothing could possibly bring him down now. Even thinks he can swing elections."

"He can," Thurgren reminded him.

"Yeah, maybe." Morosco returned his gaze to Thurgren. "But there's nobody more vulnerable than a guy thinks he's got it knocked."

Thurgren looked up at his wall calendar. "Yeah, well in about six weeks he *is* gonna have it knocked, if we don't knock him off first."

CHAPTER TWENTY-ONE

JUNE 18

HANLEY DROVE ABSENTMINDEDLY ACROSS the Tappan Zee Bridge just west of Tarrytown, bogged down in traffic crawling with the same tedious sluggishness it always did on Friday evenings. The only danger worth worrying about at three miles per hour was whether one of the countless other miserable drivers nearby would choose this particular moment to decide that humans weren't supposed to live like this day in and day out and take out his frustrations while he had a two-ton, 250-horsepower revenge machine at his fingertips.

Driving on autopilot, Hanley had plenty of time to contemplate how *he* was living day in and day out. It wasn't exactly as he'd envisioned. He'd figured that, once the money was in, he'd be able to hire plenty of people who could take the load off, leaving him free to ponder the big picture while hobnobbing with similarly situated muck-a-mucks. After all, it was the little guys, the ones who poured everything into their nail salon or carpet cleaning business or fast food franchise, who worked themselves to the bone night and day to try to keep everything together. Those were the guys who were CEO, CFO, personnel director, operations manager and accountant all rolled into one, because any of it that got farmed out cut into the bottom line, which was already thin enough that each new expense was keenly felt.

But the big corporate guys, the moguls, some of them had entire departments devoted to *parking*, so how come Hanley was spending every waking minute, and not a few of the sleeping ones, too, worrying about *Artemis-5.com*?

Because I don't know how to delegate, he thought as he exited the bridge and continued north on the Thruway. *Because I don't trust anybody else with the big decisions.* As he drove past the sign announcing the exit to the town of Suffern, he noticed that the string of red taillights in front of him had thinned out considerably, and he was up to about 40 miles per hour.

He was well aware that any pressure he'd been feeling up until now was only going to get worse. He had shareholders to worry about now, people who'd purchased stock in *Artemis-5.com* not because of any shared vision of the future or eagerness to participate in the shaping of the new millennium, but gamblers, pure and simple, who would be counting on him to load the dice and mark the cards in their favor. Hardcore gamblers weren't interested in long-term strategy or deliberate foundation building. They weren't interested in *patience*. Show them one down quarter, or even one in which everything held steady but didn't grow, and all hell could break loose. Investors didn't put money into your company because they thought your products would improve the state of education or preserve the environment, or because they'd help defend the country or ensure human rights overseas, nor did they shrink from investing just because your company made cigarettes or owned third world sweatshops or discriminated against minorities or poured hellish toxins into small-town water supplies.

They invested because they thought that eventually your share price would be higher than it was when they bought. That was it. And having left himself with a only a minority stake in *Artemis-5.com*, Hanley was as vulnerable to the anger of the stockholders as the lowliest janitor was to his supervisor. They could vote him out in a heartbeat.

Which was not necessarily a bad thing, considering he'd walk away with about ten percent of a cash-rich behemoth.

Hanley took a deep breath and blew it out loudly just as he veered off to catch the exit for the Quickway that would cut west across the heart of the southern Catskill Mountains. There were no other cars at the tollbooth, and only one behind, something with overly large, yellow-orange headlights. He slowed down just long enough to let the electronic reader take note of the E-Z Pass card stuck to his windshield. Then, energized by the blissfully empty darkness ahead, he cranked it up, noting that the other car coming through the toll plaza was doing just the same.

Hanley waited until he was up to 70 miles per hour, then eased off the gas slightly to maintain that speed, which was only 5 miles per hour above the posted speed limit and below the threshold that would get a state trooper's attention. He expected the other car to pass him, and noticed with only mild surprise that it, too, had settled into the same speed about a quarter mile behind.

They stayed that way for the next thirty miles, and Hanley wondered with some amusement if the frustrated Jubal Thurgren was having him tailed. Slowing for his exit, his suspicion was heightened when the other car slowed as well, and followed him right off the highway at the Monticello exit. Hanley was surprised at the extent of his relief when he finally lost the guy as he turned off onto the road toward the practically nonexistent town of Hurleyville. Turning once again, this time onto a rarely traveled two-lane road lit only by widely interspersed streetlamps, he caught his breath as the unmistakable yellow-orange light swept across the trees at the intersection behind him before appearing as two glowing full moons in his rearview mirror.

Hanley unconsciously sped up, then backed off as the poorly maintained road surface made its bumps and crannies felt through the suspension. In the mirror he could see the two headlights shaking as the driver of the other car ignored the rough ride and began narrowing the gap between them. Alarmed now, Hanley started to reach for his phone but remembered dishearteningly that there wasn't a cell antenna within fifteen miles of this area, which was too sparsely populated to warrant one.

Hanley pressed the accelerator and tried to forget about the wild bouncing as his car leaped forward. He couldn't tell if the lights behind were getting closer, but assumed from how severely their beams were flailing about that the driver was still accelerating. Hanley couldn't risk going any faster because even now he was on the very edge of control, his tires intermittently losing contact with the road and threatening to send him careening off into the trees, but the other driver didn't seem to have that concern, and Hanley could hear his engine clearly now, as well as the loud thumps and crunching sounds as the large vehicle thundered its way clumsily but steadily closer, and then the engine suddenly spun up into a high-pitched whine and the headlights seemed to spring forward.

The noise of the collision was as sickening as the force that slammed Hanley's head back into the padded headrest. While part of his brain fought to get his badly swerving car aligned with the road again, another part could make out the sounds of crumpling metal and shattering plastic, but he didn't have time to sort it out before another nauseating jolt tore at the car and his nerves.

Between the assailant ramming his car and his bottomless terror, Hanley was losing the battle to keep control of his car. The last impact had forced him halfway off the right side of the road, and as he fought his way back, his pursuer used the extra room to pull up alongside. It was a large Pontiac, and by the light of a streetlamp flashing by, Hanley caught sight of the driver's profile, but it was only a momentary glimpse before his eye was drawn to the man's right hand, which was not on the wheel but extended in Hanley's direction.

Just as it flashed into Hanley's consciousness that the hand contained a long-barreled gun pointing directly at him, the man's head was illuminated by a bright bluish light lancing in from behind them. Before Hanley had time to react to the presence of a third vehicle, he heard yet another crash, but didn't feel it, and saw the man's head jerk backward abruptly as the third car slammed into his with breathtaking force. The driver, badly jolted, grabbed at the steering wheel to try to regain control. Hanley saw that he was using both hands and realized that he must have dropped the gun.

Hanley was now able to drop back and watch as the second car, a large BMW, rammed the big Pontiac again, then again, until it finally flew off the left side of the road and came to rest in a ditch, swirling dust playing about it and settling quickly. The BMW screeched to a halt, backed up and stopped. A figure shot out of the driver's side and leaped out, then began running toward the ditch, which was when Hanley recognized the car as Lance Muldowney's.

Wanting nothing more than to keep driving and get as far away from there as possible, Hanley made a U-turn and drove back cautiously. Staying in the car as he slowed to a stop, he saw that the Pontiac's door was open, but there was no sign of either Muldowney or the other driver.

Breathing heavily, Hanley stayed in the car and waited, making note of the time for some future reason he wasn't yet sure of. Several anxious minutes later, Lance Muldowney stumbled out of the woods and leaned over with his hands on his knees, swallowing huge gulps of air in an attempt to steady himself. Hanley got out of his car, looked around and began walking toward him on unsteady legs.

"Couldn't—catch him," Muldowney said between labored breaths. Both of them dropped down onto the damp grass, Muldowney still heaving from the exertion, Hanley shaking almost uncontrollably.

After a minute, when Muldowney's breathing finally slowed, Hanley said, "What, precisely, were you planning to do had you caught him?"

Muldowney looked up, uncomprehendingly at first, then began laughing as he realized he hadn't had much of a plan when he'd lit out after the guy. "You at least get a look at him?" he asked when the cathartic laughter had subsided.

Hanley nodded and leaned to the side so he could pull a handkerchief from his pants pocket. "It was Paul Steffen," he said as he handed it to Muldowney. "And he was armed."

Muldowney gaped at Hanley for a long moment, then touched the handkerchief to his perspiring brow and held it there as he leaned his head on his hand. "Christ . . ." he muttered.

"My sentiments exactly."

"Although, it's kind of a relief, in a way. That Steffen was serious, I mean." Muldowney handed the handkerchief back, then stretched his neck left and right to relieve some of the tension. He could feel Hanley waiting for an explanation for that remark. "Tell you the honest truth, Jim? I always thought it mighta been you who dropped that brick on Jubal Thurgren."

"Me! I thought it might've been you!"

It seemed they'd been equally successful at shocking each other. "Why would you think that?" Muldowney asked.

"Same reason as you, more than likely. Let's face it, we both had the same motive."

"Meaning . . . ?"

"Come now." Hanley put his hands on the ground behind him and leaned back. "Both of us stand to get extremely wealthy off *Artemis-5*, and Thurgren's the only thing standing in our way." But now he understood what Muldowney had meant by the attack tonight being some kind of relief. It underscored the likelihood for him that it had been Steffen, not Hanley, who'd been lying in wait on the highway for Thurgren to drive underneath the overpass. The reason Steffen hadn't shown up for the lunch was that he'd been out demonstrating his seriousness.

But Hanley wasn't ready to accept it at face value, and he had some troubling questions. "How did Steffen know that he was being set up, that I was coming to lunch wearing a wire? How did he know that Thurgren planned to be there himself, and even what route he'd be taking to get there?"

Muldowney agreed that there were still a lot of loose ends. "But this is one very smart, very serious cookie we're dealing with."

"Why would Steffen want to kill *me*?" Hanley persisted, growing agitated again. "What's the point?"

"Could be that's what he meant with that 'Don't fuck with me' line. Either Steffen or the people he works for are giant pissed off you didn't agree to their terms after his little demonstration that he was really willing to eliminate Thurgren."

Hanley was already shaking his head before Muldowney had finished. "How would they know that when they never gave me a chance to respond? I never heard from Steffen again and I had no way to get in touch with him!"

"Oh, boy . . ." Muldowney was staring off into the distance. Then he whirled around on the grass and faced Hanley. "He *knew* you were planning to set him up! He had to, otherwise how would he know where to attack Thurgren?"

Hanley frowned and tried to recall the details of his one and only conversation with Steffen. "Everything he said led me to believe he or his people were tied in tight with the SEC. He even knew that Thurgren's big plan was to make an example of an Internet start-up. But he never exactly said anything directly, anything I could nail down."

"And then he found out you were setting him up."

It was the only possible explanation for what Steffen had done. "That was all the answer he needed from me," Hanley concluded for himself.

"And it was plenty enough motivation for him to come after you. My guess, his people weren't too happy with his failure to clinch the deal."

Hanley's mind was still swirling with connections that appeared solid but instantly eroded under the weight of baffling inconsistencies. "Still doesn't make any sense. If he wanted revenge because I reported him to the SEC, why go after Thurgren in the first place? Why not just me?"

"I don't think he was trying to kill you tonight, James. It was a message. He was just trying to scare you. When he dropped the rock on Thurgren, he was telling you that he could do it. But you'd already reported him once, so you needed convincing. Much as I'd like to take credit for saving your sorry ass, if I hadn't come along, I think he would have run you off the road and then had a little conversation to ensure your cooperation."

Hanley shuddered at the implications of "a little conversation," but still looked skeptical.

"He could have just shot you from behind, Jim," Muldowney conjectured. "He didn't have to bang you around and wave the gun."

"Well, he may have been trying to scare *me*, but he was for sure trying to kill Thurgren."

"How do you figure that?"

"Because how do you drop a cinder block onto the windshield of a car doing seventy miles an hour and not risk killing the driver?"

Hanley was right. There was no way to play the margins that close. "So, Thurgren was lucky as hell, is all."

"Yes. And if all that's true, Lanny, we're going to be hearing from Steffen again. I think we need to warn Thurgren."

Muldowney went quiet for a few seconds, then said softly, "Why, James? Just report it to the cops, and let it go at that."

"The police?" Hanley stared at him in confusion. "But I saw his face, Lance. How can I—"

"It was dark," Muldowney murmured ominously. "You didn't see shit. Don't be an idiot, James; you think you owe Thurgren something?"

They stared at each other, and Muldowney's implication was clear: Steffen could still be useful—he might still be willing to take out Thurgren—and neither Hanley nor Muldowney could be held complicit if he did. Hanley had done his duty and reported the first contact, the criminal solicitation, and if he reported this incident only as a local matter because he didn't get a good look at the perpetrator, how could he be faulted for not knowing it had been Steffen?

"Now that I think about it," Muldowney added, "screw the locals, too. Let's just get the hell out of here."

They sat without speaking for a few minutes, only the *shrknch-shrknch* of the cicadas and the throaty rumbles of frogs in the distance breaking the eerie silence of the deserted road.

"You didn't know he was only trying to scare me, Lance."

"What?"

"At first. You only surmised that later. You thought someone was trying to kill me and you never hesitated."

Hanley's gratitude needed no further expounding. Embarrassed, Muldowney got to his feet and extended a hand to help Hanley up. "Whatever," he said as he let go and began walking toward Hanley's car. "Just do me a favor and don't let's make a big deal about it, okay?"

Hanley caught up just as they reached his car. Muldowney ran his hand over the rear bumper. "Guy hardly touched you, James."

Hanley could see that must have been true. "Felt rather like a tank hitting me."

"Musta been the shock or something. Like I said, idea was probably to just throw a scare into you."

"Newsflash for you." Hanley wrapped his arms around his chest and squeezed as hard as he could for a few seconds, then let go and shook his hands and arms. "It worked."

. . .

JUBAL THURGREN'S JAW MUSCLE WAS PULSING VISIBLY AS he stared, grim faced, at nothing in particular.

"Say that again?" Lewis Morosco prompted him.

"You heard me. Not one of the companies *Artemis-5* struck deals with has been subcontracted to actually produce anything for it."

"What about the colleges? All those research labs?"

Thurgren confirmed that none of the universities with which *Artemis-5.com* had entered into technology transfer arrangements was working on anything specifically for the company, yet most of them had granted *Artemis-5.com* significant percentages of future revenues in exchange for very generous, open-ended grants. "You need to step up the pressure, Lewis. You have to get us more information on what in heck Hanley is up to."

"Muldowney's walking a tricky line here, Jubal. What if—"

"It's do-it-or-get-off-the-pot time, Lewis. Even if we have to risk pushing too hard and blowing the whole thing. We don't have enough, and time's running out."

"How do you figure that? The IPO's already over anyway."

"I know, and the longer we wait, the harder it's going to be to reset the clock on it."

"You don't really think that's possible, do you?"

There was no use conjuring up a comforting answer, because the truth was Thurgren had no way to know. "You've got to work the crowd at the Wrecker's Ball hard, Lewis. Even unsubstantiated rumors are important now."

Morosco understood. The avenues of inquiry they'd been pursuing simply weren't panning out, and what they needed right now was fresh leads. "What are you gonna be doing?"

"If it kills me," Thurgren replied, "I'm going to find out how in God's name they racked up half a billion in revenue."

JUNE 20

THESE WEREN'T THE KIND OF PEOPLE WHO got chintzy when it came time to work up a costume, and Morosco's own get-up was no lesser an achievement than some of the ones worn by the captains of commerce who really belonged at the ball.

His Tin Man costume was made of aluminized fabric and topped with a head of corrugated cardboard that had been sprayed first with a coat of primer and then with a shiny metallic auto paint. It was a beauty, and it encased Morosco's face completely, making him unrecognizable. He was getting a kick out of not identifying himself so that everybody had to speculate about who he was. There hadn't been much choice, really, since no one would have known his name, anyway, and even if they had, they might not have taken too kindly to his presence.

Only thing was, he hadn't counted on how hot it was going to get inside the thing. He couldn't drink anything without lifting the head off, and, as much as he would have liked a shot of something potent, right now a cool glass of water would have been just as welcome.

He spotted Benjamin Franklin from behind. The venerable old gent was carrying a kite in one hand and a drink in the other. He had a slight limp, favoring the left leg, and was just about the right height . . .

Morosco maneuvered to the side and confirmed that it was indeed Burton Staller. Taking care not to be obvious, he made his way in that direction and then stopped once he could hear his voice.

"Too damned right I'm gonna buy it up," Staller was saying to Louis XIV angrily. "Just filed an appeal with those damned Comanches today."

"Nuh-uh," Genghis Khan was quick to point out. "Navajos or Apaches, maybe Mescalero, but not Comanches, not in New Mexico."

Staller looked at him like a lion might look at a clam: with barely enough regard even to bother registering contempt. "Whatever. Should have kept them all on the reservation."

"So you're buying?" King Louis pressed.

"Can't. Not until this goddamned HSR approval comes in, those fuggin' feds."

"When's that?" His Highness tried to ask as casually as he could.

"July eighth. If there's anything left. Christ . . ."

Morosco estimated it would take the monarch less than three minutes to sneak away and call his broker. He spotted James Hanley, dressed as Jean Lafitte and surrounded by an admiring group of hobos, forest animals, several knights and two popes. Sidling up slowly and trying to ignore the heat building up inside his costume, Morosco listened in to some conversations but didn't say a word himself.

"Thinking of hooking on up with Mike," one of the popes was saying. When Hanley only shrugged, His Holiness said, "Yeah, not the number-one choice, but telecomms, we're running out of retailers to synch with. All the good ones are taken, know what I mean?"

"That's true," Hanley admitted. "But Mike? I don't know. Make sure you don't end up propping up his whole company after the first year."

The pontiff frowned in concern. "Yeah . . ."

"Cook up a contract provision," Hanley suggested. "Tie it to their results. After a year, should they not hit the numbers?" He took a sip of his scotch. "You take over and run it instead."

The Vicar of Christ nodded his head so enthusiastically he almost lost his miter. "You think they'll agree?"

"Sweeten the deal," Hanley replied.

"I don't know . . ."

"What's the difference if you toss in another half billion? If they perform, you're in good shape. If they don't, they're yours. That's worth a lot."

The pope still looked dubious, so Hanley capped it off with a line that was fast becoming his trademark. "Jack, in a year, you won't remember what you paid. You'll only know if it's working."

His Holiness thought about it for a few seconds, then made the sign of the cross in front of Hanley—"Go in peace, my son"—and walked away happy and with much to think about.

It went on that way, faces he'd only seen in newspapers tracking Hanley down and sharing concerns, asking questions, seeking affirmation of decisions they'd already made, running pending ones by him to see what he thought. Some were only trying to impress him, and Morosco caught some truly tantalizing nuggets from movers and shakers who should have known better than to be so forthcoming but couldn't help it. He concentrated fiercely and tried to make mental notes of it all.

IN THE SMALL STUDY OFF THE LIVING ROOM OF THEIR RES-ton, Virginia, condo—he and Genevieve had wisely decided to dump their house when he'd made the decision to resign his partnership—Thurgren agonized over *Artemis-5.com*'s terse but stunning quarterly report, trying to figure out how they'd managed to list billions in assets and hundreds of millions in revenue when he'd been unable to locate a single actual operation or identify a single *Artemis-5.com* product.

All the documents that had come in clandestinely via Lance Muldowney and surrounded him now as he pondered the mystery, had shed no light on it at all, which shouldn't have been too surprising considering how tightly Hanley had compartmentalized his company. He considered Muldowney purely a finance guy and kept him isolated from operations, which was pretty much along the lines of how Muldowney had sold himself into the company in the first place, so it was really all aboveboard.

In exasperation, Thurgren picked up the phone. "I'm gonna just call him."

"Who?" Genevieve asked.

"Ted Mangus."

"You're going to call the managing partner of Highland & Harwick at home on a Sunday night?"

"Yeah. Gonna ask him about the underlying schedules that fed these damned reports."

Mangus was an old-schooler who never quite got over the wars that had raged between public accountants and the SEC over whether an auditing firm should be allowed to perform consulting services for audit clients. The SEC had tried to take the position that this was a conflict of interest. The auditor's client was supposed to be the shareholders, the idea being for the outside accountants to objectively scrutinize the books and keep management honest when they reported results to those shareholders.

But if the same auditors were also selling consulting services to management, then management was a client, too, and what would happen when the auditors came across some questionable business practices? Knowing they could kiss their lucrative consulting fees good-bye, would they still blow the whistle?

The SEC had thrown everything it had into the battle to prevent public accounting firms from doing anything for publicly held audit clients other than examining the books on behalf of shareholders. They lost, and did so resoundingly, and now the consulting practices of some of the largest accounting firms were actually larger and more profitable than the auditing divisions.

But the battle had cost money, especially for the accounting firms, and the less visible but equally painful psychological scars had not yet healed among the older, more conservative partners, who'd resented being dragged into the public spotlight and humiliated into defending themselves. People like Ted Mangus still regarded the SEC as the enemy, and he reflexively told Thurgren that the schedules he wanted weren't public yet, and wouldn't be until the annual report was filed in another nine months.

"What about the working papers, Ted? Will you at least let me look at those?"

"Are you serious? You haven't been out of the business *that* long. You know perfectly well the danger that they might be misinterpreted prior to their finalization and certification by Highland & Harwick."

He was quoting directly from the SEC's own guidelines. "I'm not going to print them or send them to anybody, Ted. All I want is to *see* them."

Mangus knew the regs by heart and stuck to his guns. But he also knew that it still didn't pay to cross the SEC, that they were just people, after all, people with considerable authority to make his life miserable, and it never paid to unduly rankle people who were in a position to cause you grief. "Listen, if you've got some specific questions, maybe I can be helpful. Best I can do."

It was something. Grasping at this tiny straw, Thurgren thought it best not to ask the question that was uppermost on his mind at this moment, which was why the managing partner of the world's largest professional services firm would have detailed information about a single client at the top of his head. "That's great, Ted. I appreciate it. What are the major sources of the five hundred million in revenue?" *For which,* Thurgren saw no need to throw in, *there are virtually no profits?*

Phrasing his question in the plural was a natural enough assumption, but an incorrect one. "It all comes from a company they bought in Malaysia called Universal Expediters."

Mangus explained in broad strokes how the company operated, and why it showed such little profit for such enormous revenue. He had no way to know how Thurgren's temperature was rising as he spoke, and therefore no reason to modulate the matter-of-fact tone of voice he was using, as though everything he was saying was perfectly proper.

When he finished, Thurgren took several deep breaths before responding, trying to maintain his professionalism, because he needed one more piece of information. "Uh-huh, I see. What about the assets they listed?"

Again Mangus explained, and when he was through and Thurgren was pretty sure that was all he was going to get, he said, "Tell me this is a practical joke, Mangus."

"There's nothing improper about it," Mangus told him huffily, "and if you don't like it, you can tell the SEC to change its own rules. That about it?"

As Thurgren hung up, he was aghast that the firm of Highland & Harwick would let an audit client get away with something like that, but not as much as he was over the fact that the SEC didn't have rules to prevent it.

MOROSCO, HEATING UP BADLY INSIDE THE STUFFY TIN MAN costume, listened in as Hanley spoke with Dr. Mallory Compton.

". . . Rather simple, really, and you and a couple of the other board members stand to make a fair bit of money. The real trick, the tough one, is to identify the winners before anyone else does."

Compton nodded in agreement. "There are a lot of smart, eager people doing good work, James. Many of them have solid companies under way, and yes, I agree, the young people need encouragement and some financial assistance, and the foundation is surely in a—"

"Oh, blow it out your ass, will ya, Murray?" Hanley had come to enjoy sabotaging Compton's professorial demeanor with some well-timed street talk. "You think I'm giving you a piece of this kind of action so you can sit around talking like a goddamned bumper sticker? Now look . . ." Hanley cast a suspicious glance at the Tin Man and turned slightly. "Any kid who's already incorporated, it's too late. Everybody's already throwing money at him left and right, they're *competing* for him, for God's sake, and he knows it. He's working them all like marionettes and besides, by the time that all happens, somebody else is probably already stealing his idea or improving on it. Why the hell do you think they all want to go public or get bought out so fast? I'll tell you why: so they can cash in before the world discovers their brainchildren aren't worth shit anymore, that's why. What we need to do, Murray, we need to find those guys in their parents' garages while they're still *in* the garages, not once they're already on the cover of *Business Week*."

Morosco got the definite impression that speaking like a Brooklyn plumber was almost a kind of relief for Hanley, like the strings of obscenities gushed by Tourette's sufferers after an hour of forcing themselves to hold back.

He already knew what Hanley was telling Compton. The three most technical of the *Artemis-5.com* board members were also on the board of the *Artemis-5.com* Foundation for the Advancement of the Internet, and their job was going to be to use the technology transfer contracts with universities to find out what the brightest students were up to. When they spotted something with commercial potential, they could offer grants to those students in exchange for written promises to enter into joint ventures with *Artemis-5.com* later.

"Here's the thing, Murray," Hanley was saying, his arm around Compton's shoulders. "You go up to a college student, he's living on beer and pizza and hasn't got enough spare change to fill his gas tank, you tell this kid, 'Kid, howdja like a million or two tomorrow morning to get your idea going, and we don't give a shit if you put a few grand here and there in your own pocket?' What do you think he's gonna say?"

"But he's obligated to *Artemis-5.com* later. There's a string attached."

"Well, of course there's a string, Murray, except the string doesn't cost him a dime! We pay all his costs, we fund his corporation, and then we own a piece and he still gets to make more money than he ever dreamed of! All we did, we got him young, we got him *early*, and we did it before he shot his mouth off to the whole world and ruined everything. One year out of college and the pimply faced dweeb is driving a Testarossa and copping more pussy than the whole college football team . . . you think he's gonna have a *problem* with this?"

Morosco laughed to himself as the scholarly Compton reddened and was forced to admit that Hanley certainly seemed to have a persuasive point. "But what if we guess wrong, James? There's no way to know for certain if any idea is going to—"

Hanley sighed and shook his head. "You know, for being such a guru, you think awfully small, Mallory. If we fund fifty or sixty guys, dump one or two hundred million in the process, and only three or four hit, you think it's possible we can make a buck or two overall? Gee, I don't know, let's ask this nosy tin can over here. Hah? What do you think, Metal Guy?"

Morosco jerked his head around, grabbing at the top of the costume to keep it from falling off, and saw Hanley staring straight at him. "Sorry?"

"I'm going to freshen my drink, James," Compton said.

"Yeah, you go do that. Think about what I said." Hanley stepped closer to Morosco. "We know each other?"

Morosco shrugged, wishing he could stick a hand inside the costume and mop the perspiration that was running down his face. He was so thirsty he could hardly swallow, but there was no way to take a drink without lifting off the head.

Hanley peered through the eyeholes, trying to make out who was inside. "Must be rather hot in that getup, 'ey?"

The Tin Man nodded as Hanley continued to stare. Morosco tried to work up some saliva so he could speak, and even that small exertion made him dizzy.

"SOMETHING'S NOT RIGHT HERE, GODDAMNIT."

Genevieve turned away from her computer and regarded her husband with a mixture of amiable annoyance and wifely sympathy. "JT, you've been moping around about this for hours now. You're taking this very personal."

"I can't get any straight answers!"

"That's because you're asking straight questions, dopey. You're the enemy, remember? What did you expect, that the managing partner of the biggest accounting firm in the world was going to drop trou and bend over just because you picked up a phone? And why are you going that high up in the first place? Guys in the head office never know anything."

"Well, Mangus sure seemed to."

"He knows what his people tell him. You need to speak to a local guy. Holy Hannah, JT, you were a *partner* in a firm like that; don't you remember anything?"

"Apparently not." Thurgren reached beneath the lamp table for a phonebook. "Who's the partner in charge of the H&H audit practice? Not the national guy, the New York guy."

"What are you calling *him* for?"

"What am I . . . You just told me that it's the local—"

Genevieve rolled her eyes, stood up, and walked to a wing chair to retrieve her attaché. She pulled an address book out of it and said as she flipped through it, "Step back, son, yer crowdin' me." Then she walked over, sat beside Thurgren, and yanked the phone out of his hand.

"Who're you calling?"

"Timothy Seale. At home."

"Who's that?"

"Partner in charge of H&H's management consulting practice in New York."

"Management consulting? What the heck's that got to do with—"

At Thurgren's questioning stare, she put her hand over the mouthpiece and said, "Complete stab in the dark, but I'm getting bored watching you play by the rules and getting nowhere. Now stay quiet." She waved to the extension phone on her computer desk, and Thurgren hurried to pick it up before Seale answered and would hear the click.

"Mr. Seale? Faith Gogopak here, *Wall Street Journal,* how you doin'?" She lifted a *what-can-I-tell-you?* shoulder at Thurgren's raised-eyebrow stare, but couldn't tell if he was wondering about the brazen ploy itself or the rapid, clipped speech she was affecting.

"Uh, I'm okay, I—"

"Listen, sorry to bug you at home on a weekend, but what I've got, I've got this goddamned deadline, see, piece I'm doing about James Hanley over at *Artemis-5,* it's a fluff thing, you know, pillar of the community, the company's wider beneficial impact on the New York economy, the usual bullshit, and what I was wondering, can you help me out with a couple things? Give you a couple nice quotes, you know, do a little image thing for you at the same time, get me?"

"Oh, sure, sure. I can help you. What do you need to—"

"Like f'rinstance, how much consulting work is H&H doing for *Artemis-5?*"

Thurgren could feel Seale's mind getting back on track despite the promise of some ink in the official diary of the American dream. "Well, that's a little delicate, Ms. Uh, whadja say your—"

"Gogopak, yeah, I getcha, except when James said for me to give you a call, gave me your number, he seemed to think—"

"Hanley told you to call me?"

"Course. Said that nobody on Earth understood the outfit better'n Tim Seale, but if that's not—"

"Well . . ."

"You wanna keep it off the record, that it? Hell, no problem there, Tim. All's I want, just gimme the rough amount of services being performed, and"—she quickly read a note Thurgren had scratched out on a pad of paper and held up in the air—"and that'll be public eventually anyway, right? Once the audited books of the firm are released to the shareholders?"

"Not necessarily. They're not required to disclose fees like that unless—"

"Okay, I getcha, so you're saying they're not gonna be material, right? Not high enough to require disclosure? Oh, well . . ." She sounded terribly disappointed and ready to cut off the conversation. "I thought . . . James made it sound . . . say, listen, thanks anyway and—"

"Hang on, hang on. Yes, they're significant and, uh, you know, pumping more dollars into the local economy and all, well . . ." Genevieve shot thumbs up at Thurgren, who nodded and dropped the pad down, holding his pen poised above it. "I'd guess H&H stands to collect maybe, say fifteen million from its consulting work to *Artemis-5* this year."

"Uh-huh."

Trying to ignore the adrenaline shooting up his spine, Thurgren scribbled another note to Genevieve to ask what the nature of those services might be, but Seale wouldn't say anything beyond that they were of a general business nature. Thurgren started to write another note, but Genevieve held up a hand and frowned at him—*Don't push!*—and said, "Great client for you guys, huh?"

"You bet," Seale answered, pride evident in his voice. "New as it is, *Artemis-5.com* will be H&H's largest consulting client, by far."

"Good on ya', Tim! Listen, if I can't quote you on this one, I'll make it up to you when you can go on the record, okay? On account of I owe you."

When Genevieve hung up, spreading her hands triumphantly as she looked at her husband, it took Thurgren another few seconds to remember the phone in his hand and put it back on the hook.

MOROSCO WASN'T SURE HOW LONG HE COULD KEEP THIS UP. Even though he could breathe, he felt like he was suffocating. Perspiration was stinging his eyes and he tried to wipe them through the eyeholes but couldn't reach in far enough.

"You learn anything?"

Morosco managed to clear his throat. "About what?"

"About my business," Hanley said. The dizziness grew stronger and Morosco began to teeter. Hanley reached out to steady him. "Buddy, you're gonna die in that stupid thing."

"I—"

"How the hell can you drink without taking it off?"

"I can't."

"Well, there you go. You're dehydrated. That's why you're wobbling like that, because you're dehydrated. Here, sit down. Let me help you off with that—"

"No, that's—"

"Don't be crazy."

Before Morosco could stop him, Hanley let go of his arm, put out both his hands and yanked the tin head straight upward, lifting it cleanly off.

Morosco's hands flew to his eyes and swiped at them even as he drew in lungfuls of cool, sweet air. Hanley was staring at him, eyes wide and mouth agape. Morosco pushed his matted hair away from his face and waited as recognition dawned on Hanley's face.

"Muldowney?" A laugh exploded out of Hanley. "Jesus H, Lanny . . . I was wondering where the hell you were!"

Morosco blinked a few times, then mopped his brow with the back of his hand and grinned back. "Thought I was gonna die in that friggin' thing, Jim," he said. "That asshole you sent me to shoulda supplied an air conditioner with it."

JUNE 22

BURTON STALLER'S FORMAL APPEAL WAS the first thing the governor of New Mexico saw when he got home from three weeks in Malaysia, where he'd been competing in a particularly grueling adventure race in which use of any communications device was considered a distress call; he'd be rescued, but he'd also be disqualified, and the governor would rather lose his life than quit.

By the time he read the appeal the legislature, which only met for sixty calendar days in odd-numbered years and thirty days in even-numbered years to begin with, had already adjourned, the only substantive piece of legislation they'd passed being the sales tax "clarification" itself, which had been introduced by the lieutenant governor of the state by way of an amendment hidden deep inside a bill authorizing local water districts to display pictures of past governors and enacted when their chief executive's plane was still only fifty feet or so off the ground on its way out of the country.

The governor, having dutifully put in nearly a year of grinding lobbying in an effort to lure *TillYouDrop.net* to New Mexico in the first place, threatened to exercise his right to convene the legislature in a special session to deal with the matter. Since the prospect of sitting in session in the middle of summer was not something the legislators looked upon fondly, and since they'd pretty much been snookered by the lieutenant governor anyway and never really considered the proposal properly, a compromise was worked out whereby the matter was kicked into the Ways and Means Committee with a mandate to make a recommendation by mid-July. Part of the deal was that the governor, a supremely rational and remarkably apolitical public servant who would have been a lot better off running the state without the legislature's assistance, agreed he would treat it as binding since it was unthinkable to him that the now-quite-visible committee would make a recommendation that would ensure that the state's most advanced technology business would end up manufacturing birch-bark canoes by hand.

There was little doubt among those familiar with the politics of this sleepy state that the committee members, simply to stick it to the governor and make certain he wouldn't be around to ever interfere with their vacations again, would recommend retaining the sales tax.

On the other hand, it seemed pretty clear that the legislators were heartily embarrassed at having been hoodwinked by the lieutenant governor, and would surely and swiftly reverse their previous self-destructive vote rather than sound the death knell for hi-tech business in New Mexico.

Now that a binary, yes-no, up-or-down decision about the future of the sales tax—and, thereby, the future of *TillYouDrop.net*—was on the table, the whole issue became the purest kind of legal crapshoot, and it was assumed that the Wall Street Casino would be closed for business on this one. To be sure, there'd be some moderate trading conducted by the large pool of the mathematically challenged who also bought lottery tickets, but that was lunch money chaff. For the most part, the larger institutional investors would shy away from laying their clients' money on the line, because what was the point of placing a bet on a 50-50 proposition if you didn't have any inside information on the likely outcome?

Things however, were not turning out that way. Trading was more than just brisk, with the doomsayers selling shares short and the more conservative dumping whatever they had. That they would try to do so was to be expected, but what came as a complete surprise to Jubal Thurgren was that there seemed to be plenty of buyers for everything that was offered. Even more inexplicable was the fact that none of the short sellers was bailing out on the stock. People who had failed to cash in their shorts when the stock had hit bottom at $28 were still hanging on as it rose, and rise it did. Under those strange conditions it wasn't unusual that the share price would slowly but inexorably creep higher and higher, but it was statistically inconceivable that virtually *nobody* had cashed out their risky short sales.

Yet there it was. And Jubal Thurgren was not amused.

JULY 5

"Car drives like a Mack truck."

Thurgren, sitting in the passenger seat of his own car so he could eat, took a bite out of the ham-and-Swiss on rye, then chewed just enough to get his tongue around some words. " 'S'wrong with a Mack truck?"

Paul Steffen wiggled the steering wheel back and forth several times. "This really *is* your father's Oldsmobile," he said as the front wheels smartly failed to respond. He grimaced and shifted his weight on the seat.

"So what'd you drive when you were in the Secret Service . . . Ferraris? Why're you squirming around like that?"

"That shithead Morosco really rammed into me. I almost let him catch me in the woods so I could pop him one."

Thurgren smiled as he swallowed. "Gotta admit, it came off pretty real."

Steffen swung the car off the Beltway and onto Route 66 toward Arlington. "Thought you didn't even like the whole idea."

"I didn't. But, you get right down to it, Morosco thought he was falling out of favor with Hanley, and I still needed a few more details." He reached for the diet soda sitting in the console cup holder. "Now Hanley thinks Muldowney saved his life, so our agent in place is back in business."

"For how long, though?"

Thurgren shrugged. "Don't know. Couple days ago he asked me if it was time for him to come in out of the cold."

"And you told him to stay in."

"In so many words." What he'd actually said was, *Doesn't look so damned cold from where I'm sitting. You see me munching brioche at Lutéce, squiring models around in limos?* "He asked how you were doing."

"Awfully nice of the wild-ass sonofabitch. Eight years in the Secret Service without a scratch, then one job with him and I'm mainlining ibuprofen." Steffen shifted uncomfortably again. "Better hope Friedenthal doesn't find out. He thinks your whole investigation is a crock."

"Yeah, but he loves Morosco. Thinks the kid can do no wrong."

Steffen exited the highway onto North Glebe Road heading south. "That's part of your problem."

Thurgren took a few noisy sips through the straw. "How do you figure?"

The traffic light ahead turned yellow. True to his upstanding G-man image, Steffen never even considered running it, and watched in the rearview mirror to make sure the driver behind them didn't assume he would. "When Morosco came up with the idea for me to offer to whack you, Friedenthal figured that would smoke Hanley out one way or the other. When he turned me down flat, far as Friedenthal was concerned, that was the end of it."

"So he thinks Morosco's a genius for coming up with the plan, and I'm a schmuck for ignoring the outcome."

"I believe those may have been his exact words. And it didn't help that you fought him so hard on approving the idea in the first place. He thinks it's because you knew Hanley wouldn't take the bait."

"That had nothing to do with it!"

"I know that, but—"

"I just hate that kind of phony baloney setup business. Try to hoodwink a guy into hiring a hit man? That's not cricket, Paul. Not even *American*, f'Chrissakes!"

"Not American?" Steffen let out a loud laugh, then instantly stifled it and groaned.

"How are you going to bowl tonight, Paul? You can't hardly even laugh."

"Figure it'll loosen me up. Look, Jubal: First of all, you're not really hoodwinking him. If he's an honest citizen, he turns it down. And second, why'd you go along if you didn't like the whole idea?"

"Because I didn't want to discourage one of my guys from being creative." Thurgren popped the last piece of the sandwich into his mouth. "Heck," he mumbled around it, "it's tough enough keeping them motivated chasing these white-collar guys around. What happens if I stifle them down into looking at ledgers all day?"

"Okay, maybe the first time. But once Hanley reported me? Woulda thought you'd let it go."

"Like I told Friedenthal, just because he didn't hire you to kill me doesn't mean he still isn't a con man." He reached for the drink again, picking it up just as they turned onto Arlington Boulevard and hit a pothole.

"Hey, don't get that on my bowling jacket!" Steffen exclaimed.

"I do, I'll give you mine. We're the same size. Come to think of it, it's probably yours, anyway. And I thought you believed it was Hanley dropped that cinder block on my head."

"I do. But you're the one still thinks it was an accident."

"Those cops said it happened once in a while, some bored gang-banger with nothing better to do. Just a bit of random mayhem in a bad neighborhood."

"Except Hanley was late to lunch, so he had plenty of time to hit you out on the Expressway. And he let Morosco talk him out of reporting his little roadside encounter with me. What excuse is there for an honest citizen not to notify the police?"

When Thurgren didn't answer, Steffen said, "I'll tell you what he was thinking, Jubal. He was thinking that maybe my offer to take you out was still open for negotiation. That's why he didn't want me arrested." He made a final turn onto South Highland and the garish lights of the Arlington Brew 'n' Bowl came into view in the distance. "You still thinkina bringin' him in?"

"Possibly." Thurgren crushed the waxed paper into a ball and dropped it into the paper bag at his feet. "I mean, heck, we gotta do something. Four more weeks and Hanley buys himself an island in the Azores complete with his own army, and that's the end of it."

Steffen slowed the car and turned into the parking lot. "Me and Lewis got a great idea how to do it."

"Gotta do it without creating a public fuss."

"Jubal, even Hanley won't know he's coming in."

"Oh, yeah?"

Steffen pulled into a spot and threw the gear lever into park, then turned off the ignition and handed the keys to Thurgren. "What we do, we have Morosco tell the guy there's a meeting . . ."

The two of them opened their doors and started to get out. Steffen was already standing when Thurgren leaned forward between the door and the windshield and pointed to the hood. "Hey, what's this?"

Steffen looked to where he was pointing and saw a small red spot of light wavering unsteadily. It was moving toward him but then seemed to hesitate.

Thurgren looked around to see where it was coming from. "Whaddaya suppose—"

"Get down!" Steffen barked sharply.

"Huh?" Thurgren turned back just in time to see Steffen flying across the hood, his arms outstretched. Before he could fully understand what was happening, he heard the near-simultaneous sounds of a sharp crack from across the street and a metallic *clang* from the hood of the car, just as Steffen slammed into him and dragged him forcefully to the ground.

Despite the weight of the special agent's body nearly suffocating him, Thurgren stayed down until he heard the roar of a gunned engine and tires screeching.

"He's getting away!" he yelled, then shoved hard to get Steffen off of him. Scrambling awkwardly to his feet, he ran out of the parking lot and into the street, spotting a car with its lights off disappearing in the distance. He kept watching, hoping a nearby house light might illuminate the car or its plates, but the vehicle was around a corner and completely out of sight a few seconds later.

Thurgren brushed at his pants and bowling jacket as he walked back to the parking lot on legs suddenly rubbery and difficult to operate. "Couldn't read the plate," he said in a tremulous voice as he approached his car, but there was no answer from Steffen, who was still on the ground. That was strange enough, but then Thurgren noticed an oil slick pooling beneath his friend's inert body, and it took him a second to realize that oil is what blood would look like in the dimness of a poorly lit parking lot.

FBI ASSISTANT DIRECTOR HAROLD FRIEDENTHAL STOOD WITH his legs slightly apart and arms folded tightly across his chest, still as death as he listened. More experienced at this sort of thing than the badly shaken Jubal Thurgren, who was trying to describe to him what had happened, Friedenthal never looked up as Thurgren paused with every distant footfall, every door swung open, every intercom buzz and blinking light and chirping electronic phone. The Bureau veteran knew that news, when it was available, would find them quickly enough without their jumping at every false alarm.

He didn't hurry Thurgren along at those times, or tell him not to be distracted, because another thing that Friedenthal knew was that there was as much information in how the story was being told as in the words themselves. Besides, there were two things going on here, both of equal importance. One was that critical information was being conveyed while it was still fresh in the teller's mind. The other was that, by talking it all out right away, a federal enforcement officer who had never bargained on violence when he'd joined the Securities and Exchange Commission was already beginning the process of putting himself back together after witnessing a close friend and colleague get shot by a sniper.

Thurgren paused yet again, but Friedenthal saw that it wasn't as a result of a fresh distraction. Still he waited.

"What I can't understand," Thurgren said eventually, "how could Paul have known we were about to be fired on?"

Friedenthal nodded encouragingly. Thurgren was tough, he could see that, and was already rousing himself to the point of identifying issues and seeking their resolution. "That red spot," he said. "It was a laser sight targeting in on you."

"A laser sight. Don't know how those work."

Friedenthal fully extended his arm to the side and made a gun of his hand. "You don't have to aim like this," he said as he closed one eye and sighted down his arm with the other. "The laser is mounted above the barrel of the gun so it points where the muzzle points. You put the red spot on whatever you want to hit, and then you pull the trigger."

"Good God. How can you miss?"

"You can't. All you need is a steady hand, and maybe a scope on the gun so you can see the spot at long distance. Long as your hand is steady, it's a bull's-eye every time."

Thurgren shook his head in wonder and disgust, and tried to recall how that lethal spot had looked on the hood of his car. "He was hesitating."

"Paul?"

"The shooter. The spot was on the hood of the car, shaking a lot. What I think—" Friedenthal knew what he thought, but stayed quiet. "He was thrown because he'd expected me to get out on the driver's side, not the passenger's."

Thurgren stood up stiffly. His neck was starting to hurt from looking up and he rubbed it. "Paul's old Secret Service training kicked in and he launched himself over the hood." He stopped rubbing. "To protect me . . ."

He sat down again, and now Friedenthal sat beside him. "You're telling me you think the guy was going after *you*?" the assistant director asked, incredulous.

"Who the heck else?"

"Steffen, that's who! Wait a minute . . . Don't tell me you're still piddling around on that *Artemis* thing!"

"That's twice somebody tried to kill me!"

Any pretense Friedenthal had entertained about staying cool in this crisis dried up and blew away. "Jubal, *you're* the one told me that cinder block through your window was a coincidence!"

"And I believed it. Before this happened." He looked into Friedenthal's eyes for the first time since they'd met in the hospital. He hadn't been able to face him after presiding over the shooting of one of his agents. "But this one wasn't random, Harry."

Friedenthal pulled a cell phone from his jacket pocket. "I'm getting an all-points out for the shooter."

"Hold it," Thurgren said, putting a hand on the phone. "I didn't get a good enough look at the car for you to put anything useful out over the wires. If I thought there was a prayer of catching the guy, I'd say go for it. But media coverage right now would only complicate the investigation."

"What investigation?" Friedenthal said with undisguised annoyance, but then regretted it. It was possible that Thurgren's bullheadedness was the cause of Steffen's getting shot, but this was not the time make an issue of it.

Footsteps again, but different this time. They both looked down the corridor to see Lewis Morosco running toward them. "I got your call. Jesus . . . hello, Mr. Friedenthal . . . What the hell happened, Jubal?"

"I think your buddy Hanley tried to have me taken out." He waited while Morosco dropped back against the opposite wall.

Morosco, hand trembling, rubbed his brow and tried to think even as he was catching his breath. "How's Paul?" he said absently.

"Don't know," Friedenthal said, "but he mighta gotten lucky. Seems the round hit the hood of the car first before ricocheting into him."

"Is he conscious?"

"Semi. Lost a lot of blood. He's in the OR now."

Morosco let out a breath as Thurgren said to Friedenthal, "I don't think we can wait any longer to move on Hanley."

"You think we got enough?" Morosco asked.

Thurgren looked toward the operating room for the thousandth time, and prayed for the thousandth time that the physicians had just forgotten about them and were off having coffee after having trundled Steffen off to recovery all patched up and no worse for wear. "We may not be able to connect him with the shooting, but we can probably take his company down. Harry, there's something I've got to tell you."

"Let's not talk about it out here," Friedenthal said, rising. "Nurse said we can use a lounge down the hall."

. . .

"WE BORROWED PAUL TO STAGE A FAKE RESCUE," THURGREN said, mustering up his nerve after they were seated in the privacy of the lounge.

Friedenthal's face went stony. "When?"

"Two weeks ago. Lewis wasn't getting anything much good anymore, and Hanley started making some noises that led us to believe he was getting unhappy with him. We needed a way to get Muldowney back in his good graces, so we set it up for him to save Hanley's life." Without mentioning that it had been Morosco's idea, and that Thurgren himself had opposed it, he laid it all out, slowly, knowing that Friedenthal wouldn't interrupt. The longer Thurgren took to tell the story, the longer he'd postpone the assistant director's inevitable expression of righteous anger.

When he finished, Morosco stepped in quickly before Friedenthal could go off on a tirade. "I think the shooter was probably someone who'd seen Jubal up close before, Mr. Friedenthal."

"Why?"

"Because he'd been able to tell in bad light from across the street that the person getting out of the driver's side wasn't Jubal, even though he and Steffen have roughly the same height and build."

Friedenthal turned toward Thurgren, as if to confirm that estimate. "We were even wearing the same bowling jackets," Thurgren said.

"It's a good observation, Morosco," Friedenthal said with tentative approval, "except you got it backwards. I'm telling you, Jubal, it's Steffen they were after."

"Either way, sir, it might rule out a hired professional, who probably would've pulled the trigger the instant one of them had stood up enough to present a clear target. But someone who knew Jubal . . . Okay, or someone who knew Paul . . ."

Friedenthal admitted that some of the shooter's hesitancy might have come from the fact that he recognized Thurgren, too, and had been confused by it. If so, that bolstered the evidence against Hanley, and as he mused out loud, Thurgren leaped to a conclusion.

"Hanley himself must have been the triggerman."

"Come on, Jubal," Morosco said.

"Just listen! Hanley knows both me and Paul, and he would've been completely floored when he saw us together. That's why he hesitated." *Which probably saved my life . . . and Steffen's, too, because he didn't get off a clean shot even when he did finally decide to fire.*

"Sounds a little far-fetched," Friedenthal insisted. "I'm not buying it. Listen, who says Hanley is even here in Washington?"

That simple question brought Thurgren up short, and pretty much stopped the conversation altogether. "Lewis, you alright?"

Thurgren looked up to see what Friedenthal was talking about, and watched as Morosco, who had already slid halfway down the wall, continued until he was sitting on his haunches. "What's the matter with you?"

Morosco swallowed and said, "He *is* in Washington."

Thurgren and Friedenthal exchanged glances. "You sure?" Friedenthal asked.

"Positive. He's meeting at a hotel with a consortium of software companies looking for *Artemis-5*'s endorsement of some standard they're proposing. I don't even know what that means, but—"

"What hotel?" Friedenthal asked.

Morosco tried to remember. "Think it was a Marriott. Yeah, in, uh . . . Reston, that was it."

"What time?"

"Seven-thirty. That I remember because there was going to be dinner first, but Beth told them James wouldn't make the dinner, he'd be there for the meeting. But Mr. Friedenthal, it's not possible. I know this guy, and it's just not in him to—"

"Harry, it fits." Thurgren bolted upright and pointed to Morosco. "Hanley could have been waiting at the bowling alley and had plenty of time to get to that meeting."

As Friedenthal thought about it, Morosco, now helpless before the evidence, said, "If you'd just not gone to see him in New York, Jubal, he wouldn't have known your face."

"Don't start second-guessing yourselves," Friedenthal warned sternly as he looked at his watch, then reached into his jacket pocket and pulled out his cell phone. "That meeting may still be under way. I'll have a couple of agents meet us there and we'll search Hanley's car, maybe test him for GSR."

Morosco shook his head. "Waste of time," he said as he got to his feet. "Sir, Hanley's no dummy, believe me. He would have dumped the gun and also washed and changed his clothes, which would completely eliminate any gunshot residue."

Friedenthal rubbed a thumb over his phone as he considered what they should do. "If we do the search and nothing comes up," Morosco said, "we'll only alert Hanley that we're on to him."

It was a good point, and Friedenthal took it a step further. "If we ask for a search warrant on such a flimsy premise and don't turn up anything, we'll piss off the issuing judge and never get another warrant when we really need one."

"The sonofabitch tried to kill me!" Thurgren protested. "We got a chance to nail an attempted murderer and we're not going to take it?"

"Maybe he did, maybe he didn't," Friedenthal said, "But that's how it goes, Jubal. Sometimes, you just gotta—"

"Wait a minute!" Morosco interrupted, snapping his fingers. "Sorry, sir. But I've got the keys to Hanley's car. Supposing I just kind of mosey on over there and—"

Friedenthal put his hands in the air. "I don't want to hear this, Lewis!"

"But there's no issue, Mr. Friedenthal. He gave me his keys, so doesn't that imply my right to use the car?"

Friedenthal shook his head. "You're undercover. It's false pretenses."

"But law enforcement officers engage in deception all the time!"

"Of a certain type. You lie to a guy to trick him into confessing. But rifling a guy's car when he doesn't know you're the law? I don't think a court would construe that as 'permission.' You need a warrant."

"So how about this?" Thurgren said softly as he looked around the corridor. "If Lewis finds a rifle in Hanley's car, *then* we go get a search warrant."

"I don't want to know about it." Friedenthal looked worried. "What I'm wondering, how much danger is Lewis himself in? If you're right about all of this, Jubal, if you're right about Hanley, then maybe we should pull him out right now."

Morosco shook his head. "Pull me out and the operation is dead," he said forcefully. "Hanley couldn't possibly be suspicious of me. He's given me a stake in the company, in writing and notarized. I'm telling you, he *trusts* me."

"Enough to tell you he was trying to kill Jubal?"

That seemed to deflate some of Morosco's cockiness, and he had to admit that he was nowhere close to being that intimate with Hanley. "In fact," Morosco added, "he used to bitch about Jubal all the time, but he hasn't said anything at all about him for quite a while."

At that, Thurgren and Friedenthal looked at each other, realizing simultaneously that what Morosco had just described was Hanley having come to a decision to take action after some period of ruminating about it.

"I'm heading out," Morosco said.

FRIEDENTHAL LOOKED AT HIS WATCH, TRYING TO CALCULATE about what time they could expect to hear from Morosco. "How long you figure for him to get to where the meeting is?"

"You don't know about that, remember?"

"You're right. Jubal, you need to move against Hanley with whatever you have." When Thurgren turned to look at him in surprise, he pressed the point. "Why take a chance? If you're right, the stakes have just gone up and there's no way to tell when he's gonna try to take you out again. Without around-the-clock bodyguards, there's no practical way for us to protect you."

"Assuming I really was the target."

"You could take yourself off the case."

"No."

As the conversation died down, Thurgren's anxiety level continued to rise. He'd had no experience dealing with violent criminals prior to the incident in the UCLA library, and this kind of proximity to mortal danger was rattling him badly.

"Where the hell are those goddamned doctors?" Friedenthal fumed futilely. "Don't they realize Paul's got people out here who—"

Thurgren almost jumped out of his skin as the ringing of his cell phone pierced the solitude of the quiet hallway. He scrambled to grab it before it could ring again.

It was Morosco, disappointment etching his words. "I searched his car, Jubal. It was clean."

"Don't feel bad, Lewis," Thurgren told him, shaking his head at Friedenthal. "Just means he's smart, is all, just like you said."

As he snapped the phone shut, Friedenthal asked him if he had enough to move. "I know things he did that might have been illegal and are at least definitely suspicious," Thurgren replied. "What I don't know is exactly *why* he did them." He explained to Friedenthal his fear that, without a coherent structure, some core concept to hang it all on, his case may not resonate with people in a position to prosecute Hanley. "I don't think we should move on him until we can explain it, Harry."

Friedenthal sighed in exasperation. "I tell you you're full of shit? You're ready to roll. I tell you, okay, maybe you're right? And you don't want to move in." Friedenthal shook his head. "You wouldn't last two seconds in the Bureau, Jubal."

They heard the OR door swing open and turned to see a young, tired-looking surgeon in scrubs heading their way. Both of them stood up. Young as he was, the doctor knew enough not to unnecessarily delay giving news.

Especially good news. He flashed a thumbs up and nodded his head as soon as Friedenthal and Thurgren noticed him coming. As they sighed in relief, the doctor yanked his cap off, scratching at the hair that had matted underneath. "Tough sonofabitch, let me tell you. All that muscle kept the round from hitting anything vital."

"So, how come it took so long?" Friedenthal asked with some irritation.

The surgeon looked at his watch. "Hey, gimme a break. You call forty-five minutes long?"

"So he's going to be okay?" Thurgren asked hopefully.

"Yeah. Lost a lot of blood and we'll keep him two, three days, but he should be back catching bad guys pretty soon."

"Thanks, Doc. Don't mind this surly bastard over here. He just generally gives everybody a hard time."

When the doctor had gone, Friedenthal put a hand on Thurgren's shoulder. "You need to make sure Morosco's okay."

"I know."

"Not sure you do, Jubal. Appreciate you trying to protect him, but I know that bullshit rescue was his idea. It's possible he almost got Paul killed on account of it backfiring, and he's gonna tear himself up over it if you don't set him right."

"How come you think it was his idea?"

Friedenthal snickered as he turned to get his coat from the chair. "You don't have that kind of flair, Jubal. That was a cowboy play—a boneheaded one, that's for damned sure—but a cowboy move nonetheless."

He picked up the coat and slung it over his shoulder. "And you're not the cowboy on this team."

CHAPTER TWENTY-FOUR

JULY 8

THURGREN PAUSED OUTSIDE MOROSCO'S DOOR. He wasn't terribly good at this sort of thing. He liked to lead by example, by removing obstacles and letting bright young people make a few mistakes and come into their own. Overt counseling was condescending and potentially humiliating, especially to a maverick like Lewis Morosco, who would likely not take kindly to someone feeling it necessary to attend to his wounded psyche, or even presuming to think it *was* wounded.

It was one of the things Thurgren had liked least about being a partner in a big, highly visible and tightly regulated firm, all that time that he had to spend "dealing with people issues." It was a self-perpetuating and self-escalating cycle of creeping codependence. Fresh-faced kids were coming straight out of college preprogrammed to expect care and feeding by huge human resources departments, and those departments wielded great influence when it came to how partners and employees interacted. Fear of lawsuits had become the prevailing guiding principle, because legal threats could come from anywhere: sexual harassment, discrimination, unlawful termination, unequal pay, even tortious interference should anyone, God forbid, give a bad reference to a departing employee and "compromise his right to secure gainful employment." That fear warped the handling of personnel matters to such an extent that honesty in human interaction was the one thing practically guaranteed to get you into trouble.

Ultimately, it hurt the employees. Good people making a change couldn't get supportive references because that would mean that a refusal to comment on a not-so-good employee implied some hidden negative, so the standard was to "No comment" all inquiries universally. Decent people who were simply inappropriate for a particular environment were often kept on rather than let go because there was too much risk in firing them straight out. So they hung around until they figured it out for themselves and left anyway, wasting years in the process when that could have been peaceably and honorably avoided. Written policies on "inappropriate behavior" and the required use of gender-neutral language were often longer than customer service manuals, and innocently asking a fellow employee out to dinner was fast becoming a logistical nightmare roughly tantamount to requisitioning nerve gas from an army depot: By the time you worked through all the required permissions, supervisor notifications and protective rearguard interviews, the invitee would probably already be married and have kids.

In actuality, Jubal Thurgren really hadn't been opposed to a lot of the more reasonable guidelines, which explained why he'd been wildly popular among the up-and-comers who wanted to make his firm their home. It was just that the time and energy it took to deal with all of it, time that was not spent servicing clients, never got smaller, only larger.

And here he was again, ready to play the understanding and all-knowing patriarch of the Enforcement Division, when the only real lesson he would like to have conveyed to Lewis Morosco was that if he'd just listened in the first place, all this could have been avoided. "Whaddaya say, Lewis?"

"Jubal, glad you're here. Forgot to ask, did Steffen mention we had an idea for how to bring Hanley in?"

It was just before the FBI agent had gotten shot. "Started to. Never got into it." Thurgren dropped onto a small couch near the door opposite Morosco's desk. "How come you're not up at *Artemis* today?"

"Hanley's still in Washington. I'm gonna meet him later. You want to hear the idea?"

If Morosco's wounded psyche needed some care and feeding, he was hiding it well. "Sure," Thurgren said, not actually all that interested. He let his eye wander to the bookcase that abutted the couch at an angle and was drawn to an elegant leather binding with *A Financial History of New York* embossed in gold on the spine. "What's the latest with Staller?"

Morosco punched a few keys on his computer. "Seem to be a lot of people on the Street who think that committee's gonna recommend that the tax continue," he said, shaking his head. "They're still not covering their short sales."

"Why shouldn't they keep the tax?" Thurgren suggested. "Heckuva source of revenue for the state."

"Are you kidding? For one thing, it'll wreck *TillYouDrop*. Why the hell would anyone buy from a New Mexican Web site when there's a million others that don't charge sales tax? I think the state's gonna back off."

"Possibly. But—"

"They'd be cutting their own throats, Jubal. What other company in its right mind would want to be based in New Mexico under those conditions?"

"So is the Street pretty much taking a wait-and-see?" Given this kind of thinking, it seemed reasonable that there wouldn't be much activity in the stock pending the ruling, because there was no way to predict what New Mexico would do. "It's a pure coin toss at this point."

But that hadn't turned out to be the case. "Whole damned market's a crapshoot," Morosco said with an enigmatic smile. "Isn't that what you're always telling me? This one's like playing roulette."

He reported that there were massive numbers of shorted shares and "call" options being offered by people anticipating an unfavorable ruling that would badly damage *TillYouDrop.net*. "To be expected, Lewis," Thurgren said as he nodded sagely.

"Yeah," Morosco responded, anticipating Thurgren's imminent reaction. "Thing is, though, they're all being bought up, on account of people don't believe the legislature's gonna cut its own throat. The way things are moving around, you'd think this dipshit little retailer was General Motors."

Enjoying Thurgren's surprise, Morosco further reported that all of that trading was actually driving the price up, which would normally frighten short sellers and option writers who were betting on it going down, but they didn't seem to care, and kept on selling shares they didn't yet own. The people selling call options were betting that, by the time the options expired, the share price would have tanked. None of the buyers would bother to exercise the options and wouldn't be able to sell them, either, and the writers would simply keep the money they'd received for them.

Today, one week before the Ways and Means Committee was due to deliver its recommendation, the price stood at a staggering $102, and nearly a million shares had either been optioned with the promise to deliver by the end of July or sold short straight out.

What Thurgren was having trouble understanding was why nobody was moving on their positions. "Some of these people sold short at fifty. The stock's already over a hundred. Why aren't they getting out before it gets any higher?"

"Obviously, because they think it's eventually going to crash."

"So, how come the people who bought options aren't exercising them or selling them at a premium?"

"Obviously, because they think it's going to go even higher."

Thurgren shook his head. "Some people are going to think like that, sure, but some others have to be cutting their losses or cashing out along the way. Based on what we're hearing, *nobody* is doing either. It makes no sense."

"None of this makes sense, Thurgren. Why would people even be trading at all before the committee recommendation comes out, unless they have some inside scoop?"

"And Staller's dumping his stock like crazy," Thurgren said. "Is that what you're about to tell me?" Staller, who was sitting on a great number of *TillYouDrop.net* shares, could try to sell them off before the committee announcement. Although that kind of selling would start driving the price back down, he could probably come close to doubling his money by then anyway.

"He's not selling," Morosco answered. "The thirty-day hold on his HSR filing just ended and he's buying. Not just stock but options, too, and paying damned near whatever anybody's asking. Why do you think the price shot up so high?"

"Buying?" Thurgren sat up straight. "What could he possibly be thinking?" Surely Staller had to know of the huge risk.

"I don't know, Jubal. What's worse, who are all of those people who're selling to him? Sounds almost like somebody knows something nobody else does."

"Or thinks he knows." Thurgren gnawed on a fingernail as he tried to puzzle out what Staller could possibly be up to.

"So, what do you think?" Morosco said after a minute had passed.

"Something's out of whack, but I'm dipped if I can figure out what." Thurgren took a sip of coffee and made a face as the noxiously cold liquid hit his tongue, then reached for the book that had caught his eye earlier. "Sure something awfully familiar about it, though. Where'd you get this?"

"Lance Muldowney his own self got it at the Virgin. Christmas present to all the employees. You listening now, Jubal?"

"Absolutely," he said as he began leafing through the early pages. "Say, get a load of this. Did you know how Wall Street got its name?"

"Bet you're gonna tell me," Morosco sighed, giving up any hope of gaining Thurgren's attention.

"Peter Stuyvesant built a wall across the lower tip of the island to defend his little Dutch trading post, which was called Nieuw Amsterdam, by the way."

"Is that a fact?"

"Sixteen-foot logs sunk four feet into the earth and sharpened into points at the top. Separated 'em off from the rest of Manhattan."

"So, what happened?"

"The British attacked by water!" Thurgren said with a laugh as he read. "Stuyvesant wanted to fight anyway, but all the local merchants told him to stuff it; it was bad for business. So they gave up, and the British renamed the town New York. When the wall finally came down and there was a road left behind, they named it Wall Street. After the wall, see?"

"I got it, Jubal. Imagine . . . I coulda gone through my whole life not knowing that, if it wasn't for you."

Ignoring the sarcasm, Thurgren flipped through some more pages. Then he stopped and read from one in particular. He read for quite a while, through several pages.

"Jubal?"

Thurgren put a hand to his head and leaned back.

"Hellsa matter with you, Jubal? You okay?"

Thurgren held up the book. "Did James Hanley get one of these?" he asked.

"Everybody at the Virgin did. Why?"

"You mind if I borrow it?"

"Keep the goddamned thing. You want to hear this idea or not?"

"Maybe later," he said as he stood up. "Thanks for the book."

Morosco stood up as well. "Jubal, you gotta listen about how—"

"Hanley, yeah. We'll bring him in, Lewis. How, I'll leave to you."

With that authorization in hand, Morosco knew to stop selling. "How soon?"

"I'll let you know."

CHAPTER TWENTY-FIVE

JULY 10

THURGREN LEANED FORWARD AND PUNCHED at his insistently buzzing intercom. "Yes, Nan. When? Did she say—" He looked at his watch. "Well, did it *sound* like it was important? Oh, really. Okay, one o'clock. Bye." He handed the phone back to Morosco. "Katerina Heejmstra wants to have lunch."

"Today?"

"In an hour."

"WE'RE ABOUT TO TERMINATE JAMES Hanley."

Thurgren had assumed in advance that Heejmstra hadn't invited him—or, more correctly, summoned him—to lunch for something trivial, so he'd prepared himself to stay neutral no matter what it was. It nevertheless took a few seconds to assure himself his voice would remain level, time he occupied by wiping a nonexistent something from his mouth and dropping the napkin back on his lap. "You're firing the founder of your feast?"

Thurgren's amazement hadn't escaped Heejmstra's notice, but she saw no benefit in overtly acknowledging it. "There are some people who are better at starting things than seeing them through."

There weren't too many civil servants below the GS-14 salary level to be seen lunching at the decidedly undemocratic Le Lion d'Or, possibly the only truly world-class restaurant in the very capital of modern democracy. "Bit of a premature assessment, don't you think?" Thurgren asked as he looked around the room, trying to remember details he could tell Ginny about later. "Any of the other companies you're on the board of showing stock appreciation that high?"

Heejmstra ignored the implied criticism of her multiple directorships. "Doesn't have to do with that. On paper, everything is just fine and—the problem, what we're objecting to . . ."

The hesitation in the normally blusteringly self-confident businesswoman's voice made Thurgren return his gaze to her. "Is how he's going about it. So give me an example."

Now Heejmstra looked around, then leaned forward and lowered her voice slightly. "He bought this company, a Malaysian outfit called Universal Expediters."

Thurgren didn't lean forward, preferring to maintain the posture of a passive recipient of information rather than a participant in some conspiracy. He said nothing, waiting it out.

"Not necessarily a bad acquisition," she continued, "but he did it entirely on his own. Never consulted the board. Never even *told* us about it!"

Thurgren nodded his understanding. "When did this happen?"

"About six weeks ago."

"I don't remember seeing an Eight-K form in the company's filings with us. Report of a material event. No press release, either."

Heejmstra shrugged and sat up straight once again. "By now that kind of thing shouldn't surprise you. Certainly doesn't surprise any of us."

Thurgren took up a knife and reached for the butter. "What surprises me is that you were paying such close attention."

"You plan to keep throwing annoying little jabs at me, Thurgren, or do you want to have an adult conversation here?"

"What else?" He smeared a yellow blob onto a roll and bit into it, the crust crumbling into flakes that trickled downward onto his plate, making him lurch forward before they dropped onto his lap.

Heejmstra considered his deliberate refusal to deal with her irritation, then put it aside. "He bought the rights to some useless, piece-of-shit computerized goggles or whatever, again without consulting us, or even his own technical people, and it turns out the thing is obsolete already."

"Was it material?"

"Paid a million dollars for it, essentially on a whim. I'd say that was pretty damned material. He does stuff like that all the time, and we have no idea what the hell is going on. He also mistreated an attorney over some patent infringement issue, practically inviting litigation from *Whoopie!.com*, and come to find out he wasn't even really planning to use the goddamned thing!" She'd gotten to the edge of shrillness and paused to get hold of herself.

"Doesn't sound all that terrible," Thurgren said casually, trying not to show that half the synapses in his brain were all trying to fire at the same time.

"We also can't account for ten million of the venture capital money he raised before the IPO."

Thurgren set the knife down. "What do the auditors say?"

"Nothing. They've already closed the quarterlies and won't get around to it until the next cycle."

Thurgren nodded and wrapped his hand around his water glass. "So why are you telling me this, Katerina?" he said as he raised it up to his mouth. "What's Hanley say when you call him out?"

"He won't talk to us as a group. Treats everybody like shit, the arrogant bastard, and seems to enjoy getting us angry."

"And you're telling me this why?"

Heejmstra exhaled softly and looked away. "I've got a bad feeling about where all of this is heading."

Thurgren drank deeply, then set the glass down. "And you figure if you get out in front of it, if you're the first to clue me in, then maybe you won't get hurt when it all falls apart."

"I wouldn't have put it quite like that."

"Because what's going to happen," he said, ignoring her objection, "you're going to can Hanley and you'll all be left holding the bag, or else you won't can him and then you'll have to answer to the shareholders about why you let him stay."

Thurgren *harrumphed* pointedly and then dug back into his veal, aware that Heejmstra had lost her appetite even as his gained renewed vigor. "When's this going to happen?"

"In the next week or two."

Thurgren took his time chewing, sensing Heejmstra's growing nervousness. "You know that's right around the time when he can flip his shares," he said once he'd swallowed. "You fire him, he doesn't have to show the long-term flag anymore. He can cash out and be well and truly gone, leaving you all to clean up the mess."

She stared at him frostily. "Do you have anything else to tell me I already know?"

Whether he did or not didn't matter. Thurgren was so eager to get out and get to a phone it was all he could do to stop from knocking back his chair and running. When he reached for his wallet and began withdrawing some bills, Heejmstra looked at him in surprise. "I'll take care of it, Thurgren. I invited you."

He smiled as he kept counting bills. "That'd be just great, Katerina. An SEC enforcement officer treated to lunch by a company under investigation. Are we through here?" He dropped the bills on the table without waiting for an answer, then signaled the waiter and told him he needed a receipt.

This was one absurdly overpriced meal his employer would be happy to pick up.

WHILE THURGREN AND HEEJMSTRA WERE AT LUNCH, TILL-*YouDrop.net* had still been trading at \$102 a share. Ten minutes after the exchanges closed, the New Mexico Ways and Means Committee made its announcement.

State senator Righteous McCloud made it clear that New Mexico was not charging a sales tax. "What we got here is a gross receipts tax," he said on television, squinting into the glare of the klieg lights set up outside the committee room, "which we've always had, since the Gross Receipts and Compensating Tax Act. What that is, it's a tax on the *seller*, not the buyer. Now, if the seller decides he wants to pass the GRT on to the buyer insteada treatin' it as just an added cost of doing bid'niz, well, that's *his* bid'niz. But our committee doesn't see what'd be fair about exemptin' an Internet company while the resta our hardworkin' bid'niz people have to pay up."

The next morning a near-panic was under way in the trading of *TillYouDrop.net* stock, and by eleven A.M. it had cratered right back to its previous low of $28.

People who had sold short at $50 or higher were choking in near ecstasy. People who had call options looked forward to the July 31 expiration date like children awaiting Christmas morning. On that date, people who had bought the options would simply tear them up rather than exercise them, since it wouldn't make a lot of sense to buy stock from the sellers at $50 or more when they could buy it on the open market for $28. The sellers would walk away with the money they'd gotten for the options as pure profit.

But still people were buying, and the price started right back up again. James Hanley was nervous as he came in that morning and walked straight to Jackie Toland's office. She was on the phone and waved him to silence while she "Uh-huh'd" and "I see'd" a few times, then hung up.

"You're a peach, Jackie," Hanley gurgled. "Made us a king's ransom out of thin air. Soon as we cover the shorts we're going to—"

"Staller still says not to bail yet."

Hanley froze in mid-grin. "Not to—the stock's at forty-two and climbing!"

"I know. He says if we get out, we'll be sorry. Don't be just another chicken-shit loser, he said, grabbing the quick buck and getting out of Dodge."

Hanley's grin disappeared completely as he sat down slowly. "But what's he got going? He owns Lord only knows how much of *TillYouDrop*, so this has to have cost him millions already. And he's still not getting out?"

Toland shrugged. "Don't know. But he got us this far. Why don't we sit tight and see how it plays out? There's no time limit on covering the shorts, anyway."

"WHAT THE HELL IS GOING ON HERE!"

Jubal Thurgren and Lewis Morosco, prowling the communications room of SEC headquarters in Washington and trying to absorb every newswire and ticker report flowing in, were too preoccupied to respond to Chairman Peabody's rhetorical exclamation. They couldn't have answered him, anyway, because they had no idea how what they were seeing made any sense.

For some reason, there were still people out there still willing, even eager, to buy *TillYouDrop.net* stock despite the damaging news from New Mexico. What was even more shocking was that the short sellers were still hanging on and not closing out. Incredibly, as a result of the demand the price of *TillYouDrop* was soaring again.

But Thurgren knew these were paper gains only. As soon as the buyers tried to cash in their virtual profits by selling, the price would plummet again. It was possible they might not even have enough buyers for the essentially worthless shares, regardless of how low a price they were willing to accept.

Thurgren sat down and rubbed his tired eyes, then leaned back and tried for a while to catnap, to no avail. He opened his eyes and saw Morosco hopping from monitor to monitor, trying to read several at once as he stabbed at keys to change the displays. "What's the buzz?" Thurgren asked.

Morosco kept his eyes glued to the screens and hit some more keys. When the new displays appeared, he read them quickly, then exhaled loudly and turned around. "They're still buying. Price is up over a hundred."

They stared at the monitors in silence until the market finally closed.

"Something's going to break, Jubal," Peabody said. "I can feel it in my big toe, and what I want to know is, are you on top of this thing?" He tried to sound imposing and magisterial, and even though Thurgren could sense his underlying fear, there was no good to be done by exposing it.

On the other hand, there was no point in lying to him, either. "I'm afraid not, George."

Peabody blinked uncomprehendingly. "You're—*what?*"

"I'm not on top of it. I don't understand it. I know what they're doing, but I don't know why."

"Why don't you know why!"

"Because they haven't done anything illegal. At least not that I can see."

Peabody frowned and sat down. "Morosco, you any smarter than your so-called boss?"

"None of it makes much sense, sir, but like Jubal says, we don't get it. We were thinking, maybe Staller has an in on the governor's office, and he has reason to believe the recommendation won't be accepted, but—" The phone rang, and Morosco reached over to grab it.

"But," Peabody finished for him, "that still wouldn't justify the absurd prices he's paying for all that stock. Maybe another outfit's already pledged to buy the whole company from him if the sales tax disappears?"

"They would have to have filed papers," Thurgren pointed out. "A Thirteen-D, at least, and nobody has. And even if it was just an informal side agreement, it's simply not worth that much."

"All that aside," Peabody reminded him, "the committee's already made its decision, it went in the wrong direction, and he's still gobbling up stock and buying options."

Because of the rabid buying spree, the share price of *Till-YouDrop.net* had closed at an astounding $162. It looked like a simple case of market reaction, in which a group of well-funded buyers could drive up a stock price simply by increasing demand. There was nothing necessarily illegal about it, and it looked like they were sitting on a tremendous fortune. Of course, those share prices would drop once they began to sell.

Morosco hung up and turned to them, his face pale. "Brokers are starting to call in the shorts."

"Christ . . ." Peabody muttered as he rubbed the side of his face.

Probably sensing impending doom, the brokerage houses that had loaned the short sellers shares to sell were now demanding their return. Since none of the short sellers actually owned any shares, and the only place to get them was on the open market, they'd have to buy for $162 a share what they'd sold in advance for about $50. They were facing losses of over $110 per share and would be out hundreds of millions by the time they bought the shares they owed and delivered them back to the brokerages.

Option writers were in an equally terrible bind. There were only a few weeks left before the options they sold would expire, and everyone who was holding those options would undoubtedly exercise them. The option sellers would have to buy shares on the open market and deliver them up for less than a third of what they'd paid.

"Anybody have any idea how many options and short shares are out there?" Peabody couldn't keep a note of hopefulness out of his voice, even knowing how truly hopeless the question was, because the same technologies that were fueling all the growth were also making it more and more difficult to regulate.

"No way to know for sure, George," Thurgren said, confirming Peabody's suspicions. Since the advent of the Internet, more and more private trading was occurring 'off the boards,' making it near impossible for anybody to get a handle on the big picture anymore. "But based on what's been trading on the legit options markets and extrapolating? We're thinking it could be as many as two million shares."

"The only prayer they have," Morosco said as Peabody winced, "is if the buyers stop buying tomorrow and people who still have shares they want to sell begin looking for other buyers." That would cause the price to drop again, perhaps precipitously, and then the option writers and short sellers wouldn't have to pay as much when they bought the two million shares they owed.

"Still won't get the price down to its old levels," Peabody observed. "They might not get hurt as bad as they first thought, but it's still going to be a bloodbath for them."

"It's worse than that, sir," Morosco said. "Everybody on the Street knows those short sellers are going to be scrambling to buy up the shares they owe, and that'll boost demand. Personally, I don't think that price is going to come down a penny."

None of them could conceive of a scenario in which the coming mayhem might be avoided, but as they contemplated how it was likely to shake out, none had any inkling of the real catastrophe looming above them, one that would be far worse than anything they could have imagined.

CHAPTER TWENTY-SIX

JULY 18

"IN PREPARATION FOR OUR LANDING AT Washington National, please fasten your seatbelts and make certain your seatbacks and tray tables are in their full upright and locked positions."

James Hanley slammed his tray table into position with enough force to cause the passenger seated in front of him to take notice. "Spending more bloody time commuting to Washington than I am running the bloody business," he muttered in annoyance.

Muldowney dumped his Styrofoam coffee cup into the plastic bag being held open by a flight attendant. "We been over this, Jim. Keeping your shareholders happy is as important as keeping your operations running smooth."

"These aren't our shareholders!"

Muldowney shook his head and declined to

explain, yet again, why they'd accepted an invitation to attend a session of The Analyst Club, a group of elite financial professionals who periodically met with CEOs preparatory to the crafting of investment recommendations by their firms.

As both of them well knew, the price of a company's stock wasn't directly tied to its profitability or long-term potential, but to the investing public's perception of whether the price would go up or down. It was also the case that nobody on Earth other than an insider had any real notion of which way it would go, and equally true that in their bottomless hunger for information, however dubious, investors would latch on to any source with the appearance of authority. And nobody was better at projecting that authority than professional stockbrokers, despite the easily demonstrated fact that their predictions were no more accurate than flips of a coin. If they were, it would likely be because they had access to information not available to the general public, which would make it illegal insider information, and why would anybody with that kind of access tell the rest of the world about it in the first place?

Stated another way, why would someone who could really predict the market need a job as a market analyst?

Since the only brokers who ever reported on the accuracy of their predictions were those who'd been right, the public had no way to become aware of the absurdity of the whole situation except to use their common sense, but that was the same common sense that had led them to drive the capitalized value of *Whoopie!.com* to nearly $100 billion, even though the company had yet to turn a profit.

At least the investing public had a choice; CEOs of publicly held companies didn't. As much as they would have liked to tell self-important investment analysts to stick it in their ear, they were acutely aware that one negative story in *Business Week* or *Forbes* could send their stock prices plunging, even if the company's fundamentals were rock solid and profits were rolling in at record rates. They also knew that nothing in the regulations prevented them from actually *paying* fraudulent but well-coifed television analysts to push their stocks, and there was no obligation for those analysts to reveal to their listeners that they were hired flacks.

It was unbelievable that anybody listened to them, especially when they directly contradicted each other, but people did, and that's why

James Hanley was on a plane to Washington. Muldowney had been insistent, explaining that rebuffing The Analyst Club was practically an admission that your company was in serious trouble. Having avoided a lot of trouble by following Muldowney's advice, Hanley had agreed.

Which didn't mean he was going to refrain from making his ire known. "Where did you say we're meeting with these masters of the universe?"

"Hotel conference room, right next to SEC headquarters. Wanna stop in and have a nice mocha latte with Jubal Thurgren?"

"Very funny. Have you a car waiting?"

"No," Muldowney shot back sarcastically. "I thought we'd walk. It's only ten miles away."

JUBAL THURGREN AND HARRY FRIEDENTHAL WERE HOLED UP AT SEC headquarters on Fifth Street NW with a group of high-level Commission and Fed officials. Such a gathering of eagles at other than a lobbyist's cocktail party was unusual, but there was little time to dwell on it as they discussed a cataclysm sweeping across Wall Street that was so virulent, the situation would have gotten appreciably worse by the end of the meeting than it was when it had begun.

"We've been watching Burton Staller for months," Thurgren said, trying not to get distracted by the stenographer taking notes, "knowing exactly what he was doing every minute but without any idea why. Now we know, and it's almost beyond belief."

There was some eye-rolling from the jaded, heard-it-all-before meeting participants. "Don't be so dramatic, Thurgren," Federal Reserve Chairman Phillip Goldwith said. "What could be so terrible?"

"I'll tell you. As you already know, there were about two million shares of *TillYouDrop.net* sold short or optioned last month, the optioned shares due to be delivered tomorrow. For estimating purposes, we can figure most of those options were at around fifty a share."

"Like you said, we already know that."

"What you don't know is that virtually all of the options were uncovered." That meant that the people who wrote options to deliver shares didn't actually own any.

"So they have to go out and buy the shares they owe," Peabody said. "Expensive, sure, and they're going to take a serious bath, but—"

"What you also don't know," Thurgren said, hurling yet another grenade, "is that every single one of those short shares and options was purchased by Burton Staller."

The dead silence in the room gave him some small measure of satisfaction, but it was fleeting and bitter in light of what was happening in New York.

"Jesus," someone breathed. "You mean all those shares have to be delivered to Staller?"

"It gets worse," Thurgren said.

SEC chairman George Peabody III shook his head. "How can it possibly get any—"

Thurgren finally dropped the main bomb. "Burton Staller owns every single share of *TillYouDrop.net* ever issued."

ONCE SETTLED IN THE LIMO, HANLEY SEEMED TO RELAX. The magisterial buildings of the nation's capital never failed to inspire awe, as they were meant to. As did many Americans who visited, Hanley felt a thrill of pride when he considered that he owned a piece of every edifice. That pride was a bit fuller right now, because he felt he owned a hell of a lot bigger piece than he had in the past.

As was their custom when traveling together, Hanley and Muldowney/Morosco kept their cell phones turned off, preferring to take advantage of the opportunity to discuss various matters at greater length than was possible in a hectic office.

"Jackie Toland's becoming a bother," Hanley said as the Jefferson Memorial swung into view.

"She's been patient, James. Now that we're public, she's starting to wonder when she gets her end." Hanley didn't answer, but swiveled his head slowly as the beautifully sculpted white marble monument passed by. "So what do you think? She's good people."

"Good people." Hanley brought his head back around and looked down at his hands. "Only thing is, and believe me that it pains me to say this, she's not all that special."

Morosco needed no further expansion of that point, and had known for a while that it would come down to this. It wasn't an unusual situation. Toland was a competent attorney, and a trustworthy one. The problem was, she wasn't necessarily more so than any of a hundred thousand other attorneys who could have done the same work. She'd been paid at the billing rate she'd quoted when she'd first been retained by *Artemis-5.com*, so where was the justification for giving her a windfall equity position in the corporation? "From a business perspective, it makes no sense," Hanley concluded.

On the other hand, as Morosco hastened to explain, a lot of things of that ilk made no sense but had become strong precedent. Janitors at Microsoft who'd been given stock options early on had become millionaires when the company went public. Thousands of employees of no special competence or creativity had gotten rich in similar situations. It was how things worked; it was expected, if for no other reason than to keep buffed a company's patina of fairness. But was it fair to the shareholders, the real owners of the company, who had no say in day-to-day operations?

"She's not going to slink away quietly, James. Woman's got an edge to her. Plus, she's still got your power of attorney."

Hanley's features froze. "I'd forgotten about that." And about how he'd signed all the forms without reading them, as a dramatic but essentially irresponsible expression of his trust in Toland. "Do you imagine she'd risk disbarment trying to pull something vengeful?"

"No, but it still doesn't seem right, James."

"So I'll give her a fifty-grand bonus and that'll be that. And call Beth and have the power of attorney nullified immediately."

"Gonna be a fraction of what she thought she was in for."

"Let it rest, Lanny. To any objective outside observer it'd seem downright extravagant of us."

HAVING JUST ANNOUNCED THAT BURTON STALLER OWNED JUST about every share of *TillYouDrop.net* ever issued, Thurgren stopped, waiting and watching as horrified realization hit the people in the room one by one.

After the New Mexico committee decision, the option and short sellers were cackling with glee and toasting their good fortune even as *TillYouDrop.net* was gasping out its death rattle. But to everyone's astonishment, somebody had still been out there snapping up everything in sight, and sending the price back up. That somebody was Burton Staller himself.

When his thirty-day HSR delay had ended he'd swung into high gear as if to make up for lost time. Using every resource and every business connection at his disposal, he started gobbling up all the *TillYouDrop.net* shares he could get his hands on, and buying shorted shares and options from whoever he could talk into selling them. Naturally, the price kept rising as he did so, and the higher it got, the more he bought, and the more people were willing to sell him. In short order, the share price had rebounded and was still on the way up. It looked as if Staller was sitting on a fortune in high-priced stock, except that it was made purely out of paper because the underlying company was effectively vaporized.

"Staller is exercising his options, and the brokerages who backed the short sellers are calling in the shares that were sold. So now, all those people have to go out and buy the optioned shares they owe Staller, and they also have to buy the shares they owe the brokerages. That's two million shares of *TillYouDrop* that have to be purchased."

The people listening to Thurgren didn't really need to be taken through the rest of the explanation. Two million shares needed to get bought, and the only place to buy them was from Staller himself, who owned them all. That meant that the market price, although very high already, was nevertheless completely irrelevant. Since Staller was the only source, he could ask any price he wanted, and the people who needed those shares would have no choice but to pay it, regardless of their underlying value.

There was only one real question on the floor, and Peabody was the one who gave it voice. "How much does he want?"

"A thousand a share."

Held breaths were exhaled as though pummeled out of everyone's chest. "A thousand!" Goldwith nearly screamed. "That's six times what they closed at yesterday!"

"And twenty times what they're really worth!" Peabody threw in.

"More likely forty," Thurgren replied, "or more, if the company tanks altogether. But it gets worse."

"For Chrissakes, Thurgren!" Peabody nearly screamed, all sense of decorum gone. "How the hell can it get worse!"

"With one exception, the people who speculated in all those shorts and options don't have the money to cover them."

Thurgren let that sink in, then realized it might never sink in, so he explained the implications he'd already considered before he'd called the meeting. "The option writers never anticipated actually needing to deliver the shares they pledged, because they were certain the stock price would end up in the cellar. So they'd just phoned up their brokers and put in the orders." The Wall Street houses, smelling interest income and huge commissions, had blithely executed the transactions without bothering to check up on whether the sellers had the means to cover their obligations if things went wrong. "Same thing with the short sellers."

Goldwith did a mental calculation. It was an easy one, owing to the abundance of zeros: two million shares times a thousand a share. "They've got to come up with two billion."

"No," Peabody said. "Won't be that much. The day the committee decision was announced, when that stock hit bottom at twenty-eight a share?" Thurgren bit his lip and nodded, knowing exactly what was coming. "How many people covered their shorts right then? Took their profit immediately and thereby escaped this thing?"

Thurgren took a deep breath. "Essentially none, George."

Peabody looked at him blankly. "What do you mean, none?"

"Few small players here and there, but the bulk—over ninety-five percent of the shares—hung in."

"How in the hell is that possible!"

"Something's not right, Thurgren," Goldwith said. "I mean, obviously a lot's not right, but it's inconceivable more people wouldn't have cashed out the day that decision came out."

"I know that, sir. And we believe that's where the answer to how this whole thing could have happened lies."

"Two billion," Peabody breathed.

"In cash," Goldwith added.

"By tomorrow," Thurgren threw in, any nervousness he might have had in the presence of all these famous heavyweights now gone in light of the greater crisis.

"Only the option writers have to do it tomorrow," Peabody corrected him. "The short sellers don't have a time limit." People who sold short had technically 'borrowed' shares form their brokers, promising to replenish the supply later.

"They do now. As I said, all of the brokerages have called in the shares because of what's been going on."

Peabody shook his head. "No statutory requirement there. The brokerages will give them a couple of days, if for no other reason than they don't have to show a massive loss on the books just yet. On the other hand, a few days . . ." He turned a hand over as a gesture of resignation.

"A few days isn't going to make a difference," Thurgren said, voicing Peabody's unspoken thought. "And if their clients can't handle it, the brokerages will have to cover the losses for them. I don't think I'm exaggerating when I say that this could conceivably destroy several venerable Wall Street firms."

"I agree." Goldwith leaned back on his chair and tapped his chin. "And the resultant effect on the exchanges would be seriously destabilizing. The aftershocks could tear through the entire economy." It was eerily reminiscent of the 'easy credit' margin fiasco that had preceded the crash of '29, and the only winner would be Burton Staller, who would pocket the greatest windfall profit in financial history.

"Wait a minute." Peabody sat forward as he looked at Thurgren. "You said nobody could cover their shorts except for one entity. So who is that?"

Thurgren took a deep breath. *"Artemis-5.com."*

Peabody folded his arms in front of him and dropped his head down as Goldwith said, "Jubal, if you've got any more surprises, would you for Chrissakes unload them all at once before George here has a coronary?"

"How many?" came Peabody's muffled inquiry.

"Several hundred thousand shares. We don't know the details yet of what the share prices were when they did that, but they could easily be looking at a loss of"—Thurgren coughed several times—"half a billion."

"Does Hanley know what's happening yet?" Goldwith asked.

"Probably not. He's been traveling since the news broke."

"Tell me you've got a plan to deal with this," Peabody said when he was finally able to lift his head and shake himself out of his contemplation of catastrophe.

Thurgren waited. He didn't want a lot of time to be spent on detailed analysis when decisive action was called for. If he let the incipient panic intensify for a few seconds, the relief when he finally held out the promise of an out might hasten things along.

"Jubal?" Peabody prompted him, unable to keep the hopefulness out of his voice.

"A tentative one," Thurgren said. "And I don't know that there's precedent for it."

"Tell us anyway."

"We need to call a moratorium on settling up the transactions. In fact, we need to suspend any further transactions having anything to do with *TillYouDrop.net*, and freeze all funds from everything that's happened in the last six weeks. That includes the short sales and options themselves, all of Staller's straight up purchases of outstanding shares, even the commissions that were collected by the brokerages."

"Assuming that's even possible—" Goldwith started to say.

"And I frankly doubt it," Peabody cautioned.

"—what do we do in the interim?"

"We have to uncover every regulation Burton Staller broke," Friedenthal answered. "Like did he sell short on a downtick." Friedenthal, heretofore a financial novice, had learned quickly in the last few hours.

After NYSE President Richard Whitney scandalously bankrupted his firm in 1938, the balance of power on the Street shifted from brokerage houses to the SEC. Among the regulations quickly enacted was one that prohibited anyone from selling a stock short unless the last transaction in that issue was at a higher price than the one before it, known as an uptick. The idea was to prevent panicked short selling of stocks that were already in the process of plunging downward.

There were many other rules to prevent this kind of situation from developing, and Peabody brought some of them up. "He was required to file forms," the chairman said. "A Thirteen-D before he got to five percent and an HSR at fifteen. That one should have thrown him into a thirty-day hold while he waited for approval. Maybe—"

"Forget it," Thurgren said. "He's not the type to let administrative details like that slip by. You'll find all those forms on file, and the required press releases, too."

"Then why didn't anybody pay attention to them?" Goldwith asked.

"A good question. Something fishy about all of those option sellers not reviewing those. But that's for later." Thurgren turned to Friedenthal and signaled for him to take over.

"There's no way he didn't commit some major violations, and once we know what those are, we figure out a rescission solution." Everything related to the *TillYouDrop.net* debacle would get reset to where it was when the whole mess began. Staller could be forced to return every penny of illegal profits, a civil penalty known as disgorgement.

"That's not possible," Peabody said, "and there's no way we're going to even get close just because he sold short on a downtrend. Besides, he was doing the buying, not the selling, remember?"

"That was just an example, sir."

Peabody looked at the antique clock at the back of the room. "We might be able to nullify Staller's own trades," he said, thinking out loud, "or most of them. But as to the impact throughout the market, all those weeks worth of wild trading . . ." As his voice trailed off he brought his eyes back to Thurgren. "But we don't even have a prayer of trying unless we can say for sure he broke the law. And broke it big."

"He had to have broken the law, and we'll find out how."

"And if he didn't?"

Thurgren shrugged and scratched the back of his head. "Then we're fucked," he said as the stenographer dutifully recorded his answer.

Tough to castigate him for inappropriate language when all he was speaking was the truth, and nobody did.

An aide knocked and came in through a door at the front of the room. He looked at Goldwith and nodded, then withdrew.

"I think our guests are here," Goldwith announced. "Let's keep this to ourselves for the time being and deal with it afterward."

"THIS IT?"

The SEC building hovered overhead as the driver slowed and drove past it to the hotel farther down the block.

"Guess so." Morosco opened his briefcase and pulled out one of the two manila folders inside, handing it to Hanley. "This one's yours."

"Hope this doesn't take too long."

"Well, try to smile, will you?" Morosco said as the chauffer opened the door. "Try to look like you're sitting on top of a trillion-dollar baby and you're just as upbeat as all heck, by golly."

"Stuff it, Muldowney."

Morosco shook his head hopelessly and stepped out, waited for Hanley to do the same, marched confidently into the lobby of the hotel and directly to the Potomac Conference Room on the Promenade level, then held the door open for Hanley, who wondered as he walked in why a meeting of The Analyst Club would be peopled not by a room full of investment advisors but the senior staffs of both the SEC and the Federal Reserve, and why they in turn would be flanked by four armed FBI agents, and why, sitting in the middle seat of a long table, would be Jubal Thurgren, who rose and said, "Good morning, Mr. Hanley. Nice to see you again. You're about to be arrested, but I thought we might have a little chat first."

Giving Hanley time to absorb this, he turned to Morosco. "You're welcome to stay if you'd care to, Mr. Mulrooney."

"That's *Muldowney*, Mr. Thurgren," Lewis Morosco shot back defiantly before grabbing Hanley's elbow and squeezing it, as if to say, *Take an example from me and try to be strong.*

CHAPTER TWENTY-SEVEN

STATUTORILY REQUIRED IDENTIFICATIONS, disclaimers, Miranda warnings and the like were dutifully made, Hanley using the time to shake off his shock and assess the nature of his position in this gathering. He vaguely heard Thurgren telling him he had the right to counsel, and thought seriously about asserting it and ending the meeting right then and there, but he also dimly recalled being told that he was not yet under arrest and there was going to be some informal conversation first. His sensitive antennae cut through the static in the ether quickly and came to the only rational conclusion: *They don't have enough or they need to deal.* They'd probably start by trying to get him to incriminate himself. He briefly considered turning around and leaving.

No. If he did that, they would arrest him. No

way had they assembled this tonnage of brass in one room only to send everybody away if he refused to cooperate.

"Mr. Hanley?"

"Why on Earth would I need a lawyer, Mr. Thurgren?"

"Well, it's your call, and I just wanted to make absolutely sure that you—" Thurgren stopped talking the instant Hanley held up his hand, and regretted the loss of control immediately.

"Mr. Thurgren, you've just spent ten minutes droning on with a laundry list of administrivia with which every person in this room is already agonizingly familiar." Hanley could see that his words had struck home with the assembled officials. "We're all grown men here, you've already said I'm not under arrest—"

"Yet."

Hanley rolled his eyes disdainfully. "Okay . . . *yet*. Why don't we just forgo all the bureaucratic nonsense you seem to hold in such affection and cut to the heart of the matter." He looked around, knowing that he appeared calm and in command of himself. But that wasn't quite enough. "Does anybody have any objection?"

The rest of the men in the room nodded and murmured their assent, none of them having stopped to consider that control of the proceedings had just been wrested from the accuser by the accused.

It wasn't lost on Thurgren, but he didn't have a problem with Hanley stealing one small moment in the sun, given what was coming. "I appreciate that expression of cooperation, so let's get right to it."

Thurgren stood and, inexplicably, started out with what seemed to be a rambling and irrelevant dissertation. "I always wondered why Mr. Hanley named the firm after Artemis, the twin sister of Apollo. Was it because she had a strange, multifaceted nature, and the company would have its fingers in many pies? Or that she was protective of little children and mothers in childbirth, because the company was going to be spawning so many subsidiaries and funding so many entrepreneurs with new ideas?"

Thurgren could get away with such discursiveness because nobody who knew him doubted that there was a point he'd get to eventually. He had Morosco's copy of *A Financial History of New York* on the table in front of him. He picked it up and rubbed his hand across the leather cover. "A little history is in order." Hanley looked around to see if anybody else thought this a bit strange, but everybody seemed to be taking things in stride.

"In the middle of the sixteenth century," Thurgren said, pacing like a college professor in a lecture hall, "somebody had an idea to import tulips into Western Europe from Turkey, and it wasn't long before they became a craze. Rich people were obsessed with having more and rarer tulips in their gardens than their neighbors, and they were willing to pay darned near anything to do it. Naturally, the price of tulips rose steadily."

They may have been willing to cut Thurgren some slack, but they had their limits. "Jubal," said SEC Chairman George Peabody III, "surely you're not going to drag us all the way back to Economics 101, are you? I think we all know this story."

"I don't," Harry Friedenthal said, which got a mild laugh.

"It's a good story, Harry," Thurgren said with a good-natured smile. "Pretty soon, people began to buy tulips not because of how beautiful they were, or how rare, but because they thought the prices would keep going up. People who didn't even have gardens started to buy them, and sometimes they wouldn't even take possession of them but would arrange to re-sell them without ever seeing a single flower. Nowhere was tulip speculation more frenzied than in Holland, and—"

Now it was Fed Chairman Goldwith's turn: "Mr. Thurgren, I assume there's a point to this?"

"Bear with me just a bit longer, sir."

Hanley ostentatiously looked at his watch and sighed audibly.

Thurgren ignored him. "By the middle of the seventeenth century, the price of tulips had risen to astronomical heights, often many thousands of dollars. That's when somebody woke up and decided that all that money that was flowing around was completely out of proportion to the underlying value of a tulip and therefore had about as substantial a foundation as helium without the balloon. So he started selling off every tulip, tulip future and tulip option he had. Soon everybody was doing the same thing, and in very short order the local economy was destroyed and thousands of people were completely ruined. Over *tulips*."

Thurgren relished the surprised look on Friedenthal's face, and the knowing shaking of heads from the others who were already familiar with the painfully true story. "At the peak of the madness, a single bulb of a particularly rare species of tulip was sold for what in today's money would be nearly a hundred and fifty thousand dollars."

He reluctantly turned from the satisfyingly stunned expression on Friedenthal's face and settled his gaze on Hanley. "That tulip was known as *Artemis*. The price at the time was five thousand Dutch florins."

The smiles around the room turned to confused expressions. "Gentlemen," Thurgren said as he looked around the room, "there is no *Artemis-5.com*. There never was." He tapped the leather cover of the history book. "*Artemis-5.com* has no more of a foundation than its namesake tulip did four hundred years ago."

CHAPTER TWENTY-EIGHT

AFTER MONTHS OF NEARLY UNBEARABLE frustration, Thurgren had finally managed to wrest meaning out of all he'd discovered. Putting all the pieces together in the correct configuration, it was possible to come to only one conclusion: James Hanley had perpetrated what was shaping up as the most massive swindle in the history of Western capitalism.

"It makes some of the things Cornelius Vanderbilt did look like traffic violations by comparison," Thurgren summarized to his rapt audience. It was hard to restrain himself from sounding exuberant; he'd doped it all out with barely a week to spare before Hanley would legally be able to cash in all his shares of *Artemis-5.com*.

"All very dramatic," Hanley said contemptuously, trying to break the spell Thurgren had woven. "Maybe sometime during the intermission you can tell us what, exactly, you're alleging about my company."

"Your company is a paper-based fiction, Mr. Hanley," Thurgren proceeded to allege, addressing both the assembled officials and Hanley. "The company, if you can even call it that, has no assets, no products, no plans and no future. The whole enterprise is what the computer-types would call 'vaporware.' All *Artemis-5* possesses is the cash raised in its fraudulent IPO and little pieces of other companies it's bought since then."

Hanley flapped his hand dismissively and looked away.

"Mr. Hanley," SEC Chairman Peabody said, "I'd like to recommend in the strongest possible terms that you retain counsel. You may not be under arrest yet, but that in no way precludes us from using your words against you."

"I understand that, and if I planned on lying I'd get a lawyer. Come to think of it, I recommend in the strongest possible terms that *Mr. Thurgren* retain counsel, as he's likely to need a lawyer more than I." Hanley looked at Thurgren. "I'll tell you what: If you don't get a lawyer, I won't, either. Let's proceed."

As Thurgren shrugged his agreement and turned away, he sneaked a wink at Morosco/Muldowney, receiving a knowing nod in reply. "No product produced by *Artemis-5.com* has ever been offered," he said, back in lecture mode, "either in the public marketplace or privately. No evidence exists that any kind of service was provided, or even that one was contemplated." He paused, until Hanley picked up that he was being invited to refute Thurgren's points one by one.

"I was under no obligation to reveal my plans in detail," he said easily, trying to keep any smugness out of his voice. "The SEC is well aware of how vital trade secret protection is in this fast-moving market. Were I to disclose my company's plans, a well-funded copycat could beat me into the market before I got my own offerings in place. And I most assuredly don't intend to reveal it to this esteemed assemblage, which already considers me a criminal and wants nothing more than to nail me to the nearest cross."

"That's not true," Peabody said indignantly.

"Sure it is," Fed Chairman Goldwith said amiably. "What else, Jubal?"

Thurgren turned toward the two high officials. *"Artemis-5.com's* board is a sham. Not one of the directors we interviewed could even tell us what the company's business is. Nearly every one of those directors also serves on the boards of dozens of other companies, having been promised the same kinds of financial windfalls as Mr. Hanley promised them."

"I never wanted a board in the first place!" Hanley exclaimed. "It's an SEC requirement, so I did all I could. Did I stock the pond with cronies of mine, with yes-men and toadies? No! I chose the best and the brightest in the industry, and if those directors elected not to involve themselves in the affairs of the company, go indict them, not me."

"What you put together was a Strategic Advisory Board to attract venture capital money, not a real board of directors capable of—"

"And let's not forget," Hanley continued, "the stockholders always had the right to pick whomever they wanted as directors."

"Right up until the IPO," Peabody countered, "you *were* the stockholders, Mr. Hanley. And besides, as you well know, individual stockholders rarely spend time on such matters. They vote for or against a presented slate. Yes, yes, I know, it's their responsibility and they should, but that's why there are boards in the first place, to protect the little guy."

"Little guy?" Hanley leaned back so that the front legs of his chair rose off the floor. "Mr. Chairman, our largest single shareholder is SCalERS, the State of California Employees' Retirement—"

"We're familiar with who they are, Mr. Hanley."

"Then you're well aware that it's one of the biggest and most sophisticated institutional investors in the whole country. They own nearly ten percent of *Artemis-5* and you might be interested to know that they never exercised that right, either."

He brought the chair back to the floor with a thud. "As it happens, Mr. Chairman, SCalERS has a seat on the board, and their representative pestered us with a million questions about the financial condition of the company but never once inquired as to its operations, either before or after committing to shares now worth over *four billion*."

Hanley paused, pleased that nobody had a snappy comeback to that one. "In any event, the board's job is not the day-to-day running of the company. Their job is to protect the interests of the shareholders. And might I point out that no investor in *Artemis-5.com* has ever lost a dime? Quite to the contrary, the company's fortunes have gone nowhere but straight up since the day we offered shares to the public."

Peabody didn't like the way this was going. "Mr. Hanley, it seems to me that, despite the appearance of technical correctness, there is a case to be made that you did a fairly thorough job of hiding from potential investors the risks involved in buying in to your company. As I'm sure you know, the rules about disclosing potential downsides are very strict."

Thurgren winced and bit down hard on his tongue. Risk disclosure was the one topic he'd been studiously avoiding, and he silently cursed Peabody: *If you don't know the play, stay quiet!*

Hanley wasted no time leaping on it with both feet, which Thurgren expected but dismayed him anyway.

"Mr. Chairman, a valid point!" Hanley called out, trying to keep the glee out of his voice. "Might I suggest that Mr. Thurgren discuss my description of the risks involved in the initial offering? In fact, why don't we have him read that section from the prospectus—it should only take a minute or two."

"I don't take orders from you, sir."

"Not a problem at all. I'll do it." He reached into his manila folder and retrieved a copy of the offering prospectus and read out loud the exact wording he'd handed to Muldowney and told him to print as is without further discussion. "This venture is highly speculative and prone to failure. The technical hurdles are formidable and unproven, and the barriers to entry for potential competitors are virtually non-existent. There is a very high likelihood that investors will not only fail to realize any appreciation but will lose their entire investment altogether. The principals of the Company recommend in no uncertain terms that those investors who are unprepared for substantial losses refrain from purchasing any of the shares to be made available via this offering." He slapped the document back on the table and folded his arms.

Peabody was bowled over, and stared daggers at Thurgren as Hanley added, "Anybody who failed to read that clear-cut, unambiguous warning, or who read it but chose to write it off as overly conservative—uh, 'ass-covering' I believe is the traditional term—anybody who did that has only himself to blame if his investment eventually heads south, which, I hasten to add, it doesn't appear to be doing."

Thurgren was livid. "That paragraph might as well have been written in disappearing ink! Nobody pays attention to that section, especially if there's a *dot-com* hanging off the end of the company!" Even as the words left his mouth, he regretted them.

"Gentlemen!" Hanley got to his feet and put his hands on the desk, leaning forward to emphasize his resentment as he insisted that he had done everything he possibly could to try to put a cap on the lunacy, going out of his way to tell people in no uncertain terms they were very likely to lose all their money. "I went on national television to do it, on the most-watched talk show in the country. Right in the middle of the quiet period I made it absolutely clear to the investing public that buying into *Artemis-5.com* was an enormous gamble with incredible risk, with very high odds that investors would lose all their money. You show me one second where I didn't bend over backward to increase awareness of the risk and reduce the demand for our stock!"

"You did nothing of the sort!" Thurgren accused. "It was the most blatant form of reverse psychology and you know it! The more you played hard to get, the more you had people salivating!"

Hanley was in danger of losing his temper. Not really, but by appearing to be so, he drew attention to the self-control he was exercising. "Are you reading my mind now, Thurgren? What else could I have said that would have been any stronger!"

Now Thurgren got angry. "What other legitimate forty-five-billion-dollar company has less than two hundred employees!"

"Two hundred employees? We should get an award for efficiency!" Hanley waved his hand at the front of the room. "The SEC's got two *thousand* employees and doesn't contribute one red cent to the economy. We took in nearly five hundred million dollars in our first quarter!"

Thurgren, relieved that Hanley himself had changed the subject, now had his chance to go for the throat. But he didn't want to play his next card in an overheated environment, and he also wanted to exploit the moment psychologically. "I think we should settle down here a little. We're still civilized men and there's no reason why we have to shout." He expected Hanley to react harshly to this display of superior respectability, and was surprised when Hanley subtly trumped him a different way.

"You're absolutely right, Mr. Thurgren." Hanley took a deep breath and let it out slowly. "Please accept my apology."

Thurgren, of course, had been shouting as loudly as Hanley, and everybody in the room knew it. Hanley's heartfelt apology, made without any reference to his adversary's equally indecorous behavior, thus made him seem the humbler and more sincere of the two.

Thurgren considered apologizing as well, but it would have been artless and transparently calculated, so he instead moved on. "Mr. Hanley mentioned *Artemis-5's*—"

There was a timid knock at the back of the room and Thurgren paused as one of the FBI agents rose to answer it. The agent half-opened the door, nodded at someone, and then accepted a note. Closing the door, he said, "A message for Mr. Hanley."

"It can wait," Hanley said.

"Sounds like maybe it can't. It's from your secretary, and she says it's urgent."

"Do you want to take a break and return the call, Mr. Hanley?" Goldwith asked.

"I'll do it later."

The agent walked the note over and handed it to him. "She said it sounded pretty—"

"She thinks I'm in a meeting of the Analyst's Club," Hanley said icily. "It can wait. You were saying, Mr. Thurgren?"

"I was discussing a rather remarkable half-billion in revenue." Thurgren once again addressed himself to the front of the room. "That revenue comes entirely from a company Mr. Hanley bought in Malaysia called Universal Expediters. UE is a distribution facility, essentially a central brokerage operation that clears agricultural trades among international corporations. To simplify the accounting, the company technically 'buys' each shipment from the producer and takes paper ownership for a day or two, then 'sells' it to the receiver."

The accountants in the room understood instantly where this was going, and they frowned as Thurgren went on. "Since UE records each shipment to its records as a buy and a sell, it shows expenses of $481 million and sales of $482 million. Not a huge profit, a million bucks, but the profit isn't the point. What Mr. Hanley was after was the illusion of a solid revenue stream and a great amount of activity."

Thurgren dropped his notes on the table in front of him. "Universal Expediters consists entirely of four clerks and a computer in a shack outside of Kuala Lumpur, but *Artemis-5* gets to claim sales of half a billion dollars on its books. Net effect?" Thurgren asked rhetorically as he lifted his arms. "The impression—an entirely deceptive impression— that major business activity is under way." He let his arms drop. "And we haven't even spoken about the billions in hard assets the company claims."

Thurgren explained that *Artemis-5.com* treated its investments in other companies as equity shares, taking the appropriate percentage of assets as its own. "So if they own two percent of a corporation with six hundred million dollars in assets, the audited report lists it as twelve million in *Artemis-5* assets."

"Nothing improper there," Hanley argued calmly. "Show me in the rules where it says—"

"I'll show you exactly where," Thurgren interrupted. "Rule 10b-5, subsection c, which prohibits 'any act, practice, or course of business which operates or would operate as a fraud or deceit upon any person, in connection with the purchase or sale of any security.' We know you have cash, the funds you raised in the IPO. But your 10-Q quarterly also show warehouses, factories, fleets of trucks, buildings, cargo ships—"

Hanley was shaking his head. "Sounds like a judgment call to me, Thurgren."

"Maybe. But whose judgment was it not to make the required 8-K filing when you acquired that company?"

Hanley stared at him blankly.

"Report of a material event, Mr. Hanley. So everybody knows you're buying up a company. It's the—"

"I know what an 8-K is."

"So you admit you were aware of the regulation. Can we therefore assume you were also aware of it when you failed to file one for every other acquisition you made?" Thurgren had a difficult time trying to keep a note of triumph out of his voice.

"Failed to file one?" Hanley looked around, as if wondering whether anyone else understood Thurgren's point. "I wasn't required to file one."

"I think you were. There are three specific criteria, all relating to the size of the acquisition, and you met every one of them."

"Maybe. But there's an exception to all of them, and that took precedence."

Thurgren didn't say anything, so Goldwith prompted Hanley to explain. "Oh, boy," Peabody whispered to him. "I know just where he's going."

Hanley didn't disappoint him. "I don't have to file any of those notices if making acquisitions is the normal function of my business. And we happen to be in the business of acquiring other companies."

"Since when!" Thurgren exclaimed.

"Since always," Hanley answered, unruffled. "Just look at all the companies we've taken positions in since the very day we opened the doors."

Thurgren could only stare at him. Hanley had just turned Katerina Heejmstra's damning complaint, that he wasn't keeping his board informed of all his acquisitions, into a plausible defense against charges of failure to report material events. The very fact that *Artemis-5.com* had made a continual string of such purchases proved that it had just been business as usual all along.

"And according to my auditors—"

"Your auditors, yes." Thurgren nodded, more than happy for the opening he needed to get onto a new topic. "The question arises," he said, finger in the air, "why did Highland & Harwick allow *Artemis-5.com* to get away with this kind of accounting trick that generates the appearance of a real business?"

"I resent that phrase!" Hanley said sternly. "We're not trying to *get away with* anything!"

"The answer," Thurgren went on as though Hanley hadn't protested, "lies in the brawl between the accounting profession and the SEC that has been raging for decades. Public accounting firms are mandated by law to be watchdogs on behalf of the shareholders of publicly traded companies. The job of the auditor is to ensure that management is keeping the books fairly, in a manner that gives shareholders a true and complete picture of the company's operations. The auditor's obligation is not only to be fair and impartial, but to be strictly *independent* of company management."

Thurgren came out from behind the table and folded his arms as he walked. "But what happens when that auditing firm is also providing a host of lucrative ancillary services directly to management? Because the thing is, gentlemen—and this is fact—at the same time that Highland & Harwick's audit division was supposed to be objectively scrutinizing *Artemis-5*'s management, its consulting division was collecting millions in fees from that same management, namely James Vincent Hanley. In fact, *Artemis-5.com* is the single biggest consulting client H&H has!"

For once, Hanley had no quick answer, and Thurgren was free to drive the point home. "The auditors are supposed to be chosen by the board of directors speaking for the shareholders, without interference from management. But in the case of *Artemis-5.com*, the chairman of the board was none other than Mr. Hanley himself, who is also the CEO. And we've already demonstrated that most members of the board were so removed from things that they didn't even know what the company was in business for. And why should they? Half a dozen of the most famous people in the industry agreed to serve on the board because James Hanley offered them the promise of money beyond their wildest dreams for doing nothing more than signing a few pieces of paper and letting their names be used on his company letterhead.

"So what we end up with at the end of the day is an audit firm making so much money from *Artemis-5*, and working under the nonsupervision of an apathetic board under the thumb of the CEO, that the company could have been printing counterfeit money in the basement and H&H would have looked the other way."

Thurgren stopped, looked accusingly at Hanley, and let the deliciously rapt silence speak for itself.

"Well, I must say," Hanley sighed at last, shaking his head in what looked like beaten resignation, "that's the most awful thing I've ever heard. Why, it's outrageous!"

Thurgren blinked at him and tried to figure out what he was doing. "What are you talking about? We're indicting you for it!"

Hanley's eyes grew wide in astonishment. "Me?" He looked around the room to see if anybody else could believe what Thurgren had just said. "You're indicting *me*? You can't be serious! If you think the H&H auditors didn't do their job, go indict *them*, not me!"

He stood up and put his hands on his hips. "Am I to be held responsible for the actions of those who were being paid to scrutinize my books? If hiring my own audit firm as paid consultants is a conflict of interest, does Mr. Thurgren seriously expect me to be the one to raise a red flag?" He spread his hands in a supplicating gesture. "What in blazes do I know about the rules of public accounting? That's why I hired auditors in the first place!"

He turned back to Thurgren. "And while we're on the subject, is mine the only company that hires its audit firm as consultants? Well, Mr. Thurgren?"

"I'm not on trial here," Thurgren answered crossly. "I don't have to answer your questions!"

"I'm not on trial either and I'm answering *your* questions! Now you answer mine. Is *Artemis-5.com* the only company that hires its audit firm as consultants!"

"You know very well it isn't."

"And I assume you know that as well, and knew it even as you were hurling baseless accusations at me! As a matter of fact, the consulting divisions of public accounting firms are often even bigger than the audit practices, and they do *billions* in consulting for their audit clients. Isn't that right? Mr. Thurgren?"

He didn't bother to wait for an answer to a rhetorical question with an obvious answer. "And it's been going on like that for forty years. Your commission lost every single battle to get it changed, and you're going to indict *me* for it?" He sat back down. "I rather think not!"

"There's a lot more." Thurgren felt a sheen of sweat begin to form on his upper lip. "The idea that the company intended to tap into Internet backbone server traffic was deceptive. No effort to enter into an agreement with any backbone providers has ever been made, and nothing has ever shown that it is even technically possible."

"I have no idea what you're talking about," Hanley said. "The company has never stated, on any occasion or in any forum, that it intends to do anything involving backbone servers. You can't possibly have a single scrap of evidence to show that *Artemis-5.com* ever even mentioned the use of backbone servers, because it never did."

"It was in every financial newspaper and journal in the country!"

"That's not my fault."

"Perhaps not, but you didn't do anything to stop the rumors from spreading."

"Are you telling me I had a legal obligation to try?" Hanley said slyly.

Bad move, and Thurgren jumped on it. "As it happens, yes. You have a fiduciary duty to protect the investing public from false information being propagated about your company. But you didn't because it was to your advantage. For one thing, it's how you got Mallory J. Compton on your board."

"No, it isn't."

"Sure it is. You implied that you were going to tap into Internet backbone servers. You told Katerina Heejmstra you were going to revolutionize Internet retailing. Then you told Alan Pauling you'd invented a quantum computer and had it blessed by a deranged physicist nobody's seen in four years. You told your prospective board members completely different things, each one designed to push their specific buttons and make them sign on. You also went around claiming that certain people were already on your board before you ever even spoke to them—"

"I did no such thing."

"And then you went all the way to California to line up VC money instead of getting it in New York."

"Implying . . . ?"

"You were trying to get people to think you were a hi-tech company. Dr. Compton will testify in court that you claimed to have a way to tap into backbone servers, and he'll also testify that you told him Alan Pauling was already on the board, when he wasn't."

Thurgren stopped and waited. Hanley didn't look at all perturbed, which perturbed the hell out of Thurgren. "I very much doubt Dr. Compton will do that," Hanley said with perfect dramatic timing when the moment was ripe, "unless he thinks he'll enjoy looking like the biggest idiot in the industry for swallowing a patently absurd assertion like that. Besides, the board members were all sworn to secrecy via nondisclosure agreements. Should any of them elect to violate that agreement, I'd sue them straight into the ground. Come to think of it, you just told me that Compton already violated it, so maybe I'll start a suit as soon as I leave here today."

"Leave here?" Thurgren said with a chuckle. "You're not going anywhere!"

"Oh, I think I am."

Hanley's serenity in the face of the calamity awaiting him was maddening. "We have indictments! You're under arrest!"

Hanley stood up unhurriedly, as though he were about to reach for his coat preparatory to ambling out of the room. "I'm not under anything, Thurgren. There's not a damned thing any of you can do to me."

Goldwith, who had been following the salvos intently but not without some amusement, held up a hand, instantly stopping the conversation. All eyes turned to him as he leaned forward. "Mr. Hanley, you don't seriously believe that any of the semantic technicalities you've been spewing here are going to stand up in court, do you? In front of a jury of reasonable people, not just in a civil case but in criminal proceedings as well?"

Hanley smiled wryly. "You're right, Mr. Chairman. I wouldn't have a prayer of prevailing as the defendant in either a criminal or a civil suit. I was just having a little fun sticking pins in Mr. Thurgren's pompous balloon." He scratched his head idly. "On the other hand, those criminal indictments will never be handed down, and nobody is going to be taking me to civil court, either."

"I assume you're going to explain yourself, sir," Goldwith said.

"I am. But might I suggest we clear the room of everybody except the two chairmen and Mr. Thurgren?" Friedenthal and the armed FBI agents looked startled, and Hanley said, "Come now, gentlemen . . . do you think I'm going to begin spraying bullets around the room? Lance, you remain, too."

It was clear that Hanley intended to stop all conversation until his wish was complied with, and it was equally clear that he was willing to be placed under arrest if the room wasn't cleared. The underlying implication was that there was probably a pretty good reason why he wasn't worried about any of that, and so the only real option available was to do what he asked. Besides, what could be the harm?

"But Mr. Chairman . . . !" one of the agents began to protest.

"Go on, Sam, it's okay," Goldwith urged. "I can catch bullets with my teeth, everybody says so."

Once the room was cleared, Hanley reaffirmed his denial of everything Thurgren had accused him of and then, with infuriating calm, proceeded to tell the dumbfounded governmental trio why, even if it was all true, there wasn't anything they could do about it.

CHAPTER TWENTY-NINE

"FIRST OF ALL," HANLEY SAID AS HE came to his feet and stepped out from behind the table to which he'd been confined, "were *Artemis-5.com* shown to be a phantom, it's quite likely that the pandemonium that would ensue could plunge the nation and the world into the financial equivalent of a nuclear winter."

SEC Chairman Peabody relaxed instantly, and felt Philip Goldwith do the same. "You overestimate yourself, Mr. Hanley. *Artemis-5* isn't General Electric or IBM."

"Never said it was," Hanley admitted agreeably. "Barely a blip on the screen. Were it to disappear overnight, you'd have several hundred people out of work and a bunch of reckless gamblers licking their losses. No big deal."

He came around to the front of the table and

leaned back against it. "But here's the thing that does make it a big deal: In the current atmosphere, let Mr. Thurgren's groundless allegations leak outside these walls and the state of complete denial surrounding the ridiculous overcapitalization of hundreds of other Internet companies collapses. The resultant panic selling would destroy every stock market in America virtually overnight."

A sweeping statement of that magnitude ought to have ended the meeting right then and there, with the two powerful agency chairmen no longer willing to waste time entertaining the megalomaniacal rantings of a certifiable lunatic. But neither Peabody nor Goldwith said a word or moved a muscle, nor was Thurgren willing to let forth some exclamation of derision, chagrined as he was by the ashen faces of his superiors.

Hanley waited a moment before proceeding. "Millions of families and corporations who'd overinvested in those companies would suddenly be wiped out as the paper valuations evaporated, as would those ancillary and after-market providers who'd built entire companies around the 'new economy.' I daresay the failure of California's employees' retirement system alone would plunge a large chunk of that state into ruin."

Thurgren and Morosco exchanged glances, Thurgren's particularly pained as it dawned on him why the prescient Hanley had insisted on allowing SCalERS such a large chunk of stock. It was so he could hold millions of California employees and retirees hostage against a day such as this one. The bankrupting of Orange County several years prior because of overinvestment in risky derivatives wouldn't amount to a rounding error in the accounting next to a setback of the magnitude Hanley was suggesting.

"SCalERS might own a very large chunk of *Artemis-5.com*," Thurgren pointed out, "but that doesn't mean they have a large chunk of themselves in your company." He could see Peabody and Goldwith nodding vigorously at that observation. Bolstered by that, he said, "They have a hundred and seventy-five billion invested overall, only four billion in *Artemis-5*. Even if they lost their entire investment in your company, they'd still be plenty solvent."

Hanley's silence raised the level of hope in the room, but then he vaporized it altogether. "You're not listening, Mr. Thurgren. It's not just

Artemis-5, it's the entire Internet sand castle. Might I respectfully suggest that you take a careful look at all the SCalERS holdings?"

"Christ Almighty . . ." Peabody muttered.

Goldwith snapped his head toward the SEC chairman. "What is it, George?" he whispered as he held up a hand for Hanley to wait.

"I'll explain Chairman Peabody's discomfort, Mr. Goldwith," Hanley said, ignoring the command to keep quiet. "SCalERS investment managers got sick and tired of the accusations that they were a bunch of tired old men keeping all those retirement funds in stodgy, slow-growth sectors of the economy. In the last few years they've moved aggressively into hi-tech stocks, a lot of it in Internet software companies whose fundamentals violated nearly every conservative tenet they'd nurtured for decades. You think it's no big deal they've got four billion in my company?" He turned to Thurgren. "They've got *twice* that in *Whoopie!.com*, and that doesn't even begin to tell the whole story."

"You're still exaggerating, Hanley."

"Well, let's say I am, Mr. Thurgren. Do you really think the two distinguished gentlemen at the front of the room are going to let you go through with your indictments?" He pushed off from the table and pointed an accusing finger. "*They* were the ones sworn to regulate the markets. *They* were the ones whose job it was never to allow a situation like this to arise, so when several million Californians get wiped out, when a whole slew of worthwhile charities suddenly have over two billion dollars taken away from them, when the entire economy spirals into a lethal black hole, *who do you think the lynch mobs are going to go after first?*"

Thurgren whipped his head around to the front of the room. Seeing the two chairmen sitting quietly, appearing to be seriously considering Hanley's argument, Thurgren said in a nearly choking voice. "We can't just let him get away with it!"

"Get away with what!" Hanley challenged loudly. "I created a company out of thin air and brought it to a market cap of seven billion dollars. I distributed five percent to charities, just as I promised I would, and after having done so, did I then rest on my laurels?"

He walked a few steps toward the chairmen and stopped. "By exploiting the cachet *Artemis-5* had built up in the public's imagination I invested in hundreds of ventures all over the world and it's now worth nearly forty-five billion! Gentlemen, I brought my shareholders one of the highest returns in memory in less than four months"—He turned to Thurgren—"so *what is your goddamned problem!*"

"It's all on paper!" Thurgren nearly yelled. At the edge of panic, he could feel Peabody and Goldwith staring at him, almost daring him to refute these assertions that seemed to hold the promise of sparing both the economy and their reputations. "You're a lunatic," he said as he fought to maintain at least the outward appearance of self-control. "A lunatic and a criminal. Every penny of that forty-five billion rests on a house of cards that could collapse in the slightest breeze!"

"That's not true," Hanley said calmly.

"How many shares of *TillYouDrop.net* did you sell short?"

Hanley frowned, confused at the non sequitur. "What?"

"How many shares?"

"Of what possible relevance is that?"

"Pretty risky proposition, playing with shareholder money like that. Is *Artemis-5.com* in the business of stock speculation, because I didn't see that in the prospectus."

"Every sizable company has a corporate finance department whose job it is to manage the money. What of it?"

"Why that particular security? What made you so sure it was going to drop that you'd risk selling short?"

"It's what I pay Mr. Muldowney for. Do you want to get into the profit we realize from the soda machines in the cafeteria, too?"

"No, you're quite right." Thurgren folded his arms and tried to relax against his chair. "What are you going to do now, Mr. Hanley? How do you plan to maintain the same illusion that led to all that money being invested in a nonexistent company?"

"It is not an illusion, and as for how the company will be run from here on in?" Hanley walked back around the table and picked up his manila folder. "It's not my problem. I've been fired, remember?"

"You planned it."

"I did what?"

"Planned it," Thurgren said. "You sold off majority interest in the company just so you *could* be fired by the board. You made some reckless and unlawful acquisitions and invested in dubious technology, but at a relatively harmless level, then proceeded to deliberately provoke members of the board so they'd vote you out."

Thurgren turned to the front of the room. "If Hanley leaves before the annual report is issued, he flips his shares and disappears with four billion dollars, leaving his board holding the bag when it all falls apart."

"I didn't plan anything, except—"

A knock at the back door again. Hanley pressed his lips together and waited, then closed his eyes as the FBI agent said, "Sorry Mr. Hanley. It's—"

"Would you call her back and tell her to wait, please!"

"It's not your secretary, sir. It's Schumann-Dallis. She told them where you were."

Goldwith crooked a finger at Thurgren as the FBI agent handed the note to Hanley. "Message from the Virgin?" he whispered as Thurgren leaned in to listen. "Dollars to doughnuts it's about Staller's bear trap. Should we tell him what's happened?"

Thurgren turned to watch as Hanley wrote something on the back of the note and returned it to the agent. "No. We'd have to cut this meeting short and this may be our only crack at him when he hasn't got a lawyer. He'll find out soon enough."

Goldwith nodded his agreement and Thurgren straightened up as Hanley turned back toward them. "Everything okay, Mr. Hanley?" Goldwith asked solicitously.

"Fine. As I was saying, I didn't plan anything except how to run the company for the benefit of my investors, just the way I've been doing. Now?" He spread his hands, as if in helpless supplication. "You're free to speak to the board of directors that terminated me. I believe they're considering soliciting tender offers for outright purchase of *Artemis-5.com*."

"The numbers don't add up," Peabody said. "What makes you think any company in its right mind would buy *Artemis* and make your investors whole?"

"I've got a real good feeling about it."

"What happens to the ten percent you kept for yourself?" Thurgren asked.

"A modest fee for making a lot of people a lot of money. And don't look so shocked: I'm a businessman, not Santa Claus." Hanley dropped the folder back on the table and addressed himself once more to the chairmen. "Everybody wins, including all the charities involved, nobody gets hurt . . . who could possibly have a problem with that? Do the people in this room really want to go to the American Cancer Society, the AIDS Foundation and a dozen children's charities and tell them they have to give back the largest windfall in their histories? They've been flipping their shares and doing handsprings over all that cash coming in."

Hanley dropped back on his chair. "And let's face it, fellas: If you were really prepared to bring the hammer down on me, why didn't you just come to my office and arrest me? What was the point of assembling all this brass and then trying to impress me by trotting out all your evidence in advance?" He leaned forward, elbows on the table. "It's because you wanted to offer me a deal. My silence for what . . . a light sentence? Television privileges in Lewisburg? Well, let me save you some time. Whatever you're offering?" He stood up abruptly and folded his arms. "I decline. Now, can I go?"

Despite some emotionally delivered objections by the thoroughly mortified Thurgren, the two chairmen really had no choice. Hanley stood, buttoned his jacket, and handed his folder to Morosco, then started for the door, where he paused and turned back.

"When you really stop to think about it, even if Mr. Thurgren's absurd allegations had merit, how much harm did this strictly hypothetical sleight-of-hand really do, especially in comparison to what Mr. Thurgren might refer to as the *legitimate* companies plying the Street?"

Thurgren made a show of gathering his papers and ignoring Hanley, but the chairmen were listening as Hanley answered his own question. "I took advantage of a market atmosphere of *your* making, not mine, and while a slight bit of misdirection is perhaps undeniable, the fact is that it didn't cost anybody anything. I'd even put forth the proposition that I treated my investors better than those *legitimate* giants of the Internet world. After all, which is worse . . . the *Whoopie!.com* model, with a hundred billion worth of stock outstanding for a company grossing two hundred million a year and which has virtually no tangible assets to speak of? Or my company, which strategically reinvested its IPO money to the eventual benefit of those who bought in?

"*Whoopie!.com* could easily disappear tomorrow and wipe those investors out completely. There's an unlimited supply of very smart, very well-funded hotshots out there who have no problem stealing somebody else's idea and executing it a lot better. They're the people who put the first spreadsheet out of business by making a better one, the people who stormed the walls of the IBM castle, stole the PC and made it their own, the people who raided a lab full of brilliant scientists but lousy businessmen and made their graphical interfaces commercially viable. All those new Internet companies squatting at the top of the ziggurat right now? In two years they're going to look like slide rules, because there is no deadlier sin in this industry than complacency . . . except maybe arrogance. Or maybe they're the same thing."

Hanley seemed to think about that for a second, then shrugged it off. "Either way, it's the only sin you're likely to get punished for. The rest can be forgiven, so long as you make enough money for your investors. And anybody with nothing more than a fancy Web site who thinks it's really worth a hundred billion dollars is not only deluding himself but the rest of the world as well. The only reasons it's worth that much is because people *think* it is, and the only reason they think that is because everybody else thinks so, too. It's nothing but a glorified Ponzi scheme, a catastrophe waiting to happen, and when it does, the crash will echo all the way back to 1929. And you call *me* a criminal?"

Hanley chuckled mirthlessly and shook his head. "*Artemis-5*'s money is safely diversified all over the world, carefully invested and earning returns for all those who bought in, so you tell me: Which of those two companies is taking better care of its stockholders?"

Thurgren, not to be intimidated, and finding Hanley's lecturing condescending and irritating, tried to counter his position. "At least those other companies are providing a real service."

"A real service?" Hanley said, incredulous. "There's a company that came up with a piece of software that can figure out—*barely*—what a user is really looking for when he does a Web search. It doesn't do a damned thing the user couldn't do for himself with hardly any extra effort. I've got *presentations* that are better than that product."

Thurgren knew the company. It had been underwritten by Schumann-Dallis and Hanley himself had worked on the offering. "So?"

"So, they just got bought for two billion dollars. And you know what the whole two billion is really based on? It's based on keeping Internet users stupid. Because you could print search instructions on an index card that would be ten times more useful than that piece of junk, and for free, and put that company out of business in a heartbeat. So before you tell me I built my company on a house of cards, why don't you have a little chat with Arnold Plotkin?"

"They didn't go public, Hanley. They were bought out by another company before their IPO. It's not our concern."

"They were bought out by a *public* company! Chairman Peabody, do you not have a problem with the fact that the corporation paid two billion of its shareholders' money for some laughable piece of junk that only works if the customers stay ignorant?"

"None of our business what they spend their money on—"

"Then why is our short sale of *TillYouDrop* your business!"

"—so long as nobody cheats anybody," Peabody finished. "Which you did, Mr. Hanley."

"No, I didn't. And as far as how my investors will fare, well, you yourself should know this better than anybody, sir: The market bats last." Hanley turned and waved over his shoulder. "So long."

He motioned to Morosco, who hadn't said a single word since the meeting began, to follow him. Morosco cast one brief glance at Thurgren, scrambled to gather up his papers, then left in Hanley's wake. Thurgren and the two chairmen, stunned into speechlessness, made no move to stop them.

Outside the room, the FBI agents stepped forward as soon as the door opened, but they stood aside upon a hand signal from Peabody. Hanley and Morosco walked off unmolested, leaving Thurgren livid with helpless rage. The last thing he saw before the door closed was Hanley put a cell phone to his ear and dial as he read the note from the Virgin, his brokerage.

GOLDWITH WAS THE FIRST TO SPEAK INTO the painful silence. "He's right, you know."

Thurgren got ready to come unglued but the chairman waved him down. "Not about all that self-serving balderdash. He's a criminal eighty ways from Sunday. I'm talking about the effect on the markets, the whole economy, if the public gets wind of what he's done."

"They're going to eventually," Thurgren said.

"He's done a damned good job of concealing it so far," Goldwith fired back.

A door opened and Harry Friedenthal came into the room. "Only with the collusion of his auditors," he said.

"You hear everything?" Peabody asked. Friedenthal nodded that he had.

"There's no way he can keep this up," Thurgren insisted. "As soon as they file an annual report with detailed notes, it's all over. And that's less than six months away."

"He doesn't have to keep it up," Goldwith reminded him. "He's out, remember?"

"Doesn't mean we couldn't still prosecute him," the volatile Peabody said. "I mean, for Gods' sake, everything the commission stands for has been blatantly and arrogantly violated!"

"Prosecute him for what, George?" With his slightly more cynical and jaundiced view of the world, Goldwith couldn't see that happening. "Like he said, everybody wins. At least they did on his watch."

"Let me respectfully disagree, sir," Thurgren said. Having stage-managed this meeting with the expectation that he'd have *Artemis-5.com*'s chairman in a jail cell by day's end, he'd been ready to snap Hanley's neck with his bare hands. "First, it's patently impossible to maintain the deception. Second, just because Hanley's out doesn't mean he didn't break the law when he was in, and with terrible consequences. When *Artemis-5* fails, the ripple effect will be catastrophic. We can't sit by and pretend it isn't going to happen."

"Who're you going to call as witnesses?" Goldwith asked. "If nobody's been hurt, at least not so far, who'll testify against him?"

"And another thing, Jubal," Peabody said. "The very act of prosecuting him might end up being the *cause* of that catastrophe you're talking about."

He'd pretty much driven to the heart of the matter, which was Hanley's own strategy for being left alone. "What you're saying," Thurgren protested, "everything will be okay if nobody says anything. If we all play ball, keep the fraud a secret, don't blow on the house of cards, everything will turn out all right. We breathe a sigh of relief, James Hanley walks away with his ten percent, and so long as nobody finds out, none of us goes to prison for malfeasance because of our failure to act as officers of the court."

"Well, I wouldn't have put it quite that way," Peabody said.

"But that's the way it is," Goldwith asserted. "And there's one other thing we seem to be forgetting."

Thurgren nodded. "This 'everybody wins' thing is baloney."

"Exactly. All those stock increases Hanley was yakking about.

Every company he invested in saw its share prices go up, purely as a result of *Artemis-5*'s interest. Well, that's illusory as well, and if that's the source of the profit he plans to return to his investors, there's an awful lot of other people who are going to get creamed when that all levels out." He turned to Peabody. "Jubal's, right, George. We either get out in front of this thing and try to control it, or stand on the sidelines as it happens by itself. Because it *will* happen, and soon."

They stayed quiet for a few seconds, each lost in his own thoughts, until Goldwith spoke up and brought to the fore one of Thurgren's nagging anxieties. "What's the story on your boy Morosco, Jubal? He still on the side of righteousness?"

The issue of where Morosco/Muldowney stood in the whole mess had been keeping Thurgren up nights. "I'll handle it."

"Should we cut off his pay?" Peabody wondered.

"No," Thurgren said. "Let's keep him on the payroll for the time being. Might work to our advantage."

Goldwith grunted and pushed his chair back. "Not hard to see why you hate this Hanley character so much."

"Hanley's not what I hate." Goldwith paused to hear what Thurgren meant by that. "What I hate is this lemming mentality, this mob behavior elevated beyond absurdity. Stick a dot-com at the end of a company's name and people will go after it like an addict after a fix. Why? Is it because they have the vision to extrapolate current trends into the future and foresee the implications?

"No. It's because they know other people are going to be buying up the stock. Almost a quarter of the investors who bought *Whoopie!.com* don't even own a computer and wouldn't know a browser if it jumped up and bit them in the behind. But as long as other people are going to be snapping up shares, the price is going to rise. And why are those other people doing that? Is it because they're able to integrate the new offering into the context of a developing cultural shift and grasp the way it fills a gaping niche?

"No again. They're doing it because *they* know everybody else is going to be doing the same thing, and that's the only ingredient necessary to affect a stock's price. So demand is already in place by the time the offering hits, which boosts the price immediately, and that confirms that all the predictions were correct, which further increases the demand and the price jumps even higher, and that just enhances the illusion even more, and so forth until the whole things snowballs into a full-fledged feeding frenzy.

"Except that there aren't any *fundamentals* at work here, see? Nobody's doing the analysis to try to predict things like future earnings, market share, competitive threats . . . nobody gives a rat's ass, because the only thing that counts is the demand for the stock. Who cares if a company worth a hundred billion dollars has no more revenue than a corner candy store if people are willing to fork over four hundred bucks a share to buy in?"

"You're being a little simplistic, Jubal," Peabody said as Goldwith relaxed on his chair and stayed seated.

"You think so? Look at the ripple effect when Katerina Heejmstra left *Whoopie!.com*'s board to join *Artemis-5*'s. The single-day loss across the market was over *half a trillion dollars*, all because someone left the board of one company to go to another that hadn't even issued its own stock yet. Is that the kind of tenuous thread we want to be hanging from? Five hundred billion up in smoke and nobody even had any idea what business it was in!"

"Man's got a point," Friedenthal said.

"And how does all of this lunacy get rationalized? How does the analyst explain it all when he's interviewed on CBN and knows he'd get fired as soon as he got back to the office if he happened to let slip that there's no there there? He mumbles a few tired chestnuts about *generation of primary demand* and *complex new market paradigms* and *novel analytical foundations that more effectively incorporate current technological realities* but what he's really saying is, 'Come on, folks! Come on everybody, clap your hands! Clap 'em real loud, and if you believe, deep in your hearts, if you really, *really* believe, well then . . . Tinkerbell will live! She really will, and all you have to do is believe! So come on, folks . . . !' "

Thurgren caught himself getting carried away and calmed down. "And Tinkerbell lives, even if she's got terminal leprosy, because it's not too damned difficult to believe in her when she starts the day at fifteen and closes the afternoon at over three hundred. Except that someday— and that day is not too far away—someday somebody's going to notice a really bad rash on little Tinkerbell's butt, and she's going to be dead by the close of business along with every other Tinkerbell who stayed alive only by the grace of misplaced faith, and all those addled pixies crashing to earth are going to take the entire economy with them."

Thurgren turned back to his table to get his coat. "Gentlemen, you can only pretend that chicken poop is chicken soup for so long. And *that's* why we need to take Hanley and his bullshit sham of a company down."

Peabody and Goldwith exchanged glances, and then the SEC chairman said, "Jubal, one thing you have to promise me not to forget."

Thurgren turned around to face him, pretty much guessing what was coming.

"Whatever you're planning," Peabody warned, "however you get this done, don't forget that your first duty is to protect the overall integrity of the securities markets. Hanley himself is small potatoes by comparison."

"He's a criminal. If we let a criminal continue to operate, what kind of integrity is that?"

Peabody wasn't about to fall into a semantic trap; *integrity* in the rules meant structural soundness, not moral rectitude.

Nor was he about to debate the point. "This isn't up for negotiation. James Hanley is your second priority. Your first is to keep the markets on a steady heading. If I don't have your commitment on that, tell me now and you're off the case."

"Even if it means he walks?"

"Flips his shares and disappears with four billion dollars?" Friedenthal threw in.

"Even if it means he walks," Peabody confirmed.

Thurgren sneaked a glance at Friedenthal and got a barely perceptible nod in return: *He's right, Jubal, and if I fight him, he'll win. But whatever you need, you got.* "You do realize we have exactly one week in which to get this done," Thurgren said to Peabody.

"Then I'd suggest we break this up so you can get to work."

Neither Thurgren nor FBI assistant director Harry Friedenthal had ever mentioned to either of the chairmen the attempt on Thurgren's life the week before. Without hard proof, it would only muddy the waters, and there wasn't any time left to let the matter get any more complicated than it already was.

"Jubal, you have a minute for me?"

Thurgren looked up to see the Fed chairman motioning him outside to his waiting limo.

PHILLIP GOLDWITH WAS ARGUABLY THE MOST POWERFUL MAN in the United States. Even the Chief Justice of the Supreme Court needed at least four other votes to craft an opinion that could profoundly change people's lives without the benefit of legislative mandate, while Goldwith could do it solo just by ratcheting interest rates up or down or fiddling with the money supply.

"Three presidents served under Goldwith," SEC Chairman Peabody had once joked. So when he spoke, people listened, as Jubal Thurgren was doing now.

"This is important," Goldwith was saying, "even dire, in some respects."

They were alone in a small lounge on the second floor of the SEC building. When Goldwith had waved him aside following the larger meeting, Thurgren was sure his career was about to come to an abrupt and ignominious end, as though this were all somehow his fault. "I know that, sir. It just took us a while to put it all together. He was pretty devious about—"

"What I wanted to tell you, Thurgren, is that it's not the end of the world. The shit'll hit the fan, there will be much gnashing of teeth . . ." Goldwith lifted his hands and let them drop on the table between them. "Life will go on, believe me."

Thurgren looked at him in disbelief. "Mr. Chairman . . ." he began, but then didn't know where to go.

"You were about to tell me I don't understand." Goldwith smiled at the chagrin on Thurgren's face. "Don't worry about it. If I knew half of what people think I know, I'd be twice as smart as I really am."

"A lot of people could get wiped out, Mr. Chairman."

"Fuck 'em. Let 'em get wiped out." Goldwith took in the look of shock on Thurgren's face for a second, then grew sober. "What are we talking about here, Thurgren, people who sweated and slaved and worked their fingers to the bone for years to build a boiler factory or lay railroad track to the Yukon?"

It was purely rhetorical and Thurgren didn't bother to answer. "You're talking about people who sit in front of a computer screen," Goldwith continued, "and make bets on the outcome of what other people do. They buy stocks in technology companies without knowing the difference between a computer chip and a potato chip. There's no difference between laying a hundred bucks on Microsoft and laying it on eight the hard way."

"But they study fundamentals. They—"

Goldwith screwed up his face in contempt. "Gimme a break! Whatever fundamentals are known, they're already reflected in the stock price. The only time a short-term speculation isn't a crap shoot is when you have inside information. Somebody buys a stock, they shouldn't do it with money they can't afford to lose. And if somebody sells a stock short, betting the price will go down?" He shrugged. "Tell me why you should feel sorry for him, when you don't feel sorry for a guy who bought a short and lost however much the seller gained."

Emboldened by the chairman's nonchalant style, Thurgren took him on. "You're not seriously trying to tell me that the capital markets don't serve a vital purpose."

"Of course they do, but that doesn't mean that individual speculators are to be admired for their contributions. Look, beggars are vital to Islam because without them there'd be no way for Muslims to fulfill their charitable obligations, but it doesn't mean you have award shows for them. So why do you feel beholden to somebody who sees the market as nothing more than a legal roulette game? Some schmuck bets the grocery money on a quick killing, he needs to be prepared to get killed."

Thurgren wasn't about to argue with that, a point he agreed with. "But people at least have the right to expect that other people are going to behave lawfully. If somebody like Staller illegally manipulates the market—"

"Then we crash down on him like a ton of bricks. Don't get me wrong, Thurgren, we're going to do that. And we'll try to make the victims whole. But that's not why I called you in here."

"You were telling me I shouldn't worry, that it wouldn't be that big a calamity."

"Ah, yes. That was it." Goldwith dropped back against the chair. "I hear that the sky is about to fall maybe three, four times a month. Thing is, the system's a lot more resilient than most people seem to realize. At least if guys like you are on the ball."

Thurgren couldn't tell if that was a compliment or a criticism. "If Staller winds up taking down some firms . . . ?" he suggested ominously.

Goldwith waved it away. "You're talking a couple billion dollars. Big deal. I sneeze to the left instead of the right and *fifty* billion changes hands." They both smiled at the truth, and the idiocy, of that. "Know what?"

Goldwith leaned forward and reduced his voice to a conspiratorial whisper. "Every once in a while I come to the office real late, scowling and ignoring reporters, just to watch the kinds of bullshit that ends up on the financial talk shows. I look all pissed off and the Dow drops fifty points . . . ?" He grinned broadly and sat up straight. "I'm high for the rest of the day!"

Thurgren laughed and shook his head. "Tell me I'm not hearing this!"

"You're not."

"Let me ask you something, Mr. Chairman: Are you really not that bothered by all of this craziness with hi-tech stocks, like you're always saying in interviews?"

"Ah, listen. The markets have seen this kind of exuberance before. When World War I started, General Motors jumped from eighty-one a share to five hundred. Bethlehem Steel began the year at forty-six and went as high as six hundred."

"War is good for business."

"Sure is. Demand is through the roof, nobody questions prices, and speculators have a field day because the betting situation is ideal. During the Civil War, prices would zigzag like crazy after each battle depending on whether the Union or the rebels won, and if your information was a few minutes fresher than someone else's, you could make a fortune. Brokers on the Street had their own agents in both the Union and Confederate armies whose only job was to get them that information as fast as they could. Wall Street knew the outcome of the Battle of Gettysburg before Lincoln did."

"Now you're exaggerating."

"You should read more history, Thurgren, but to get back to the point, all those price run-ups didn't hurt anything, and I'll tell you something else: People are worried about how big some of these outfits are getting, all these crazy mergers? When J. P. Morgan organized U.S. Steel just after the turn of the century, it was capitalized at a billion and a half dollars. All the manufacturing in the entire *country* at the time was only nine billion, so how's that for a five-hundred-pound gorilla?"

"But the Internet is different. You have to admit that."

"It may be, but getting crazy over business isn't. Long time ago a guy named Jay Cooke was selling bonds for the Northern Pacific railroad and wanted to attract German investors, so he got North Dakota to name its capital 'Bismarck.' "

Thurgren started to roll his eyes, then realized that Goldwith wasn't kidding.

"And frenzies aren't new, either, Thurgren. Hundred and fifty years ago investors bought up shares in railroads, even for companies that hadn't yet put any rolling stock on the rails. When they finally did and reality set in, the stocks crashed. In the late twenties speculators gobbled up shares of airline companies that had never flown a single passenger and some that didn't even have any planes yet. Outfit called Seaboard Air Lines saw its stock price get run up until people realized it was just a railroad with a poetic name. The sixties? One look at McDonald's and franchising companies fell over each other coming out of the starting gates, and hardly any of them succeeded."

Thurgren leaped on the point. "And every single one of those stock segments—railroads, airlines, franchises—every one of 'em crashed after reality set in."

"And we recovered every single time," Goldwith countered easily.

"You call the Great Depression a recovery?"

"Haven't got time for an economics lesson, Thurgren, but if you think the crash caused that, then you really do need to read more history. By the time the Depression began, the market had already recovered; whole crash thing was over inside of ten weeks. The boys on the Street knew how to take care of business, and it was idiots in the federal government who blew it. Fed sat on its ass, let the money supply shrink when it should have been flooding the Street with cash, and then, just when it seemed things couldn't get any worse? That schmuck

Hoover pushed through the greatest tax increase in history. Got so bad, the interest rate on Treasury bills went *negative*."

Thurgren knew about that. People were so distrustful of cash, they bought Treasury bills at more than their face value. When the bills matured, they were worth less than their cost, hence the negative interest. "You're much more optimistic than I would have guessed, sir."

Goldwith peered carefully at Thurgren to make sure he was listening. "The market is much more resilient than you might believe, Jubal. No matter how hard it gets hit, it has a way of sorting itself out, often returning even stronger than it was before. Why? Because the market is a reflection of the people. It's greedy, grasping and covetous, but at rock bottom there's a sense of fair play and a yearning for equilibrium and stability."

Thurgren wished he could be that confident, and found it hard to believe that Goldwith could be this optimistic. "So what *are* you worried about, Mr. Chairman? You surely don't think everything's just hunky-dory."

"What am I worried about?" Goldwith folded his hands in front of him and grew thoughtful. "Every boom contains within it the seeds of its own destruction. You may think optimism about the future of technology is fueling this market, but that's not the only thing."

"What else?"

"Consumer spending. In a red-hot economy people buy stuff like crazy, that drives prices up, that puts more money in their pockets, they spend more, and so on and so on. The *real* problem we got here, Thurgren, is that what they're spending are gains that exist only on paper, but they think they're real, so they feel free to save less, extend their credit card a little more, refinance their homes . . ."

It was very much akin to James Hanley's televised warning about the Internet business model based on advertising as a source of revenue. Thurgren knew the rest, the scenario Goldwith had referred to in private as "The Horror" and which made him hold his breath every time the market experienced a setback. If there was no rebound, if the Warlords of Wall Street could no longer make people believe that a crash was a just a healthy "correction" as a slide kept on sliding, then the capital markets would stop funneling money into new companies that created jobs. Paper profits would evaporate into the nothingness whence they arose, and consumers already flush with cars, homes, stereo systems and closetsful of other toys would stop spending money.

Unable to hawk all the goods they'd geared up to manufacture, companies would be forced to lay off massive numbers of employees, the same people they'd been counting on to buy all that stuff they were making. Housing prices would plummet, as would the market for office space and business-to-business services, and foreign capital would leave the United States like vegetarians fleeing a barbeque, leaving Treasury bills unsold and interest rates rising. Ultimately, high inflation and high unemployment would combine to produce a recession as bleak and catastrophic as its precursor was buoyant and filled with hope.

Goldwith raised his eyebrows and shrugged. "I raised interest rates six times but the only thing that slowed down was my rate of invitations to dinner parties. It hurt older industries I never wanted to touch, but the dot-coms defied the laws of economic gravity and kept rising. So, you asked what worries me, and that's it. Burton Staller?" He closed his eyes and shook his head. "A pimple on the ass of progress. Small potatoes."

He reopened his eyes and pushed his chair away from the table. "But anytime you create wealth absent a foundation of real value," he said as he slowly stood up, "something's eventually gotta give."

Thurgren stood as well, and reached for Goldwith's coat. "So we're helpless as it happens?" he said as he opened it and held it out.

Goldwith turned and began slipping his arms into the coat. "No, not helpless. But the challenge is to let it down slowly, so it eventually settles where the fundamentals dictate it should. Kick the stool out from under it and it'll plunge way below that line, and we'll be staring at the crater for the next ten years."

He turned back to the table to pick up his briefcase. "You did a damned fine job, Thurgren. If ordinary folk understood any of this, you might even go down as a hero. This *Artemis-5* business, James Hanley, and whatever?" He began walking toward the door. "Don't get carried away, okay?"

"I won't, sir."

Goldwith paused, hand on the doorknob. "But don't let them pressure you out of doing what you think is right, either. You let me know if you need help dealing with anybody."

"Shouldn't I be leaning on Chairman Peabody?"

"That's who I was referring to. You'd be amazed at what kinds of strings the SEC can pull—hell, Joe Kennedy was its first chairman—but sometimes you got to kick 'em off the tower first. When are you leaving for New Mexico?"

"Soon as we're done."

Goldwith nodded and opened the door. "We're done," he said, then turned to see James Hanley standing in the doorway flanked by two FBI agents.

"Said he had to see you, sir," one of them said.

It didn't take Goldwith long to understand why. Hanley's face, heretofore the very picture of vaunting hubris and unshakable self-confidence, was bloodless now, the arrogance in his eyes replaced by some nameless dread that made Goldwith take a half step backward.

Thurgren would later feel guilty at the small thrill of pleasure he took from noticing that the antenna sticking up from Hanley's cell phone was vibrating as the hand that held it shook uncontrollably.

"There's a problem," Hanley said in a choked and trembling voice.

CHAPTER THIRTY-ONE

JULY 20

"DO YOU HAVE AN APPOINTMENT?"

Thurgren eyed the secretary to see if she'd meant the question as an icy preamble to a curt dismissal, or simply as a perfectly innocent inquiry preparatory to being cooperative. He decided that the latter was extremely unlikely. "Do I have one on your desk calendar there, Ms."— He leaned backward to take a read of her nameplate—"Ms. Baker?"

Ms. Baker, administrative assistant to New Mexico State Senator Righteous McCloud, didn't bother looking, nor did she in any way alter the business smile on her face. "No, Mr. Thurgren. You don't."

"In that case, no, I don't. Is the senator in?"

"He's very busy, sir, and—"

"I bet he doesn't have any appointments right now. See? Look right here and you can see for—"

"Look here—"

"Ms. Baker, please tell Senator McCloud that someone from the Enforcement Division of the Securities and Exchange Commission is here to see him, and that as of right now that someone isn't carrying an indictment."

Ms. Baker blinked, then leaned to the side and waved her hand toward the doorway behind Thurgren. "And who are these people?"

"Friends of mine," Thurgren replied, not turning but hearing the shuffling sounds of people entering the room and settling into visitors' chairs with easy familiarity.

"Wait just a moment." Ms. Baker rose and walked toward the large doorway behind and to the side of her desk. She made a small show of opening the door only wide enough to slip through without affording her pushy visitor an opportunity to see past her, and then closed it firmly.

The latch had barely clicked shut when the door reopened and Ms. Baker came back out, lips firmly set, not looking at all happy at having clearly lost what promised to be only the first of many such skirmishes. Thurgren assumed it was one of hundreds she probably fought every day against people who didn't even realize they were at war, and who were vaguely aware only of some sort of unpleasant one-upsmanship that seemed to be under way whenever they were forced to interact with her.

"He'll see you right away. Please go in."

Thurgren turned and walked back to the people seated near the door, then bent to talk to one of them.

"He's waiting!" Ms. Baker demanded officiously.

Thurgren turned to regard her. "What was he doing before I got here?" he said, then resumed his whispered conversation before heading for the senator's inner sanctum. "Make sure she isn't listening through the keyhole," he called over his shoulder. Stifled laughs came back at him as Ms. Baker's jaw dropped indignantly.

Porter "Righteous" McCloud, a quarter-blooded Zuni whose wall was festooned with tribal memorabilia but who wouldn't know a teepee if one fell on him, came around his desk with his hand extended. "So! To what do I owe the pleasure?"

Thurgren shook his hand and, unbidden, took a seat facing Mc-

Cloud's desk as the senator returned to the big leather chair behind it. "It's not going to be much of a pleasure, Senator." *Please don't ask me to call you 'just Righteous,'* Thurgren silently prayed.

"That so?" Even before he was fully seated, McCloud's fingers began nervously drumming the arm of his chair.

"Mr. McCloud, I'd heard you were a pretty straight shooter." He'd heard no such thing. He'd never even heard of McCloud until three weeks ago when the Ways and Means Committee's recommendation on the tax had been announced. "So let me come straight to the point."

McCloud nodded his agreement. A sheen of sweat appeared on his upper lip.

"We've got us a bit of a problem in the stock exchanges," Thurgren said.

"That so? And what might that be?"

Thurgren looked at him without speaking for a few seconds. "You don't have any idea what I'm talking about?"

Now McCloud stayed quiet as they eyed each other. The sheen was now a thickening film that threatened to begin dripping soon. "Well, lessee. You mean maybe that business with, uh, that Innernet company, whatcha call it there . . ."

"TillYouDrop.net," Thurgren said.

McCloud snapped his fingers. "That's it! That what you mean?"

Thurgren didn't answer right away, but shook his head slowly, stood up and began removing his jacket. "Yeah, that's what I mean, McCloud." As he turned to drape the jacket over the back of another of the three visitors' chairs, he stole a glance backward just as McCloud wiped the sweat from his lip with the back of a forefinger.

"Bad business, that."

Thurgren sat back down. "Yeah, bad business. Now would you like to tell me all about it?" McCloud didn't answer, but Thurgren could see slipping away the last small vestige of the hope the legislator had been harboring that this visit wasn't what he thought it might be. "Okay, then. I'll tell you what I know and then you can tell me if I got it right, okay?"

"Suit yourself," McCloud said, the noncommittal response of a practiced politician. *Talk all you want, but I haven't admitted a thing.*

"Couple of months ago," Thurgren began, "the state legislature here decided to implement a sales tax on anything sold over the Internet by companies based in New Mexico. It was aimed squarely at *TillYouDrop* which—"

"Whoa, hold it!" McCloud held up his hands and pumped them forcefully toward Thurgren. "It warn't aimed squarely at nobody. And it warn't no sales tax, either. My colleagues and I simply thought it wholly unfair that our shopkeepers had to—"

"Senator, I don't really give a damn why. But let's agree that it was *TillYouDrop* that was going to feel the brunt of it."

McCloud let his hands drop back to his lap. "It's your story, feller. I'm not agreein' to dick."

"Fine. Anyway, Burton Staller, who was a major stockholder of the company, filed for an appeal of that decision and it was thrown to the Ways and Means Committee to decide one way or the other."

"That's true."

"And you're on that committee."

"Proud to say I am. Yessir."

"Proud and happy, yes. Now, as soon as your committee received the mandate to study the issue, the market got flooded with people selling the stock short and writing options against it. You know what that means, Senator? Selling short? Writing options?"

"Well, lessee now: Sell it before you got it, hope it goes down, then buy it at lower than you sold it and deliver up the shares. That about it?"

"Best explanation I ever heard," Thurgren said, nodding his approval. "I think you understand it perfectly, Senator." McCloud gulped at the implications of the compliment. "So if, say, I don't know . . ." Thurgren waved his hand around as if searching for something, then seemed to find it. "Say your committee recommended keeping that sales tax."

"I told you—"

"Okay, the gross receipts tax. Now if that happened, the price of *TillYouDrop* shares would plummet, and all those short sellers and option writers would be one big happy bunch of campers, am I right?"

"Well . . ." McCloud tried to laugh, shifting in his chair as he did so. "Now you're a little beyond my expertise there, Mr. Thurgren. Hell, I'm just a—"

"You were one of those people selling short, Senator McCloud. So were five other members of your committee, and so were a bunch of your friends and relatives, and some businessmen and state officials to whom you owed political favors. Two million shares altogether, every last one of them by the bunch with you and your colleagues in the middle."

"Horsepucky!"

"Horsepucky? You and those other committee members agreed that you'd vote to keep the sales tax, knowing it would practically destroy *TillYouDrop*. Which was fine with you, because you got a hundred million dollars from the shorted shares and options and you'd all get rich when it cost you a fraction of that to cover them."

"You have no proof. You can't tie those short sales to us!"

"I will before the day is out."

"How!"

"You're going to tell me."

McCloud felt a ray of sunshine forming somewhere high above. This was what Thurgren was counting on for proof? "Very funny."

"You're going to give me all the details, and everybody's names, and you're going to swear to it in an affidavit."

"You been sneakin' into peyote ceremonies or are you just a natural lunatic, Thurgren?"

"Whatever. But here's the thing: Five minutes from now I'm either taking your deposition or I'm on my way down the hall to the next guy on the committee, offering him the same thing I'm offering you."

"Which is?"

"Transactional immunity."

McCloud knew without being told exactly what that would mean: a complete and total walk, no fear whatsoever of prosecution. He'd be thrown out of the legislature, of course, but that was better than spending the rest of his life in prison for half a dozen impeachable and felonious offenses. "You're gonna need a federal prosecutor to make that offer," he said, licking his dry lips. "And a court reporter."

"Waiting in your outer office, Senator. We do it now, right now, or I'm on my way to the next guy on my list. First guy to bite, he gets the walk." Thurgren could see in the corrupt legislator's eyes that it was as good as done. "But we want it all, McCloud. Everything. Names, dates, brokerage receipts . . . and I want to know which one of you came up with the idea."

McCloud's dead eyes flickered for a second. "Which one . . . ?"

Thurgren nodded. "Staller tricked you into selling all those shares short. All along, you and your crooked friends thought you were in cahoots with him, because you thought the stock price would plummet, and all the time he was sticking it to you. He ran the price of the stock up and down at will, cornered every share in existence, and now you have to buy your shares from him to cover your shorts and your options."

"Have to—what? What did you say?"

"Thing I couldn't figure out? What was giving me so much trouble?" Thurgren shook his head as he recalled his mystification. "How come none of the option and short sellers had cashed out when the stock bottomed out? How was it possible that virtually *nobody* covered the shorts or sold off their options, everybody kept hanging on? Didn't make any sense."

McCloud kept silent and waited.

"It's because you and your bunch had all of them, and you kept them because Staller told you to. He assured you *TillYouDrop* would go bankrupt and you'd get to keep all the money from your short sales. Well, you heard me right, McCloud. Staller now owns every share."

"He—"

"Who did you think was buying them, Senator . . . elves? Now you have to buy your optioned and shorted shares from Staller so you can turn around and deliver them right back to him, and he wants a thousand a share." Thurgren stood up and retrieved his jacket, preferring not to see McCloud's face as it dawned on the public servant that he was about to be completely wiped out. He'd also declined to let him know that *Artemis-5.com* was in similar straits.

Thurgren had felt all along that there was something familiar about the strange goings on in the market since July, but hadn't been able to put his finger on it. It was only when he realized that a classic 'bear trap' was under way that he knew Staller must have committed a series of highly illegal acts. A bear trap hadn't been pulled off since Cornelius Vanderbilt cornered every share of the Harlem Railroad and then demanded delivery of shares owed to him which nobody could buy except from Vanderbilt himself. But while everything he'd done back in 1864 was within the law at the time, subsequent regulations made the bear trap impossible to pull off legally, which meant that Staller had to have committed a variety of serious civil infractions along the way, in addition to the handful of felonies which were now being uncovered. For one thing, he'd bought hundreds of thousands of shares through a blind intermediary while the thirty-day HSR hold had been in effect, the kind of charge it was easy to prove once you knew that the crime had actually occurred.

From there it had been relatively easy. "Somebody working for Staller had to have planted the idea for you to sell short, and I want to know who was approached—"

"Stu Rawlings," McCloud said. "Chairman of the committee."

A good sign. Thurgren already knew that, so he knew McCloud was telling the truth and would likely continue to do so. "And who came to see him?"

McCloud slumped back in his chair. "Burton Staller."

Thurgren felt lightheaded and fought to keep his voice under control, trying to give the impression he already knew everything and was just testing McCloud. "Staller came himself."

McCloud nodded. "Said we would all get rich, him included, if we sold short and voted in favor of the sales tax, and that he'd arrange for people to buy the shorted shares."

Thurgren was still holding his jacket, and started putting it on slowly. "And who did you think was doing all the buying?"

"Had no idea. What the hell did we care?"

Good question. "But the price kept rising as your shorts and options kept getting bought. Didn't that worry you?"

"Why? Soon's we came out with our recommendation, it was bound to tank."

Which it did; the share price had dropped all the way down to $28. "So why didn't you sell right then? Your profit would have been enormous."

McCloud gritted his teeth in real pain. "Staller told Rawlings to hang on. Because it would go down even further. Might even drop to zilch if *TillYouDrop* went out of business altogether."

You mean if you drove them out of business, Thurgren thought. He finished shrugging his jacket on. "And now you know it was Staller who'd been gobbling up all the shorts and options."

"All the real shares, too," McCloud added through clenched teeth.

"And your gang owes him two billion dollars."

At the sound of that figure, McCloud closed his eyes and shuddered. "That thieving sonofabitch," he hissed.

Thurgren tried to keep from laughing at the absurdity of the remark, coming as it did from somebody who thought he'd been colluding in that thievery until discovering he was really its victim. "I'll need a minute with my people, McCloud." What he didn't say was that he needed to let the assistant U.S. attorney know that they'd have to cut some kind of a deal with State Senator Stuart Rawlings as well. It would be his testimony that would land Staller in a federal penitentiary and, Lord willing, eventually allow the SEC to clean up the mess his incredible scheme had left behind.

Thurgren thought of letting McCloud know that the SEC had declared an emergency moratorium on settling up stock transactions involving *TillYouDrop.net* and that, at least for the moment, the crooked legislators were under no obligation to close out their positions.

But then he considered the years it would take to litigate the case while the senators fought with every legal trick known to man, and he decided that, since McCloud was getting a walk, a day or two of slowly twisting in the wind would be Thurgren's fleeting but nonetheless personally gratifying bit of punishment for such a reprehensible violator of the public trust.

PART THREE

On Wall Street . . . the measure of eternity is the end of the current quarter.

—JOHN STEELE GORDON,
The Great Game

CHAPTER THIRTY-TWO

JULY 26

JUBAL THURGREN AND FBI ASSISTANT DI-
rector Harold Friedenthal sat in the viewing gallery of the bureau's basement rifle range. In
another hour the seats would be filled with tourists
agog over demonstrations of handheld firepower
taking place on the other side of the glass wall.

Right now it was empty and quiet and private,
a fitting venue for mutual commiseration. "My
guess?" Thurgren said in response to a question
Friedenthal had asked. "Morosco's had a taste of
the good life. A good long taste, as it happens, and
my bet is he quits the SEC and teams up with
Hanley for real."

"And without him on the inside, you're out in
the cold."

"That's about it. I need a way to nail Hanley,
and I need your help."

Without answering directly, Friedenthal asked if they should put surveillance on Hanley. "Kind of use you like bait, Jubal, and protect you at the same time. If he tries to hit you again, we'll be there."

Thurgren had already anticipated the question, and now vetoed the idea. "After the performance he just put on, he's got no reason to take me out anymore. Right now, he thinks he's won. And as a matter of fact—"

"As of right now he has. I know." Friedenthal sighed and looked at the ceiling. "I want him bad as you, now that he's made assholes out of all of us."

Thurgren's pager went off. He looked at the display but didn't do anything about it. "Genevieve says we should put every accountant in the entire commission to work tracing *Artemis-5*'s actions, and then set some of our lawyers to detailing precisely which laws and regulations Hanley violated."

"Good woman, your Ginny, but naive when it comes to bad guys. Too much faith in the law." Friedenthal returned his gaze to Thurgren and shifted position on the uncomfortable seat. "Problem you got here, most of it's going to be 'appearance of impropriety' stuff, judgment calls, and you'll never get a hard indictment based on that. Best you can hope for is some piddling fine and a promise not to do it again, and my guess is Hanley would fight you tooth and nail even on those."

Thurgren knew he was right. The Enforcement Division's primary legal weapon was the injunction, which would forbid a bad guy from doing again whatever he'd done that was illegal in the first place. The standard consent agreement was basically a three part statement by the perpetrator: We didn't do it; even if we did, it wasn't illegal; we promise never to do it again. There were other civil remedies as well, but they still wouldn't be enough to punish Hanley for what he did . . . and was still doing.

The FBI special agent on shoot-the-guns-for-the-tourists duty that morning entered the glass enclosed range and waved to Friedenthal. "There's only one other possibility then," Thurgren said. "We have to prove Hanley was the one who tried to kill me."

Friedenthal watched as the agent picked up a submachine gun and began inspecting it. "You really believe he was the shooter?"

"At one time I had this gut feeling that Hanley was no killer. When we tried to set up the sting with Steffen, it was Hanley who picked up a phone and called us right away. He was the one willing to wear a wire. If he'd wanted me dead, all he had to do was accept Steffen's offer and not report it to us."

"Good point. But if not Hanley, then . . ." He waited until Thurgren turned toward him. "Morosco?"

If he expected this to shock Thurgren, he was disappointed. "I'd thought about it, Harry. Cozy as he was with Hanley, ambitious, and with all those stock options? That's an awful lot of money to ignore in favor of your duty to God and country. But if he wanted to leave the SEC and join up with Hanley for real, he was already in perfect position, so what would be his motive for taking me out?"

"Stop you from screwing it all up with your investigation. He knew how intent you were on nailing Hanley, and if you succeeded, Morosco's back in Washington, another GERB working for peanuts. You were a problem, Jubal."

Thurgren smiled at Friedenthal's use of the acronym for "government-employed rat bastard," a highly derogatory condemnation of career civil servants. "Heck, there's easier ways he could compromise the investigation without whacking me. For one thing, he could be as much of a spook for Hanley as he was for us. He stays on the payroll, we think he's still our boy, and all the time he's spying on *us*. Then, when the time is right . . . Harry!"

Friedenthal twisted back around to face Thurgren. "What?"

"What if Lewis is trying to frame Hanley? What if he's the guy but he's making it look like it was Hanley?"

Friedenthal's mind, well lubricated with years of experience in postulating similar scenarios, worked through the implications quickly. "Doesn't work."

"Why?"

"Because he's got no reason to do that. He's in Fat City without the risk of violence, so why take the chance?"

"Because he's more ambitious than that? He wants it all?"

Friedenthal shook his head. "Still doesn't play. If Morosco was trying to frame Hanley, why didn't he plant the gun he'd used on you in

Hanley's car that night? It would've been a piece of cake. Morosco had the keys and he could have dumped the thing in the trunk while Hanley was in his meeting."

Thurgren knew that Friedenthal was right. "Wouldn't even have to do that. He's the one who volunteered to search the car himself, remember? All he had to do was come back with the rifle and say he found it in Hanley's car."

"But he didn't."

"No. He told us there was no gun. Morosco's not the guy, Harry, as convenient as that would have been for us, and then when he showed up at our offices, still on the job and still ready to work the investigation? All he had to do was stay with Hanley and not come back."

"So the only guy left is Hanley, and all the evidence points to him, even if Morosco defects. You need to handle that page?"

"It's Nan. Probably a paper clip emergency." Thurgren said it tongue-in-cheek, since they both knew it would take an armed invasion to rattle his secretary. He took a cell phone from his jacket pocket and hit a speed-dial button. He listened for a few seconds, his eyes growing wider, then thanked her and folded the phone shut.

"You win the lottery?" Friedenthal asked.

"Sort of. Morosco just walked into SEC headquarters."

Friedenthal's eyebrows rose to register his own surprise. "Whud he do?"

"Asked where I was, got a cup of coffee, then went to his office and started doing some paperwork."

Friedenthal smiled and stood up. "Knew I had that boy pegged right. Shame on you for suspecting him!"

"Me? You're the so-and-so who said it first!"

"By the way, what are you going to do about the Staller situation?"

Thurgren got instantly depressed upon hearing the question. "Just wrote a memo on it. Best idea I've come up with so far? We force the company into bankruptcy."

"Is it really totally worthless?"

"There are no real liquidatable assets to speak of, mostly a few bucks in obsolete inventory and some obscure patent that turns out to have nothing to do with their business."

"So how does nuking the company help anything?"

Thurgren rose and flipped up his seat, as well as Friedenthal's. "None of the brokerages who are owed shares would demand them back, since they'd be worthless. Nobody who owed them would have to go to Staller to buy them, which defeats that part of the bear trap. And Staller himself wouldn't make a dime."

"What about the options, though? People would still have to go to him to buy the shares they'd promised."

Thurgren nodded grimly. "Didn't say the idea was perfect, Harry."

"THOUGHT YOU'D GONE OVER TO THE ENEMY, LEWIS."

Morosco looked up startled, then broke into a grin as he recognized Thurgren standing in his doorway. "Damned sight better perks than this shithole, and—" The grin disappeared as another figure appeared by Thurgren. "Oh, Mr. Director. Sorry, I didn't, uh—"

"And well you should apologize, son. We don't use such language in the Bureau." He waited for Morosco to relax, then said, "Think you can bring yourself to call somebody as important as me just Harry? At least in private?"

"Would that be Harry *sir*, or just plain Harry?" Morosco motioned to the couch. Despite Friedenthal's offer of familiarity, it wouldn't have been seemly to have the two of them sit in visitors' chairs while he stayed behind his desk. He came around and turned one of the chairs toward the couch. "Sorry it took me so long to get back to you, Jubal. Hanley's had me going a mile a minute and I didn't want him looking at me cockeyed."

"Not to worry," Thurgren assured him. "You read my memo on how to handle the bear trap?"

"Yeah. Didn't like it."

"Wasn't too crazy about it myself. Doesn't consider the option problem."

"Wasn't so much that. Problem with the bankruptcy idea is that all of the short sellers would get away with murder, on account of they already got the dough for the worthless shares."

"You're right," Friedenthal said. "And aren't most of those people the New Mexican guys and their cronies? We might be stiffing Staller but are those crooks the ones we really want to protect?"

"Won't happen," Thurgren reminded him. "We can force them to disgorge illegal gains."

"And don't forget that there are a lot of people who bought the short shares innocently," Morosco added, "and they're going to get devastated because all they'll have to show for it is a pile of worthless paper. And then there are the options . . ."

"Already thought of that," Friedenthal said, proud of his acumen in having spotted that flaw.

"So what's the answer?" Thurgren asked.

"Isn't one," Morosco said glibly. "Of course, the one good thing about forcing *TillYouDrop.net* into the dumper is that it solves the matter of trying to sort it all out. Everybody just walks away and licks their wounds and we can forget about it. All *we* can do is nail bad guys."

"Doesn't seem to be a way to do that, either."

Not expecting much by way of positive response, Thurgren wasn't prepared for Morosco's answer. "Matter of fact, there is. Good that you're both here at the same time, on accounta this one could take some juice."

"Right up there with getting my agent shot, is it?" Friedenthal said lightly.

"Close, as a matter of fact, but safer this time."

"Speaking of that," Thurgren said, "we were just wondering about something. You have any idea why Hanley didn't accept Paul's original offer to take me out? When they had lunch in that Thai place?"

Morosco stretched his legs out in front of him and put his hands in his pockets as he thought about it. "Probably because he's much too smart. Why give away all those shares and risk dealing with an unknown third party, or end up beholden to murder-for-hire gangsters?" It was the same thought Thurgren himself had had.

"You'd already thought of that, Jubal," Friedenthal reminded him, "and now you've got to deal with it. Lewis, does Hanley still trust you?"

"Apparently. Only thing is, he's never brought up this business of taking out Jubal with me. He hints around about it, but won't give me any specifics. And what I'm thinking, if I push it, he might get suspicious."

"That's because your little rescue scheme ended up backfiring," Friedenthal said.

Morosco looked at him in surprise. "We been through that . . . Harry. I didn't mean for Paul to get—"

Friedenthal waved it away. "Not talking about that, Lewis. Jubal here thinks Muldowney so endeared himself to Hanley with his heroism that the guy probably decided to protect him from knowing about the rough stuff. He doesn't want you to know the truth about *Artemis-5* and he doesn't want you to know about him trying to take Jubal out." Friedenthal could tell from Morosco's expression that he'd not considered that possibility before.

A string of emotions played themselves out on Morosco's face, ending up on a note of new-found reticence. "Sure doesn't make me feel real good about being undercover against him."

"Either way," Thurgren said, "Lance Muldowney is the key, and he's still inside. But we don't know how long that's going to last, so I think it's now or never."

Morosco nodded his agreement, albeit reluctantly. "Your problem," Friedenthal offered, "is that your evidence is largely circumstantial. We had more against DeLorean and he got acquitted. And Lewis' testimony by itself won't stand."

"I know that. We've got to figure out how to make a hard case against Hanley."

Morosco stood up and went around behind his desk. "I already figured that out. That's what I wanted to tell you about."

"You're getting to be pretty good at that kind of thing," Friedenthal said. "So what's the big plan?"

"If the case doesn't exist—and it doesn't, Jubal—we have to create it. We've got to set up a situation we can control completely, set out some bait and hope he takes it." Morosco sat down and tapped a finger on the writing tablet he'd been making notes on when they'd come into his office. "And when he does, we have to prove that he did it with no holes left open. No doubt whatsoever."

Friedenthal looked down at his shoes and chewed on his lip, waiting for Thurgren's reaction.

"We've only got one shot, Lewis," Thurgren said. "This one's for all the marbles."

Friedenthal nodded, but barely perceptibly. "Let me know what you need on my end, Jubal."

JULY 27

Hanley, his secretary, Beth, and Muldowney were in the *Artemis-5.com* break room watching a financial news show attempting to analyze the implications of the shocking indictment of IdeaConnexion CEO Burton Staller. That five New Mexico state senators had also been indicted was barely mentioned, since that had nothing to do with business.

They were trying to stay positive despite the devastating implications for *Artemis-5.com*, which stood to lose nearly half a billion dollars unless the federal government could figure out a way to negate the effects of Staller's machinations. Hanley's triumph at the SEC was already beginning to fade in light of the news he'd gotten just as he and Muldowney had walked out of that meeting.

"Reminds me of that great *Wall Street Journal* gag headline somebody had hanging in their cubicle at the Virgin," Muldowney said during a commercial.

"What was that?" Beth asked him as a crawl at the bottom of the screen announced that a news conference was under way in Washington.

"WORLD TO END . . . DOW DROPS THIRTY POINTS."

As Beth laughed, Hanley stood up and changed the television to an all-news station which was covering the conference.

In addition to Staller and the legislators, half a dozen Wall Street brokers and a whole gang of assorted conspirators had been charged with a long list of securities violations. Hanley and Muldowney exchanged glances when Jubal Thurgren was identified as the principle SEC investigator, but the publicity-shy enforcement official had apparently declined to appear in person.

"How did Staller corner every share in an open market?" Beth asked. "And doesn't he have to file something if he intends to acquire more than—"

"He did," Muldowney replied, "and nobody paid any attention since—Hang on!"

As Beth started to say something else, Muldowney *shushed* her and pointed to the screen. SEC Chairman George Peabody III was speaking about that very point, indicating that Staller had used an illegal manipulation called "matched orders," but he offered no further explanation and Beth was still confused.

So was Muldowney. "Is that like painting the tape?"

Hanley nodded. "Staller was in collusion with a brokerage firm," he said to Beth. "He sells them a hundred thousand shares, a thousand at a time one right after the other, then he buys them back for a higher amount, then sells them again to the same outfit for an even higher amount, and so forth."

"What's the point?"

"Anybody watching would think there was a full-scale feeding frenzy in progress," Hanley said, "when in fact nothing was really happening at all. Pretty soon, everybody jumps on the bandwagon and the stock shoots through the roof for real."

"And that's called painting the tape?"

"From the old days," Muldowney explained. "Back when they used stock tickers. You'd see all that ticker tape flying out of the machine, all those shares trading hands and the prices rising with every trade."

"Somebody was just painting a misleading message on the tape," Beth concluded for herself.

"The SEC also announced it was looking into new rules that would prevent this kind of market manipulation," one of the talking heads said as the press conference got boring and the station cut away.

"Locking the barn door?" his sidekick ventured radiantly with a Solomonic smirk.

"Sounds like it, Juniper. Only trouble is, they thought they'd already done that back when Cornelius Vanderbilt laid the first 'bear trap.' "

Juniper Raintree, one of the new breed of drop-dead gorgeous "money honeys" who dressed up financial talk shows, expertly looked at the teleprompter with her *do-me* violet eyes without appearing to have looked at it at all. "And that was when, Marshall?"

"Eighteen sixty-three. Well, it seems certain now that a handful of New Mexican legislators and several dozen of their political cronies will be doing some fairly serious time in federal penitentiaries—"

"And a goodly number of unscrupulous Wall Street stockbrokers will be thrown out of the profession and ordered never to handle a share of stock again. Shades of Mike Milken, right, Marshall?"

"You bet, Juniper. But let's move on to another piece of this incredible story."

"Let me guess. You're talking about *Artemis-5.com*, am I right?"

"Right as rain, Juniper."

"Did you see that?" Muldowney exclaimed. "She guessed what Marshall was thinking! God, what a woman!"

"Quiet down!" Beth said. "Here comes the good part."

"—back when," Marshall Stratton was saying, "the mystery startup unaccountably declined to recruit Staller to its board of directors. It had been well known that the legendary financier was high on *Artemis-5.com*'s short list, but there were rumors—"

"—and we're not reporting them as facts, Marsh."

"You bet, Juniper."

"But we're reporting them nonetheless," Muldowney said, "trusting all of you out there in television land to disregard every word."

"Quiet!" Beth hissed.

"—were rumors at the time," Stratton continued, "that the *Artemis-5.com* principals had some suspicions about Staller."

"Hadn't passed James Hanley's sniff test, isn't that what *Business Week* reported?"

"I believe you're right, Juniper. Hadn't passed the sniff test. Let's go to Chizelwa Farnsworth on the floor of the exchange for some reaction. Chiz?"

"Thank you, Marsh. I'm here on the floor of the exchange, which is of course closed now, and I'm here with Robert Schumann, chairman, president and CEO of Schumann-Dallis Investments. Bob, James Hanley used to work for you at the Virgin, didn't he?"

Schumann hated it when people called his beloved company the Virgin. "Absolutely, Chuz. One of the best bond traders we ever had." The only thing he hated more was losing money or prestige because of a principle, so he let it go.

"You were a bond trader?" Beth asked Hanley.

"No. Institutional sales."

"Then how come—"

"He didn't know who I was when I was there. We never met until I was already out of the firm."

"—knew at the time that Hanley had an uncanny sixth sense," Schumann was saying, "and we'd come to rely on it, so I can't say it was a surprise that he managed to sniff out this bad apple who had fooled so many people."

"This is too good," Muldowney remarked.

"Yeah," Beth responded, "until she points out that the Virgin handled all of Staller's business."

"She won't," Hanley said.

"Why wouldn't she—"

"Watch."

"—comes along, when we've struggled so hard for so many years to make sure that everything we do is on the up and up."

"So you think these indictments will give the Street a black eye, Bob?"

"Just the opposite, Chaz, because the most important thing to keep in mind here is this: The system works. It was designed to catch people like Burton Staller and every time it does, we should all feel better about those safeguards we built in to ensure the overall integrity of the markets."

Hanley chuckled softly. "She also won't point out that Schumann-Dallis alone spent sixteen million bucks fighting every one of those safeguards."

"Couldn't agree with you more," Farnsworth said, using all the razor-shop investigative reporting arrows in her quiver. "Do you think we'll see more of this amazing kind of foresight from James Hanley and *Artemis-5.com*?"

"No question about it, Chaz."

"Well, there you have it, Marshall and Juniper. One of the most respected names on Wall Street weighing in on this extraordinary, developing story about one of the hottest companies around." She declined to remind her audience that one of the other most respected names on Wall Street was the one that had just been indicted.

Hanley aimed the remote at the set and turned it off. "So why didn't she go for his throat?" Beth asked.

Hanley thought about how to explain the various topics that were taboo for financial reporters. How it was absolutely forbidden, for example, for any financial reporter under any circumstances to review anybody's track record in making predictions. Were they to do that, it would become painfully evident that nobody on Wall Street actually knew anything about anything—Robert Schumann himself had predicted seventeen of the last three recessions—at least not legally, and that it was demonstrably impossible to actually predict anything with more accuracy than by throwing darts at the stock tables. If they could, they certainly wouldn't be telling anybody else about it on television and thereby cutting their own throats. But, since nobody could anyway, bringing up that minor point would mean that there would no longer *be* any financial reporting, since nearly all of it was devoted to convincing the audience that they were getting useful data. Tell them the truth and you're out of a job, and all the gurus you regularly interviewed would lose the free advertising they got by appearing and pretending to be more prescient than they actually were.

"They need each other too much," Hanley answered simply, and left it at that.

"But doesn't Schumann have to disclose that he's on your board?" Beth asked.

"Nope," Muldowney answered, enjoying Beth's surprised look. "It's just television, not an SEC filing."

"I find that hard to believe," she persisted. "Even if it's television, there are still regulations about that sort of thing. Aren't there?"

Hanley stood up slowly and stretched. "Beth, even if the guy is getting a fee to push a company's stock he's not required to disclose it."

Disbelieving, Beth turned to Muldowney, who only shrugged his confirmation. She shook her head and also stood up. "So that's why none of them ever run for office."

Hanley laughed and turned to Muldowney, who was still seated. "You saved our bacon with Staller, boosted our credibility about eighty points, and I got all the credit."

Muldowney regarded him thoughtfully, letting him worry for a second about what his response might be. "Fuck the credit," he finally said. "All's I want is a piece of that eighty points."

"I was wondering," Beth said. "Whatever happened to those two nice young boys who invented those goggles?"

"They'll be fine," Hanley answered as Muldowney smirked and turned away. "I understand Burton Staller helped them invest their money."

Engrossed in their conversation, they hadn't noticed a small follow-up item on the newscast. Since the New Mexico legislature had behaved criminally, the canny governor had seized the opportunity to unilaterally declare that henceforth and forever more—or at least for the duration of his administration—there would be no sales tax on Internet purchases, effective immediately.

CHAPTER THIRTY-THREE

JULY 29

"GODDAMNIT, JUBAL, DON'T YOU DO THIS to me!"

Morosco had indeed come up with a complex, daring plan to get Hanley to incriminate himself. Thurgren, admiring Morosco's thinking and bothered by his own earlier suspicions about him, had confessed that he'd suspected Morosco might have 'gone over the wall.' This didn't come as a complete surprise, Thurgren having already cracked a semiserious joke about it in Harry Friedenthal's presence, and Morosco was unable to hide that he'd been bothered by it. But as Thurgren had said, which was how Friedenthal had said it to him, sometimes you have to be hard in this business, you have to consider all possibilities, and they'd let it go as Morosco's sting began to take shape.

They'd spent the entire morning talking through the plan, considering contingencies for every variation they could think of, and the more it came together the more excited they got, and then Thurgren put a torpedo through the hull. "You know, Lewis, until we laid it all out like this, I didn't realize how much we really had on Hanley."

Morosco looked up from the papers and diagrams scattered on the conference table. "Goddamnit, Jubal . . ."

Thurgren seemed not to have heard him as he continued thinking out loud, staring upward. "What I'm wondering, is it possible we might be able to get him to cop to a plea without going through this risky setup."

"Jubal, what the hell are you—we got four days left! You can't get cold feet now!"

Thurgren looked away. "Things have changed, Lewis," he said distractedly.

And it had taken only seconds. The moment the governor of New Mexico had declared the Internet sales tax null and void, *TillYouDrop*, still owned nearly 100 percent by Staller, was suddenly a viable concern once again, so there was no justifiable way to force it into bankruptcy. Predictably, brokerages who'd loaned shares to short sellers and who might have walked away once Chapter 10 bankruptcy was declared under Thurgren's plan, now wanted them returned once again.

"No, they haven't. The only thing that changed was the need for your plan, which wouldn't have worked anyway."

Thurgren brought his gaze back to earth in surprise. "I know you're hot for this sting, and it's a good one, don't get me wrong. But let's not lose sight of the objective here."

"The objective is to smoke him out once and for all, is what I thought it was, and this here's as surefire as we're gonna get!"

"Like I said, it's a good plan, but let's not kid ourselves it isn't risky as all get-out. What I'm trying to tell you, now that I look at everything all laid out, I think there's a good chance that if Hanley hears all the evidence, without a dozen guys staring at him and challenging his manhood, he might see how bad it looks for him and be willing to discuss some kind of plea bargain, which is the only way we're going to get him to cooperate and prevent mass market panic."

"What it'll do, it'll tip our hand."

"I don't think so."

"What are you going to do?"

"I'm going to go see him."

Morosco threw his pencil on the table and got to his feet. Tie askew, collar unbuttoned and sleeves rolled up, he paced the length of the conference room, rubbing his neck. "He'll never cop to trying to kill you."

"May have to let him go on that one."

That didn't surprise Morosco, Thurgren having already made it clear that he was trying to keep his eye on the more important mandate. "If you're convinced, let's figure out how you're gonna do it. It's a tricky play."

"Yep. Biggest question we got—"

"Do you tell him Muldowney is really me. That'll shock the living crap out of him, all right." Shock value aside, letting Hanley know that 'Muldowney' was really an undercover operative and confronting him with all the related evidence would go a long way toward helping him to realize his case was hopeless. "But I don't think you want to do that."

"Why not?"

Morosco turned and put his hands on the table, leaning forward. "Because if you fuck this up—and I think you will—we still need me on the inside."

THURGREN'S SECRETARY PUT THE PHONE AGAINST HER CHEST. "She said, and I quote, 'Nobody comes to the man but that he comes by me.' I think that's Matthew seven, verse three."

"It's John fourteen six, and I didn't ask to speak with Jesus Christ, just James Hanley." Thurgren reached for the phone.

"Don't blaspheme," Nan said as she handed it over. "My brother-in-law's barber said *Artemis-5* is going to make him a small fortune."

"Only if he started with a large one." Thurgren took the phone and put it to his ear. "Jubal Thurgren here."

"Mr. Thurgren, I tried to explain to your girl—"

"Good morning, Miss Toland."

"Sorry?"

"I said, good morning."

Nan smiled as she listened, knowing her boss all too well.

"Oh. Uh, good morning to you, too."

"And the *girl's* name is Nan."

"Fine. Shall we continue with the etiquette lesson or do you want to get down to business?"

"Sure. It's very simple. I want to speak with your boss and set up a meeting."

"As I told *Nan*, I'll set it up once you've told me what it's all about. And he's not my boss."

"Oh really? I thought you were the lawyer."

"Outside counsel. I'm not on the company payroll."

Thurgren waited for a moment, then said, "So is Mr. Hanley your client?"

There was a slight hesitation on the other end. "Obviously. Which is why I'm getting in the middle of this."

"So Hanley himself is your client, not the company. Is that right?"

Hesitation gave way to open wariness. "Why?"

"Doesn't matter why. You've got no shield against disclosing the nature of your representation once you've taken steps to intercede between a client and a law enforcement official, and you're interceding now. So you can advise your client all you want but you don't have a choice about informing him of my proposal to meet. Unless I'm mistaken about legal ethics."

Thurgren paused as Nan applauded silently, and waited.

"Oh, come on now, Mr. Thurgren, there's no need for that." Thurgren rolled his eyes at the ceiling and waited out the limp attempt at some sort of personal rapprochement now that he'd successfully asserted himself. "Just tell me what the nature of the meeting is, James and I will put our schedules together and see what's open—"

"You plan to be there?"

"I think his attorney should be present."

"So you *are* his personal attorney, okay fine. Then this is what I'd like you to tell him: Tell him it's in his own best interest to meet with me alone. If he wants you standing by, that's fine with me, but we start alone."

"Not going to cut it."

"But you have an obligation to put it to him. If he rejects it, fine, but you tell him the proposal."

"Mr. Thurgren—"

"And get back to me within an hour. Will that be okay, Miss Toland?"

"We're a little busy around here."

"I imagine you are."

"No, what I mean—we filed a federal lawsuit against Burton Staller."

"What kind of lawsuit?"

"Seeking restitution for the half billion he cost us."

Thurgren was too startled to respond immediately, and took a second to make sure his voice would sound casual. "You're admitting you had inside information?"

"Nothing of the kind. Our hands were clean on the short sales, but it was Staller's illegal actions that cost us all that money."

"He hasn't cost you anything yet. There's a moratorium on settling those transactions."

"That can't last more than a few days, so we need to get our ducks in line on this suit."

Thurgren tried not to laugh into the phone. "You know, George Washington once said to his gardener, I want you to plant a row of cedar trees in front of the house tomorrow, and the gardener, he said to Washington, Are you serious? Those trees will take a hundred years to grow! Washington thought about it for a minute and then said, Well, you'd better plant them today, then!"

After a moment of silence, Toland said, "That's charming. Is there a point?"

"Yeah, there's a point. You're going to be fighting that lawsuit for the next century. I think His Nibs can spare me a few minutes. I'll see you tomorrow."

CHAPTER THIRTY-FOUR

JULY 30

THURGREN WAS EARLY, AS USUAL. WHEN-
ever there was an airplane or New York City traffic involved, he always left plenty of time. Today
he'd gotten lucky: The shuttle from Washington
was barely an hour late and the cab had covered
the distance from LaGuardia to Manhattan at an
average speed of almost twelve miles per hour, the
Gotham equivalent of Chuck Yeager's supersonic
ride in the *Bell X-1*, only much more exciting.

It gave him the chance to indulge one of his
least secret vices, a streetside Sabrett hot dog, lib-
erally bedecked with that unique mustard that ri-
valed anything from Dijon and awash in soggy
onions in an orange-colored sauce of unknown
but probably extraterrestrial origin. Washed down
with a Yoo-Hoo beneath the approving and be-
mused gaze of the outwardly jaded but inwardly

pride-filled pushcart vendor, there was nothing in the entire Escoffier canon that could touch it. Curbside hot dogs were to a New Yorker what grits were to a Southerner: Everybody ate them as a matter of course, the locals never gave them much thought, and only non-natives swooned openly about how truly delicious they were.

"Damn, that's good," Thurgren enthused.

" 'Course it's good, whaddayou, kiddin' me? 'Nother one?"

"Oh yeah." Thurgren pointed to an apartment across the street where half a dozen uniformed police officers were herding some hand-cuffed people out the front door. "What's going on over there?"

"Gambling bust," the vendor answered without turning around. "Every couple weeks they break it up. Damned shame, scum like that messing up a nice neighborhood."

"You don't like gambling?"

The vendor pulled up the top of the mustard jar. A stick the exact length of a hot dog was attached underneath, and he expertly smeared a line of the fragrant yellow paste down the length of the bun. "Terrible habit, s'why it's against the law."

As he ladled out a generous scoop of onions, Thurgren pointed to a torn piece of paper lying on top of a pile of discarded napkins in the trash bag hanging off the cart. "Looks like an option slip."

The vendor nodded. "Expires tomorrow. Stock took a freakin' nose-dive."

"Iogamma, Inc.," Thurgren said, twisting his head to the side to read the name of the company. "What do they do?"

"Beats the shit out of me. All's I know, they lose money."

"Actually," Thurgren said as he gratefully accepted the steaming hot dog, "they had a great quarter."

"What can you do?" the vendor said with a shrug. He turned at the sound of a door slamming shut on a police cruiser. "Animals in this neighborhood," he muttered in disgust. "Kids don't eat right, they piss away money like that."

Biting into the dog and feeling it had already been worth the trip, Thurgren headed for the temporary offices of *Artemis-5.com*.

· · ·

"Understand you've filed a lawsuit against Burton Staller."

"Soon as he's found guilty," Hanley said, "it'll be an easy matter to win a civil case."

"How're you going to collect any money from him? *TillYouDrop.net* isn't worth squat."

"It's coming back, now that there's no more sales tax."

Thurgren waved it away. "It's worth peanuts. And Staller doesn't have anything else because he used it all to pull off his bear trap."

"They've got to have some inventory, some other assets . . ."

"Hanley, you got stung for *half a billion dollars*! That piddling company's got some Garden Weasels and Chia Pets rotting away in a warehouse, a couple of dozen obsolete PCs and some obscure patent. It isn't worth enough to even cover your preliminary court filings."

"What patent?"

"How should I know? Some useless piece of junk right up there with a nose hair clipper."

"I sure appreciate all this sage business counsel, Thurgren, but was there perhaps some other reason for this delightful visit?"

The niceties had clearly been concluded. "Matter of fact, the FBI is considering pressing charges against you for failure to report a crime."

"What crime? What are you talking about?"

"Paul Steffen tried to kill you in upstate New York. Bumped your car, waved a gun. Lance Muldowney ran him into a ditch, and you never reported it."

Much as he would have preferred to maintain a cool demeanor, Hanley's eyes betrayed his surprise. "How did you—What makes you think that?"

Thurgren scratched idly at his chin. "Steffen's an FBI agent, Hanley. He's doing a little work for us, kind of on loan. But then you knew that already, didn't you." *Because you saw him with me at the bowling alley.*

Hanley appeared too stunned to speak, and seemed to be flailing around mentally. "You had an FBI agent try to kill me?"

"No, just scare you. Guess it didn't work."

"You sonofabitch!"

Thurgren stayed patient and let him seethe for a few seconds.

"So that's why nobody from the SEC or the FBI was willing to comment at a press conference," Hanley finally managed to whisper hoarsely. "And it's how Steffen knew that he was being set up, that I was coming to lunch wearing a wire." He nodded to himself, as if to indicate that things were starting to fall into place. "I thought it was because he had somebody inside the SEC, and I guess he did at that." He put a hand to his head.

"Yeah. He had himself. You okay?"

"Just trying to think."

"Well, you do that. Take your time. And let me know when you get to the part about how we both know it couldn't have been Steffen who tried to kill me."

Hanley pulled his hand away and sat up straight. "Sure it was! He knew you were planning to be in that surveillance van, and he even knew what route you'd be taking to get there!"

Now it was Thurgren's turn to become disoriented: "I just told you, Hanley . . . he was working for us!"

"But that's perfect, don't you see? You think he's setting me up, but he's really out to kill you and get his hands on my stock!"

"And then he lets himself be taped? For Pete's sake, Hanley, get a grip on yourself!"

"Taped? He knew you weren't really going to tape him, and besides, he never showed up! It was a perfect scam!"

"Have you completely lost your mind!"

"Oh yeah?" Hanley was warming to it now, and Thurgren was having trouble figuring out whether it was possible the man had slipped into some kind of psychosis and actually believed what he was saying. "Why'd you even have surveillance there at all, Thurgren? If it was all bullshit, why'd you drag out a van and a guy to run it?"

Thurgren noticed that Hanley's cultivated mode of speech was fading in and out at random. "Had no choice. Frankly, I thought you were going to take the offer from Steffen, in which case we were going to wire *him*. So the van and the technician were already on site. Then when you called the SEC, I had to see it through or you'd figure out Steffen was a phony. The equipment in the van wasn't even turned on, and the technician sat inside reading the racing forms all afternoon."

"I don't believe you."

Thurgren laughed, partially from the relief that the weird fantasy had ended. "Hanley, Steffen's practically my best friend. We go bowling together, for Pete's sake!"

"Yeah, well, your bosom buddy even tried to kill *me*. Hell, if Muldowney hadn't shown up in the nick of time . . ."

Thurgren held back on any visible reaction. He couldn't tell Hanley that his take on Steffen was wrong without revealing that Lance Muldowney was really Lewis Morosco. But maybe he wouldn't have to. "Hate to tell you this, but we set that up too. Steffen was just supposed to scare you, and then your boy played Batman and ran him into a ditch. But here's the important part: You never filed a report, either with us or the local police."

With his dubious defense now thoroughly crushed, Hanley started scrambling pitiably. "I didn't know it was Steffen. It was dark, and—"

"Forget it. His report said you got a clear look at his face."

"You can't prove I did!"

The more excitable and desperate Hanley grew, the calmer Thurgren became. "Even if you didn't know it was Steffen, you should have told the police. That's the law."

"I was scared. Steffen's car was in a ditch. It could have been traced. If I reported him, he would have come after me for sure!"

Thurgren nodded and turned away slightly, as if thinking it over carefully. "And that's why you didn't file a report?"

"Definitely!"

"Okay. So what'd you do with the gun, James?"

"What gun? What the hell are you talking about now!"

"The one you tried to kill me with at the bowling alley in Washington. And let's stop pretending that Steffen being an FBI agent is new news to you, okay? Because he's the guy you hit when you thought you were taking a shot at me, and then you went off to your meeting. But you dumped the gun somewhere—we know, because we searched your car—so where is it?"

Blinking rapidly, trying to think, Hanley's eyes darted back and forth but Thurgren had rattled him good and his normally glib backtracking wasn't working. "You searched my car?" he said hoarsely.

"Where'd you dump the gun, Hanley!"

But Hanley didn't seem to have heard him. A quizzical look came over his face and he slowly sank back on his chair.

"You searched my car?"

HALF AN HOUR LATER, UPSET AND DISTRACTED, THURGREN left the *Artemis-5.com* offices and walked a few blocks before hailing a cab, phoning up Morosco after he'd had a chance to think.

"Couldn't shake him," he said after he'd been put through.

If Morosco was sorry to hear that, he didn't do a good job of showing it. "Aw, gee, that's too bad! Real surprise, too. You hit him with everything?"

"Yeah. Both barrels."

"So we're still on, right? Still gonna play it out?"

There's no other way, Thurgren assured him. Morosco reported that everything was in place. As they'd agreed, he'd proceeded with setting things up, just in case Thurgren didn't get anywhere with Hanley.

"Thought it might be a good idea if we all packed some heat," Morosco said. "Harry agreed. That okay with you?"

"Oh sure, let's carry guns. Why not have a little fun at the same time, right?"

"Come on, Jubal, don't be grumpy. You tried your best, it didn't work, but the good news is, we're still in the ball game."

"I'll try to be more positive, Lewis."

"That's the ticket! See you when you get back."

"Hold it! I need you to do something."

"Sure. What?"

"I want you to call *TillYouDrop*'s auditors."

"Highland & Harwick?"

"Right. Same as *Artemis-5*'s. Call Ted Mangus directly, and ask him if *TillYouDrop.net* is carrying the *Artemis-5* lawsuit on its books as a contingent liability."

"They're not. We already know that."

"I know we know that. What I want is for you to drop a real strong hint that they should."

"Why?"

"Because if their books are burdened down with the possibility of losing a massive lawsuit, the company's as good as dead again. And dead is the only way it's going to help us out of this mess."

"Still think you're crazy, but anyway, since when do auditors take hints from us?"

"When they're scared to death they're going to get nailed to the wall right along with their criminal client, that's when. Mangus is already sweating bullets and looking for any opportunity to be a good guy in our eyes."

"I'm not comfortable with this, Jubal."

Thurgren sighed and pinched the bridge of his nose. "Then forget it. I'll do it myself."

CHAPTER THIRTY-FIVE

AUGUST 1

THURGREN STARED AT THE PHONE BUT MADE no move to pick up the handset. A rhythmic sound made him look across the room, first at Harry Friedenthal, then at Morosco.

Morosco's foot was tapping a staccato beat on the floor, betraying his poorly constrained excitement. "Something wrong, Jubal?"

Thurgren looked back to the phone. A shaft of morning sunlight streaming through his dusty window lit it up like a museum display. "Point of no return here. I pick up the phone and dial? We're committed."

"Kinda why you spent all of last week cooking it up, isn't it?" Friedenthal asked.

"Could've been planning a bungee jump, too. Doesn't mean you're not going to get a tad nervous when you're standing on the bridge looking straight down."

"Come on, Jubal," Morosco huffed in exasperation, his knee still pistoning up and down. "You know you're gonna do it, so just pick up the damned phone"—he mimed the motion with his hand, nodding in approval as Thurgren reached for the handset—"and make the call."

Thurgren hesitated for another moment, then inhaled deeply and punched the buttons, sending his overeager subordinate into a scramble to get his headset on. Hearing it ring at the other end, he let out the breath and sat back, swiveling away in order not to get distracted. "Mr. Hanley, please," he said a moment later. "Jubal Thurgren calling." He put his hand over the mouthpiece and said over his shoulder, "Least she didn't ask what it was about. I would've told—Mr. Hanley?"

Morosco tried to force himself to relax. It was all in Thurgren's hands now.

"Mr. Thurgren?"

"Yeah. How are you?"

"Aboveground and not in prison. Yourself?"

"Same, I guess. Got a minute?"

"For my favorite G-man? Always."

"Um, I thought it might be a good idea for you and me to kind of have a last go at being civil, see if there's not something we can work out that makes it best for everybody all around."

"You're trying to put me in jail, Mr. Thurgren. How's that going to be best for me?"

"Listen, can we basically agree we both got a little heated, maybe went a little overboard trying to make our cases?"

"Did I get heated?"

"In your own way."

"You trick me into a confrontation with the top financial watchdogs in the country, accuse me of trying to destroy the entire capitalist system, blindside me so I have no opportunity to prepare . . . and all of this after you tried to fool me into accepting an offer to have you killed. I rather thought I was being fairly rational under the circumstances."

"Well, I've got to admit, that was one heckuva performance you put on down in Washington. Looked for a second there like you almost had those people believing it."

"They were prepared to indict and arrest me on the spot, and they let me walk instead. I'd say I was pretty convincing."

"The only thing you convinced them of was that you weren't going to go quietly. Don't tell me all this time you've been thinking they actually fell for that fantasy you spun."

Thurgren swiveled back a bit to see if Friedenthal had caught the hesitation at the other end. The FBI assistant director nodded his approval of the way things were going, then Thurgren turned away again when he heard Hanley start to speak.

"Mr. Thurgren, I assume you didn't call to chin wag over old times. Is there something I can help you with?"

"Maybe we can help each other. I wanted to—"

"Do you watch a lot of television, Thurgren? I'm just wondering, because it's the only place you might have gotten this notion that somebody with an IQ higher than a dustcover's could fall for this I'm-going-to-do-you-a-favor line of rubbish. What are you now, my best buddy, calling up to lend me a helping hand?"

"No need to get excited."

"Why don't you let me be the judge of that. Why did you call? And do us both a real favor this time and skip the government-issue malarkey, if that wouldn't be too much trouble."

"Fair enough." Thurgren swung around to face forward again, glancing at Morosco and Friedenthal in turn, as if seeking some kind of support. "Mr. Hanley, the federal prosecutor has agreed to hand down indictments against you. They're going to be served Monday."

"I thought we already—"

"They'll also be serving Lance Muldowney and your lawyer, Jacqueline Tobin."

Silence at the other end. Then, "Toland."

"What?"

"Her name's Toland. And she's not my lawyer, she does some work for my company."

"Whatever." Thurgren tried to buy a few seconds as he hastily jotted something down.

"You don't have a case against us. I already explained why."

"And a fine speech it was." Thurgren dropped the pencil and sat back, returning his concentration to the task at hand. "But while your lucid explanation may have satisfied you, it didn't work for anybody else. I think we do have a case, and so does the U.S. attorney, and the only way we're going to find out how strong it is, we're going to ask a jury what *they* think."

"There's no way you're ever going to—"

"The discovery requests are almost complete, and you'll get served with those after you've been arraigned. It will require you to turn over every single scrap of paper that was ever—"

"I know what discovery is, Thurgren. We'll fight every paragraph with everything we have."

"That's your right as an American citizen, Hanley. I fully expect a vigorous and spirited defense."

Silence again. Thurgren looked at Morosco, who was thinking the same thing as he: What was going through Hanley's mind at this moment were visions of tidal waves of paper swelling every corner of *Artemis-5.com* to the breaking point, hordes of lawyers with their meters on tripping gaily and unconstrained through the meadows of the company's books, endless press stories grounded on the flimsiest speculation and masquerading as news, and the fires of scandal stoked to white hot incandescence by a media community for whom the misery of others was more coveted than their own souls.

Thurgren also believed that Hanley was envisioning his own long-term incarceration.

"Are you proposing some sort of accommodation?" Hanley said at last, and Morosco clenched a fist.

Thurgren wondered how much of that long interval Hanley had devoted to ensuring that his voice, when at last he spoke, sounded even and untroubled. "Of a sort. Maybe."

"Then you have doubts about the strength of your case."

"None whatsoever. I don't think you have a chance in the world."

"And you have nothing to lose by prosecuting me, whereas we both know it'll turn my company upside down even if I'm acquitted."

"Actually, I have a lot to lose. The whole case is premised largely on my say so, and I guess that means I'm betting my whole career on this one. If we blow it, I'll probably be out on the street. And I suspect you'll come after me for malicious prosecution, defamation and God only knows what else."

"You can pretty much count on that."

"Well I don't give a hoot, Hanley. We're fully committed to moving ahead."

"So why are we talking?"

"Because the SEC still has a strong interest in not disrupting the markets. The chairman's already decided to risk it if it comes down to that, because there's no way they can let you ride after what you did—"

"I didn't do anything!"

"—but if there's a middle ground that still serves justice and doesn't toss grenades into the exchanges, he's willing to discuss it."

"Sounds a little—"

Thurgren saw Morosco pump a fist toward the phone—*Timing's right . . . drop the hammer!*—and nodded his acknowledgment. "Listen, Hanley," he said abruptly. "Doing the baloney bolero with you is starting to bore me, and I don't have the time or the patience for it anymore. If you're willing to sit down with me and try to work something out, I'll meet with you, but I want this to be real clear: If we don't come to an arrangement, you'll be taken into custody Monday morning. We'll let you surrender on your own, as a courtesy, but heck or high water, we're cracking down on you with everything in the arsenal from fraudulent conveyance to conspiracy, and I'm going to dedicate the rest of *my* life to putting you in Lewisburg for the rest of *yours*."

There was no snappy comeback from the other end, just the barely discernible sound of rapid breathing. Friedenthal held his hands up, palm toward Thurgren, who got the message and kept quiet as the seconds ticked past.

"I'm not admitting anything," Hanley said at last. "But I'll meet with you."

"Just you and me, Hanley. No lawyers, no Lance Muldowney or any other flunkies"—Morosco smiled sheepishly—"and no wires."

"And not at your offices, either."

"Nor yours. But I'll come to New York tomorrow morning. How about that new building of yours?"

"It's only half completed."

"That's the point." Neither of them would have to worry about the other one having it bugged, and on a Saturday they'd have it all to themselves.

"Okay. Ten o'clock?"

Morosco waved his hands frantically to get Thurgren's attention, then jabbed a thumb into the air.

"Make it eleven. I'll bring the coffee." Thurgren jerked his head up as a click sounded in the receiver. He held it away and looked at it stupidly. "Did he just hang up on me?"

"Whadja expect him to do?" Morosco pulled the uncomfortable headset off and rubbed his ears vigorously. "Ask about the family?"

Thurgren dropped the handset back onto its cradle. "So that's it then."

"That's it." Friedenthal stood and arched his back, then swung his arms back and forth a few times. "You played it beautifully, Jubal. Doubt the poor sonofabitch is gonna get much sleep tonight."

As he retrieved his jacket from a peg behind the door, Thurgren turned to look out his window. "Makes two of us."

CHAPTER THIRTY-SIX

AUGUST 2

FUTILE AS HE KNEW IT WAS GOING TO BE to try to sleep, Thurgren leaned back against the headrest and closed his eyes anyway. The throaty rumble of the jet engines vibrating through the airframe was soothing in a way, even more so than silence would be because silence would do nothing to drive the swirl of maddening thoughts from his head.

The very instant he began to feel the slightly disorienting headiness that signaled the first ticklings of sleep, a sharp crackling sound from the seat to his right jarred him out of it. He tried to ignore it but it recurred, more insistent this time. He opened one eye just as FBI Assistant Director Friedenthal finally managed to separate a single piece of something from a plastic array of similar somethings. He shoved the rest of the blister pack back into his jacket pocket and set to work trying, noisily, to slip a fingernail under the foil tab.

"Every time I try to get one of these goddamned things open, it makes me want a cigarette," he muttered, which was when Thurgren recognized the recalcitrant package as one that contained a piece of nicotine-laced Gasp-Away gum, part of the comprehensive Gasp-Away stop-smoking 'system' that also included brochures that nobody ever read and counseling that nobody ever used.

"You think it'll work, Harry?"

The foil wrapper snapped open and the gum within popped into the air and clattered to the floor. "Shit . . ." Friedenthal bent over to retrieve it, grunting as the seatbelt cut into his middle. "My money back if it doesn't. Says so right on the package."

"The meeting, Harry. I'm talking about the meeting."

"How should I know?" He got his fingers around the gum and straightened up. "If you've done all the prep work you can, you just ride it out like you scripted it . . . piece'a cake. 'Course, I don't know all the details."

"Piece'a cake, yeah." Thurgren closed his eyes again and tried to wiggle into a more comfortable position against the almost non-existent padding of the badly worn seat. "So how come you're already on your third piece'a chewable cigarette since we boarded?"

Friedenthal wiped the small square against his pant leg and regarded it disdainfully. "I don't get it anyway. Swallowing nicotine's supposed to be better than smoking it?"

"Like drinkin' no-alcohol beer, you ask me," Paul Steffen said from the third seat in their row. "Hell's the point?"

"You pipe down. You belong back in the hospital, and you're giving me health lectures? Tell me again why I'm even on this boondoggle, Jubal," Friedenthal demanded irritably. "I mean, don't get me wrong, I love shuttling up to New York to see my quota of filth and depravity, but am I necessary?"

"Told you, Harry: I need reliable witnesses."

"And Steffen isn't reliable?"

"He's not credible. Come on, it's practically entrapment, what with him and Hanley having met up before."

"Then why's he here at all?"

"'Cuz I deserve it, that's why," Steffen responded. "See that prick go down."

"And for this the department pays your expenses? Least you could have done, you could have driven up with Morosco."

"I'm not getting within five hundred yards of that maniac, he's got his hands on a car. Besides, this is a lot damned cheaper than that two-thousand-a-day nursing home you had me in."

"But you—"

"Look, Harry." Steffen sat up straight, grimaced as something tugged at his fresh stitches, and turned to Friedenthal. "One more word outta you and I'm going on disability for the next twenty years. You want *that* in your departmental budget?"

Friedenthal shook his head. "This better work, Jubal."

"Thanks for the pep talk." Thurgren held up a hand. "No, really, Harry. It gave me shivers."

"WHERE'VE YOU BEEN, MULDOWNEY!" HANLEY DEMANDED AN-grily.

"Washington, where else?" Morosco answered. He cast a quick glance at Hanley, making note of the tremor in his jaw, the nervous opening and closing of his fist, and several other signs of incipient panic. "You got any idea at all how many rules and—"

"We've got troubles, Lanny. Big troubles, you and me both, and Jackie, too. I just—"

Morosco held up his hand, and Hanley stopped speaking. Walking to the door, Morosco closed it, turning the handle before it finally shut in order not to alert Toland that something was going on. "Where's Beth today?"

"Sent her home. Listen, Lanny, something's come up, and I don't think we're likely to clever our way out of this one."

Morosco nodded and, with what Hanley considered maddening deliberateness, pulled a visitor's chair closer to the desk and sat down, wiping imaginary lint from his pants before folding his hands. "You got a call from Thurgren at the SEC. He threatened to indict you again and suggested a meeting."

"Your buddy at the SEC throwing little tidbits our way again?"

"Mmmm . . ." Morosco rocked his head back and forth as he considered the question. "Not exactly, Jim."

FRIEDENTHAL LOOKED AT HIS WATCH. "MOROSCO MEETING US at the airport? Save us an expensive cab ride?"

Thurgren sighed, any hope of a catnap gone in the face of Friedenthal's transparent attempts to hide his nervousness by chatting away mindlessly. "If he has time. He's busy."

"Busy? Doing what?"

Steffen sniggered, and as Friedenthal started to turn toward him to find out what was so funny, Thurgren said, "He's in Hanley's office," and Friedenthal returned his attention to him instead.

"CLOSE YOUR MOUTH, JAMES," MOROSCO SAID. "YOU LOOK ridiculous."

Hanley did so, then opened it again. "You what?" he managed to splutter.

"I work for Thurgren. Have for two years. Yo, Jim!" Morosco snapped his fingers a few times. "You with me, buddy? Jim!"

Hanley nodded his head weakly, not at all aware of the fact that he resembled a fish newly landed on a dock, gasping for air and not quite sure what had hit him. Morosco bent toward his attaché on the floor and pulled out a bottle of water, twisting off the cap and handing it across the desk. "Take a swig. You'll feel better."

Something about that command had a vaguely familiar feeling. *Who had said something like . . . ?* Barely aware of what he was doing, Hanley grasped the bottle and did as he was told—*It had been Paul Steffen, in the Thai restaurant*—but got his breathing mixed up with his drinking and coughed violently, water spraying from his nose.

"Jesus!" Morosco yelped, shoving his chair back. "Get a grip, will ya? It's not as bad as you think!"

Hanley managed to clear the water from his lungs and nose.

Breathing rapidly, he closed his eyes and tried to calm himself, to regain some of his cherished rationality and deal with this . . . this . . .

He pointed to Morosco's French cuff with a trembling finger. "Your name . . ."

Morosco followed his eyes to the monogram at his wrist. "Oh, yeah. Same initials. So I wouldn't have to buy a new wardrobe. My real name is Lewis Morosco."

Hanley finally swam back into focus, and tried to replay the last year of his life in order to assess the damage. But the complexity and the implications were far too overwhelming for him to grasp in just a few seconds, so he gave up rather than risk retreating into incoherence again. Instead, he decided to forgo sequential thinking altogether and stick to the one solid thing he could latch on to, which was how much he despised the traitorous piece of scum sitting opposite him, and how little time it had taken him to work up to that level of hatred.

Morosco felt the raw power of Hanley's revulsion as clearly as if the man had been throwing daggers at him. That wasn't necessarily a bad thing, given the situation. "I was undercover at the Virgin. My assignment was to get the goods on Burton Staller—" He waited for a few seconds, until Hanley could process that and integrate it with how Morosco was able to give him advance warning of Staller's troubles "—then you and *Artemis-5.com* came along. So there I was, kind of an agent in place already, and, well . . ." He lifted his hands and let them drop into his lap with a loud slap.

Hanley's brain, already in danger of meltdown, sought to protect its host by testing out another line of defense. "I don't believe you. This is some kind of a trick. You can't prove any of this, and don't . . . don't . . . !" Hanley held out his hand to stop Morosco from reaching into his pocket. "Don't bother showing me identification, either. I could get a dozen of those made up before lunch."

Morosco put up his hands in mock surrender. "Okay, James, okay. Tell you the truth, it never occurred to me you wouldn't believe me. So let's see . . ."

Hanley seemed to be holding his breath, his eyes darting back and forth rapidly as if seeking something firm to hold on to. Morosco knew he had to get him calmed down or else none of this was going to work.

And the best way to get someone like Hanley calmed down was to help him arrange his world into a reasonable structure. In a situation as complicated as this one, the only way to do that was to tell the truth. Anything less, and there was bound to be a misstep somewhere.

"Do you remember when I warned you to report Paul Steffen to the SEC?" Morosco asked, receiving a nod in response. "Turned out to be a pretty good call on my part, didn't it?" Another nod. "Because now you know Steffen was an FBI agent trying to set you up."

He stayed quiet as Hanley drank it in and tried to assess the implications. "How did you know I knew the truth about Steffen?" Hanley asked.

"Don't get stupid on me, James." Morosco saw resignation begin to seep into Hanley's eyes. "You already had this conversation with Thurgren. Way back when, I warned you to report Steffen, remember? I told you not to take any chances, to turn him in right away, to agree to wear a wire."

"Because you knew it was a setup."

Morosco shrugged. "It was my idea. When I first came up with it, I thought there was a chance you'd go for it, and that would have been the end of you and *Artemis-5.com* both."

"And then you sabotaged your own sting? Why?"

Morosco laughed. "Isn't it obvious?"

Now they were on ground Hanley could relate to easily, and he didn't need any counseling from Morosco to get where he needed to be. "Because you got a taste of the possibilities, that's why. You knew my company was going to be a power and you wanted in."

Even as the words came out, Hanley felt his world start to click back into place. Greed, ambition, the manipulation and exploitation of a man's basic needs . . . as familiar as an old pair of slippers and as predictable as the dawn. "You were a double agent, Lanny."

"Lewis."

"Both ends against the middle and protected either way." Hanley smiled for the first time that day, then dropped back against his chair and laughed. "Certainly got to hand it to you, kid. Not sure I'd have done it any different, had I been sitting in the catbird seat like you were."

Morosco returned the smile and started to relax. "If anyone could appreciate it, I knew you could, Jim."

As they regarded each other with the easy affability of two veteran bullshitters admiring each other's guile, Hanley's smile began to fade, continuing its downward slide until it was gone altogether.

Morosco knew exactly what he was thinking. "I didn't really save your life that night, James. When you thought Steffen was trying to kill you."

"You were in on that setup, too."

"I'm sorry about that, bud. Truly I am. It was Thurgren's idea, because he thought you were starting to lose faith in me—"

"He was afraid he'd lose you on the inside. Needed to get you back on my good side."

"I hated it, but I had no choice. If it's any comfort to you, I did give Steffen a good case of whiplash."

Hanley shook his head and looked away. "Jesus . . ."

Morosco waited a few seconds, then said sharply, "We need to talk some business."

"Business?" The sheer audacity of this punk was just too much, but Hanley drew strength from it, using it as a lever to ground his thinking. "You want to talk *business*, you slimy—after what you did to me?"

"What I did to you?" Morosco slammed his hand onto Hanley's desk and stood up. "If it wasn't for me there wouldn't *be* an *Artemis-5*! You would've fallen for the Steffen setup and gone to jail, you would've put Burton Staller on your board and then watched him get indicted, not to mention that I worked my ass off night and day to make sure every last goddamned detail of the IPO went off without a hitch!"

It was true, and Hanley couldn't argue with any of it, but there were other things, too. "Why'd you let me fall for Staller's bear trap?"

"We didn't know what he was doing. Anything else, James? Because you really need to get over this in a hurry."

"Why are you telling me this . . . *Lewis*?"

Morosco sat down again. "Because I want to stay with the company, and you, for real." He could see the skepticism leaping onto Hanley's features. "There's no reason not to believe me, James. You now know good and goddamned well I could have shut this place down dozens of times, and I didn't."

"So what's this now . . . you confessing to clear your conscience before I make you a billionaire? Is that it? Because we both know that all your shares really belong to the government, not you. Unless . . ."

"They don't know what I own. We both know that you could tell them, and that'd be the end of me. The ten million in Switzerland, too. I never reported that either." He could see Hanley wavering as he tried to juggle the myriad pros and cons and sort them out. "Don't forget that as far as Thurgren is concerned, I'm still working for the Enforcement Division. Your company doesn't have a more valuable asset anywhere on the planet than me inside the SEC."

"You're willing to do that? Stay with them and keep playing this out?"

"Hell, yes."

"And how do I know I can trust you?"

The fact was, if Hanley turned him down, Morosco could still wreck *Artemis-5.com* and be a hero at the SEC. There was no proof he ever considered doing otherwise. But it would be better if that extortionary aspect of his leverage over Hanley remained unspoken, to perpetuate the illusion that they were going to be two mutually trusting business partners. "You already think I'm a grasping, overly ambitious opportunist, James. Presented with the choice of being a government wage slave or an entrepreneurial billionaire, which way do you figure I'm gonna go?"

It was a powerful point, he could see that, and Hanley was teetering right on the edge. Morosco just needed to tip him over. "You're going to be indicted Monday morning, James. I can turn that around, but there's no reason for me to take that risk unless I'm going to be *Artemis-5*'s Number Two."

Realistically, Hanley had no choice in the matter, and they both knew it. And Morosco was right: *Artemis-5.com* would have no better asset, not just because he'd be playing the SEC to the company's advantage but because he was in fact an extremely astute businessman who'd steered Hanley through a complex process with masterful aplomb. Besides, as an old client once told him, caring, altruism, generosity and charity were all admirable qualities but essentially unreliable. Greed, on the other hand, you could bank on. Appeal to a man's greed, feed it regularly, and his loyalty was assured.

"Okay, Lewis. If you want to become a born-again capitalist, I could use you. We both know that." He flipped up his hand and let it drop back to the armrest. "So what's your big idea?"

"Not a new concept, really." Morosco sat back and prepared to do some heavy conversing. "You're going to kill Jubal Thurgren."

CHAPTER THIRTY-SEVEN

LIKE AN ESCAPING PRISONER WHO FIGURED he finally had it made only to run right into his captors' arms, Hanley thought he'd gotten a firm grip on this situation just in time to have it take another macabre turn.

Most behavior results from the accumulation of experience, with entire sections of the brain devoted to abstracting from that experience things that might be relevant to the situation at hand. But there was nothing in Hanley's data banks remotely related to what was happening to him now. Aside from his fear and disorientation, which were real, he found himself feeling and acting according to some mechanical interpretation of what might be appropriate under the circumstances rather than to the spontaneous dictates of normal emotions.

The upper hand had once more shifted to

Morosco, and there was no telling how many more grenades he still had fastened to his ammo belt. "You don't have to say anything yet. Just hear me out."

He leaned forward and rested his elbows on Hanley's desk, gesturing as he spoke. "Thurgren's handed us the key himself. He wants an off-the-record sit-down, just the two of you. No lawyers, no regulators, no wires, just man to man. You with me?"

Hanley nodded his understanding, but not necessarily his commitment.

"Okay. So there you are, on the ground floor of a building under construction. It's Saturday, there's nobody else around. He said he'd bring the coffee and doughnuts, right?"

Of course it was right. Any last vestiges of doubt as to whether Morosco really worked for Thurgren hissed out of Hanley's head and into the ether. The only remaining uncertainty was how much Morosco knew about *him*.

"There'll be a table and a couple of chairs. You'll sit opposite each other. An hour or so beforehand, you give me a key to the lock on the fence surrounding the site, and I tape a handgun underneath the table. Two strips of adhesive, with the barrel facing away from you, the base of the stock pointing left and wrapped in some more tape. All you have to do is reach under and it'll come into your hand in ready position. You just tear it away."

He pushed away from the table and sat back. "No conversation, no hesitation, no nothing. You point it at him and you pull the trigger."

It was clear that Morosco wasn't going to be volunteering anything further absent some sign that Hanley was still a sentient being. "Why don't I just start negotiating with him? Hear him out, see if there's some wiggle room?"

Morosco regarded him silently for a second, then snickered and turned away. "Thought you were a lot smarter than that, James." He stood up and walked to the window, looking out at the brown haze hanging over the city. "For one thing, he'll be wired."

"How?"

"His tie. The battery and transmitter are hidden in the knot, the microphone is one of his collar buttons, and the antenna is a metallic thread woven right into the tie itself. You'd never find it."

"So why don't I just make him take off the tie?"

"Why don't you just tell him I came by here and told you about the wire?" Morosco turned away from the window and looked back at Hanley. "Chrissakes, Jim, use your brains!"

"Sorry. So what's supposed to happen next?"

"He'll tell you he's going ahead with the indictments."

"He hasn't got anything on me!"

"Sure he does. It may not be enough, but it'll make for one hell of a public show. He'll tell you he's going to go after your auditors at the same time, but quietly, and he'll let them plea bargain if they cop to what you did, complete with all the backup documentation."

"They won't do it. If they admitted anything, the implied civil liability would be enormous. And without them, Thurgren can't win." It was a good point, but Hanley said it without conviction, seeming to have little of the swaggering self-confidence he'd displayed at the confrontation with Peabody and Goldwith.

Morosco sensed the hesitation and bore in on it. "He doesn't give a shit, Jim. He doesn't want it to come to that, so he's going to offer you a deal: You resign from *Artemis-5.com* for health reasons, and he slowly liquidates the company and returns all the money to the investors."

Hanley sneered at the suggestion. "He must be out of his mind to think I'd do that!"

"He expects you to refuse, but he'll try to draw you into a conversation in which you incriminate yourself."

"That's why you said no conversation. So my voice wouldn't be taped."

Morosco leaned against the window sill and folded his arms. "Exactly."

"That's one dilly of a plan, Lewis."

"Thank you."

"Why don't you shove it up your ass, and then go fuck yourself."

"What?" Morosco's aplomb threatened to join Hanley's swagger out in the ozone. "I don't . . . What's the—"

"I'm not going to shoot anybody, you fucking moron! Are you completely and totally insane?"

"It's the only way, James! Unless you got a better—"

"First of all, I'm not going to risk a murder rap! Second of all, even if I did, how do I get away?"

"You just walk away! There's nobody else around so you just—"

"Who's picking up the wire!"

Morosco pushed off the sill and waved an arm to the side. "Those guys'll be half a mile away. You'll be long gone by the time they even figure out what the hell is going on!"

"And then what?" Hanley demanded, unaware that his affected linguistic façade had completely disappeared. "Half the goddamned SEC knows I have a meeting with Thurgren, so where's the first place they're gonna look when they find him splattered all over my new building?"

"I got that figured out already. What happens is—"

"*Fuck you,* Morosco! You hear me? You want to be a billionaire, *you* figure out how to get us out of this and leave me the hell out of it!"

"Jim—"

"I'm not going to do it! Finished!"

Morosco leaned back against the sill again. "You sure?"

"Bet your sweet ass I'm sure!"

A deafening silence suffused the space between them, neither seeming to know what to do next, and then Morosco laughed quietly and shook his head.

"What's so funny?" Hanley demanded crossly.

"I told him you wouldn't do it."

"Told . . . what? Told who!"

"Thurgren." Morosco slapped his thighs and straightened up once again, turning to look out the window and folding his arms. "Yep. I said to him, I said, Jubal, trust me on this. James Hanley isn't going to go for it."

"WHAT THE HELL ARE YOU TALKING ABOUT?" FRIEDENTHAL asked Thurgren. "What do you mean, he's in Hanley's office?"

"You'da come and talked to us when we asked you to," Steffen said with a malicious grin, "you'd know all of this. But no-o-o-o, you don't get messy in the details."

As the plane banked into a gentle turn, Friedenthal popped the newly cleaned nicotine gum into his mouth and turned to his right.

"Steffen," he said as he began chewing the gum as fast as he could, "you don't gimme the skinny on this thing pronto, I'm gonna bust you down to the fingerprint filing section before this plane touches the ground."

"Harry."

Friedenthal felt a finger tapping his arm and whipped his head back toward Thurgren.

"Morosco's telling Hanley how to kill me when we meet tomorrow."

"WAY IT'S SUPPOSED TO WORK," MOROSCO EXPLAINED, "you fire at Thurgren, and he tumbles over backwards while he breaks a vial of red dye number two and splatters it all over the place. You drop the gun, you bolt, the FBI guys pick you up outside and you go down for attempted murder."

"And he'll be wearing a vest."

"A vest, yeah. Are you a complete idiot? What if you shoot him in the head?"

"Blanks, then." This time, there was no need for Hanley to wrestle his sanity back. This time, things made perfect sense. Except one thing.

He looked carefully at Morosco. "They think I'd do that? Shoot Thurgren?"

"Why not, Jim? You tried to kill him twice before." Morosco held up a hand as Hanley started to protest. "Yeah, yeah, I know. It was the tooth fairy. Listen, I don't give a shit one way or the other. Point is, they'll know in advance you're going to go for it because I'm supposed to report back to them, then we get the shooting on tape and you're dead. Not a bad plan, actually."

"Who came up with it?"

"I did."

"Great. I really appreciate it, Morosco. But since you turned out to be such a prick, why don't we bypass the bullshit and get down to the only two things that matter in this conversation. The first one is you telling me how I'm supposed to boomerang this operation back on Thurgren. What's your idea, that I pick up a brick and bash his skull in while nobody's looking?"

"I thought of that, but—"

"Goddamnit, I was just kidding!"

"Wouldn't work anyway. Thurgren's going to be armed with a real gun, just in case you try to play outside the script. It'll be in his waistband."

Hanley felt a chill as the cold-bloodedness of the man he once thought of as his friend made itself increasingly apparent. "If he's armed, won't I find it if I search him?"

"I already told you: Don't search him. Part of what I'm supposed to be telling you is that there's no need to."

"I can't believe this is really happening to me."

"You better believe it, Jim, because right now I'm your only way out. You still listening, or you want to blubber your life away because it's all so unfair?"

"I'm listening. What do I do?"

"Simple. Just call his bluff."

"How?"

"Look, you were right all along. He really doesn't have enough hard evidence against you, which is why he's going through all of this." Morosco was starting to relax again as he began to draw Hanley in. "Tell him you've done nothing wrong. Sound sincere, and don't forget for a single second that you're being taped. He'll give you the old, Come on, it's just the two of us, you can tell me, it's off the record. But don't fall for it. Stick to your innocent guns no matter what. You're running a legitimate company, you won't be pushed around by somebody who's just trying to make a name for himself. You believe in the justice system, you're willing to take your chances in court, all of that hearts and flowers crap. Take the high road all the way, Jim, no matter what he throws at you."

"I don't have to pretend, Morosco. I've always taken the high road."

Morosco stared at him for a few seconds, then smiled. "I'm not wired, Jumbo. You want to search me?"

"I didn't say you were."

"Then save the speeches, okay?"

"So I call his bluff. Then what?"

Morosco sat back and spread his hands. "You walk out. End of story. Thurgren won't indict you."

"He won't? How can I be sure?"

"Because I'm telling you, that's how. This scam is his last chance.

If you don't take the bait, he has to fold his tent and go home. He won't have a choice. It's a direct command from above."

Hanley thought about it, trying to work through the ramifications. "There's a problem, Morosco."

"What problem?"

"He thinks you're here now telling me about a gun you planted. You're supposed to know before you leave here if I agreed to shoot him. So if I show up and don't do it, if I give him this rah rah speech, how do you explain it?"

"I don't have to. *You* explain it."

"What are you talking about?"

"Turn me in. Just like you turned Steffen in. Tell Thurgren about that idiot Muldowney who concocted this insane scheme. Here you are, a legitimate businessman, and this madman expected you to shoot down a federal officer in cold blood. Show him the gun, get a good speech down on tape, then storm out in self-righteous fury. That's the last you'll ever hear from Jubal Thurgren and the SEC."

Hanley smiled for the first time, and received a smug, self-satisfied smile in return. "Your troubles are about to end, Jim," Morosco said.

"Maybe. You seem to have thought of everything. But I said there were two things that mattered in this conversation, and we only covered one."

"Yeah. That kind of brings us to the last point, which I almost forgot."

"I bet you did. So let's deal with that. Why don't you tell me what you get out of all this, Lewis? I mean exactly, and how do we do it so nobody gets wise?"

Morosco inclined his head slightly in acknowledgment; black belts in bullshit at it once again, negotiating terms, each knowing it was already a done deal with only minor details remaining to be worked out.

He walked away from the window, hands in his pockets. "I'll show up here a few days afterward, consumed with guilt and remorse for ever having doubted you. I will have resigned from the SEC because of my shame at having participated in a scam to blacken the name of an American hero, and beg your forgiveness, which you will generously bestow upon me."

"How generously?"

"In addition to naming me *Artemis-5*'s Number Two, you vest in me all of the equity you'd already pledged to Lance Muldowney."

"Ah." Hanley folded his hands across his belly. "I'm going to do all that, am I?"

"You already said Muldowney did a bang-up job for you while he was here."

"Gotta admit, you were a good man."

"Well there you go. We don't have to be friends, Jim. It's just a simple business deal, and look at it this way: You save the company as well as yourself, and you don't have to give up a damned thing you haven't already given away. Except you give it to me instead of Muldowney."

"I thought you said you were going to stay with the SEC. Be my inside man there."

"That was just to see if you'd let me back in to the company before I laid this all out for you. Besides, there isn't going to be any need for me to stay there once this is all over. Thurgren's name will be mud, and nobody there would dare lay a hand on you after all the time and effort he will have wasted. Now." He walked back to the desk. "Have we got a deal?"

"I don't know. Not sure I like being blackmailed into a partnership." Hanley regretted it instantly. He knew he had no real choice in the matter, so why poison the waters unnecessarily?

Fortunately, Morosco played the game better than he did, and found a way to smooth things over. "Don't look at it that way, James. Look at it from a business point of view. It's a good deal for both sides."

"We're bound only by mutual self-interest, is that it, Lewis? The reason I should trust you is because of what we both have to gain?"

"That's it, Jim. Can't think of a better basis for a partnership. So have we got a deal?"

He held out his hand.

Hanley shook it.

"YOU GOT GOOD MEN ON THIS, STEFFEN?"

"The best, Harry." Steffen held open the door of the cab as the assistant director got out. Thurgren took another second to sign the voucher for the cab driver, who'd been waiting for them at LaGuardia, then got out and slammed the door shut.

"Local men?" Friedenthal asked.

"Yeah," Steffen replied as they began walking toward the building housing the New York field office of the FBI. "They know the area, and by now they know every brick at the construction site too."

"Jubal!"

They turned in unison to see Morosco striding rapidly across the plaza toward them. "Keep your fingers crossed," Thurgren said to Friedenthal.

"How'd it go?" Steffen asked when Morosco pulled up.

"Better than we could've imagined."

"He buy it all?"

"Hook, line and sinker." Morosco turned to Thurgren and poked him in the chest. "Get ready to watch a man cut his own throat."

"How'd he take it when he found out Muldowney and Morosco were the same guy?"

"I thought he was gonna puke. Just between you and me, though, I gotta tell you . . ." He cast a sly glance at Friedenthal. "It was kind of fun."

"Just between you and me, Lewis," Thurgren responded, "I know it was. I told him about Steffen, remember?"

"Glad you cowboys are having so much goddamned fun," Friedenthal said irritably as they came up to the lobby doors. "Now I want to hear every detail of this operation, right down to how many steps it takes to get from the door of that room you're gonna be in to the table."

CHAPTER THIRTY-EIGHT

AUGUST 3

THE SITE OF THE NEW ARTEMIS-5.COM
building was on the edge of an abandoned rail
yard that nestled against the Hudson River. It
was the last major parcel of undeveloped land
in the middle of the island of Manhattan other
than Central Park, but unlike that venerable piece
of sacred ground that was statutorily off-limits
to developers, the rail yard was awaiting only
vision and money appropriate to its potential.
Some years beforehand, the city's most flam-
boyant real estate developer had proposed building a city-within-a-city there, complete with a
mile-high tower that would guarantee that he had
the biggest one on earth, but the notion shriveled
and went limp along with his fortunes during the
minicrash of the late eighties. While his fortunes

had recovered, the erectile dream hadn't, for reasons not publicly known.

Hanley was convinced that such a parcel could not endure in its present state, tantalizingly rich in unrealized possibilities, not when unprecedented amounts of cash were becoming available at such a dizzying rate that it was a full time job just figuring out how to spend it all. While the present investment climate didn't favor traditional bricks and mortar construction—why spend a couple hundred million on a risky building whose income potential was limited to rent and appreciation when you could spend it on tradable equities whose income potential was limitless?—it was inevitable that the rail yard would someday yield to development of some sort. Fallow land, like a taxicab sitting in a garage with its meter not running, was anathema to the business sensibility, an affront to its notion of what constituted an orderly universe.

Hanley wasn't interested in developing anything, but he was interested in staking his claim in an adjoining neighborhood in order to slurp up the droppings of whatever horse eventually decided to partake of the oats the rail yard offered. While the site of the new *Artemis-5.com* building barely lay on the fringes of what was considered prime real estate in New York, the fact was that, in the digital age, you might just as well build in Moustache Bend as Manhattan anyway. The need to be in any particular location was a near-irrelevant consideration when you had no raw materials you needed to buy, no product you needed to manufacture, no goods to ship and no labor that couldn't be performed remotely.

When you got right down to it, Hanley didn't even need the building, except as some kind of a symbol to provide comfort to those shareholding pains in the ass who took solace in such traditional icons.

Standing in an interior room with only three or four drywalls already up, Friedenthal heaved a metal carry-all onto the table and snapped open its latches. He lifted the lid to reveal several handguns resting within foam cutouts. "Nine millimeter Glock, you said." He lifted it out and handed it over.

Morosco hefted the weapon, warming to its weighty lethality. "Perfect." He pushed a release button with his thumb and caught the magazine as it fell out of the bottom of the grip, pressed the top round to make sure it was free against the spring, then slid it back in and snapped it home with a satisfying metallic click.

Friedenthal raised his eyebrows at this display of easy familiarity. "Hey, Cisco, remember, the idea's to have it, not to use it."

Morosco dropped the gun into his shoulder holster and seated it firmly with an extra shove. "Gotcha."

Friedenthal took out a small Beretta and handed it to Thurgren who, in contrast to Morosco's eager acceptance of the Glock, handled it gingerly. "You really think these are necessary?" he asked for the hundredth time.

"What if he's armed?" Morosco answered for the hundredth time.

"But why would he bring a gun when you're supplying him with one?"

"Jeez, we been all through this, Jubal!" Morosco said in exasperation. "You can't very well search the guy, so why take a chance?"

"Kid's right," Friedenthal said. "You're certified in small weapons, so what's it hurt to carry a little insurance? Here, turn around."

As Thurgren did so, Friedenthal lifted his jacket and tucked the Beretta into his waistband. "Case he's looking for a bulge. You can even take the jacket off if it looks like he's suspicious. Just don't turn your back to him."

"How many times are you going to tell me that, Harry?"

"Till I think you got it. Now look: Don't forget to make sure you sit down on your side of the table right away. We don't want him crawling around underneath trying to find the damned thing."

Thurgren grinned, mostly to try to hide his nervousness. "I got it, Harry."

"You okay, Jubal?" Morosco asked as Friedenthal sat down and reached his hand underneath the table to make sure one last time that the gun was taped in the right position.

Thurgren took a deep breath and let it out slowly. "I'm supposed to be an accountant," he answered. "How come I keep winding up around guns?"

Steffen and Morosco laughed. "You'll be fine," Friedenthal said, then handed over a thermos and a paper sack. "Jelly doughnuts. Right, Morosco?"

"Practically all he eats. Nice touch."

"I'll walk you out," Thurgren said, leading the way back to the front entrance.

"Who was his location scout?" Friedenthal wondered out loud as they stood just inside the lobby framing and looked out at the surroundings. "Bela Lugosi?"

"It was cheap, and it was available," Morosco responded. "Why waste shareholder money on frills?"

"Frills is one thing," Friedenthal observed, "but this is carrying fiscal responsibility to extremes."

"Perfect for us, though." Thurgren slapped his hands together to try to rid them of the cement dust that seemed to be everywhere, then looked at his watch. "Ten o'clock. We better get out of sight. Lewis, Harry . . . see you guys later."

"What's the hurry?" Friedenthal said. "Thought the meeting wasn't until eleven."

"My guess," Morosco explained, "he's gonna do a drive-by first, make sure there's really nobody else here. I know he has a conference call scheduled for ten, but it'll be a short one."

"Nothing else you guys can do, anyway," Steffen agreed.

Friedenthal took another look around, as though reluctant to leave. "Check your tie again, Jubal."

"For Pete's sake, Harry, we checked it ten damned—"

A tinny voice rasped out from somewhere in the vicinity of Friedenthal's head. He slapped at the side of his neck and yanked an earpiece out by the wire, then lifted his collar toward his mouth. "Alright already!"

Thurgren grinned at Steffen. "Guess it's working. Why don't you disappear now. Lewis, go hide."

"Have fun," Morosco said as he turned to re-enter the building.

"We're listening every second, Jubal," Friedenthal assured Thurgren. "Slightest thing out of script and we're—"

"I know, Harry. Don't worry."

Friedenthal took a last look around. There was no evidence that anybody but Thurgren was here. All the other cars were parked blocks away.

"Good luck, Jubal," he said. "Try not to get hurt, will ya?"

TWENTY MINUTES LATER HANLEY'S MERCEDES SLOWLY PULLED up outside the safety fence. It sat there with the engine running for nearly a minute before Hanley finally turned it off and opened the door. He looked around carefully before closing it.

He moved slowly toward the building, gingerly picking his way through the usual kinds of rubble that littered construction projects. He paused at the doorway, looking around once again, then seemed to hesitate before steeling himself and entering.

Down the corridor, seventh door on the right, Thurgren had told him. The interior was dank and dim, illuminated only by sunlight that came through window openings and managed to bounce its way into the hallway. Hanley counted rooms as he went: *three, four, five* . . .

"Jim!" someone whispered urgently from off to his right.

Hanley jumped to the side in alarm, raising a clatter as he banged into a half-installed aluminum door support. A shadow moved into the hallway and gradually resolved itself into Lewis Morosco. Hanley's eyes grew wide but he stayed quiet when he saw Morosco's finger at his lips.

"Mr. Hanley?" a voice called out from two doors down.

In response to Hanley's questioning stare, Morosco pulled him into a room and drew close. "Tell him you're coming!" he hissed urgently, then shoved him halfway out into the hallway.

Hanley cleared his throat. "On my way!"

Morosco pulled him roughly back. "Stay here for a second!"

"What the hell's going on, Lewis!"

"Slight problem. I can fix it. Just stay quiet."

"But—"

"Trust me!"

Without waiting for acknowledgment, Morosco turned and stepped into the hallway, making no effort to be quiet as he made his way toward the seventh door on the right.

SITTING AT THE TABLE FACING THE DOORWAY, THURGREN opened the bag Friedenthal had given him and took out several doughnuts, two cardboard cups and several napkins. As the footsteps drew closer, he unscrewed the top of the thermos. "Hope you don't take cream, Mr. Hanley," he called out. "Sugar I got, but no—"

Lewis Morosco stepped into the doorway.

Before Thurgren could say anything he saw Morosco press a finger to his lips, a command to be silent. Morosco flicked a finger upward. Thurgren set down the thermos and slowly stood up, staying quiet as Morosco tapped his finger against his lip again and again, warning him to be quiet.

Still not speaking, Morosco motioned him away from the table, then twisted slightly and pointed to the small of his back. When Thurgren didn't respond, Morosco stepped forward and whispered, "Trust me!" then grabbed him by the shoulder and turned him around. Before Thurgren realized what was going on, Morosco lifted his jacket, yanked the Beretta out of his waistband and shoved him roughly away, pulling the button microphone off at the same time.

Thurgren stumbled and tried to regain his balance. He turned back around and saw Morosco pointing the Beretta at him. The panic in Thurgren's eyes only increased when he saw the deadness in Morosco's, but he had little time to contemplate it.

Morosco put his other hand around the grip, extended his arms, and fired three shots in quick succession.

Thurgren was thrown backward by the force of the powerful weapon, hitting the far wall and collapsing in a heap on the ground.

He'd barely landed before Morosco ran to grab a small steel bar that had been leaning against the side wall. Hearing footsteps scrambling over loose rocks, he tossed it toward Thurgren's lifeless body, then turned around and flipped the table over, scattering the thermos and doughnuts.

The footsteps came closer. Morosco turned the table so the underside was facing away from the door.

The footsteps stopped. "Jesus Christ! Oh, Jesus Christ, Lewis! *Lewis!*"

Morosco stepped to the doorway and clapped a hand over Hanley's mouth. "The sonofabitch tried to kill me!" he whispered as he grabbed hold of Hanley's arm and dragged him into the room.

"Tried to—"

"This is bad, James," Morosco said loudly. "Very bad."

"Bad? Of course it's bad! What do you mean he—Oh, shit, Lewis! Is he dead? Oh my God! Is he dead?"

"I don't know!" Morosco replied, panic choking his voice. "Holy shit, I gotta get the FBI guys! I don't fucking believe this!"

"What FB—what the hell are FBI guys doing here? What the—" Even while he was blabbering incoherently, Hanley couldn't take his eyes off the limp body lying on the opposite side of the room. "Is he dead?"

"I don't know, James. Look . . ." Morosco lowered his voice and turned away from Thurgren's body. He pressed the Beretta into Hanley's hand. "Keep him covered, just in case. You hear me? I'm gonna get the agents in here right away!"

Hanley, too frightened and confused to resist, accepted the gun and let it hang limply from his hand.

"Keep it on him, James!" Morosco whispered, then ran out of the room.

MOROSCO RAN DOWN THE CORRIDOR, TURNED LEFT AND WAITED. Several seconds later he stepped out and almost collided with Friedenthal, who was entering from an adjacent hallway after running down the stairs.

"He got off three shots!" the assistant director said in amazement as they sped down the hall together. "Three shots, can you believe it?"

"You get good stuff on the tape?" Morosco asked breathlessly.

"Not a damned thing. All we heard was paper crinkling. Something must've gone wrong with the wire. Doesn't matter, though . . ."

Morosco slackened his pace and let Friedenthal get ahead, staying close as the FBI man turned into the doorway of the room, hanging back as he came to a stop.

"Drop it!" Friedenthal cried out, drawing his weapon.

Morosco stepped up behind him and looked in to see Hanley cowering in a corner behind the table, gun in hand, terror writ large across his perspiring features. "Wh-*what*?"

"I said, *drop it!*"

Hanley let the gun fall out of his hands. Staring at Friedenthal, he dropped back against the wall, arms raised.

Friedenthal looked over toward where Thurgren lay still, then back at Hanley. "You filthy bastard!" he growled through gritted teeth, then pointed his gun at him.

"No!" Hanley screamed, his hands shaking uncontrollably. "It wasn't me! I didn't do it, I swear to God." He pointed at Morosco. "It was—"

"Keep those hands up!" Morosco ordered.

"*He* shot him, not me! I wasn't even in the room! Ask him, go ahead!"

But Friedenthal was no longer listening. He was staring at the floor near Hanley's feet, confusion creeping up over his features. Ignoring Hanley's simpering pleas, he stepped forward and kicked away the gun Hanley had dropped, then bent to retrieve it.

"A Beretta?" he said, befuddled. "Oh, no . . ."

He ran to the far side of the room and knelt down, placing two fingers on Thurgren's neck. He went still, then turned to Morosco. "He's dead."

Morosco stepped into the room, stared at Thurgren for a second, then went after Hanley. "I'll kill you, you dirty—!"

But Friedenthal jumped forward and stopped him. "You don't understand, Lewis. He's really dead." Friedenthal held up the Beretta.

Morosco looked at him stupidly, then shoved him away and stepped to the table lying on its side. He moved around it and stared at the underside for a long second, then reached out and yanked away the gun that was still securely taped there.

Two special agents appeared in the doorway. "Take him into custody," Friedenthal said, pointing listlessly at Hanley without looking at him.

"For the love of God, you've got to believe me!" Hanley wailed piteously. "Morosco shot him, not me! I wasn't even here! Goddamnit, will you listen to me!"

One of the agents dragged him roughly to his feet as the other withdrew a pair of handcuffs from inside his jacket. "You have the right to remain silent . . ."

"Lewis, you can't do this to me!"

"Anything you say can and will . . ."

"*Morosco!* You bastard! I'll kill you!"

He was still screaming as the agents dragged him down the corridor.

"There was a struggle," Friedenthal said, surveying the overturned table, scattered doughnuts and napkins, and spilled coffee. "What the hell do you suppose happened? How could it have gone so wrong?"

Morosco shrugged helplessly, then looked around. "What's that?" he said, pointing.

Friedenthal walked over and picked up the steel bar, then slapped it on his open palm several times. "I had to guess, I'd say Hanley used this to get the gun away from Jubal." He looked at Thurgren's body. "He didn't want to carry a gun in the first place. Hated the damned things. Ah, Christ . . ."

CHAPTER THIRTY-NINE

OUTSIDE THE BUILDING, IN THE INCON-
gruously brilliant sunshine, Morosco and Friedenthal sat quietly on a pile of bricks and watched as
Hanley was shoved roughly into an FBI van.
Friedenthal held out a pack of cigarettes and Morosco accepted one gratefully. "What happened to
your gum?"

Friedenthal shrugged out a cigarette for himself and pulled it out from the pack with his teeth.
"Fuck the gum," he said around the cigarette as
he fumbled for a light.

Morosco tapped his cigarette against a
knuckle a few times, looking around sadly.

"You suppose Hanley smelled he was being
scammed?" Friedenthal said as he flicked open a
lighter.

"Don't see how," Morosco answered as he

leaned forward toward the flame. He lit up and drew a deep lungful, then straightened up. "I mean, he already knew he was being scammed—Hell, I told him so. But how could he have figured out I was really planning to double-cross him and load his gun with blanks?"

Friedenthal lit his own cigarette and thought about it. "Maybe he didn't."

"What do you mean?"

Friedenthal cocked his head to one side. "Maybe he didn't know one way or the other. Maybe you were really on his side, maybe you were on ours. He had no way to know for sure."

"I don't get you."

"Don't take this wrong, Lewis, okay? But the fact is, you gave him the perfect way to kill Jubal."

Morosco had the cigarette halfway to his lips and stopped. "What?"

"Two guys, alone, no witnesses. It's a Saturday, nobody's hanging around a construction site. Hanley puts a couple slugs into him and walks away. Tries to kill him just like he did twice before, and we can't touch him. Why? Because we don't have anything on tape. Hanley never said a word, and all we have is suspicions."

"Because I told him about the wire. Ah, Jesus . . ."

"Like I said, don't feel bad."

"But why did he use Jubal's gun? Why not the one I planted?"

"In case you were scamming him. He didn't know for sure. But Jubal's own gun? He knew that one was for real."

Seeing how awful Morosco felt, Friedenthal was quick to lighten his load. "But at least we caught him, Lewis. That was your doing, telling him the surveillance was half a mile away when we were upstairs all the time. Wasn't for that, he might've gotten away."

"Or he might not have shot Jubal at all."

"You can't think of everything, kid. It's part of the business we're in."

"Yeah," Morosco said, as though trying to convince himself. "Thurgren was on the job, he knew the risks."

"Sure. Comes with the territory."

Morosco brightened noticeably. "Important thing is, we got the guy. The operation was a success."

"That's the spirit! You've got a real career ahead of you, son."

Morosco looked at him curiously, wondering over the federal agent's seeming callousness following a botched assignment in which one of his colleagues and friends got killed. "Unfortunately, I'm not sure that's gonna be possible."

"How do you figure?"

Morosco inhaled and blew out a cloud of smoke. "The Fed chairman made it real clear, Harry. The most important thing is not to let the markets get rocked by all of this. Jubal wanted to trick Hanley into a deal that would let us slowly liquidate the company. Well, that didn't work. We might've let Hanley get away with his little white collar crime, but now he's a murderer. He has to go away."

"So?"

"We can't let the company collapse. It would defeat the whole purpose, and Jubal will have died for nothing."

Friedenthal scratched at his chin, then nodded slowly. "You're a right clear thinker, Lewis. We need to maintain perspective here. But what's it got to do with your career in the Enforcement Division?"

"I don't want to brag or anything, Harry, but I'm the only person alive who can run *Artemis*. We both know that."

"Ah. I get what you mean. You've got to take over the whole shootin' match."

"You see another way?"

"No, I don't. You're absolutely right. Sure do admire you, kid. Imagine having to give up a career in securities law just to fly around in corporate jets, live in a Fifth Avenue co-op, chase expensive tail all over the world . . ."

"Well you don't have to get sarcastic about it," Morosco said as he looked away.

"Nice try, kid."

It wasn't Friedenthal's voice. Morosco snapped his head back toward him. Catching something out of the corner of his eye, he twisted around even further to see what it was.

Jubal Thurgren was standing behind the brick pile, brushing himself off and staring at him.

Morosco gasped and went rigid, but recovered with admirable

speed, leaping to his feet and whipping out his gun in barely a half second. He pointed it at Friedenthal and Thurgren, trying to hold them both back while buying time to think.

As he glanced around frantically sizing up his escape options, Friedenthal calmly took the cigarette out of his mouth and flicked it onto the ground. "You didn't really think we were going to give any of you clowns real guns, did you, Lewis?"

Morosco looked at the gun, blinked, then spun around and took off toward the fence. Two very large special agents who'd been stationed just behind a Porta Potti were waiting to grab him, handcuff him and throw him into the back seat of a bureau vehicle, where he would tearfully confess everything on the slow trip to the federal holding facility in downtown Manhattan.

But in the same instant that his world began to crumble, Morosco knew that his apprehension had been planned for. There was only one possible way out of this site for him so he spun on his heel and ran in the other direction, right past Friedenthal and Thurgren, neither of whom was in any kind of shape to stop a twenty-something bullet train trying to escape a life sentence. Just to make sure, Morosco ran straight for them, veering off only after the two older men, startled by his unexpected action, reflexively jumped out of his way.

"Shit!" one of the two special agents yelped as they took off after him, a sentiment echoed by Friedenthal as he pulled a radio from his jacket pocket.

As one of the agents paused to get his own radio, Friedenthal shouted, "I got it! *Go!*" and began issuing rapid-fire instructions as the agents continued their pursuit.

Thurgren hurried to the side so he could get a glimpse of what was happening. Morosco had about a fifty yard lead as they headed for the ten-foot fence that protected the back side of the construction project, and he was nimbly running over a low pile of rubble. One of the agents yelled something, probably an order to halt, but Thurgren couldn't make out the words and Morosco didn't seem to care as he launched himself off the top of a broken cement block and hit the fence.

The slower of the two agents shouted again and then went down on one knee, arms straight out and pointing toward the fence. Just as the sun glinted metallically from his clasped hands, Thurgren heard *"No!"*

screamed at high volume from just off to his left, twisted to see Frieden-thal gesturing wildly, and then turned back to see the agent point the gun straight up and fire it into the air.

Morosco never even flinched, but was now spidering his way up the fence, barely bothering with firm toeholds as he jammed his feet against the links as best he could and climbed mostly with hand and upper body strength. As he reached the top and threw a leg over, the faster agent reached the bottom of the fence and slammed into it, rattling the flimsy temporary barrier. Morosco's body shook with the impact and his leg slipped off the upper pipe, but his hands had a firm grip. He waited out the vibration and once more got his leg over the top, quickly pulling himself up and over.

Again the agent shoved hard into the fence, and once more Morosco hung on and waited it out. Then he pushed back with his feet, let go, and dropped to the ground on the other side.

"Ninth Street!" Friedenthal said into the radio, then, "Stand by . . ."

Morosco whipped his head first to the left, then to the right, made a decision and took off.

"South!" Friedenthal shouted, then he grabbed a fistful of Thur-gren's jacket and tugged. "Let's go." As they started back toward the front entrance of the project at a fast walk, he said, "How'd you figure Morosco?"

"When I went to see Hanley," Thurgren answered, surprised at his shortness of breath, "tried to get him to cop to a plea. Expected him to crumble like a stale cookie when I told him who Paul Steffen really was, and he kind of did, but when he picked himself up off the floor it was my turn to come apart."

Friedenthal's radio crackled but he ignored it. "Because . . . ?"

"He said that it was Morosco who'd made him report Steffen to us."

"Morosco blew the scam?" Friedenthal stumbled slightly and slowed down. "But it was his idea!"

"Yeah," Thurgren said as he reached for Friedenthal's elbow. "But he set *us* up, too, don't you see? By making Hanley out to be a good citizen, he not only sealed himself in Hanley's good graces, he stopped us from shutting down *Artemis-5*. Then when he staged that bullshit rescue and pretended to save Hanley's life, he locked it up even further. He had us believing it was all in support of nailing Hanley, but the real reason was so that Morosco could eventually take over the entire company, which was his plan all along."

"And you were his last obstacle." They reached the front entrance and stopped, breathing heavily. "Problem is, there's no way to prove one way or the other that it was Morosco who told Hanley to report Steffen. Hanley isn't exactly a reliable witness."

"Especially considering he didn't report that phony rescue to the police. And it was Morosco who convinced him not to."

"But Morosco's covered himself on that one," Friedenthal saw right away. "He can say he was just doing his job, setting Hanley up for an obstruction charge."

"It was actually a whole lot more devious than that, Harry, but you're right again. There was no way to prove it. What are we doing?"

"Waiting for a ride. You were saying . . . ?"

Thurgren leaned against the fence and wiped his brow with the back of his sleeve. "Even after I told Hanley about Steffen, he and I both knew I didn't have enough against him yet, so I hit him with the shooting at the bowling alley. Told him he had the motive and he sure as heck had the opportunity because he was right there in Washington at exactly the right time. That left me with only the method to account for, the rifle. I asked him what he'd done with it. You know, flat out, just like that, so he'd fall apart and confess everything."

"Good tactic. Hang on." The radio had crackled again, and this time Friedenthal replied. "Usually shakes a guy up pretty good," he said to Thurgren when he'd finished. They heard the sound of an approaching car. "So?"

"He says to me, what the heck are you talking about? What rifle? And I tell him we searched his car and it wasn't there, so where did he dump it?"

The bureau car pulled up and screeched to a stop. "I think we got him cornered!" the driver said. "Let's move!"

"You told him that?" Friedenthal exclaimed as the two of them got in as fast as they could. The car squealed away from the curb before they'd barely gotten the door closed. "Jubal, it was an illegal search!"

"He's running along the wharves, sir," the driver reported. "We got him, 'less he decides to swim for Jersey."

"I don't want—"

"The agents know that, sir. He's got no place to go and he's getting winded. We'll be there in a minute, soon's we get around the closed streets."

"OKAY. LIKE I SAID, JUBAL, IT WAS AN ILLEGAL SEARCH. Hanley's car."

"Maybe. Maybe not. Hanley himself gave Morosco a spare set of keys."

"We've been through that."

"Christ!" Thurgren grabbed hold of an armrest as the car careened around a corner. "Doesn't make any difference anyway, Harry, because there was no search. It never happened."

"Sure it did. Morosco—"

"He never looked in the trunk. Never even went to where Hanley's meeting was."

A confused look started to overtake Friedenthal's face but it was short-lived. "Okay, sure, because Morosco already knew there'd be no gun there, since he himself took the shot, so why should he bother? Except you can't *prove* he didn't go and actually look in the trunk."

"Yes I can. Y'see—"

The car suddenly ground to a stop, Thurgren and Friedenthal both holding out their hands to keep from ending up in the front seat. "There they are!" the driver said, pointing to half a dozen scattered agents moving rapidly along an abandoned and crumbling pier building.

"He's climbing it," Friedenthal said as he opened the door and got out. "Dumb schmuck. You never go *up*."

"Too bad," Thurgren said. "I already approved his transfer to the Bureau."

"You're a real card. Let's go."

They came up to the base of the rotting pile of timbers masquerading as a building just as the agents began slowing down, seeing that Morosco was trapped. Two of the men stepped into the structure, then yelped as a piece of blackened board hurtled down and crashed into the wooden floor nearby.

"Hang back," Friedenthal ordered as everybody looked upward, searching for Morosco's exact location. "Where's he gonna go?"

The two agents obeyed, scrambling back out and onto the paved ramp abutting the building. A creaking sound from overhead and to the side made them all look in a different spot. "Come on, Jubal," Friedenthal said. "Let's go see if we can talk him into not getting himself shot down like a squirrel."

AS THEY CAREFULLY MADE THEIR WAY AROUND THE SIDE OF the structure, another piece of wood slammed into the ground. "What the—Lewis!" Thurgren shouted upward. "How much dumber can you possibly get!"

"You got nothing on me!" came the answer.

"Then how come you pointed a gun at me and Harry and took off! How come you're throwing sticks at us right now?"

"You guys scared me, that's why! Got the wrong idea and I wasn't about to stand there and try to explain!"

Thurgren looked at Friedenthal in amazement, then turned his face upward once again. "You tried to *kill* me, you sonofabitch!"

"Your word against mine!"

Thurgren looked down at his shoes and shook his head. "You believe this?"

"It was Hanley!" Morosco called down. "He's the one tried to do Jubal! You hear me, Harry?"

"That's *Mr. Friedenthal* to you!"

"He knows Hanley couldn't have shot me at the bowling alley, Lewis," Thurgren called out, "so why don't you just—"

"He ditched the rifle, Harry! That's why it wasn't in his trunk. I told you, he's not stupid, he must have—"

"You didn't look in the trunk, Lewis," Thurgren said.

"The hell I didn't!"

"You couldn't have!" Thurgren lowered his voice and said to Friedenthal, "He lied to us that night, pure and simple."

Friedenthal turned to Thurgren, mystified. "Say what?"

"What I was trying to tell you before. When I told Hanley we searched his car, he laughed right in my face."

"What made him so confident?"

"He didn't have his car in Washington. He'd flown down and taken cabs."

Friedenthal's eyes grew wide and he grabbed Thurgren's arm. "Can we prove that?"

"I've got the airline receipts and the cab company logs. It's a lock, and you and I both heard Morosco say he searched the car."

"Let's step off to the side."

"Where the hell are you going!" Morosco shouted down as he watched them move off.

"Don't answer," Friedenthal said. "Let him think we're giving up and the tough guys are gonna take over."

"Hey! I know they're not gonna shoot me!" A note of panic crept into Morosco's voice. "You wouldn't let 'em shoot me before! Goddamnit . . . !"

They came to a stop out of Morosco's sight line. "Let him get nervous," Friedenthal said. "So, you're in Hanley's office . . ."

"As soon as I heard that," Thurgren said, "about how his car couldn't have been searched, I just needed to get the heck out of there as soon as I could, so I made out like he'd called my bluff and won, and tried to slink away looking like an idiot."

"So why'd you go through all of this?" Friedenthal waved his hand around, indicating the whole complex setup that had occupied them for a full week. "We had Morosco right there, dead to rights."

"No, we didn't." Thurgren started to lean against a piling, then pulled away quickly when he realized it was covered with old protective pitch. "We didn't have enough that was hard and fast. It was all circumstantial, or conversations between just two people, and I wanted to nail this bastard with no loose ends. Gotta tell you, Harry, at that point, Hanley seemed downright harmless compared to Morosco."

"I can see that. So that's when you cut a deal with Hanley. So he'd cooperate in getting the goods on Morosco."

"Nothing of the sort. I didn't tell Hanley anything."

Startled, Friedenthal returned his gaze to Thurgren. "You mean to tell me he wasn't in on this last bit?"

"Had no idea."

"But how come?"

"Just in case I was wrong. In case I'd made a mistake in my thinking."

"Jubal!" came another desperate shout. "Where are you!"

Friedenthal stepped away and yelled back, "Will you shut the hell up? We're trying to have a conversation here!"

"*Jubal!*" came the answering, anxiety-choked cry.

Friedenthal moved back and folded his arms, then slowly began to nod his understanding. "Whole idea was to smoke out the real guy."

"Yeah." Thurgren took a deep breath and let it out. "Whichever one of them took the bait and shot me? That was our guy."

"Nice. But what about Hanley? He's still being held for attempted murder and he still thinks you're dead!"

"I'll tell you later. Can we get this guy down?"

"Huh?" Friedenthal seemed distracted for a second. "Oh, yeah, sure. MacNeil!"

An agent holding a high-powered rifle with a scope mounted over the barrel came running up. "Get him down," Friedenthal said, holding up a hand to stop the suddenly horrified Thurgren from protesting.

Thurgren knew there was no way to gauge the depth of Friedenthal's hatred of Morosco. The assistant director felt betrayed on several levels, not the least of which involved his error in judging the young man's character and placing so much faith in him.

But he wouldn't have him shot, would he?

The marksman smiled knowingly and walked unhurriedly around the side of the building. Shouldering the rifle and taking careful aim at the ceiling, he fired half a dozen rounds in quick succession. The deafening sound of the exploding rounds caromed off the brick buildings across the West Side Highway as a shower of splinters rained down out of the corroded rafters.

"*Holy fuck!*"

The screeched epithet rebounded its way out of the ancient ceiling, followed by a sound not unlike rats clawing their way across a pile of dried leaves. Several seconds later Morosco tumbled out of the woodwork and landed in a dusty heap on the floor, making no move to flee again as the rest of the agents moved in.

"Can we get a minute with him?" Thurgren asked Friedenthal.

The assistant FBI director waved the agents away, and he and Thurgren walked toward Morosco, who was sitting on the floor rubbing the side of his leg. Random bits of sawdust continued to sprinkle down nearby.

"WHY DON'T YOU GET UP OFF YOUR ASS," FRIEDENTHAL said, unable to hide the scorn in his voice. That he had harbored ambitions for Morosco only to see those hopes dashed, coupled with the demonstration of his fallibility in judging character, did nothing to improve his disposition.

Morosco rolled to his other side and stood up gingerly, wincing as he put weight on the leg, but he was able to get to a nearby sawed-off piling with only minor limping. He sat down and continued rubbing his leg, unable to meet the eyes of the two men who stood in front of him.

"We've known it was you for a while, Lewis. No sense wasting time denying it."

"Bullshit. You don't have a thing on me."

Friedenthal sighed, a sarcastic and faux-weary sound that telegraphed clearly his deep derision. "Okay, here we go," he said as he stepped over to a caved-in counter and leaned against it. "Einstein here's going to talk us into letting him go. Might's well give up right now and beat the traffic home, Jubal."

Thurgren looked around and located an empty packing crate. He dragged it over and sat down so he was facing Morosco. "The reason Hanley was late to that lunch with Steffen, when I got a cinder block dumped on my car? It was *your* idea for him to be late, to show Steffen he wasn't being intimidated. Meanwhile, you zipped yourself on over to the Cross Bronx Expressway and waited for me on the overpass, and because Hanley showed up late for lunch, I was supposed to think it was him." He waited a second. "But it was you, Lewis." Thurgren purposely used Morosco's first name to see if there was any personal feeling left at all, to see if there would be even the slightest expression of remorse.

"I didn't tell him to be late, and there's no way you can prove it. It's his word against mine! He was late because he was out trying to bash your skull in, so of course he's gonna try to pin it on me!"

"Maybe. But you're also the one who told Hanley to turn Steffen in when he first showed up. You knew the setup, you helped plan it, and then you deliberately blew it. That right there's good for ten to fifteen."

"That's a complete—"

"And after you talked us into setting up that phony rescue, you talked Hanley out of reporting it to either us or the police."

Morosco stopped rubbing his leg. "Bullshit again! Why would I do that?"

"Two reasons, starting with the fact that the plan was for you to bump Steffen's car a little, and then he'd drive off. Except you got a little enthusiastic and drove him right into a ditch. If you'd let Hanley report it, the police would have found the car, traced it, and that would have been the end of your plan to be a hero in his eyes."

Morosco frowned slightly. "So, good for me. I saved the whole scam, that bit of clear thinking. What the hell's your point?"

"Let's talk about *your* point instead. The real reason you didn't want Hanley to file a report was so I'd think he was the one who wanted me dead, that he wanted Steffen on the loose to finish the job of eliminating me in exchange for a piece of *Artemis-5*."

Morosco grunted and started rubbing again. "Chrissakes, Jubal . . . you gonna try to prove what was in my head?"

"Yeah, I am. You're the one who set up the time and place for Hanley's meeting with those software companies in Washington. It was just three miles from where I was going bowling, and at just the right time, too. That's something you knew but Hanley didn't."

"Still pretty flimsy, Jubal. You can't prove any of this." He was showing signs of starting to act smug, suspecting that maybe Thurgren didn't really have the goods.

"You're right. But I don't have to prove it, Lewis. Fact is, I don't really give a hoot who knows. I'm just telling you how I put it together. Like you searching Hanley's car while he was in that meeting, and we both know he didn't have his car in Washington."

"Well, I'll give you that one. I got lazy and didn't really go to search his car. I figured Hanley was smart enough to dump the rifle, so that's what I told you. Poor judgment, maybe, but you sure as hell aren't going to pin Steffen's shooting on me. You haven't even shown any motive, for Chrissakes! Why would I want to have done any of this!"

"You got a point there, Lewis. But all of that aside, how do you plan to worm your way out of the slugs you thought you were pouring into me back at the construction site?"

When Morosco didn't respond, Thurgren said, "The whole setup wasn't to nail Hanley, Lewis. It was to nail *you.*"

"So . . ." Friedenthal said as Thurgren stood up and kicked the carton away. "You want to talk a deal right now or take your chances at trial?"

Morosco stayed quiet for a few seconds, then looked from one to the other of them and laughed. "You got nothing, Harry. You don't even have a tape, remember?" Morosco could tell from Thurgren's expression that he was getting to him. "Far as anybody else knows, it was all just part of the sting, our little way of pinning it all on Hanley. Hey, you know what?" Warming to it now, he stood up to face them. "Now that I think about it, *you* were the one who masterminded framing Hanley for an attempted murder! Pull a scam like that, a federal officer? You'll die in prison!"

"Yeah, right." Thurgren shook his head and turned around, waving to the agents who were standing by out on the asphalt ramp. "See you in court, Lewis."

Morosco called his bluff and let him go. "Lookin' forward to it, Jubal."

As the agents moved in to arrest Morosco, Thurgren slumped heavily against the bureau car that had brought them to the scene.

"You okay, bud?" Friedenthal asked as he came up alongside.

Tight-lipped, Thurgren looked down at the ground. "May not have him as sewn up as we'd like, Harry. Can I have this car for a while?"

"Sure. You going to see Hanley?"

"Not yet."

"Good idea. Let him sweat a little."

"Yeah." But that wasn't the reason at all.

AUGUST 10

"HEY . . . !" THE GUARD YELLED, leaping forward to catch Hanley just as he was starting to fall over.

While the badly disoriented would-be mogul was trying to reacquire his grip on reality, or at least get back to a sitting position, Thurgren took a few seconds to pull himself together as well. "Didn't you have any pants his size?" he asked.

"Fit when he came in," the guard answered, one steadying hand on the teetering prisoner's shoulder.

It was difficult for Thurgren to believe that a human being with no physical ailments could have deteriorated so rapidly. Hanley's complexion had gone sallow and pasty, his dark eyes having taken on a paranoid, hunted look as they'd sunk deeper into his thinning face. A vein pulsed near his jaw, and his once-proud bearing had eroded into the hunched retreat characteristic of terrorist kidnap victims who feared random, unprovoked beatings.

Even as his world tried to swim back into focus, Hanley's eyes darted about frantically to assess imminent threats until they alighted once more on Thurgren. He started to sway again, but the guard's hand held him upright and may even have transmitted some strength into him. "I thought you were dead!" he whispered hoarsely.

"Yeah, sorry about that. Didn't anybody tell you?"

Hanley answered with a slow shake of his head, apparently not having caught that it was a sarcastic, purely rhetorical question.

"You okay now, pal?"

Hanley twisted toward the guard, figured out who he was, then nodded unconvincingly. The guard patted his shoulder and took his hand away.

"Man's a damned mess," he said softly as he walked past Thurgren. "I'll be right outside."

As the door clicked shut, Thurgren shrugged off his coat and draped it over the back of the chair facing Hanley across a small aluminum card table. He could sense the prisoner clicking through the implications presented by the startling reincarnation of a man he'd spent the last five days assuming had been shot to death, and also autonomically girding himself for a battle of wills.

"I thought all along it might have been you who tried to kill me at the bowling alley," Thurgren said as he loosened his tie and sat down, "but to tell you the truth, I didn't think you had it in you." He waited until he could sense a reaction in Hanley's eyes, then said, "Guess I was wrong."

Already stretched to the end of his rope, Hanley was unprepared for the sudden plunge back into the psychotic abyss. His eyes grew wide as he struggled to find his voice. "You were right there!" he choked. "You know it was Muldowney who shot you! I mean, who tried to . . . who thought he . . . Thurgren, you know I didn't pull the trigger!" He half rose out of his chair. "I wasn't even in the room!"

Thurgren waved him back down and waited until he obeyed.

"James, Muldowney's real name is Lewis Morosco. He works for me. Has for the last two years. He didn't try to kill me; he was just helping to set you up."

Hanley's fevered brain was in no shape to deal with what Thurgren was telling him. The more he tried to fit the pieces together, the more he felt he was drowning in confusion. Lance Muldowney had already confessed to him his dual identity. Thurgren supposedly knew he was doing that. Then Lewis Morosco, or whatever the hell his real name was, tried to give him a way to get out of the trap that was being set, except that all he'd really been doing was setting it further. But was pretending to shooting Thurgren part of that, or . . . ?

Wait. *Wait.* Thurgren had just told him that Muldowney was really Morosco. But Thurgren knew that Morosco had already told him that. Why did he think this would be news? Unless that's part of the scam. Yeah, that's it! *He's trying to confuse me!*

Except he knows I didn't shoot him, so what's the point? Lunacy. All of it, just madness. *Except Thurgren isn't a lunatic and he isn't an idiot. And therefore . . .*

Ah, Christ . . . "You're trying to pin attempted murder on me!"

"Now why would I want to do a thing like that, James?"

"Because you don't have anything else, that's why!" Hanley blinked rapidly to try to clear his head and at least give off an aura of lucidity. "You had no case, so you and Muldowney are framing me for attempting to kill you. Don't bother to argue, Thurgren, because you and I both know I didn't so much as point a gun at you!"

"But you were going to."

"Bullshit. *Bullshit!* I had no intention of killing you!"

"Then why did you agree to—"

"Because I knew you were coming wired, that's why! With half a dozen FBI guys listening I was going to sing a song of innocence and make you look like a complete idiot!"

Thurgren rocked his head back and forth a few times. "I'm not buying it."

"Thurgren, will you listen to me? Morosco's your criminal! He's the one that engineered this whole thing!"

"Of course he is! That's what I've been trying to—"

"No, no! That's not—He wants to take over my company, don't you see? That's what this is all about!"

Thurgren laughed and leaned back on his chair. "He's a federal officer, Hanley. How many times do I have to tell you that!"

"Just listen, goddamnit!"

And as Thurgren rolled his eyes and shook his head and hauled out a half dozen other expressions of incredulity, disbelief and derision, Hanley laid it all out, everything Thurgren needed to perfect indictments against the spectacularly larcenous and cold-blooded Lewis Morosco.

It was Morosco who'd convinced Hanley to report the first Steffen approach to the feds, Morosco who'd gone off to drop a cinder block on Thurgren's car while making it look like Hanley had done it. Thurgren mentally filled in some other details Hanley couldn't have known about. It was Morosco who had shot Steffen in the bowling alley parking lot, and the only reason he hadn't planted the weapon and framed Hanley for it was because he'd neglected to check if Hanley had driven his car down rather than flown.

And Thurgren realized one other thing as Hanley ranted on: Morosco had probably been going for both him and Steffen at the same time. The only reason he hadn't succeeded was because of the hesitation when he'd been surprised by the two of them having switched places in the car.

As Hanley ended up his diatribe with the only possible bottom-line conclusion that fit all the facts, Thurgren knew for a certainty he was right. "He betrayed you and the Commission on his way to engineering the complete takeover of *Artemis-5*."

Hanley had been accurate in every detail, providing the complete picture of Morosco's means and motives he'd partially worked out since he'd been arrested and was finally able to fill in today.

Thurgren was quick to reward his diligence appropriately. "Yeah, whatever."

As Hanley sat back, mortified and seized with helpless desolation, Thurgren continued, "Are you through now? Because I'm here to offer you a deal: ten years in exchange for your complete cooperation in quietly dismantling *Artemis-5*. That's against a certain life sentence for trying to kill a federal law enforcement officer." He leaned in and whispered. "Maybe you didn't shoot at me at the construction site, but you're the one who dropped a brick on me and tried to shoot me at that bowling alley."

"It wasn't me, Thurgren!" Hanley bleated once again. "You were a pain in my ass, but I never wanted you dead!"

"So let me ask you this: When Paul Steffen ran you off the road and you thought he'd tried to kill you, why didn't you report that to us?"

"Muldown—Morosco told me not to!"

"So what? Was he your lawyer?" Thurgren shook his head dismissively. "You should have reported it, James. Thing is, you figured that maybe Steffen would still try to kill me, which would be doing you quite a favor, wouldn't it? Because with me dead you had no more obstacles in your way."

"That's not true," Hanley said halfheartedly.

"Maybe, maybe not," Thurgren responded casually, relishing the moment, "but look at it this way: Ten years for the scam you pulled with *Artemis-5* is a damned good deal. You should be happy you're getting off that easy."

Hanley, thoroughly beaten, still had enough of his marbles left to know he had no real choice. "How do we do this?"

"You're about to get a tender offer. Somebody wants to buy your company."

"Yeah? Now why would I want to accept an offer like that?"

"Because if you don't, we're going ahead with our indictments. You'll lose—you already know that—and you'll spend the rest of your life in a federal penitentiary."

"And if I cooperate I just do ten years." A glimmer appeared in Hanley's eyes. "Doesn't smell right, Thurgren. If you have me dead to rights, why are you offering a deal like that?"

Because the federal government doesn't frame people. Or at least I don't. "So you'll stay quiet. That's part of the bargain. Open your mouth and we'll throw you down a black hole forever."

"And your way, nobody gets hurt."

"That's it. Well, if you don't count Morosco. Him we crash down on with the vengeance of God."

Hanley's ears perked up. "Yeah. He tried to kill you."

"Maybe. But he played us both for suckers. The only side he was on was his own." What Thurgren realized and Hanley hadn't come around to yet was that Morosco had had the whole thing wired so that no matter which side came out on top, he'd come out smelling like a rose. "Why do you think he set up that little rescue bit?"

"He said that was your idea."

"I bet he did." Thurgren told Hanley that Morosco talked him into letting him stage the rescue, ostensibly to get himself in tighter with Hanley so he could be a better spy. But Morosco's real reason was to ensure his own position in the company once he realized the SEC might not be able to stop Hanley.

If the government won, Morosco would be a hero at the SEC. If Hanley won, he'd be the number two guy at *Artemis-5.com*. When Hanley's confrontation with the SEC ended, Morosco had an open choice to either stay behind with the government officials or leave with Hanley, depending on who came out on top. He'd left with Hanley. "And he might have stayed there, too," Thurgren finished, "except that being number two wasn't good enough. He might've gotten away with everything if he wasn't so damned greedy."

"But he took a huge risk," Hanley said. "He had to know that if I ever found out about it I'd kick him out on his ass. Didn't he think you'd tell me at some point, just out of spite if you couldn't indict me?"

"Of course. That's why he framed you for attempting to kill me." *And I couldn't have told you even if I wanted to,* Thurgren declined to explain. *Revealing the identity of an undercover operative would land me in prison so fast I wouldn't know what hit me. And, frankly, we don't like to publicize failed operations.*

Despite his predicament, Hanley had to smile in admiration of Morosco's deviousness. Thurgren knew Harry Friedenthal had judged that aspect of his personality correctly.

"How do you plan to fund a forty-five-billion-dollar tender offer anyway?" Hanley asked.

Thurgren had at first given some thought to simply suspending trading in *Artemis-5.com*'s stock and forcing a liquidation. Once he'd identified all the assets and frozen them, he could sell them off and distribute the proceeds along with the company's remaining cash. But aside from the huge amount of money that current shareholders would lose, the effect on the market of such a dramatic and unprecedented maneuver might have been devastating. There would hardly be a tech stock unaffected, and the cancerous lack of investor confidence would metastasize throughout the whole system. Healthy companies would suffer right along with the ones that were more deserving of an early demise.

That thinking had given Thurgren a possible path to avert the disaster. He had asked himself, who were the companies most likely to be adversely affected by the inevitable crash, and who among them had the means to help prevent it?

"It's not going to be a forty-five-billion-dollar offer," he now explained to Hanley. "More like thirty or thirty-five." SEC representatives had descended on three dozen CEOs of the biggest, cash-richest and most heavily capitalized technology companies and informed them that the gravy train was about to run off the side of a mountain. The only way to stop it, the SEC people said, was for all of them to form a consortium and buy *Artemis-5.com*, which they'd be able to do for much less than the current value of all the outstanding stock, and divide the assets from a quiet liquidation among them.

"Why doesn't the government bail *Artemis-5.com* out," Hanley wanted to know, "just like it did that car company a while back?"

Because the automaker was a vital national asset, came Thurgren's answer, with several hundred thousand employees and whole communities dependent on its survival, and it was worth preserving. *Artemis-5.com*, on the other hand, was a fraud, and Uncle Sam was not about to dip into his cookie jar to support a fraud that was doomed to fail regardless.

When the proposed consortium members asked what would happen afterward, they were told that *Artemis-5.com* would simply cease to exist, and instead of $45 billion worth of vapor assets residing within a single company, one billion would be housed in each of thirty-five companies. If they worked it right—and the SEC would take pains to help them in that regard—they might not be any worse off than before they'd bought into the consortium. At least on paper. And since paper was all many of them were worth anyway . . .

"You'll hear the screaming all the way to Washington," Hanley protested. "Shareholders will go berserk when they find out the company was sold out from under them at less than what it's worth."

"Your little *dot-bomb* of a company isn't worth the powder it would take to blow it to hell."

"The investors don't think so."

"A chance we'll have to take."

"And the board will never approve it, anyway."

Thurgren laughed at that one. Not only did they approve it, he told Hanley, they each signed over all of their personal shares. "Just as you're going to do," Thurgren said as he reached around to get some papers from his jacket pocket. "It's that or they face indictment on charges of colluding to fraudulently manipulate the stock market. We'll announce the tender offer tomorrow, which will anger the investors, but at least they won't lose everything. Most of them will get seventy or eighty cents on the dollar."

"They won't get anywhere near that!"

"I'm talking about a percentage of what they spent to buy the stock, not what they think it's worth now."

"But they were betting on vastly more."

"Tough. It's not like they worked for it. All they did was log on to some *dot-com* broker and hit a few keys. The uproar will die away quickly."

"What makes you so sure?"

"Guess we'll see, won't we?"

Hanley still hadn't made a move to look at the papers. "One thing I don't understand: When Muldowney—okay, Morosco—when Morosco left with me after the SEC meeting, how come you didn't expose him right there?"

For one thing, Thurgren hadn't been dead sure Morosco had turned. And if he had, Thurgren wanted to wait until he could prove it for certain and nail him right along with Hanley. Even if they couldn't get Hanley, Thurgren was going to see to it that Morosco went down anyway. "I did make sure he kept getting his paychecks, though. Gonna make it easier in the end to bust him for obstruction."

"Obstruction?" A light went on somewhere behind Hanley's eyes. "That's what you have him on, after all of this? Obstruction of justice?"

Thurgren shrugged. "What about it?"

"You don't have a case against him, do you, Thurgren!"

"What are you talking about! Of course we—"

"No, you don't! If you did, you'd be hitting him with attempted murder and three dozen other serious charges! Except you can't charge us both with attempted murder at the same time, so"—Hanley pulled repeatedly at his lower lip, his eyes darting back and forth until they settled once again on Thurgren—"you don't have a damned thing you can prove!"

"I was an eyewitness, remember?"

His desultory tone let Hanley know he wasn't convinced. "You were the only eyewitness, Thurgren, and you're not entirely credible. You've been out to get me for months, and who's to say you didn't stretch things a little to make a case? And as for young Morosco, well, betrayal can make you do some pretty questionable things. When a jury learns what he did—or what you allege he did—how much faith do you think they'll have in your testimony against him?"

Hanley was at least partially right. In a sense, Thurgren had been hoisted by his own petard, because he'd been so clever about ferreting out who'd been willing to kill him that he may have left some holes when it came time to actually making a solid legal case. "Yeah, well, we can talk about Morosco all day, but what's important right now is that *you're* history, and you know it." He shoved the papers toward Hanley and dropped a pen on top of the stack. "Sign, before I lose my patience." In reality, Thurgren was disconsolate beneath his bravado. Although it was over for Hanley, since there wasn't actually going to be an attempted murder charge, his troubles with Morosco might not be. Hanley was right about the problem in pursuing a successful prosecution.

Hanley fingered the documents but made no move to lift the pen. If he had any awareness of how fast Thurgren's heart was beating in anticipation of getting his signature, he didn't show it, but just sat there, gazing at the documents. "How long do you figure you can maintain the myth, Thurgren?" he finally said.

"What myth?"

"All of it." Hanley waved a hand to the side, as though meaning to encompass the enormity of everything outside the walls of the jail. "The whole illusion. All the sweet-sounding lies and the fairy tales we all want to believe in."

Thurgren pressed his lips together and forced himself to calmness, not wanting to betray his anxiety. "What are you talking about?"

Hanley picked up the pen and tapped it on the table. "Experts troop across the television all day long, from three hours before the market opens until well after it closes. Financial reporters are forever asking brokers what it all means, what should people be doing." He looked up and smiled strangely. "They ask *brokers*, Thurgren! Asking a broker if people should be in stocks is like asking an auto salesman if this is a good time to buy a car. In the entire history of financial reporting no broker ever advised getting out, because they only make money if people stay in, and yet nobody ever calls bullshit on them! Now why is that?"

"You really want to talk philosophy right now?" *Even though I agree with you a hundred percent.*

"When the market's up they tell us to buy and ride the wave. When the market's down they tell us this is a great time to find bargains, to buy *on the dip*. Every day when the market closes the tube is flooded with people telling us precisely why things happened during the day, and how it was all so easily foreseeable, except that none of them foresaw any of it until it was all over, like those guys at Caltech who tell you how easily predictable the earthquake was after it happened. They've even got us thinking a crash is a good thing because we've been trained to call it a *correction* instead."

Thurgren stayed quiet, so Hanley continued on his own. "Truth is, Thurgren, nobody knows anything."

"So how come people on the Street make money?"

"The only reason a Wall Street big shot makes more money on the market than a cab driver is because he's using other people's dough. Market goes up, he makes money. Market goes down, he still makes money."

"And all those guys who buy the right stocks?"

Hanley laughed, then shook his head and smiled ruefully. "When I was growing up in Brooklyn, there was this guy with nothing but a phone number who'd pick horses for you for five bucks. What he did, he gave all his customers different horses, so he had the whole field covered. One out of every nine of his customers thought he was a genius when they won, and would keep paying him five bucks even when he kept losing for them. But every time he picked a winner, they were more convinced he was a genius and they kept on paying. And obviously a few of them won often, and won a lot, and they thought he was psychic. But it was all complete bullshit, just the natural consequence of simple statistics."

The smile disappeared. "Nobody knows anything, and the name of the game is getting people to believe you know it all. Just ask yourself this, Thurgren: Why on Earth would anybody who can predict the market ever tell anybody else? If any one of those fraudulent fuckers really knew what he was talking about, the last goddamn thing in the world he'd be doing is telling *us* about it!" Hanley picked up the pen again and twirled it in his fingers. "What about the Staller situation?"

A throbbing began in the back of Thurgren's neck. "Still unresolved. Everything's frozen, including covering short sales and option settlements."

"A rescission solution? Setting the clock back?"

Not even remotely feasible. For one thing, Staller was fighting the charges against him with everything he had, and there was no way to start ordering anybody to take back trades unless he was convicted or confessed. For another, things had gone too far and even tracking every transaction was only a pipe dream. Because of the use of the Internet to bypass traditional channels, there was no central mechanism for recording trades and deals, and therefore no way to retrace what had happened. It was even becoming apparent that the SEC would have to let settlement of short sales and options take place, then freeze everything again and hope to get it sorted out even as Staller went to trial. "Not looking too good."

Hanley nodded his understanding and drummed his fingers on the table. "I can bail them out," he said after a long silence.

Thurgren had guessed that Hanley would get around to that sooner or later. Fed Chairman Phillip Goldwith had been vehement in his opposition to letting anybody rescue the participants in the bear trap, especially since doing so would mean delivering truckloads of money to the patently criminal Burton Staller.

Thurgren had argued with him, taking the position that shares of *TillYouDrop.net* still had to be returned to the brokerages who had loaned them out to the short sellers, and those brokerages had not taken part in Staller's scheme, so why should they get hurt? Furthermore, Staller had offered to cut his thousand-a-share demand in half if the charges against him were dropped. It would then take only a billion to cover everything and stop several firms from getting killed when they were forced to cover for the essentially penniless New Mexican legislators.

"What do you mean?" Thurgren asked.

"I mean, I can make this situation go away. And please, don't give me any more bullshit about some ridiculous consortium of tech companies, because that scenario is about the dumbest goddamned thing I've ever heard, although I do appreciate the first good laugh I've had since you had me locked up in here."

The consortium was a truly brilliant plan, and every company approached about the idea had essentially—and in some case, literally—told the SEC officials to go jump in a lake. Even as a phony story to try to get Hanley to confess and avoid a dangerously public trial, it was obviously already a failure; Thurgren had no intention of sticking to it any longer. "Bailing everybody out will cost in excess of a billion dollars. You can't spend that much of *Artemis-5*'s money and—"

"I don't have to.

"—and besides, you've been fired, remember?"

"Actually, no, I haven't."

"Figures. Just another piece of your fraudulent—"

"I can make it happen," Hanley said, as if Thurgren had never interjected a snide comment. "I can fix the Staller thing. To my investors, I'm still a hero."

"Nothing's going to happen."

"You're going to let those firms go down? Or let Burton Staller end up owning them?"

Thurgren had lost the argument with Goldwith, who'd offered to wager a considerable sum that the brokerages didn't have clean hands but probably commingled their own accounts and funds with those of their clients, effected short sales contrary to exchange regulations, and at the very least failed to exercise due diligence in assessing whether their clients could cover their short sales of *TillYouDrop.net* if things went south. "They saw the quick buck and they went for it," the chairman had said. "Cut their own throats, and I'll be damned if we're going to let Hanley steal a billion smackers from his own shareholders to buy his way out of prison by making them whole."

There was another problem, one that Thurgren preferred not even to think about, and that was how they were going to make the case against Staller. None of his victims, including Hanley, would testify against him because to do so would mean admitting they'd willingly taken part in an insider trading scam, even though they hadn't known how it would be turned against them. The only exceptions were the two New Mexican state senators who'd been promised transactional immunity, and their former colleagues had already mounted a campaign to discredit them.

As Friedenthal had told him on many occasions, "If you're going after a king, you'd better make sure you kill him." Given all the people who Staller had made rich, merely harassing him without incontrovertible proof of serious lawbreaking might start an insurrection that could set the SEC back fifty years.

Hanley eyed Thurgren slyly. "You know what I think, Thurgren? I think you don't really want to see me in prison."

"Is that so."

"Yes. You used to think I was a killer, and when that turned out not to be the case, I think some of the wind went out of your sails. In fact, I'm guessing some part of you may even have a little admiration for what I managed to do."

"You're no different from Burton Staller."

"Don't compare me to Staller! He's a thief and a gangster who conspired with corrupt politicians to con people out of their money."

"And you conspired with yourself to do the same."

"No I didn't! If all of you had just kept your hands off nobody would've gotten hurt. *You're* the ones responsible for what's going to happen to all those people, not me!"

Thurgren had no immediate response forthcoming, and Hanley leaned back on his chair and eyed him carefully. "This marketplace you preside over was not of my making, Thurgren, nor was the avarice it feeds on. In your quiet moments, do you ever step back and consider what's really at play here?"

"I have no idea what you're talking about." He knew exactly what Hanley was talking about.

The broken and dispirited ex-mogul sighed and looked down at his hands. "You know, there were a few years there when I really thought things were changing. People were looking beyond themselves, or at least trying. They started to worry about the environment, and people outside our own borders, old people and poor people . . ."

He turned and looked at the small window, so grimy he couldn't tell whether it was sunny or cloudy outside. "But it seems like, I don't know . . . once we finally put a man on the moon, we don't give a shit about things that really matter anymore. For a while there it was almost embarrassing to be rich. People scaled down their cars, their houses, they wore simpler clothes, less jewelry . . . and now?" He looked back at his hands. "We're back to worshipping money, and it's worse than it ever was. People build houses that would have embarrassed a Roman emperor and we admire them for it. They buy Ferraris and sports teams and private islands and people pay them money to give speeches to learn their secrets. Sure, they give to charities, but it's just a contest to see who can afford to give away the most money, and every donation comes complete with its own press conference."

"So what the hell makes you any different, Hanley? Aside from the fact that you blew it, I mean."

"Not a damned thing," Hanley answered in a voice that threatened to break. "That's the whole thing, don't you see? I got caught up in it and didn't think for a single second *why*. Because there aren't any brakes anymore. There's nobody out there criticizing all this hell-bent-for-leather frenzy to get rich as hell, quick as hell, because everybody's too goddamned busy trying to do the same thing!"

"Well . . ."

"You think you're any different, Thurgren?"

"I—" Thurgren shifted uncomfortably. "I'm not saying that—"

"Forget it. You want to know why you hate me so much?"

"I never said I hated you."

"It's because I'm you without the chains."

The concurrency of the Staller matter with that of *Artemis-5.com* had predisposed Goldwith toward some leniency with respect to Hanley who, after all, hadn't set out to rake his investors over the coals, had treated his people well, at least if you didn't count Jackie Toland, and had in fact been exceptionally magnanimous with several worthy charities. In addition, he'd been genuinely horrified by Paul Steffen's ersatz assassination proposal, and taken steps to address it. "So nick him a little," Goldwith had said. "Disgorge all his profits, leave him a pittance, throw him out of the business . . . but why lock the guy up?"

"He made a load of helium look like forty billion dollars!" Thurgren had retorted.

"So did half the tech companies on the NASDAQ. In ten years they'll be making movies about him, Jubal, and you and I will look like a couple of putzes."

Hanley waited to see if Thurgren would respond to the last barb he'd thrown, and then played his last card. "Let me walk and I'll not only help with the Staller situation, I'll give you Morosco."

"Give me—" Thurgren couldn't keep surprise from capturing his features. "What do you mean, give me Morosco!"

"I mean, give you evidence that could put him away, because you know you don't have a case yet. If I give you one, you cut me free."

Thurgren tried to hide his excitement by making it look like he needed a moment to think. "Only if we convict."

Hanley shook his head. "Too much out of my control. What if you decide to let him go, or he beats it on his own?"

"Then let me hear what you've got."

"You must be kidding. Where's my assurance you'll hold up your end?"

"Don't you have anything you can hold back?"

Hanley thought about it, then nodded his assent. "He stole ten million dollars from the company."

"Really." Thurgren was immediately deflated by the obvious desperation move.

"Yes, really. Back when things were moving so fast nobody had time to make sure the proper controls were in place, he had a check for ten million drawn out of one of our investment capital accounts. It ended up in a Swiss bank and Morosco was the only one with access to it."

Thurgren's heart rate rose again. "And you can prove that?"

"He put down the company address instead of his own, maybe because he was already planning his move to that fancy duplex. The bank sent a confirmation slip once the check cleared, and it got back to the office before Morosco did. I opened it, and I still have it. You get it when we have a deal, and I'll agree to testify."

Thurgren tried to think of a flaw even while hoping he couldn't. "He could always say he was doing it on the company's behalf. To protect some cash in case something went wrong. Or that it was evidence for the SEC once we decided to prosecute you."

"Oh, yeah? Then I guess he must have reported the withdrawal and transfer to you. Right?"

Wrong. "And the Staller bear trap?"

Hanley, growing more confident by the minute, stood up and stretched. "You remember telling me *TillYouDrop* owned an obscure patent . . . ?"

EPILOGUE

God has made us the master organizers of the world to establish system where chaos reigns. It is God's great purpose made manifest in the instincts of the race whose present phase is our personal profit, but whose far off end is the redemption of the world and the Christianization of mankind.

—ALBERT BEVERIDGE,
Senatorial campaign speech, September 16, 1898

What the hell was *he* smoking?

—PHILLIP GOLDWITH

CHAPTER FORTY-ONE

"BULLSHIT!"

Thurgren polished off the last of his beer and raised the glass to the bartender, who was pre-occupied with a financial talk show on the over-head television and didn't notice. "Swear to God," he said in response to Friedenthal's epithet as he waved the glass back and forth.

A sound like a hammer hitting a piece of hard wood came from behind them, followed by a frustrated cry of *"Shit!"*

Friedenthal winced and hunched down without turning around. A few seconds later a fist appeared between them and pounded the bar, causing the bartender to turn around.

" 'Nother gutter ball?" Thurgren asked.

"Hell did you expect, wiseguy? You try bowling with fresh stitches."

"Chrissakes, Steffen," Friedenthal said. "Been four weeks and those stitches have been out for three. When're you gonna stop feeling sorry for yourself?"

"When my disability runs out. Bullshit what?"

The bartender finally tore himself away from the television and poured two beers. "Hit my bar again, you're gonna bowl lefty," he said to Steffen as he slid them over.

"Bite me. You want this place audited? Bullshit what?"

"Morosco swears Hanley *told* him to deposit that ten million in Switzerland," Thurgren explained. "Says he came back and delivered the confirmation slip to Hanley himself."

Steffen took a long slug of beer and wiped his mouth on his sleeve. "Bullshit is right. Next thing, he's gonna tell us Hanley killed Kennedy."

"It's like a divorce," Friedenthal mused. "Two people so in love suddenly doing their damnedest to tear each other's throats out. Wonder where Hanley's gonna turn up next?"

"He's forbidden from going anywhere near a share of stock for ten years," Thurgren said.

Friedenthal responded with a cynical snort honed over his many years in law enforcement, "I still don't understand how he got that Staller business straightened out. Something about a patent?" He shook his head and reached for some salted nuts. "Too complicated for me."

"Not complicated at all. The patent was on these goggle-type thingies for looking at computer displays in three dimensions. Staller bought the invention in *TillYouDrop*'s name so he'd have it when he dumped everything else he owned. From what Hanley told me, the darned thing's worth billions."

"Hanley would tell you your spit's worth billions."

"Except in this case, he may be right."

Staller had settled Hanley's civil lawsuit by selling *TillYouDrop* to *Artemis-5.com*, complete with the rights to the CyberSpex device. With the stroke of a pen in a judge's chambers, *Artemis-5* was transformed into a legitimate technology company with the rights to a phenomenally valuable invention and exclusive development agreements with universities and research institutions throughout the world, which Hanley had negotiated and paid for early in the company's genesis, even though he'd had no idea at the time what he'd end up using them for.

As part of the deal, Hanley agreed to distribute blocks of *Artemis-5.com* shares to the brokerages that had fronted shares of *Till-YouDrop.net* to short sellers but never got them returned. That, along with the illegal profits that had been seized from the New Mexico legislators, added to the proceeds from the forced breakup of Burton Staller's vast empire, would pretty much get everybody back to square one at about seventy-five cents on the dollar, the other twenty-five cents being a fairly modest tuition fee for having learned an important lesson and not gotten completely wiped out in the process.

"So," Steffen said, "is young Lewis going to one of those cushy country club prisons?"

"He's going to Sing Sing."

"Sing Sing!" the FBI agent gasped. "Does *he* know that?"

"He never asked," Thurgren replied helplessly. "What can I tell you?"

Along with a new promotion for Thurgren at the SEC, they were celebrating the withdrawal that morning of two lawsuits that had been filed in federal court and which had threatened to undermine everything Thurgren and the Fed had worked out.

The first one was aimed at preventing the forced bankruptcy of *TillYouDrop* and had been filed by the small handful of its shareholders who were not Burton Staller. The suit had become moot once the company had been sold and those shareholders had been paid off in enough *Artemis-5.com* stock to keep them from pressing the case. They didn't get all of their money back but, strangely, were not complaining, which probably had something to do with the fact that few of them would have survived the audits of their personal finances that Chairman Goldwith had assured them would be an integral part of the government's case should they persist in their protests.

The now-defunct suit had been handled by Jackie Toland and Nicholas Simonson, who'd joined up to form Cyberlegis, the first law firm ever not to be named after any of its attorneys. They'd sought to capitalize on their recent, prestigious corporate stints at *Whoopie!.com* and *Artemis-5.com*, keeping off their resumes that Simonson had been fired and Toland had run the instant she'd smelled trouble. More cynical observers raised the question of why those two corporations, which at various times used the services of nearly every major law firm in New York, treated Cyberlegis like a legal leper colony and wouldn't so much as let one of their janitors get a will prepared by the firm, but it passed quickly.

The other suit had been more troublesome. It was a class action to block the transfer of *Artemis-5* stock to brokers who had inadvertently funded Staller's bear trap. Along with several hundred individual investors and brokerage firms, plaintiffs had included board members such as the SCalERS employee retirement system and several of the biggest and most powerful charities in the country, along with Caltech and four other prestigious universities, all of whom had benefited enormously from the company's largesse and stood to lose a good deal of it if so many shares were given away. The suit claimed that *Artemis-5.com* had never violated SEC rules even though it had no products because it was a legitimate 'mutual fund' no different in substance or structure from thousands of others that simply invested money on behalf of clients, and there was no justification for forcing its participation in whatever cockamamie plan had been devised to save the markets.

Goldwith was not interested in sharing with the plaintiffs all the details of what had happened, and how close these investors had come to losing their shirts. For one thing, he didn't feel it prudent to explain why, if it wasn't for this arrangement, they'd owe Burton Staller half a billion dollars. For another, owing Staller that money would actually be beside the point because they'd have no company in the first place.

But despite his reticence to reveal matters better left unspoken, the suit had been abruptly and inexplicably withdrawn anyway and nobody seemed to have any idea why.

Not even Jubal Thurgren.

"Why?" Friedenthal asked.

"Beats me," Thurgren said. "What I'm guessing, those *Artemis-5* investors somehow got themselves around to taking a cold, hard, business approach to the situation. You look at it that way, they're probably a lot better off living with the arrangement Hanley engineered than taking their chances with a possible total loss, but, like I say"—he took a deep swallow of his fresh beer—"I'm just guessing."

The people gathered in the bowling alley this night didn't really much care what the reasons for dropping the suit were, since they'd had little to celebrate for quite some time. Friedenthal's mild curiosity departed as quickly as it had arrived, and they soon forgot the matter.

FED CHAIRMAN GOLDWITH HAD BEEN RIGHT IN HIS ASSESS-ment of the market system as a self-correcting and essentially stabilizing force, especially when it was policed by tenacious keepers of the faith and protectors of the public weal. He more than anyone had appreciated, and been greatly amused by, the irony of a newly-born and already healthy *Artemis-5.com* having been crafted out of the chicanery of two of the greatest con artists in Street history.

As a cornerstone of making the master plan work, Goldwith had banked heavily on the fact that nobody involved had really learned anything at all during the riotous imbroglio. He was not disappointed. Within hours of the announcement that *TillYouDrop.net* and its Cyber-Spex technology were to be sold to *Artemis-5.com*, the share price of the newly structured company rose so spectacularly that each time its stock symbol rolled off the right edge of the moving ticker board, it was worth more than when it had appeared on the left. Goldwith suspected that hardly anybody who was lining up to buy the stock at any price had the slightest understanding of what that technology was or what it was good for, but he was moderately confident that, this time around at least, there was some real value to justify the company's existence . . . at least until somebody else came along and one-upped the invention, but by that time perhaps *Artemis-5.com* would be rich enough to buy that one, too.

Just about every player involved had powerful motivation for licking its wounds in silence and not making too public a clamor about how badly they'd been screwed, said screwing having been largely of their own making.

The board of directors of the born-again *Artemis-5* got themselves busy casting about for a new CEO following a closed-door session with George Peabody III and Phillip Goldwith. The substance of that private meeting was never revealed, but it coincided precisely with the dropping of the lawsuit to prevent shares of the revivified company from being given away to various brokerage houses. Rumor had it that the two chairmen had made it abundantly clear that they were fully prepared to destroy the entire economy and plunge the whole planet into the financial equivalent of the Stone Age if any of those large voting blocs, who seemed to have forgotten how close they'd come to catastrophe and were now indecorously grasping after nickels and dimes, took it upon themselves to interfere with the overall plan that had been devised to prevent their own destruction.

They were further warned away from questioning too closely exactly how *Artemis-5.com* managed to Phoenix its way up from the ashes, why it had been able to acquire *TillYouDrop* lock, stock and barrel for a total cost of one dollar, where exactly the hell James Hanley was right now and why the illustrious and revered Burton Staller was spending his afternoons on the putting green of the minimum-security federal prison camp in Pleasanton, California, and not giving interviews.

Brokerage houses that were to receive shares of *Artemis-5.com* to cover the *TillYouDrop.net* shares they'd lost were not only deliriously happy to receive one new share for every two they'd blown, but equally thrilled not to be called upon to account for why they'd behaved so irresponsibly in blithely lending out those shares in the first place.

The big institutional investors were further induced into unquestioning cooperation by advance notice from Peabody that every single share of every single thing that Burton Staller owned would soon appear on the market following a disgorgement order from the SEC, the proceeds to be used to finance as much of a return to normalcy following Staller's market tampering as was feasible. (Staller, as it happened, approved enthusiastically, as part of a deal that reduced his stay at the Milken Suite from thirty years to ten. He could have tied the matter up in court for years, but would have been managing the case from a prison cell, so his choice was an easy one.) Peabody, upon Goldwith's urging, had decreed that execution of the entire plan had to be completely concluded within seventy-two hours in order to prevent lawyers, consultants, financial managers, program traders and brokerage houses from swinging into full gear trying to figure out how to profit unfairly from the unprecedented fiasco.

Following that session, Goldwith had casually mentioned to Peabody that the venerable SEC chairman should resign, since it was a fate preferable to the beheading that Peabody in fact deserved. Seeing the wisdom in this advice, Peabody dutifully tendered his resignation to the president, who, with his characteristic, uncanny ability to see directly to the heart of an issue, asked him acidly whether he really thought it a good idea to resign in disgrace when everything had turned out okay, which would only invite unwanted speculation that could make everything unravel.

So Peabody went back to his office, promoted Jubal Thurgren to head of the Enforcement Division, and, with the kind of humble self-sacrifice characteristic of the very best in American leadership, resigned the prestigious chairmanship of the SEC in order to become interim CEO of *Artemis-5.com* and see to it that this vital cog in the new economy got onto a solid footing as quickly as possible.

AS FRIEDENTHAL SNICKERED OVER MOROSCO'S FUTURE HOME in upstate New York, Steffen said, "Hey, Jubal . . . where's your bowling jacket?"

"Paul," Thurgren answered as he took a last sip and stood up, "I'm never wearing the same jacket as you again as long as I'm walking on this Earth. Now . . ." He put a hand on the FBI agent's shoulder and pushed him away, clearing a path for himself to the lanes. "Stand aside and let me show you how this is done."

Thurgren paused as the bartender turned the volume up on the television. Robert Schumann, chairman, president and CEO of Schumann-Dallis Investments, was being interviewed by Billy O'Malley. ". . . Good question, Billy, and here's what I think," he was saying. "If there's a wave of profit-taking tomorrow, you can pretty much bank on prices taking a dive during the morning. But if investors feel this is a good time to be buying on the dip, count on a sharp increase across the board. I feel very strongly about this."

The bartender was nodding in approval. "Smart guy, that."

Thurgren looked at him, dumbfounded. "What'd he say the market's going to do?"

"Huh?"

"Is the market going up or down tomorrow?"

"Shit, Jubal, you heard him yourself. Depends on what people are gonna do."

"Well, I'll be damned. I never knew that."

"See?" The bartender nodded and grinned with satisfaction at his point having been made. "Smart, that guy. Say, listen . . . you got any good tips?"

Thurgren had already turned and begun walking away. "What?"

"Daughter's college fund. You got no idea what that costs nowadays."

"Stay in for the long haul," Friedenthal piped up, tossing off one of the oldest and most respected pieces of advice in the business. "Can't go wrong if you're patient."

"And whyzzat?"

"Stocks always rise in the long term, is why. In't that right, Jubal?" Friedenthal turned, fully expecting to be complimented for his wisdom.

"Not necessarily. Depends on what you mean by long term and when you decide to measure your position. What happens if you need your dough during one of those times when the market hits the skids, which for darned sure it's gonna do once in a while?" Thurgren pointed to a picture of the bartender's thirteen-year-old daughter taped to the cash register. "If you know you're going to be needing that dough when she's eighteen, cash out in the first up-market after she hits fifteen."

"Jeez . . . Get out when things are really cookin'?"

"Listen: If you think that not squeezing every last penny out of a boom market is a mortal sin, then you shouldn't be in the game at all. You want a really good tip?"

"Yeah!"

Thurgren nodded and pretended to consider it carefully. "Treasury bonds," he said finally, walking away.

"Treasury bonds?" The safest, lowest-yield, most unglamorous imaginable investment instrument in existence, an issue so bland it made a savings account in a local bank look like plutonium futures. "You're shittin' me!"

Friedenthal tapped the side of his empty glass with a knuckle. As the bartender shook his head, picked up the glass and walked toward the taps to refill it, the assistant FBI director assured him in no uncertain terms that he couldn't remember a time when Jubal Thurgren had been more serious.

Wire service report, December 16, 1999:

SCHEME TO FRAUDULENTLY AFFECT STOCK PRICE, SEC CHARGES

Three men in Los Angeles net $364,000 using UCLA library computers to manipulate stock of obscure company.

———

LOS ANGELES—According to federal government sources, three Southern California men were charged Wednesday with stock fraud for using the Internet to post messages about a fictitious merger in order to manipulate the price of a tiny stock for a $364,000 profit.

What makes this case especially noteworthy is that it is the first time charges of stock manipulation have been brought against individuals who are not in any way affiliated with the company involved.

Erich Schwartz, SEC assistant director of enforcement, revealed that the three men, two of whom are recent graduates of UCLA, posted hundreds of messages on the Internet over a single weekend falsely claiming that NEI Webworld, Inc. was about to be purchased by another company. The messages were posted from computer terminals available to the public at the UCLA Biomedical Library, enabling the men to keep their identities secret.

The three conspirators bought thousands of shares of NEI Webworld, a little-known company trading for as low as 13 cents a share. Following those purchases, the trio posted hundreds of phony messages about a pending takeover in three popular financial chat sites, Yahoo! Finance, Raging Bull, and Free realtime.com. The well-orchestrated barrage of messages claiming that NEI Webworld was about to be bought generated enough enthusiasm to drive the price as high as $15.31 by Friday, November 12.

The following Monday morning they unloaded all their shares, at an enormous profit over 100 times their initial investment. When no merger was actually announced, the stock quickly fell back to its previous pennies-per-share level.

Apparently, the trio's choice of a company through which to work its scheme was motivated as much by the company's name as its low share price: Despite sounding like it involves the Internet, NEI Webworld, a Dallas company that is now going through bankruptcy, is actually in the commercial printing business. The "web" in its name refers to a type of high-speed printing press used by newspapers and other high-volume printers.

According to court documents, the three men enhanced the apparent legitimacy of their posts by using dozens of different screen names and a sequence of messages that gave the impression that there was an excited and frantic conversation going on among a large number of investors. "It made it appear this information was emanating from a large number of people." Schwartz said. "It had the appearance of a widespread dialogue."

The very manner in which the stock was manipulated led investigators to the men now in custody. Unusual activity in a stock is often flagged by the surveillance units of the various markets, and the sudden rise in the price of the moribund NEI Webworld got the attention of the National Assn. of Securities Dealers. Regulators logged on to various Net chat rooms and discovered the barrage of messages, then subpoenaed Yahoo! to supply the Internet protocal address of the computer from which the messages were sent. (A protocol address is a number that identifies a specific computer connected to the Internet.) Once the source was identified as the public computers in the UCLA library, recordings made by security cameras there were used to identify the three.

Use of the Internet to fraudulently boost the price of obscure stocks is a growing problem for regulators. The U.S. attorney alleged in an affidavit that at UCLA alone several such schemes had taken place. Federal officials have taken pains to warn investors to take what they read on the Internet with large grains of salt, especially reports of huge pending gains in cheaply traded issues on the OTC Bulletin Board.

Gruenfeld, Lee

The Street

DUE DATE   C174   23.95
